KILLER INSTINCT

ALLAN EVANS

Stillwater Story House

S T I L L W A T E R
STORY HOUSE

A Stillwater Story House production

First Printing, 2026

© 2026, Allan Evans
evanswriter.com

Book Cover by Kailey Anne Roberts, Emperor Arts

ISBN: 979-8-9942569-0-9 (Kindle Edition)
ISBN: 979-8-9942569-1-6 (Paperback)

To family and friends.

1

Someone was going to die today. Frank Perlmutter sincerely hoped it wouldn't be him.

The Hotel Theodore's lounge had all the usual suspects: dim lighting, business types networking over pricey cocktails purchased with expense accounts, disinterested staff half-glued to a poker tournament on widescreens, and yacht rock softly pumping out tunes that hadn't been cool since Jimmy Carter called the White House home. Wearing an unremarkable dark suit—surrounded by men in dark suits—Frank was virtually invisible. Which was important when you were hiding a weapon meant to kill someone.

He wasn't worried. Frank was the guy no one noticed. That was his gift—the art of being forgettable.

Which, of course, was fine with Frank. Being decidedly average and wholly unremarkable was an asset for someone in his line of work. He was taller but not tall. Not particularly thick or thin. Average. He had brown hair, the color of beige houses everywhere. His eyes had flecks of blue, green, and of course, brown, and had the knack for blending in with whatever color was nearby. He had a dad's face and the body to go with it, which rendered him invisible to over ninety percent of the world's population. His was the voice of a C-SPAN narrator, not the voice of a news broadcaster or salesman. Certainly not a voice that would cause a woman to swoon. Not surprisingly, no woman had ever swooned within spitting distance of Frank.

Frank was in the hotel lounge because his Alpha—agency speak for his primary target—was here. Chen Dazhao, a stocky Chinese national with mean eyes, was in Minneapolis for a meeting with a North Korean contact. The concern was that Dazhao, a prolific cyberterrorist, might have another plan in the works. The North Korean remained a mystery—curious, but not enough to earn Beta status.

Dazhao shook hands with the unidentified man in a tailored silver suit that screamed money and menace. At his nod, the stunning woman beside him stood and walked away—her dismissal a clear signal the meeting was about to begin. Three men remained, looming nearby. Muscles packed into suits a size too small. Bodyguards.

The woman strolled—slowly and exquisitely—to the bar and took a seat. Legs crossed, lips pursed, eyes scanning the lounge of the Hotel Theodore.

Frank swallowed hard.

All curves, confidence, and don't-even-think-about-it energy, she was striking. Black dress tailored to perfection. Going in where it needed to and back out again to accommodate her eye-catching curves. Red-soled heels that added four inches to her height. The way she moved, elegant, composed, graceful. Frank was captivated.

"I'm going to talk to her." He spoke quietly, his words not meant for anyone around him. "She can tell me who Dazhao's meeting with."

"Are you sure? Speaking to women hasn't exactly been your strength." The voice in his head wasn't self-doubt or even his conscience. It was his handler.

Tom Waters was Frank's handler. A quiet voice in his earpiece, Tom watched through the micro-camera in the International Mayors Conference pin on Frank's lapel. They had a strange chemistry, like an old married couple that bickered constantly but still managed to make things work. Tom had saved Frank's life more than once—sometimes from enemies, most others from Frank's singular lack of eptness.

If he was being honest with himself, Frank knew his longevity in the field owed more to Tom's guidance than his own instincts.

"Given the operational security around the meeting, she may be our best chance to learn more," Frank whispered. "I'm going to try to talk to her."

"She's a looker. Need backup?"

"I've got this." Though with women he often didn't. Frank's track record with women wouldn't inspire confidence at the annual meeting of the Optimists Club.

The elegant Asian woman sat at the bar, poised and sophisticated, her presence commanding the room like a perfectly struck note in a Mozart concerto. Her dark eyes glimmered under the soft light, aloof yet irresistible. Frank hesitated, his pulse quickening.

He couldn't take his eyes off her. But when he took a step toward the bar—realizing he should've looked both ways—he collided with a hurrying businesswoman. Her oversized purse exploded across the floor.

"I'm so sorry." Wanting to avoid attention, Frank dropped to his knees to help her gather her stuff. Lip gloss, hand sanitizer, a pack of gum, a tangled set of earbuds, a half-eaten protein bar, and—of course—a rogue tampon scattered across the floor. Something cylindrical rolled under a nearby table. He reached for what looked like a toothbrush case.

But when he lifted the object, he realized he'd been badly mistaken.

"Oh my," said the woman at the table.

"Maybe leave your toys at home," her husband added.

The businesswoman snatched the offending item from his hand and stormed off.

"Now that was awkward," Tom said, laughing. "Can we get back to it? You can't leave a woman waiting. Especially one who looks like she walked off the cover of Vogue."

Indeed, she stood out like a priceless work of art in a Home Depot. Knowing his window was closing, Frank's nerves popped faster than a 4th of July backyard celebration in rural Alabama. He hesitated, convinced that women could smell fear.

"Don't be shy," Tom said in his ear. "Women don't like shy. They want a man who knows what he wants."

"What do I want?" Frank asked quietly. "Am I supposed to know this?"

"Buddy, the one thing you don't want is to stand in front of a girl talking to yourself. That's creepy. Not the vibe you're going for. Just walk over and say hello. Tell her you'd like to buy her a drink."

Frank forced a breath. Their eyes met as Frank approached.

"Hey, I'm—"

"Don't say your name," Tom hissed.

"Frank," he blurted before Tom could stop him. "I'm curious about the man you came in with. The one in the silver suit."

Up close, she was even more dangerous looking. Her eyes were dark and deliberate. Every part of her said: *I know what I'm doing. Do you?*

"That's my boss, Mr. Fang," she said, studying him. Her fingers toyed with an earring, her eyes locked on his. She leaned in, a whisper just for him. "Can I trust you?"

Frank hesitated.

"Say yes, you idiot." Tom didn't sound pleased. Not for the first time.

Forcing himself to hold her gaze, Frank nodded. "Yes, you can trust me."

She gestured for Frank to take the stool beside her. When he sat down, she leaned closer, her perfume far more intoxicating than the commercials suggested. "My boss is involved with dangerous men. I need your help."

Frank blinked. "I don't even know your name."

She hesitated, before offering a soft, guarded smile. "Rose. Rose Park."

Before he could reply, she added, "You have kind eyes, Frank. That's rare from where I'm from."

"She's laying it on thick. I don't trust her," Tom warned. "And you shouldn't either."

But Frank was too far gone. Women like this didn't live in his world. They lived in spy movies and diplomatic entourages. Private villas and VIP airport lounges. Not next to guys who'd peaked in high school intramurals.

"I'm in trouble. I think they know I know." Her voice trembled just slightly as her eyes began to shine.

Don't create a scene. Keep your head down. Don't get involved in anyone's problems. Frank's mantras ran through his head as her eyes pleaded with him. They were not the kind of eyes he could easily ignore.

"Hey, meeting's over," Tom barked.

He was right. Fang and his ready-for-business bodyguards were headed Frank's way. Their hands underneath their jackets. Eyes on Rose. And him. Dazhao, Frank's Alpha, was behind them, moving toward the exit.

"They're coming your way," Tom said. "Time to make your exit. Don't lose Alpha."

For every person, there's a major decision point—the proverbial fork in the road—when a choice between options is required. Time stood still for Frank as his moment arrived.

Fork number one: Complete the assignment. A single bullet would drop Dazhao, and Frank could slip away in the pandemonium. Mission accomplished.

Fork number two: Help the woman. Her eyes would forever haunt him if he left her behind.

Fork number three: Do both.

He knew better but called an audible anyway. He was going with fork number three.

Time. Slowed. To. A. Halt.

The security detail closed in.

Rose at his side. Leaning into him. The delicate scent of her perfume teased his senses.

The security detail drew their pistols first as Frank reached for his.

"Hurry!" Rose shouted.

The silencer caught on his waistband. Determination won out over his Men's Wearhouse suit pants, and the gun popped out.

"They're going to kill me." Panic in Rose's voice.

Frank stayed calm; this wasn't his first rodeo. Four shots would do. One for Dazhao, then one for each of the bodyguards. It was simple in theory.

She was by his side. "Shoot them!"

But as Frank aimed his SIG-Sauer P229, the woman redirected his aim. A subtle nudge perfectly timed.

A dull *thut* echoed, sounding more like a heavy stapler snapping shut than a gunshot.

The redirected 9mm bullet hit the nearest bodyguard. He fell back, eyes wide in surprise, blood arcing from the hole in his throat.

"Kill them all!" she screamed.

No choice now, Frank pivoted and fired at the approaching bodyguard.

The second man crashed into a table, dragging a wave of suits down with him.

The third ducked behind a table, but Frank put a bullet in his brain when he popped back up.

Thut. Even suppressed, everyone knew the sound and the business crowd panicked.

Chaos. Screams. Panic.

Dazhao was gone. Fang was out of sight. The job was past saving.

"Abort, abort!" Tom shouted. "You lost Alpha!"

As Frank hesitated, seeing the disaster around him, Rose grabbed his hand.

"Come on!" she shouted.

Knowing his best and possibly only chance to find his target again was with Rose, Frank—assassin, forgettable middle-aged nobody, man of mantras and rules—ran with her.

2

Skeeter's location turned out to be a Starbucks in Cottage Grove.

Cade Dawkins squinted across the mostly empty parking lot shimmering in the late-morning sun. He dropped his FJ Cruiser in an adjoining lot and climbed into Rob's Ford Maverick. The pickup looked a few weeks overdue for a car wash, not unusual for Minnesota. The weather taking its revenge on clean vehicles. He bumped fists with Rob. "What's happening?"

"Remember that guy who went to ground in the semi-truck parts case? Skeeter Morris—the parts hustler who'd vanished when things got hot after we grabbed the shipment. He came up for air and is currently enjoying coffee and breakfast inside."

Rob nodded toward the Starbucks.

"I could use your help. You pull off 'mean' better than I can."

They were both plainclothes investigators with the Minnesota State Patrol, ex-cops from other worlds—Rob from St. Paul PD, Cade from the Minnesota Bureau of Criminal Apprehension. The BCA, as it was known, was the CSI of Minnesota, a multi-division agency combining extensive forensic laboratory services with field investigations. Cade had been a special agent working in the field. Both found a new home working together with the Patrol.

Broad-shouldered with a frame that could've made him a natural bouncer or lineman, Rob carried his size without menace. His smile came easy, disarming people who might otherwise have expected him to lead with brute force. He preferred sharp observation over sharp elbows, and in most cases, his intellect did the heavy lifting long before his muscles were ever needed.

Where Cade was quick with a sardonic edge, Rob played the steady anchor: unflappable under pressure, methodical in his thinking, and unexpectedly insightful when the investigation hit a dead end. He had a knack for noticing the overlooked detail and asking the question no one else had considered, which made him an invaluable partner. Some mistook his relaxed demeanor for indifference, but Cade knew better—Rob's calm was gravity, keeping the team grounded when the chaos of a case threatened to pull them apart.

Cade stood a shade over six feet, athletic enough to pass for someone who spent time at the gym but not built like he was trying to prove it. He didn't look like anyone's image of a cop. Maybe it was the dirty-blonde hair that always seemed to have a mind of its own, or the gentle blue eyes that made him appear more barista than badge. People underestimated him because of that, and he let them. It worked in his favor. The same man who could be mistaken for taking latte orders had apprehended four serial killers, and though Cade never wore that history on his sleeve, it showed in the way he carried himself—calm, watchful, always ready for the moment when everything tilted toward danger.

"I can do mean. Let's go rattle his cage."

Inside, only two tables were in use. One had a young woman with her nose in a laptop. Based on the thick textbooks surrounding her, she was a student. The other table had a man with scraggly dark hair in the Business-in-the-front, party-in-the-back style, an unkempt goatee, glasses, and rumpled work clothes. He held a cup in both hands as he stared at a cell phone on the table. A video of dancing cartoon animals played. This had to be Skeeter.

Jamie, the barista, handed Cade a cup and he slid a chair over to join Skeeter. Rob loomed behind.

Reluctantly lifting his eyes from his phone, Skeeter looked Cade over. "Whatever you're selling, I don't want any."

"Not selling anything, Skeeter," Rob said behind him.

Hearing his name, Skeeter Morris straightened and studied Rob. "You're a cop," he pronounced. However, after a glance at Cade, he shook his head. "Not you, though. I think you were my server at Friday's. Brought me the wrong salad."

"You don't look like the salad-eating type, if I'm being honest."

Skeeter didn't appear to know what to do with Cade's observation. He shrugged and leaned back, waiting.

"We have a few questions." Cade folded his arms. "We understand you're in the midnight truck parts business."

Skeeter's eyes narrowed.

"I'm not here to bust your chops, necessarily."

"Necessarily," Skeeter echoed, staring at Cade. "So, you're the bad cop in this scenario?"

Rob shook his head. "He's not the bad cop. But he sure as hell isn't the good one, either."

Cade leaned forward, his eyes unflinching. "Remember you agreed to help us when Trooper Swanson caught you acquiring parts for an order?"

Skeeter nodded slightly.

"We need to know about that particular order. Parts were not the only thing in that shipment."

Skeeter held up a hand. "Hey, I don't know nothing about drugs. That's not my thing."

Rob shook his head. "It wasn't drugs. There was currency in the crates along with your parts."

"Not my parts."

"And that's why it's called theft," Cade pointed out.

Skeeter looked irritated.

"Hey, you were the one stealing," Cade said, making a face.

"Hey, you were the one stealing," Skeeter said in a bad imitation. "Where's all your bling? Isn't that a thing?"

Cade was getting annoyed. "I don't work at Friday's. Just shut up and listen."

Skeeter shut up.

"I need to know who the shipment was for. Where it was headed."

Skeeter cocked his head. "Just how high up the food chain do you think I am? I'm the one getting the parts, not making the decisions. If I made them, I sure as shit wouldn't have chosen me to be the one risking his ass procuring them."

"You mean stealing them."

Skeeter waved Cade off.

Cade cleared his throat. "You know this is the part where you can actually help yourself. You were caught "procuring" truck parts," he said, making air quotes.

"Caught on video. Now you help us and then we help you. Give us something, and your consequences can go away. Keep being a stubborn asshole, and you'll be headed for lockup after we finish our coffees." He held Skeeter's gaze. "Dealer's choice."

Cade watched the man's eyes flick to the entrance, sizing up his chances. Skeeter looked to be around fifty, with a tweaker's thin build and the soft frame of someone who'd either let himself go or had never found the energy to go in the first place. When his shoulders slumped, Cade assumed Skeeter had accurately done the math.

Skeeter's voice was quiet and even. "Fine. We've been moving currency for nearly a decade now. Truck parts was a side gig to hide it."

"Wait, the stolen truck parts were a front for moving currency? You hid one crime behind another one?" Cade scratched his head.

A shrug from Skeeter. "I guess."

Rob laughed. "Skeeter, most criminals hide their activities behind a legitimate business. I'm not sure what this says about you guys. It doesn't sound like you were exactly criminal masterminds."

"Maybe so, but we've been getting away with it for nearly ten years. Not sure what that says about you law enforcement guys."

Cade laughed, shaking his head. "Touché."

Rob took a sip, waiting for the laughter to die down. The student had paused her schoolwork and was listening. "We're interested in finding out more about the currency we seized. Do you know where it originated from?"

"The crates were from the Port of Montreal and came through the Great Lakes to Duluth. That's where we got involved. But before Quebec, I have no idea. The final destination for the currency was here. We were going to repackage it and hand it over."

"That's a lot of money. What was it for?"

Skeeter burst into laughter. "Are you kidding me? You think we ask people what they plan on using the money for? That's a great way to end up dead."

"Am I right?" he asked the girl at the other table who had been listening with interest, her studies forgotten.

"Sounds stupid to me," she agreed, closing her laptop.

Cade felt the interrogation going off the rails. There was a reason these things were usually done in private. "Thanks for your input, but we have it from here," he told her. Turning back to Skeeter, he asked, "You think this is a game, Skeeter? Start cooperating or your name gets leaked. How was the transfer supposed to happen?"

"Typically, when we're ready, we call the number on file and arrange something."

"Okay, we can work with that." Rob nodded. "I'm going to need that number."

Skeeter held up a hand. "No way. That's going to hurt our reputation. In business, reputation is everything."

Cade set down his cup. "Skeeter, you already lost their money. It doesn't get worse than that." He glanced to the young woman, who'd lost all pretense of not eavesdropping. "Tell him handing over their number won't make things worse."

"He has a point. I'm pre-law," she added with a shrug. "Been reading about criminal enterprise structures. Dumbest thing you can do is stay loyal to someone who wouldn't hesitate to burn you." She scooted her chair closer. "And actually, it may help you to have them in jail. They can't leave your business a bad review if they're in prison."

"See?" Cade gestured toward the girl. "You should listen to ..."

"Isabelle."

"Listen to Isabelle and life will be better."

Skeeter looked to her and back to Cade before nodding.

"Okay."

Skeeter sighed like a man signing his own execution order. "Fine. I'll get you the number. But if anyone asks, this never happened in a Starbucks."

Later that afternoon, Cade and Grace walked hand in hand, taking in the picturesque Crosby Farm trail along the Mississippi. The trees were a kaleidoscope of red, orange, and yellow. Songbirds sang. With the nearby river reflecting the fall colors, it was beautiful and serene. Exactly what was needed. Cade had known her for years, but recently, their partnership had blurred into something messier, riskier, and far more personal. It was as exhilarating as it was dangerous, like dating a loaded gun.

Grace had the kind of presence that turned heads without her trying. Long brunette hair spilled over her shoulders, glossy waves framing a figure built on unapologetic curves. She carried herself like she knew exactly how much space she took up—and dared anyone to comment on it. Her smile had a bite, her eyes sparked with mischief, and her irreverent streak meant she was just as likely to tease Cade as she was to kiss him.

That was part of the draw. Where Cade carried himself with quiet intensity and a sarcastic edge, Grace was pure fire, unpredictable, brash, and unwilling to play by anyone's rules but her own. She cut through his defenses with a single look, and when she laughed, it undid him. For all his experience facing down killers, it was Grace who could disarm him with nothing more than a raised eyebrow or sly smile.

"This is nice," he said, giving her hand a gentle squeeze. "Darn near romantic even."

She shrugged. "You might say that."

"I did say that. That was me just now."

"I thought I recognized the voice." She smiled.

Cade was smiling, too. "I was thinking..." he began.

"It's better if you don't. Think, that is," Grace said. "Relationships are best when they're not overthought. The moment you define something, people obsess over that label. Know what I mean?"

He nodded. "I'm just surprised you used the R word."

"*Shhh,*" she said, pointing at a deer that had wandered out from the woods. It held its ground, watching, waiting. After a few moments, it turned and bolted, heading for the cover of the trees.

"It must have been scared off by your blatant use of the R word," Cade said, giving Grace a sly look.

Laughing, she squeezed his hand. "It's not that I'm afraid of a relationship, I'm simply wary of labels."

"Without labels or names, it would be complete anarchy. You don't want that kind of guilt hanging over your head," Cade said.

"That's true," Grace admitted. "I'm not a big fan of guilt. Except for the occasional guilty pleasure."

Cade lifted a hand. "I would never stand in the way of your guilty pleasures."

"So, you'll watch Dancing with the Stars with me tonight?"

Well played. He could only shake his head.

In a bold move, he tried changing the subject. "Any excitement at the lab lately?"

"Just the usual blood stains and bullet casings. If it weren't for true crime podcasts, I'd have gone stir crazy. How about you?"

"So quiet. I almost wish another killer from that site would come challenge me to a duel or something."

Not so long ago, three serial killers had answered a website challenge and come to the Twin Cities to try and best him. It hadn't worked. Cade was still here, but the killers were not.

One of them was dead, one was in Oak Park Heights, Minnesota's only level 5 maximum security prison, while the third was killing time in Saint Peter, the Minnesota psychiatric security hospital. Patients there had been civilly committed as mentally ill or dangerous. Jarn had been both.

Grace laughed. "It really has been slow around here, if you're wishing for a serial killer to come to town. Nothing from your friend, the governor either?"

Cade made a face. Ritter was the very definition of a political weasel and Cade bristled every time he was in a room with the man.

Governor Winston Ritter had the sole authority to activate Minnesota's major crimes task force. But, to Ritter's irritation, the Department of Public Safety chose Cade to lead it—and the two had clashed at nearly every interaction since. Irreverently dubbed Five Below, the name stuck, and the unit was formed after serial killers from the Orbiting Cortex dark website had surfaced in the Twin Cities. The work forged the team into more than colleagues—Cade, Rook, Grace, Lorie, and Kristen had become a close-knit partnership.

"Nope, nothing large or unusual happening anywhere in our state. Everyone's hunkering down waiting for winter to shit on us." Cade knew by experience that in November they were living on borrowed time. The weather could turn cruel at any moment.

"True that," she said. "Though Minneapolis had a weird incident last night."

He turned to her. "How's that?"

"Just before 11 p.m. last night, a 27-year-old bartender was attacked as she headed to her car after her closing shift. She was injected in the neck with a tranquilizer, dragged nearly a dozen feet across the parking lot—then left unconscious and alone."

"Okay, that's odd, I'll give you that. Is she all right?" Cade asked.

"Physically, she's fine. But she's shaken and confused."

"Her attacker must've been scared off. Why just leave her there after going to the trouble of drugging her?"

"If so, we don't know by who. She was found by a dog walker. The guy hadn't seen or heard anyone as he and his dog walked the alley."

Cade's instincts stirred. Random attacks rarely felt this organized. "Injecting someone with a tranquilizer shows premeditation. Someone wanted this woman."

"Yet, he left her behind," Grace pointed out.

They walked in silence, both pondering.

When Cade's phone buzzed in his pocket, he hesitated. Checking the screen, he showed it to Grace. It was the Governor's office.

He considered ignoring it. "It might be nothing."

Grace raised an eyebrow. "But if it's not, I'll be here when you get back."

When Ritter called, it meant something had happened.

Usually something bad.

Someone dead, someone missing, or something about to explode.

But it also meant Cade answered.

3

The Governor's residence sat on Summit Avenue, St. Paul's most prestigious street—an average-sized mansion surrounded by above-average ones. While the rest of the city blended historic charm with modern energy, Summit clung to its past. Its homes stood like monuments to a more formal age, a corridor of frozen elegance untouched by time.

Cade waved to the trooper at the gate. With the State Patrol handling the governor's security, getting in was easy.

Outside the Governor's office, he found Governor Winston Ritter's assistant. "Hey, Sarah. Sounds like something urgent has come up."

Sarah, Ritter's executive assistant—who looked like she'd seen it all and wasn't impressed by any of it—nodded. "He's on a call with Rochester, but he should be done shortly. Coffee?"

Cade hated the whole hurry-up-and-wait routine. At least the coffee was decent, and the post-colonial Schneiderman's decor gave him something to silently judge. The framed photographs in the waiting area all had a theme. The governor. In every picture, the governor posed with celebs, local media, politicians, and the occasional dog. Pretty much anyone who would pose with him, Ritter took a picture of them, framed it, and stuck it here.

Cade didn't have a lot of respect for the man. None, really. In the past, Ritter had made it clear he was all about image. His own. Like someone slurping down a jumbo plate of spaghetti, it was disgusting to watch. When Ritter dealt with the media, he could be incredibly charming. Anyone else, they were basically pond scum.

"Okay, Governor Ritter is off the call. I'll tell him you're here." Sarah knocked lightly and pushed the door open, Cade following.

"Special Investigator Cade Dawkins from the Minnesota State Patrol is here."

"Send him in," Ritter said, eyes still on his laptop. "Might as well get this over with. The guy bugs me."

"I love you, too," Cade said, already stepping inside.

Ritter's head popped up from his laptop screen, clearly surprised that the Patrol man was already in his inner sanctum.

"Dawkins, you weren't meant to hear that." Not much of an apology if it indeed was one.

"So, you called this meeting..." He sat across from Ritter. "Something happened, you said."

Ritter looked over the screen. "Earlier today, three men got themselves gunned down in Minneapolis."

"Unfortunately, that doesn't narrow it down."

"You're not here because of a routine gang shooting," Ritter said. "This was at the Hotel Theodore, where a trio of bodyguards were gunned down. They were protecting a well-connected Korean businessman."

"So there are international implications," Cade said.

"You don't know the half of it. The International Mayors Conference starts Monday—over a thousand mayors flying in from across the globe. One bullet in the wrong direction and we're a diplomatic punchline. The eyes of the world will be on us and the absolute last thing we need is to have an international incident that destroys Minnesota's reputation on the global stage." He paused. Maybe for effect, possibly out of regret. "That's why I'm activating the major crimes task force."

The Blonde Killer case had nearly collapsed under a jurisdictional tug-of-war. Cade first worked it under the State Patrol when the deaths looked like accidents, but once it became clear a serial murderer was staging the crashes, the Bureau of Criminal Apprehension had taken over. That decision backfired when the killer carved the word "fraud" into the chest of the BCA's lead investigator. It was a public mockery of the state's jurisdictional infighting.

The governor had put Cade back in charge, and his work eventually exposed the killer as a member of the governor's own staff. The bloody conclusion left scars—some not belonging to the killer—and proved how dangerous the jurisdictional infighting had been.

In the aftermath, the Department of Public Safety had created a Major Crimes Task Force: a unit built to bypass politics and red tape in high-profile cases. Cade, with the credibility of stopping the Blonde Killer, was picked to lead this new task force, plucking whoever he needed from the law enforcement community. Besides Grace, he'd found a few trusted people who came aboard to help stop the killers from the dark web hosted site.

"Dawkins, this mayor's conference is a big deal. As before, you're granted authority to pull in whoever you need to solve this case."

Cade nodded. "What do we know about the Korean businessman? Was he here for the conference? And why would he need multiple bodyguards?"

Ritter had returned to his screen. "I can't speak to that, but yes, I believe he's here for the conference. You'll need to talk to Minneapolis PD, though. They're not going to be happy you're on their case, but c'est la vie. Find a way to work with them."

"Will do. But you know the feds will be all over this too. They love this international shit." Cade stood, more than ready to leave.

"I'm sure they do. It has to be better than chasing another white collar dickslap for six months and then have their high-priced attorney settle for three months in the Martha Stewart suite at a minimum security facility." Ritter had his nose buried back in his screen.

"We're leaner, meaner, and screw up less than the feds."

Ritter looked up. "Just don't get in a pissing match with them. We don't need any publicity. Put this one to bed quickly and quietly."

"Understood." Cade edged toward the door. There was something about being close to Ritter that made him feel like showering.

"One more word."

Ritter always had to have the last word. It was a power play move.

"Are you still banging that news anchor, Reynolds DeVries?"

Despite the Governor's expectant look, Cade shook his head. "I'm not having this conversation with you. This is my personal life."

Ritter closed his laptop and folded his arms. "There's no personal life when you're in the spotlight. You should know that." He stood. "I'm trying to teach you something here. You can leverage that relationship with DeVries to shape the story for the media."

It had been Cade's experience that whenever someone talked about leveraging something, that someone was an asshole. Of course, he already knew Ritter was an asshole.

He had him at banging.

"I'm not. We've both moved on." He glanced at the door, yearning for the escape it offered.

"Well, then, watch yourself around the media. They can be a fickle bunch and to be honest, you're rather naive." He shooed Cade away with a flourish. "Get out of here, go stop this conference from blowing up in our faces."

Cade didn't need to be told twice.

Outside, Cade exhaled, the cold November air cutting the governor's stench of self-interest. He pulled out his phone and dialed Rook. "Hey, Minneapolis," Cade said. "You're being drafted. Five Below is activated."

Rook, a sharp-eyed Minneapolis detective with the Violent Crimes Investigations Division, had a sarcastic streak and an aversion to paperwork. He and Cade had clicked during the task force's first case. "About damn time," he said. "If I have to hear about one more gang beef over a TikTok video, I might start selling timeshares."

Cade laughed. "We all need some variety in life. You can't keep dealing with the same shit day in, day out. It must be frustrating with the gang shootings."

"It's heartbreaking to see lives wasted over what? Colors? Turf? None of that matters as much as a life, but those kids don't see it. Not yet, they don't. Getting older gives some perspective, but I don't know if they will make it that long."

"For me, it's the collateral damage," Cade said. "Innocents caught in the cross-fire, families torn apart. It shouldn't be this way."

"Agreed, but I don't see things changing anytime soon. The streets are flooded with guns." Rook paused, and Cade gave him time. "But you're calling to offer me a break. Please tell me it's not another serial killer."

"It doesn't sound that way," Cade said. "Interestingly, there's an international component to the case. The deceased were a trio of bodyguards for a foreign national here for the International Mayors Conference. Ritter said the conference will bring in a thousand mayors from around the globe. He's worried about the disaster potential for the state's reputation if the killings continue."

"He's worried about his own ass, as usual. *His* reputation."

"Not going to disagree," Cade conceded. "But we need to get the situation under control before the conference begins. Before the shooter has another thousand targets to aim for."

"Agreed. Where to first, boss?"

"Hotel Theodore. The shooting happened there."

"Looks like we're back in the saddle," Rook said, his excitement palpable. "See you soon."

4

Frank sat on the edge of the bed, trying to make sense of what the hell had just happened, though he shouldn't have been surprised by the blown mission. Deep down, Frank knew his mission—and life—had veered dangerously off-script the moment the sultry stranger had asked for his help. Despite his inner monologue of mantras that so far had kept him alive and out of trouble, he'd ignored them the first time a beautiful woman had paid him any real attention. The woman—Rose, he reminded himself—hadn't said a word since the hotel. Neither had he. Tom had done enough talking for all three of them.

"What are you doing? Why did you shoot the man's security detail and not Dazhao? Where's the woman?"

Frank's target was Chen Dazhao, a Chinese national involved in the cyberattack on the Hatch nuclear plant in Georgia. You know that attack that nearly melted down the reactor's core and rendered the entire southeast of the United States completely uninhabitable for the next century? Yeah, that never made a single headline. Same as a lot of close calls in the last decade.

Though ninety-eight out of a hundred people might peg him for an accountant, Frank was an assassin for a government agency. Not the CIA, but close. The kind of agency that didn't get invited to testify before Congress.

When diplomacy failed, people like Frank were called in.

People assumed that assassins found their way into their vocation because they were cold-blooded killers with no empathy. Not Frank. He'd started at a desk. And happened to be available when a situation went sideways. Even though he'd been one for nearly a dozen years now, Frank Perlmutter was not a born killer—or particularly apt at it.

Truth be told, he was not looking forward to his next performance review.

"Not going to say it," Tom said, "But holy hell, Frank. If she finds out, Sheila Ann's going to have our heads."

Sheila Ann Bettendorf was Frank's boss. Ruthless, ambitious, and not fond of failure. Known around the office as the Dragon Lady, she ruled her little domain with an iron fist and the bad temper of a hungry two-year-old. Her tirades were legendary.

"I know, I know." Frank looked at his feet. He didn't want to say anything else.

"How can I help you if you don't talk to me? Don't go into your shut-down mode, Frank. You know I hate that."

Frank disconnected the link and sighed.

The mission hadn't gone as planned. But that was the thing with plans—they rarely did. That's why you built in contingency plans for your contingency plans. And Tom insisted on having contingency plans for those as well. For those following along at home, when plans A, B, and C went sideways, well, that's what plan D was for. But none of those accounted for when Frank deviated from said plans.

It was the woman. Hauntingly beautiful with dark brown eyes and cinnamon skin, Rose sparked something in him. Maybe it was those pleading eyes, maybe her dangerous curves or toned legs. Could even be her intoxicating perfume. Who knows? But something had pulled Frank off the plan.

He knew better. Together with Tom, his mantra had guided him past his worst instincts. *Keep your head down. Don't make a scene. Stay focused. Don't get involved in anyone else's problems.* That mantra had kept him alive. If he listened to his own internal dialogue, he might just live long enough to retire. Retirement in the Florida Keys—sunshine, fishing, and no surveillance vans—was his idea of paradise.

Yet, he'd just become involved.

It was only going to bring trouble. London had taught him that lesson the hard way.

Frank had been tailing a target in London. This target was an especially bad man, having been behind the recent Southampton shipyard bombings. The bomb's signature matched the Norfolk attack, hence his assignment. Frank's two goals: follow Alpha to the bomb planter they knew almost nothing about, and, if the chance came, take them both out.

Following his target at a discreet distance down a quiet side street near Covent Garden, the sign on the building read Lamb & Flag. The dark mahogany bar screamed old English pub with its creaky wooden floorboards and low ceiling. Surprisingly, it was packed.

"Hey buddy, I know you get a little thirsty when you're out following terrorists, but maybe the pint could wait until after work. Just saying." Tom was watching through the poppy pin on Frank's jacket, the camera lens small and subtle.

"Alpha is leading the way. I'm just here to observe."

"I know. Watch and learn. Have one for me."

Frank worked his way through the crowd, keeping Alpha in his sight. He glanced over his shoulder, situational awareness drilled into him. Unfortunately, he had looked at the wrong moment.

"Watch out—" Tom shouted in his ear.

The collision with the waitress sent her tray flying. Glasses of beer tipped and fell all over Frank, soaking him.

"I'm so sorry," the girl said. "I never even saw you."

People never seemed to notice Frank. His nondescript looks combined with his dad bod guaranteed that ninety-nine percent of the planet wouldn't give him a second glance. That could be both good and bad. At the moment it was bad. People stared in his direction. "Where's the bathroom?" he asked, anxious to get out of the spotlight.

The server gestured toward a dim corridor branching off from the bar area. He passed the women's bathroom as he headed to clean up in the men's room. The light was out at the end of the corridor, and it was a murky mass of shapes. After wiping himself off, Frank hurried to catch up to his target, hoping he was still there. As he rushed down the hall, he heard something behind him and stopped.

It was dark enough that he couldn't see anyone. Alpha crossed the room in front of him and headed toward the exit. He started moving.

But then he heard it again. It sounded like a whimper. He paused.

"What are you doing, Frankie?" Tom said in his ear. "Don't let him get away."

Again, Frank took a step forward, but there it was. A whimper, unmistakably female. He turned around. He had to do something.

"Frank," Tom warned.

Ignoring the voice in his ear, he moved down the hallway toward the sound. It was still too dark to make out much.

"Frank, this is not your mission. Alpha is going to slip away."

"We know he's going to be at the tube later," Frank said quietly. "I can get him then."

He took a step forward. As his eyes began to adjust to the dim light, he made out a figure beyond the stacks of chairs lining the hallway. "Are you okay, miss?" he asked the dark hallway.

Only it was a man who answered. He had a hint of a Russian accent, and a tone steeped in menace. "Keep going, mate. This is not your concern."

As Frank felt around in his pocket for his mini flashlight, Tom spoke again. "Frank, you do not want to wake the sleeping bear. This will create a scene. Scenes are bad, remember?"

Frank hated scenes more than most. Not calling attention to himself was ingrained in him. It could lead to unintended consequences, both professionally and personally. But what about when someone needed help? What to do then?

He didn't remember being this conflicted since his ex asked if her new pants made her butt look big. That argument had lasted three days.

He clicked on the flashlight.

"Oh, man," Tom said quietly.

The beam of Frank's flashlight illuminated a man who'd be more at home in a zoo or a carnival freakshow. Standing close to seven feet tall, the man's shirt hung open, revealing more tattoos than skin and more muscles than his local gym on Steroid Saturdays. There was a long scar running from his eye to his lip. Frank assumed the person responsible was now at the bottom of a nearby river.

Frank's light glinted off a blade of a knife that belonged in a butcher shop specializing in unusually large cows.

"Oh, man," Frank said quietly.

"I bet you'd rather it was a bear that you woke up," Tom said.

The man raised the knife and took a step toward Frank, who was thinking a strategic retreat might be his best option. Better to bolt now so he could fight another day.

That was, until he saw the girl cowering at the man's feet. She looked barely old enough to drink, let alone buy cigarettes. Her dark hair hung in her face, but there was terror in her eyes.

And now he was going to break his number one rule: Don't make a scene.

"Why don't you let her go," Frank offered it as a suggestion, thinking it would be better received than a command. Less attitude, less confrontation, less of a scene. He was dead wrong.

With a growl, the man lunged towards him with the knife. Frank grabbed a chair, just in time to block the blade. It slammed through the seat, knocking him flat. Four inches of steel missed his chest by one. Frank had a gun on him, of course, but the suppressor made it longer, which meant it was stuck down the back of his pants. He could feel it digging into his lower back. Although it was comforting to know it was there, it would be so much better if it were in his hand.

The giant plucked the chair from Frank's grasp like he was stealing a toy car from a small child, which he was sure the man did on a regular basis. The massive man didn't exactly radiate kindness. Frank glanced around while the man preoccupied himself with trying to pull the blade from the chair.

"Now's your chance," Tom shouted in his ear. "Get moving."

Frank got to his feet and reached for his pistol but stopped with his hand on the grip. A crowd of people had pushed into the hallway. They were no longer alone. That changed his plans. He'd wanted to put several rounds through the man's forehead, but you can't always get what you want.

"You've got police swarming the front and rear doors. Get out of there."

The bathroom had a window, but he'd need to get past the man with the knife first—without using his pistol. Help came from somewhere unexpected.

"Uncle Vlad," the girl said, and when the giant turned, Frank darted past him into the restroom.

Uncle? Had he misread the situation that poorly?

Without hesitation, Frank shot out the glass of the large frosted window over the sink and used the gun's barrel to knock away the worst of the shards. Not seeing another option, he backed up and ran. The dive took him through the window and into an alley behind the pub. It wasn't his most graceful landing, but he was still operational and made his way away from the danger.

The wail of the London police sirens filled the night. He slowed, not wanting to call attention to himself. Taking stock of his appearance, Frank saw his jacket was ripped, his shoulder was bleeding and his left wrist felt like it was swelling. Fortunately, he shot with his right.

"Any idea where Alpha has ended up?" he asked Tom.

"Sorry, man. He bolted as soon as you created that international incident back there."

"International? That's a tad extreme."

"Frank, the man was Russian and you're American. You're fighting on British soil. It doesn't get much more international than that."

Frank couldn't argue with him. And it was pointless anyway. Tom's chatter could be relentless, nagging in his ear like a mosquito on steroids, until Frank had to give in. Such was the power of a captive audience. Frank assumed most handlers eventually were murdered.

"I'm coming for you, just rounding the corner. Let's get you out of there before you get picked up."

And that's where the London trip ended. Alpha was a no-show for the underground meeting, vanishing off-grid without a trace. Frank never got another shot at him. He'd learned a valuable lesson that day: Keep your head down. Don't cause a stir. Other people's problems aren't your problems. Stay locked on his retirement goal: sunshine, fishing, and no complications.

After London, he'd vowed never to play the hero again.

Yet, here he was again. With Rose. Her perfume clouding his judgment and his peaceful retirement drifting further out to sea. Beautiful, sexy, dangerous. Frank couldn't take his eyes off her. She hadn't lost an ounce of elegance since the shootout.

Frank could feel all his future fish slipping off the hook.

He didn't completely trust her, but for now he was willing to see where things went.

Rose held his gaze, looking deep enough into him that he couldn't look away. She drew a long breath, let it out slowly, and finally spoke. "What I'm about to tell you could get us both killed."

5

The Hotel Theodore sat tucked away mid-block, a street over from the cavernous Minneapolis City Hall and police headquarters. Not a likely location for a shootout, yet here he was. Cade left his FJ Cruiser on a side street and jogged the block and a half. Official vehicles surrounded the luxury hotel.

Flashing his ID, he was allowed into the hotel to join the uniformed officers and suits. Cade was wearing jeans, hiking boots, and a flannel shirt under an open dark peacoat. His dirty blond hair was worn longer than most of his fellow law enforcement officers. He didn't look like a cop, which explained why a uniformed Minneapolis officer headed him off.

"This is a crime scene. You're going to have to leave." Officer Hester, as his nameplate read, didn't look like he'd mind a confrontation and stepped closer.

"Yo, Hester. He's one of us," Rook said, walking over. The officer seemed surprised but stepped aside.

"Hey, boss. Good to see you." Terrance Rooker—Rook to pretty much everyone—was a Minneapolis cop. Despite his questionable reputation, he'd been instrumental in Five Below's previous case. Cade found him to be more than capable, and they'd become friends. Rook was a black man, just shy of Cade's six feet in height, but he had a good 45 pounds of muscle that Cade didn't. Sporting a shaved head, close-cropped beard, white sneakers too clean for real work, and a leather varsity jacket that hadn't seen a football field since the Bush administration, Rook had a swagger.

They shared a quick fist bump and looked around. "Who's in charge?" Cade asked.

Rook nodded at the uniformed officer holding court by the lounge area. "That's Commander Fish. He's the man."

Cade headed over.

Commander Fish paused mid-sentence, eyeing Cade like he'd tracked dog shit across his new carpet.

"I suppose the Governor sent you." He had the wary look of a small dog protecting his bone from a German Shepherd. "Yeah, I know who you are. You're here to take over. Governor Ritter doesn't much care for our department."

Cade shook his head. "That wasn't my impression. The way I see it, Ritter's only concerned about one thing—himself. With the International Mayors Conference days away, he wants this handled fast and quiet. No headlines, no chaos. His only concern is his reputation."

Fish's eyes narrowed. "Are you saying we can't do our jobs?"

"Not saying that. We're not here to take over—we're here to help. Ritter considers the Five Below task force another resource to throw at the problem."

"That's a stupid name for a task force."

"That's your opinion," Rook said. "Since when were you the branding expert?"

Fish ignored him and addressed Cade. "If you're here to help, I've got assignments."

Cade shook his head. "We're on our own. Think of us as independent contractors, here to fill in the investigative cracks."

"There are no fucking cracks."

"Didn't mean there were. The task force is meant to work alongside your investigation. Another set of eyes can't hurt. We're not here to take anything away from the Minneapolis PD. We're not here for credit, just results."

Fish still looked like he'd eaten a lemon. Rook broke the tension.

"Don't get your undies in a bunch, Commander. We're on the same side," he said.

Cade recognized a pissing match when he saw one and stepped between them. "But we'll need access to evidence and witnesses. Let's begin with the victims. What do we know?"

"You can talk to Miller about that." He turned and called out, "Miller, come talk to the Governor's lap dogs." He walked away without a glance in their direction.

"That went well," Cade said.

"He's an officious prick." Rook clearly didn't like the man.

A woman in street clothes marched over. A detective shield hung around her neck. "You the lap dogs?"

"I'm no one's lap dog, Miller," Rook said. "Fish doesn't see the value of having an independent task force working alongside the department."

Cade spoke up. "The Governor activates the task force, but we don't answer to him." He held Miller's gaze. "We're here to stop a killer. That's it. Tell us what you know about the victims, please."

"It's not much, but fine. One shot in each chest. An economical shooter."

"Or a professional shooter," Cade pointed out. "They don't tend to waste a lot of bullets."

Miller continued. "Victims were here on South Korean passports. Part of Chou Fang's entourage. Both were armed and had their weapons out when they died."

"Self-defense?" Rook asked.

"Doubt it. Not after talking to Fang."

"Why bring armed guards to a swank place like this?" Rook asked.

"Swank. Now, there's a word you don't hear often." Cade shook his head.

"Usually, the word is attached to a gentlemen's club," Miller pointed out. "Like, Spearmint Rhino, the swankiest of gentlemen's clubs."

Rook folded his arms. "I'm not going to apologize for having a sophisticated vocabulary."

Both Miller and Cade looked at Rook with skepticism. "Oh, yeah, that's it. Sophisticated." Miller laughed.

"Anywho, Fang is a South Korean businessman here for the International Mayors Conference. The dead men were, apparently, his security detail." Miller nodded towards the lounge area. "We've got the witnesses corralled over there if you want to chat."

"Perfect. Thanks for your help." Cade went to shake her hand, but she turned and walked away. He and Rook walked over to the witness holding area.

"Start with Fang?" Rook asked.

Cade looked over at Fang, who sat like royalty among peasants, unmoved by the buzz around him. Cade shook his head. "Let's get the lay of the land first. It'd be better if we knew the situation before talking to someone like Fang."

Rook frowned. "Someone like Fang?"

"Someone who may have something to hide. Someone who may not be telling the truth, the whole truth, and nothing but the truth. Would he really travel from Asia with two armed bodyguards if everyone he's involved with is on the up and up?"

"Fair point," Rook said. "Then, who's first?" He gestured to the group caught up in the moment of violence.

"Her," Cade said, nodding to a young woman checking her watch. Wearing the uniform of the hotel's servers, she looked to be college-aged, with blonde hair past her shoulders and a lean runner's build. "She looks restless. Restless people like to talk. That works in our favor."

They introduced themselves and pulled her aside.

"What's your name?" Cade asked.

"Wynn Hesscrist."

"Walk us through the events."

"The place was busy, especially with the big conference starting in a couple of days. Many people fly in early to meet and make deals. My section was busy, business types like to drink."

"Expense accounts help with that," Cade said.

"They usually tip well. But I learned early on to mention a goal I'm trying to achieve. They always tip better if I say I'm in school or saving for a trip to Europe." She looked at her shoes. "Whether I am or not."

"Like it. That's intelligent use of psychology." He smiled. "What did the shooter look like? Tall? Short? Average?"

Wynn thought about it. "The guy was average. Not tall, not short. He looked like a dad. Nothing remarkable."

"What was he wearing?"

"A suit coat. And jeans."

"So, business casual," Rook said.

Wynn looked at Rook. "I never would've picked you for being a fashion expert."

"What's that supposed to mean? I have flair," he said, touching his jacket.

"That's a great jacket. Back when it was in style."

"It's timeless." Rook made a show of clutching at his heart.

"It's time was 2007."

"Witness is being belligerent," he narrated as he typed into his phone. "And clearly suffers from impaired vision." He gave her a look. "Girl, I could teach you about style."

"Really." Wynn looked as skeptical as someone encountering a "fresh fish" special on a Monday.

"Style is more than what you wear. It's how you live. How you carry yourself, and how you treat others. And no matter how refined your killer outfit, if your energy is out of alignment, your style is too."

"This is getting too new age for me. Can we get back to the shooter?" Cade asked. "How old was he?"

Wynn shrugged.

"How much do you think he weighed?"

Wynn shrugged.

"Any facial hair?"

Wynn shrugged again.

"You're not very good at this," Rook said.

"It's not that. There just wasn't anything special about him." She dragged her hands through her hair, fingers knotting in the strands before letting them fall with a sharp exhale.

"So, you're saying he didn't look like a stone-cold professional killer from the movies?" Cade said as he looked up from his notepad.

"No, just a dad. The kind you see pushing a lawnmower or cheering on the sidelines of a soccer game."

"Okay, tell me what happened next."

Wynn leaned forward and clasped her hands. "He was talking to an Asian woman at the bar, and that's when I saw the two men with guns pushing through the crowd. Next thing I knew the man had a gun too, with a suppressor like in the Jack Ryan show. Like spies use."

Rook and Cade exchanged looks.

"Then what?"

"Pure chaos. Everyone was screaming. The man disappeared in the commotion." Wynn shook her head.

Cade asked a few more questions, but didn't learn anything new, and cut her loose.

"What do you think?" he asked his partner.

"I think the man was a professional."

"Agreed. Not just because of the suppressor, but how he blended in. She really couldn't describe him at all. Put him in front of seven witnesses, and I bet no one could pick him out of a lineup."

Next, they found Fang. Pulling over chairs across from him, he stared back without expression.

The man was Asian, late forties, with close-cropped dark hair with a hint of gray at the temples. He wore an expensive navy suit with a subtle pinstripe. The burgundy silk tie was knotted perfectly and matched a pocket square that stuck out of a breast pocket. He wore a series of titanium rings, three on his left hand and two on his right.

Cade spoke first. "I'm Special Investigator Dawkins. This is Terrance Rooker. We're with Five Below, the major crimes task force."

The man didn't look impressed.

"What's your name?" Cade asked.

"Fang. Chou Fang."

"You're from...?"

The man looked back. Saying nothing for a long moment. "South Korea."

"And those men that were shot? Also from South Korea?"

He nodded.

"Were they traveling with you?"

Again, he hesitated. Cade had the sense that the hesitation was more disdain and weariness than lacking cooperation.

"They worked for me. They are my security detail." His English was surprisingly good. "Well, they *were* my security detail. I have replacements on the way."

"That's cold, man," Rook said. "Why do you need security in the first place?"

Without looking at Rook, Fang answered. "Their deaths speak to the necessity of their presence." There was a smugness to his demeanor that rubbed Cade the wrong way. One glance at his partner showed he wasn't the only irritated one.

Leaning forward, Rook growled, "Clearly, you're up to something. We all know you don't need armed security if you're playing by the book."

Thinking it might be best to diffuse things—getting more flies with honey and all that—Cade stepped in. "I understand you're here for the International Mayors Conference. I'd imagine that if you're in international business, this is the place to be."

Fang looked at Cade as if seeing him for the first time. "You are correct. Being an international trade consultant, access is everything. When I have so many current and potential clients in the same city, it's a boom."

Rook perked up. "Boom? Like gunshots?"

"In this case, boom is the sudden, rapid growth and expansion of my business."

Rook perked back down.

"I can understand why you would want to be here. But why bring a security team? Surely, using armed bodyguards is not normal in your profession?" Cade asked.

"I come from Korea, where there is much order. Life is regimented to a great extent. In the West, disorder increases. With trade, comes much capital and risk. To not prepare for any eventuality is not to be prepared at all."

Nodding, Cade asked, "Why did your men have their weapons out when they were shot?"

"They were protecting my assistant. She is striking and at times attracts unwarranted attention. However, the outcome was surprising."

"I'm sure. Have you ever previously seen the man who shot your team?"

"No, and I only got the briefest of glances from across the room. Unremarkable."

"Where is your assistant right now?" Cade asked.

Fang studied his hands for a long moment. He looked as if he was going to answer but instead held his tongue.

"Mr. Fang," Rook prompted.

"She disappeared in all the commotion."

"Your assistant vanished? Did she have any contacts in Minneapolis?"

Fang shook his head. "Rose is from a small fishing village. She's a simple girl, albeit a beautiful one. She wouldn't know anyone here."

"Did you see who she left with?"

Fang again found his hands interesting. "The shooter. It appears she left with him."

6

Rose had him the instant she whispered, "What I'm about to tell you could get us both killed."

She shifted forward on the bed, posture poised but intimate, eyes locked on Frank. It was the first time she'd spoken to him with that kind of directness, and it unsettled him more than he cared to admit.

"My story," she began, her voice soft, accented but deliberate, "is one of survival. To Mr. Fang, I was the flawless assistant—always polished, always ready. I managed his schedule, arranged his travel, answered his calls. It looked like servitude, but it was something else entirely. For a girl from a fishing village, it was the chance to step into another world."

She spoke like she was confessing, but her words carried weight, crafted with precision.

"Fang insisted I dress the part. He gave me an expense account and sent me to a clothier who imported Western designs. The dresses were tailored, the heels were exquisite, and soon I understood the power of presentation. A woman who looks untouchable is treated as untouchable. And so I became... untouchable."

Her smile was subtle and fleeting, but her eyes never left Frank. She didn't need to twirl for him to know the effect she could conjure. She let the silence stretch, forcing him to sit with the image she had painted.

"The heels became my signature," she continued, her tone now edged with a sly undercurrent. "Jimmy Choo, Kate Spade, Christian Louboutin... red soles, sharp lines, weapons disguised as beauty. Fang thought I was dressing for him, but I was dressing for me. Every inch of height, every sharpened silhouette, made me harder to dismiss—and easier to underestimate. That was my greatest advantage."

For a moment, her expression hardened, the sweetness stripped away. "Clothes and charm are masks. They distract. They let people see what I want them to see."

She let that hang between them, then softened again, the mask sliding back into place with a practiced grace. "But not everything was good."

Frank was riveted by her story.

"Recently, I've seen changes in Mr. Fang. He'd become preoccupied and was constantly stressed, becoming irritable at the slightest provocation. He began to hide his meetings and would shoo me from his office for certain calls. That was something he'd never done in the eighteen months I worked for him."

Frank leaned forward at the edge of his chair. The sensuous smell of her perfume wafted over him. He'd always prided himself on his professionalism, but it was getting more difficult by the moment. He decided to ask a question before a problem arose. "What did you do? Did you ask him why things had changed?"

Rose shook her head and said, "No, that would have been inappropriate of me. But eventually, my curiosity got the best of me, and I began to listen at his door and read his emails whenever he was away. And I didn't like what I saw." She looked down at her hands.

"Rose, what did you see?"

"My village upbringing stuck with me, and I knew I couldn't ignore the evil that was planned. My grandfather had a saying. To ignore evil is to condone it."

"Rose, what did you see?"

She lifted her eyes—those amazing eyes—to his. Maybe it was his imagination, but Frank thought he could see her worry and pain plain as day in her eyes.

"Mr. Fang has involved himself with bad men. They are planning a series of infrastructure attacks. These attacks are not ideological in nature; they are profit-driven using the stock markets."

She paused, watching Frank just a moment too long. Her expression was unreadable—was it fear? Calculation?

Frank wasn't sure.

His experience with the stock market consisted of looking at his monthly 401(k) statement and shrugging. A higher balance meant more time fishing. He was never curious how the balance increase happened as long as it did.

"They plan to use stock options, betting that utility and energy stocks will nosedive after the attacks. Much like Osama bin Laden was suspected of doing prior to the September 11th attacks, they want to use put trading to make windfalls in the global markets."

Talk of stock options made Frank's eyes glaze over faster than a donut on a Krispy Kreme conveyor belt. And now he was thinking about glazed donuts.

"I thought this conference, with all the conspirators gathered, would be the moment. Opportunities like this don't come twice." Rose's voice was soft, but there was no tremor in it—each word was weighed and measured.

She leaned closer, her hand brushing his—not tender, but deliberate, as if staking a claim. "I am not helpless, Frank. Don't mistake me for some village girl dazzled by the men she serves. I survived Fang because I learned when to smile, when to flatter, and when to sharpen the knife. But what comes next, I cannot do alone."

She let the words linger, then tilted her head, studying Frank as if she were assessing a weapon she wasn't sure she wanted to use. "I need someone outside Fang's circle. Someone reckless enough, clever enough... useful enough." Her fingers brushed his hand, a casual touch that felt calculated.

Her smile was faint, almost playful, but her eyes told a different story—sharp, measuring, dangerous. "So, tell me, Frank, are you the man I can use? The one I can trust to stand beside me when the ground shifts?"

It was charming. Maybe even sincere.

Or maybe it was just what she thought he wanted to hear.

Frank had never been anyone's shining knight, and despite himself, was enthralled by her plea. "I'll do my best. Do you know who these men are? Do you have their names and descriptions?"

Nodding, Rose said, "I can do better than that. I have Mr. Fang's meeting schedule. I know exactly when and where these men will be."

Rose looked at Frank thoughtfully. "Can I ask you something?" Frank nodded. "Why did you have a gun at the hotel?"

Frank hesitated. It was a hell of a story—and he wanted to tell her—but it went against everything he believed in.

Do not call attention to yourself.

His entire career had been built on blending in. If he was tailing a corrupt broker on Wall Street, he looked like just another harried accountant late for a meeting. Following a drug runner through a packed outdoor market in Cairo, he was the sunburned tourist haggling for spices. Slipping into a Moscow gala? He became the forgettable man lurking by the shrimp platter. Frank was decidedly average—and that was his superpower. He had a gift for never standing out.

But a part of him yearned to be more than average. Especially to this woman.

If only he had his handler's confidence. You wouldn't ever look at Tom with his stocky build and horn-rimmed glasses and think ladies' man, yet Frank had seen it for himself.

They'd been out at a D.C. night spot. A twenty-something blonde server had stepped up to the server station next to them. Tom made a show of looking her up and down. "They didn't make them like you when I was in college."

The blonde gave him serious stink eye. "They didn't make electric lights then, either."

"That's cold. What have I ever done to you?"

"Nothing, but you wouldn't be able to keep up with me. Not at your age."

"I'm like ten years older than you. But don't get your undies in a bunch. You're not my type, honey."

"You mean I'm sober." She'd rolled her eyes, tossed him a napkin, and walked away. But the napkin had her number.

Frank's last relationship was really about convenience—hers, not his. He suspected that had kept him around for social events when she needed a plus one. No love, no passion. Not the stuff of romance novels for sure. It had ended with a whimper.

He pushed the thought aside. Now wasn't the time to reflect on past mistakes—not with this woman staring at him like she saw something worth saving. "There's no easy explanation." He hesitated.

Her eyes positively sparkled staring back at him. "Are you a security officer?"

She was giving him an out—a perfectly gift-wrapped lie. All he had to do was nod. He hated lying. But he hated screwing things up even more. "I am." He left it there. Safer that way.

He supposed his conservative mindset had started with his father.

Frank's father, Percy, had been a salesman. He was with the same company for his entire career. As salesmen go, Percy was middle of the road. He was never going to be a rainmaker. "Let the young bucks make the splash," he'd often tell his young and impressionable son. "I'm happy to stick with my regular customers. They're always going to order the same thing every month." The other salespeople saw Percy as more of an order taker than a salesperson, but management didn't seem to care, let alone notice.

Over the years, Percy survived upheavals and reorganizations, most likely due to his low profile as much as his positive numbers in the monthly balance sheet. Managers came and went, CEOs were brought in and often ushered shortly back out, but nothing trickled down as far as Percy.

New management always offered fabulous incentives, such as new cars and trips to exotic locations to the salespeople who brought in new business. If Percy was jealous of the younger salespeople showing up to work in their brand spanking new Ford Taurus after returning bronzed and refreshed from Bali, he never let on. He was eagerly awaiting retirement so he could walk the beaches in plaid shorts dragging a metal detector.

And then, something changed.

One of Percy's accounts swallowed up a smaller company on the industrial food chain. As it turned out, this new company needed a new source for a specific widget. This widget was exactly what Percy had been providing his regular customers for years and he was referred to the new company. This would be Percy's first new customer in over a dozen years. If that wasn't enough for management to raise an eyebrow, the size of the order was.

This new company needed a lot of widgets. It was the single largest order of Percy's career. When he walked into work the next day, things were different. People noticed Percy. Secretaries, staff, and management who had ignored him for years said hello. They actually called him by name. Other salespeople came to him for advice. Percy walked with a swagger for the first time in his humdrum life.

Frank saw the change in his father. At first, it was the fact that Percy began talking about the people at his work. This was new. Then Percy began getting his shirts pressed and starched. He bought his first new tie in a decade. It was shortly after his father came home with a new Subaru that Frank realized he hadn't mentioned retirement for weeks. For once, he seemed to look forward to going to work.

His father was a new man.

But then, as Frank's father was taking newly confident strides forward, someone kicked his legs out from underneath him. It all crashed when another salesman claimed Percy's new account fell in his territory. Management listened. Considered. Decided.

Percy lost the client, the commission, and the future he'd just begun to dream about. He came home a broken man.

Frank never forgot it. Lesson learned: keep your head down, don't get noticed, and never dream too big.

Frank looked at the woman across from him—hauntingly beautiful, with cinnamon-toned skin and eyes that could undo a man. Getting noticed by her was more than enough. He didn't need or want anything else.

"When you say infrastructure attacks, what do you mean exactly? Cyber attacks? Physical attacks?"

Rose's face went tight, and she squeezed his hand. "They are planning simultaneous attacks that are both physical and cyber. They want these utilities and energy companies brought to their knees in a very public way. These men have the means and motivation to create significant disruptions. The more chaos, the more the stock prices drop."

All thoughts of donuts long evaporated as Frank nodded. "So, what do we do? Go to the authorities?"

Rose held his gaze as she looked into his soul. "They are not going to believe a secretary and a rental cop," she said. "No, we need to stop them."

This didn't feel like the kind of low-profile situation Frank preferred to be involved in.

"How do you suggest we do that?" he asked, but he already had an idea where this was going.

"You have a gun, don't you? You go to the meetings and shoot them dead."

Nope. Not low profile at all.

7

Rook spoke confidently. "We need to find the woman. If we find her, we have the shooter."

"Genius plan. How do you suggest we find her? The conference is starting soon, and the city will be flooded with politicians from around the globe." Cade ran a hand through his already messy hair. "Like we needed more."

Rook gazed out to the lobby as a whirlwind of activity went on around them. The bodies were leaving through the front entrance—never good for business—and more police than ever had come in. The Minneapolis Police Department believed in safety in numbers.

"I got nothing," Rook said after a moment. "Since Fang said her phone was dead or turned off, maybe we should look at her hotel room. See what we can learn about her."

Cade nodded. "It can't hurt. And better than staying here. I wouldn't want to step on anyone's dick. There's a cop every two feet pissing on the crime scene." It was starting to feel like a golden shower of jurisdictional pride.

"Yeah, it's a dominance thing. They don't teach you about it at the academy, but it's the Wild West. Every precinct and division competing against each other. Everyone wants to have power. Social dominance theory suggests—"

"You *did* go to college."

Rook's eyes narrowed. "May I continue?"

Cade laughed and waved a hand. "Please do."

"Social dominance theory," Rook continued, "means the big dogs get the toys, the underdogs get the crap work. The dominant precincts and divisions get the financing and better assignments, while the less dominant ones—"

"Such as your violent crimes division."

Rook flashed him a look and continued.

"The less dominant ones get the scraps and crap assignments."

"You mean like dealing with gangs, murder, assault, robbery, and criminal sexual conduct?"

Cade got the look again.

"Yeah, kinda like that. Kinda exactly like that."

"I see. I'm assuming this theory wasn't created to explain the disparity in policing?"

"No, man. It explains how the exploited are continually exploited." Rook was getting more and more passionate as he spoke. "The theory suggests that prejudice legitimizes and maintains the existing social hierarchy."

"Meaning?"

"Y'all keeping the black man down."

"Not me. I hand-picked you to be my number one, remember?"

Rook grinned. "Okay, not you. You're alright."

Cade laughed. "You're alright too. Let's go check out Rose's hotel room. Maybe we'll get lucky."

Frank reconnected Tom's link as he took a seat in the lobby away from everyone else. The large space wasn't crowded—just the usual lobby-sitters with nothing better to do than hang out in a hotel. Opening up a newspaper and leaning back, he spoke softly, "Tom. You with me?"

The response was immediate and loud enough in his earpiece that he winced.

"Frank, what the hell? You can't go all rogue on me. That's not how we play this game."

"Tom, I—"

"Listen, you need to be on point with the mission. Where are you now?"

"I'm at the hotel."

"Looks like a dump. Where is the woman?"

Frank cleared his throat.

"Wait, she's there with you? Show me."

"No, she's up in the room."

"Your room?"

Frank didn't respond.

"What are you thinking? Do I have to remind you about protocols?"

Frank shook his head.

"I'm assuming you're shaking your head. Remember, I can't see you. I can only see what you see when the link is live. And don't go turning it off again, Frank."

Frank mumbled.

Tom sighed. Exasperatedly. "Give me a sitrep."

Taking a deep breath, Frank said, "Alpha is alive. Chou Fang's two bodyguards are dead. His personal assistant, Rose, is currently in my hotel room. In my interrogation, I learned that Fang is collaborating with Alpha and a number of unknowns to attack the global energy infrastructure for financial gain. The attacks will be simultaneous as both cyber and physical assaults will be employed."

"Do you have a sense of timing on these attacks?"

"Not yet, but Fang has meetings scheduled with the men over the next several days. All are here in Minneapolis." Frank watched the hotel security officer as she moved across the lobby, taking in every person there. He subtly moved the newspaper to obscure his face.

"Is there a greater purpose to the financial gain? Is the money being used to finance a terror organization, for instance?" Tom knew his stuff.

The plainclothes security officer had stopped and taken a position near the elevator. She had her head cocked and stole a glance toward him.

"Rose said the purpose was not so much ideological as it was financial."

"Can you trust her?"

"From what I gather, she's a simple fishing village girl from North Korea who was noticed by Fang and hired to be his assistant."

"She looked pretty sophisticated, if you ask me. She was totally killing that outfit at the bar."

Frank laughed. "Her boss wanted her to dress up and paid for her clothes. She said that's her favorite part of her job. She was really shaken up and seemed genuinely concerned about her boss's plans. I want to believe her."

Tom wasn't having it, though. "Frank, this isn't my first rodeo. On the international stage, no one is who they seem to be. You can't trust anyone."

The security woman had edged a little closer.

"I'll look into the other men Fang is meeting, see if I can ID them, but I need to go. Hotel security is lurking."

"Give them something insubstantial. Maybe use the Paris scenario."

Frank slipped out his cell phone and, even though it wasn't turned on, slid it up to his ear. He lowered the paper a little.

"Of course, LeRoy. I'm not checking out the Minneapolis boys, promise. Yes, I miss you too, stud muffin."

The woman turned away smiling and Frank took the opportunity to head for the stairs.

"Nice touch, Frank. I always wanted to be a stud muffin." Tom broke out laughing as Frank broke the link.

From what Cade could tell, the Le Méridien Chambers was a hotel disguised as an art gallery. Or maybe it was an art gallery disguised as a hotel. Either way, the lobby was filled with art and looked substantially different from the last hotel he had stayed at—though he wasn't sure the Le Méridien Chambers would leave the lights on for him like the other had promised.

After showing their badges at the front desk, then again to the security officer and finally the supervisor, they were led up to the fourth floor. Rook and Cade traded glances as the security officer stared at the elevator display.

"Hey, man," Rook said. "Do you like your job?"

Without looking away from the display, the security man said, "Most days."

"I get that. What's with all the art? I saw a painting downstairs that was nothing but splatters. It looked like a crime scene photo after a chainsaw store dust-up."

Cade grinned.

"Chainsaw Store Dust-up: band name. I called it," the officer said.

"Your talents are being wasted here," Rook said smoothly. "I can see you're an idea man. Have you thought about getting into law enforcement? There's a real need."

The man nodded as the elevator doors opened. "Thought about it," he said, finally glancing at Rook. "But cops have rules. Me, I like being the guy who notices the weird stuff nobody else does. Here, I write it down, call it in, and go home. Out there?" He gave a small shake of his head. "Out there, you take it personal. And once you take it personal, the job owns you."

"That's not all bad, either," Cade said, stepping around them into the hall. "Passion is the special sauce in life. But, c'mon, let's get this investigation moving."

The security officer opened the door with his keycard and stepped aside. Weapons drawn, Rook followed Cade into the room. Within a moment, they cleared the room. The woman—and killer—weren't there.

The room was modern with a muted palette of white, black, and grays, with the occasional accent piece. A red chair, a red lamp, and a red throw pillow added the color pop that only an expensive interior designer could think of.

Under the watchful eye of the security officer, they went through the room. Rose's closet held a dozen silky dresses and expensive-looking designer heels lined the carpet below. Rook went through the dresser drawers and held up a handful of silk panties.

"How long was she planning on being here? This would last me a month."

Cade shook his head. "I don't know if that says anything about her as much as it does about you."

"I'm a man of utilitarian style. Never more than I need."

"I see you have three extra magazines for your service weapon," Cade noted as he pointed to the magazines on Rook's belt. "That's over 50 rounds. You *need* that many?"

"Yeah, I'm a really bad shot."

"Okay then. I won't stand down range from you then." Cade pulled out the woman's impossibly coordinated luggage and laid them on the king-size bed. Going through the compartments one by one, there was the usual travel debris: receipts, old luggage tags, hair binders, gum, stuff like that. Nothing out of the ordinary.

Rook moved to the bathroom and started going through her toiletries and even checking the toilet tank. Cade peeked under the mattress and crawled along the bed. Again, nothing.

Cade looked up at the security officer. "You've been in all these rooms hundreds of times. Do you see anything out of place?"

Rook came out of the bathroom as the officer sidled into the room, hands on his belt. He looked around for a long moment as he hummed something that sounded like it belonged in a funeral march. After a minute of meandering, he had the ghost of a smile. "Two of these things are not like the other."

Cade pinched his nose and shot a glance at Rook.

"I love your keen observation skills, but we're not going to play a game of hot or cold, man. What do you see?"

He sighed—the kind of sigh you give when someone tells you to quit bluffing and play your damn cards. Security Officer Sharma, as his nameplate read, pointed to the painting over the couch. "It's crooked."

Cade sat on the bed next to the woman's matching suitcase set while Rook went over to the painting. An oblong splash of nothing, the colorful painting dipped on the left side. Rook lifted the painting off its mounts. A plastic baggie dropped onto the couch and landed on the cushion. Setting aside the painting, Rook leaned close before turning back. His eyebrows rose.

"What is it?"

"It's a scooby doobie."

"What?"

"You know. A wizard stick. A tokemon. A spliff."

"Do you mean a joint?" Cade asked and Rook nodded. "Why didn't you just say so?"

"I did, but you weren't understanding. You should work the streets more. You'll learn lots of colorful language."

Cade laughed. "Of that I have no doubt. But I do doubt the street drug belonged to the woman, it could have been there for a while. Either way, it's irrelevant."

Rook turned back to the security officer. "Okay, what else do you have? You mentioned two things."

He pointed toward Cade.

Rook laughed. "I already knew something was off with him."

Sharma walked past Cade and nudged one of the suitcase wheels. "The color is different on this one."

Cade leaned over and examined the wheel. The color was off a bit by a shade of gray. And it didn't look quite as scuffed as the others.

"Nice catch," Cade said. "You're like the Sherlock Holmes of luggage wheels." But he didn't think he'd ever have noticed it—even if they had been playing a game of hot and cold. He could have been stuck on *burning hot* and still not have spotted the wheel difference.

Cade pulled on it and the caster popped free from the mounting on the suitcase base. He turned it slowly in his hand, examining it. The third time around he noticed a delicate seam with a minuscule black screw flush with the surface.

"Can you get a fine screwdriver?" he asked Sharma. The security officer nodded and stepped out into the hall.

"There's something in here," he told Rook as he shook the wheel. There was a soft rattle.

"Can't be much, not at that size," Rook said.

"It's not the *size* that matters," Cade said, deadpan, without looking up.

"Spoken like a true cracker—"

Cade held up his hand to cut him off.

"Fine, but if you don't like my witty banter, I don't know if this is going to work out," Rook said with a shake of his head. But he was grinning.

The chime of Rook's cell interrupted. "Yo, Miller. What's up?"

Rook's eyes hardened as he listened. He walked to the window and back before ending the call.

"Looks like the feds are getting involved in the case too."

Cade shrugged. "Not unexpected. The victims were foreign nationals after all."

"So, Minneapolis PD, the feds, and us are all investigating the same case?"

"Looks that way."

Rook shook his head. "I can see this becoming a shit show a mile away and even a blind man at a fish market could smell this one coming."

"Yeah," Cade said. "But it's our shit show."

The security officer returned with an older man in tow. He had the uniform shirt of maintenance men the world over. Of course, his name patch read Walt. Every building has a Walt. Likable, wise, capable. And they all knew how to pick locks and dismantle bombs.

"Heard you needed some assistance," Walt said as he rolled out a collection of fine tools on the side table.

"Yep." Cade reached for the tools, but the maintenance man waved him away.

"I got this. You catch the bad guys, I use the tools. Union rules, you know. Besides, this is far better than fixing toilets."

"I see," Cade said and handed over the wheel. He pointed to the tiny screw.

Within a moment, Walt had the cover off and turned it over to empty the contents onto the table. Small black discs with wires sticking out. They had an insect-like appearance.

Walt looked confused. "Wait, those are bugs?"

"That's exactly what they are. A rare species of imported listening bugs." Smiling, Cade added, "And they're highly invasive."

8

This wasn't how it was supposed to go.

Francis Perlmutter—Frank, if he'd had friends (he didn't)—lived life under the radar. It was almost a mantra for him: *Keep your head down. Don't make a scene. Stay focused, don't get involved in anyone's problems.* Yet, here he was. Heading for the W Hotel to find the South Korean contingent. The gun in his coat pocket, ready to kill.

He blamed the woman.

Frank was fast approaching fifty, not at all the time to be upsetting the applecart. If he listened to his own internal dialogue, he might just live long enough to retire. His goal was to quit the business and enjoy his retirement fishing in the warm Florida sun. Yet, here he was, wearing an Arctic Circle-rated parka in the frozen tundra of Minnesota.

It was definitely the woman.

She was why he'd tuned out the steadying voice in his head. And then—worse—he'd gotten involved.

Large flakes filled the evening air, making it difficult for Frank to see further than a block away. On the plus side, it effectively made him anonymous. Everyone was bundled and walked with their heads down. But really. Who had the bright idea of holding a conference here in the land of ice and snow? In November?

Up ahead, he spotted the welcome glow of the W Hotel. A snowplow roared by and launched a snow tsunami across the sidewalk. At the same time, a four-wheeler swept the sidewalk for the hearty folks walking downtown Minneapolis.

Inside, Frank pulled off his hood and sized up the situation. Beyond the immediate lobby with the front desk of disinterested staffers, was a large open area filled with groups of people spread around the tables. These people seemed oblivious to the weather carnage happening outside. Frank grabbed a seat at a small table as several men in suits vacated it.

His feet cold, Frank watched the spreading puddle as the snow melted off his dress shoes.

"You really should be wearing boots if you're walking outside."

Frank glanced up to find a server. The man looked to be in his twenties and his nameplate read Taylor.

"You may be right. I don't know how you are supposed to get around here." Frank shook his head.

"We take the skyways." Taylor accurately read his confusion and laughed.

"The skyways are how we avoid the weather. Think of it as a habitrail connecting the downtown buildings on the second story. You can get all over downtown Minneapolis through the skyways without ever stepping outside."

Because what's better than walking through a giant hamster tunnel when it's minus 12 outside?

"That's genius, but wouldn't you rather live somewhere better suited for human habitation?"

Taylor's look said *not another coastal guy with opinions.* "Like where?"

"I'm thinking Florida might be a good place."

"Too many crazies in Florida," Taylor said as he shook his head. "Pretty sure every news story where someone does something crazy, you'll see it was in Florida. Or maybe California."

"But I could fish every damn day in Florida."

"This is the land of 10,000 lakes," Taylor said. "You could fish every day here in Minnesota at a different lake. It would still take you over 27 years. Of course, you'd have to cut a hole in the ice for half the year."

Frank shook his head. "I'll pass, thank you. I'd rather take my chances with the crazies. Besides, I'm better armed than they are."

Taylor gave Frank an appraising look, no doubt deciding if he was kidding or not. He chose wrong and laughed. "Ha, good one. So, what can I bring you?"

After Frank ordered a hot tea, he sat back in the pretentious yet uncomfortable chair and scanned the room. The W had that Mad Men vibe—if Don Draper was into plastic plants and overpriced cocktails.

He was searching for his target, who he knew would be part of the South Korean group in town for the International Mayors Conference. It didn't take long to find them—about twenty gathered in a side lounge around a long table, all dressed in suits with serious expressions. A few men with earpieces lingered just outside, scanning the room with military-grade suspicion. Clearly security. Frank looked away—he didn't need to draw their attention. He'd already put two men in the morgue this week. Adding more bodyguards wouldn't help anyone.

Taylor returned with his tea and Frank sipped the warm drink while taking surreptitious glances into the side lounge. Waiting for Chou Fang to arrive. The man he would meet with would become his target. And then...

He sighed.

It felt wrong doing this without Tom. The voice in his ear could be grating—sarcastic, smug, occasionally superior—but it was also a tether. A lifeline. Over the years, Tom had earned that rare status: indispensable. He could guide Frank through an escape route in real time or summon the cavalry when things went sideways. He had eyes in the sky—access to CCTV, databases, and encrypted feeds Frank didn't pretend to understand. And maybe most importantly, Tom knew how to keep him invisible. Off the grid, out of sight, under the radar. But without him, Frank felt exposed. He didn't relish the idea of being a solo act without a net.

He activated the link bringing audio and video online.

"Are you there?" Silence, though the sound of rustling papers could be heard. "Tom, I know you're there. Talk to me."

The paper rustling got so loud, Frank suspected he was doing it on purpose. After a while of working together as handler and asset, tension had been known to creep into relationships. The term *old married couple* had been used but only quietly. No one talked so openly in front of someone who killed for a living.

"Tom. I'm in the lobby of the W Hotel with a view of the South Korean contingent. That's the large group over there." Frank turned in his chair so the IMC pin camera pointed toward the group. "Fang is scheduled to meet one of the members. My intel says that person is conspiring to attack infrastructures. That person will be my alpha."

The paper rustling stopped.

"Excuse me. Dazhao is your Alpha. Do you have any idea what Sheila Ann's reaction would be if you went off mission?"

"*Umm.*"

"Do you know how livestock are castrated?" Tom didn't wait for an answer. "Surgical castration is performed by making a large incision in the bull's scrotum. Once the scrotal sac is opened, each testicle is grasped individually to isolate the spermatic cord, and an emasculator is used to crimp and cut the cord. The emasculator stays clamped on the bull's nuts for nearly a half minute to help control bleeding."

Frank swallowed, even though his mouth had gone dry.

"Do you want Sheila Ann coming after you with an emasculator?"

"No. Not in the least," Frank managed to croak.

"Okay, here's what we're going to do. Stay and identify the person Fang meets with. Once we have an ID, we can track him and verify the woman's information. I shouldn't have to remind you—but clearly I do—this is a low-profile, intel gathering only mission. Afterwards, it's back to Dazhao."

Frank nodded.

"Use your voice, Frank. I want a record of your submittal."

There was never going to be a recording, Frank knew that. No one wanted a permanent record of a government-authorized assassination. But he answered anyway. "Yes. Intel only. And then back to Dazhao."

"Frank, I'm concerned about the hornet's nest you stirred up at the Hotel Theodore. The local authorities are bad enough, but now a high-profile major crimes task force has been activated. From what I've researched, they are devastatingly effective."

"They're after me?"

"They're after the shooter who executed two South Koreans at an upscale hotel a block from the police administration." Tom sighed dramatically. "But this isn't totally unexpected. I knew they were likely to get involved if this dragged out at all. I've been looking into ways to slow them down. Shift their priorities."

"Okay, thank you." Frank glanced around.

There was movement in the Korean contingent. One of the men, thickset with a horseshoe mustache worthy of Pulp Fiction, stood and moved to the bar. It was crowded with mostly men in suits, women in suits, and the occasional more casual interloper. The man walked past the bar and took a seat at one of the high tables that flanked the area. Pulling out his phone, he started typing. After a minute, one of the men from the bar stood up and walked over, sitting across from the man. The trouble was, at no time did he offer a view other than the back of his head.

Sighing, Frank stood.

"I need to get a look," he said quietly as he carried his tea across the room.

"That's right, just a look." Tom sounded exasperated. It was a tone Frank knew well. "If that's Fang, you get me a clear view of the man with the mustache, and I can run facial recognition. Once identified, we'll know how best to proceed."

"*Umm.*"

"Frank. Sheila Ann. The emasculator. Do I need to say more?"

Tom didn't. But he could hear Rose's voice in his head, pleading with him. "My boss is funding terrorists, and I set up the meetings. You have to stop it from happening."

In the part of his brain that still reasoned, he knew that trying to make everyone happy was never going to succeed and no one would end up happy—least of all himself. But he needed to try.

Pulling out his cell phone, he put it up to his ear and started talking.

"Yes, dear. I miss you too." His imaginary wife was very loving. Unlike the real women in his past. He walked around the back side of the bar where the restrooms were located, pausing to let a server cross his path before continuing.

"Have you put Charlie to bed yet? Can I talk to him?"

The man came into view. It was Fang.

"Charlie, how was school today?"

He moved the phone to the other ear to better obscure his profile. He was confident Fang wouldn't recognize him but being careful was ingrained in him. *Keep your head down. Don't get noticed.*

"That's great. You'll have to show Daddy when I get back from my convention."

His face and eyes stayed averted as he passed the table.

"When did you get so good at drawing? I'm proud of you."

Frank sat at a table near Fang and his guest. They looked intent in their conversation and neither gave him a second glance.

"Lean a little to your left. I can almost get him in frame." Tom's view was limited to where the camera concealed in the conference pin was pointed. It had surprising resolution for being so miniscule. But that was government tech for you. They were good at what they did. At least in matters of tech. Yet for some reason they hadn't been able to figure out how to create a pothole free road in Virginia.

There shouldn't be potholes in the Florida Keys, Frank mused.

"Yeah, horses are tough to draw." Frank leaned to his left.

"A little more," Tom said.

"I once drew a horse. Although my mom thought it was a tractor. Still, she hung it on our fridge for two years." He leaned over further, careful to keep the pin aimed towards the man.

"That's it. I have a clear image. Running facial recognition." Tom's AI sifted through thousands of faces, matching key features in seconds. "I'm sure it was a nice horse."

"There was no horse."

"There's always a horse, Frank. Until you come to terms with that, your childhood trauma will continue to fester and cause issues in your adulthood."

"You mean I may want to shoot someone?"

"Good point. Hold on, we have a match here."

Fang slid a flash drive across the table. The other man casually picked it up and slid it into his breast pocket.

"His name is Roger Featherstone, a Canadian national. He's forty-two years old and married. According to his passport scan, he arrived at Minneapolis Saint Paul yesterday from Montreal."

The men were getting up from the table.

"Do me a favor, check where else Mr. Featherstone has been."

Frank adjusted the phone at his ear as the two men passed by.

"Daddy needs to get ready for his meeting tomorrow. I have lots of pens and lanyards to give away."

Tom spoke quickly. "Frank, there are no other destinations for Featherstone. He's never been anywhere. I checked his address, and it shows up as part of a strip mall. Waxing the City, to be precise."

The men separated by the bar, Fang going one way, Featherstone the other.

"No surprise he entered the country with false credentials. He's leaving the hotel now, which means we may never know who he is or what he's planning. What would you like me to do?"

The man was headed across the foyer towards the entrance. He could disappear into the storm and never be found again. Rose's plea to stop these men echoed in his mind.

"Shit fire and light a match," Tom spat. "Go after him."

Frank didn't hesitate. He dumped his tea, pulled his hood up and followed the man outside as the wind slapped his face like a wake-up call. He pulled his parka tighter and pushed into the stormy swirl.

9

As it always does, word got out quickly about the shooting in Minneapolis. Secrets in law enforcement were about as safe as a plate of Oreos in a room full of toddlers. Everyone couldn't help themselves. Sharing was caring, after all.

And now, the media had sunk their teeth in, already turning it into a major story.

"Yesterday's double homicide took everyone by surprise. It happened at an unlikely venue, downtown Minneapolis's upscale Hotel Theodore." A brunette woman reporter stood in front of the hotel. On screen, the text read, Alex MacCarthy reporting.

"Compared to this same time a year ago, violent crimes are trending down through the first nine months in Minneapolis. But yesterday's double homicide at the Theodore in Minneapolis raised more concerns than a possible reversal of the welcome trend. Chief among those is the proximity to the upcoming International Mayors Conference."

"A spokesman for the conference met with us and didn't seem to be concerned with the deadly shooting."

A well-dressed man with salt-and-pepper hair was on screen speaking with a British accent. "The primary objective of our conference is to stimulate positive and constructive relations between mayors internationally, based on interlocking interests and concerns. While it was a tragic event, what happened yesterday had nothing to do with the International Mayors Conference. Based on our inquiries, it appears to be a business disagreement among non-governmental individuals. We are, and will continue to be, a beacon of positivity in global economics and politics."

On screen, images—likely lifted from the hotel's website—depicted the hotel's elegant interior.

"So far, the Minneapolis Police Department hasn't shared details on the two victims, citing the ongoing investigation and a desire to notify relatives first. The men are believed to be from South Korea."

A world map came on screen and South Korea was highlighted.

"Police believe the man responsible was acting alone and may have left the area. Police Chief Isla Pilkington."

A uniformed woman with her hair pulled back wore a serious expression as she addressed reporters.

"As with most ongoing investigations, facts and assumptions are fluid and may change. We believe the shooter had a disagreement with the security contingent for a foreign businessman. As such, the risk to the public is minimal. We have marshaled all resources to bring this shooter to justice. Among those resources brought to the case is the Five Below Major Crimes Task Force. Led by special investigator Cade Dawkins, they were responsible for the apprehension of the out-of-state serial killers in this year's unprecedented attacks in the Twin Cities. We'll be working with his group and welcome their assistance."

An image of Cade Dawkins, followed by ones of Grace Fox and Terrance Rooker, were displayed.

"Many viewers will recall the high-profile Blonde Killer case—the one that brought Detective Cade Dawkins to national attention. Working alongside BCA crime scene specialist Grace Fox, the two stopped Marlin Sweetwater in the middle of a brutal killing spree. Following that case, Dawkins was tapped to lead the Governor's newly formed major crimes unit. That unit—dubbed the Five Below Task Force—was rounded out by Minneapolis PD's own Terrance Rooker and two St. Paul detectives, Lorie Thao and Kristen Bednarek. As Chief Pilkington mentioned earlier, it was the task force's first—and only—case."

The screen returned to the reporter outside the hotel with a split screen showing television anchor Ava Anderson. She had blonde hair and striking hazel eyes.

"Alex, has anyone from Five Below spoken up? Police are calling it a business disagreement, but the Governor sent in a major crimes task force. That doesn't add up."

"That's a fair point. Is it a major crime or a violent end to a business dis-agreement? No one from the task force has been made available and answers will have to wait. But stay tuned, I'm Alex MacCarthy, and I'll stay on this story as it develops. Back to you, Ava."

By the time the news clip ended, Cade and Rook were already back at Le Méridien Chambers. Standing in the lobby, Cade gestured outside. Snow swirled like the inside of a snow globe. "It's really coming down out there. I didn't realize we were expecting weather."

"It's Minnesota. We're always expecting weather."

"Then why aren't you dressed for it?" Cade gestured to the white shoes and Rook's varsity jacket. "That doesn't look exactly warm."

"It's my aesthetic. It's form over function."

"Say what?"

"I'd rather be cool than be warm."

"Gotcha. Well, let's grab a spot and talk about next steps." Cade pointed out a bench that sat before a painting of a Paris café. It made generous use of ultramarine blue with flicks of Venetian red.

Rook studied the painting of the people enjoying their breakfast in sunny Paris. "I'm hungry," he said after a moment.

"Let's focus on the case. And then we can grab a bite."

"But not here. This is too rich for my cop salary."

Cade took in the ambiance and had to agree. "Let's start with the woman. Rose Park. Executive assistant to Korean businessman Chou Fang. A simple woman from a remote village, or so we were told. She wouldn't know anyone here, Fang said. Yet she was seen leaving with the shooter."

"Maybe she's not as simple as she seems. She had a cache of high-tech listening devices hidden in her luggage, after all."

"Or maybe she hadn't realized she was a mule." Cade pointed at a pair of businessmen pulling suitcases. "Would either of them even know if their luggage had been tampered with? Who checks the wheels of their suitcase?"

"Not me, but if they belonged to her boss or the deceased security team, would those bros have had access to her luggage when they needed their bugs?"

Cade shrugged. "Seems unlikely."

"It would have been far easier to hide the devices in their own suitcase. So, what's the simplest explanation, then?" Rook asked.

"The devices were hers. Then it's likely that she planned to use them on someone." Cade took a beat. "And I have an idea who."

Rook waited for Cade.

"Aren't you going to ask?"

Rook shook his head. "Nah, man."

"You're supposed to ask. It's part of the social contract we all adhere to."

Rook looked stubborn.

"You must. Don't screw with tradition."

Sigh. "I swear, one of these days, but fine. Who was the wayward executive assistant going to use the bugs on?"

"I'm glad you asked. Here's how I figure it. If the assistant left with the shooter, whom, you'll recall, shot and killed her boss's security detail, then she's in opposition to her boss. And since you generally only listen in on the opposition, it stands to reason she planned to use them on her boss."

Rook gave a golf clap. "Well done. I can't fault your reasoning. Now that we have the who, let's figure out the why."

Cade leaned back in the chair. The wind had picked up, swirling the snow outside the window. It was beautiful. "Fang arrives with a pair of armed bodyguards because he's wary. He expected trouble, which he found. But was it the shooter he was worried about?"

Rook shook his head. "That doesn't feel right. His security men were approaching a man sitting with Rose when they were killed. The man wasn't going after Fang."

"So, it's unlikely the bodyguards were there to keep an eye on our simple fishing village girl. This intervention by the shooter was unexpected." Cade paused to mull things over.

"We have to think faster. My stomach is rumbling."

Cade nodded, unhurried. "The thing I keep coming back to is the woman. Rose Park. A simple fishing village girl doesn't carry listening devices. I'll have Grace check—see if they shed any light. But what would be her motivation in all this?"

Rook offered a shrug. "One thing's for sure. We find her, we find the shooter and the answers."

"Why don't you go back to the Theodore and study the surveillance footage. Look for any and all interactions with our three main players. The shooter, Fang, and Rose Park. See who they talked with, who they looked at, and who was watching them. Maybe we get lucky and connect some dots."

"No problem. After we eat."

Cade laughed. "Of course. It's hard to be brilliant on an empty stomach—but not much easier to be brilliant on a full one, either."

"Sometimes I think you like to hear yourself talk," Rook said.

"Someone's hangry," Cade observed.

"Whatever, man. What are you going to be doing while I look through the video?"

"Head for the BCA to have Grace look at these bugs. Then I need to wrap up a case with the Patrol. It should just be a couple of hours with Rob. But until the shooter or Rose makes an appearance, we might be stuck waiting." Cade stood and stretched. "And I hate waiting."

"That's what I'm saying," Rook said. "You're making me wait to eat."

"Then let's go," Cade said laughing. "Let's get you fed—before you shoot someone and blame me for it."

Frank followed Featherstone out of the W into the snowy night. Snowflakes swirled thick and heavy around him.

"How can you see anything?" Tom asked. "All I see is white."

"That's pretty much what I'm seeing as well." Pulling on his hood, he cinched it up as the wind fought to take it back off. He'd only made it half a block before he stopped. "He's gone. I lost him."

"Figures. Would've been too convenient for him to take the skyway like a civilized fugitive."

"You know about skyways?"

Tom laughed. "Sure do. I know the Twin Cities well."

"Wait, are you here? In Minneapolis?"

"Someone's got to make sure this operation doesn't become a complete shit-show. I've been here for a while now. It's not only your ass on the line. Remember Sheila Ann?"

"The emasculator. Got it."

"Don't forget about it, then. You can stake your life on it that Sheila Ann won't."

10

Cade made the snowy crawl from Minneapolis to St. Paul in under thirty minutes, which wasn't terrible considering the weather. Most drivers had slowed and decided they'd rather be late than be in a ditch. But there were some of those, too. He counted four, all SUVs, that had ice-danced off the road. Being big didn't mean you wouldn't slide when you hit your brakes.

He took the exit after the spaghetti junction of downtown St. Paul and then wound his way through the curvy neighborhood streets to the BCA. He dropped his truck in a visitor spot and headed inside. He found Grace in her lab, wearing a lab coat, of course. She wore it over an emerald dress. Her scar from the Blonde Killer was still visible.

"What brings you my way?" she asked as she took a stool at the main table. "You don't usually drop by unless you have—"

She stopped and cocked her head.

"Wait—the governor got the band back together?"

Cade nodded. "Let the chaos begin."

"This is awesome. Task force cases are so much more interesting. A girl gets tired of reading blood spatter, you know." She leaned forward, her eyes positively sparkling with anticipation. "What do you have for me?"

"I'm not taking you away from anything important, am I?"

Her eyes flashed with impatience. "You're killing me here, Smalls. Tell me."

Cade relented. "We've been given the case of the two foreign nationals executed in Minneapolis. Two shots. Silenced. In a crowded hotel lounge. Not exactly amateur hour."

"A professional assassin?"

"Sure feels that way."

"What do we know about the dead men?"

Cade shared what they knew about Fang's men. He mentioned that Rook was reviewing surveillance footage at the hotel. "But one thing that's thrown us off is that Fang's executive assistant, Rose Park, appears to have left willingly with the shooter."

"That is interesting." Grace pulled her hair back and wrapped it in a hair binder. "It's always the anomalies that interest me. We usually learn more from them than from the patterns. What do you know about her?"

Cade stood and began pacing. "Rose Park is from a small Korean fishing village. Her boss described her as simple, yet she was intelligent enough to help run his business."

"How did she dress?"

Cade studied Grace, curious about the why behind her question. He'd known her long enough to know that anything she asked about meant something. "Judging by her closet, she liked designer labels more than fishing nets. Her shoes alone would be more than two months of my meager public servant's salary."

Nodding, Grace rubbed her chin. "She may not be as simple as she was described. Sophisticated tastes are often indicative of intelligence."

Cade paused and reached into his pocket. "And there are these," he said, scattering the devices on the counter in front of her. "We found them concealed inside a wheel of her luggage. There's further evidence she may not be a humble villager."

"Fascinating," Grace said, picking one up and examining it. She carried it over to a microscope device that displayed the magnification onto the massive screen mounted above the table. Grace rotated the bug with a pair of tweezers. "This is a listening device, but I'm sure you knew that. This is the microphone here. The wires are for transmitting the signals to the receiver, which would likely be within a relatively close distance. I'm betting it would go to someone's smartphone, maybe via a relay device of some kind."

"Can you determine the origin of these bugs?"

"Of course," Grace said brightly. "Says right here on the side, made in China."

"You're kidding me."

"Of course, I'm kidding you. These aren't mass-produced and sold to the public. They're likely made by a specific spy agency."

"That would explain the 'For Surveillance Use Only' sticker."

Grace groaned, but she still had a hint of a smile. "I can research through my databases and see if they've been cataloged previously. I'll get back to you on this."

"That'd be great."

She took a sip of her tea. "So, what do you know about assassins?"

Pausing, Cade thought about it. "Not much, really. Only what I know from the movies. But one thing is for sure, they're all elite."

Smiling, Grace nodded. "Of course, that goes with the territory. And they're very focused on their craft. Because this is what they do. Sure, cops and spies kill people, but it's not all they do. Even soldiers, mercenaries, and terrorists, although they kill people, they are usually using the murder to accomplish something larger. But assassins are a rare breed."

"And who hires these killers?" Cade wondered. "I suppose it's like most professions in that you may work for one employer, say a government or crime family, and they keep you busy with all the people they need whacked."

"Did you really just say whacked?"

"I did. It's a technical term."

"I see." Grace had a sly grin. "But these professional whackers may also be working freelance. Someone needs a spy terminated, and they call our freelancer. Or maybe there's an informer within an organization discovered and bingo, it's whack-a-mole time."

Cade dropped his head, clenching the bridge of his nose.

"What?" Grace asked. "That was brilliant."

"Don't mind me. I'm rethinking my life choices."

Grace punched his shoulder playfully. "You just wish you'd thought of it."

"Maybe," Cade said quietly.

Her smile was all Cade needed. "So, let me know what you find with the listening devices, and I'll keep you in the loop on what Rook discovers. But we need to get a handle on this soon. With politicians from around the globe descending on the Twin Cities for the International Mayors Conference, it's a powder keg waiting to blow if the shooter isn't done."

Grace grabbed his hand and went in close, her lips brushing his neck. "Later."

The goosebumps were still there as he climbed into his truck—and he was sure it wasn't from the cold.

Rook walked into the Hotel Theodore, expecting something different, but finding only normalcy. Friendly staff, happy guests, but no sign of two men having been murdered hours earlier. Life and death moving on.

He was greeted at the front desk by Carli, a smiling staffer dressed in a blue blazer. "Checking in, sir?"

Showing her his ID, Rook said, "I'm here to check out the video surveillance of the shooting—"

"Incident, you mean." Her eyes flicked to the suburban-looking couple talking to the other clerk. Her meaning was clear.

"If you'll take a seat," she gestured to the adjoining sitting area for those people who like to hang out in hotel lobbies. "I'll have Ms. Gennaro come out to see you."

"Thank you," Rook said. He took a seat and looked around. There was a steady flow of staff and guests traversing the lobby area.

Thirty-one seconds later, a woman dressed in the same cerulean blue blazer approached. Lean and fit, her strawberry-blonde hair was pulled back into a ponytail. Her nameplate read H. Gennaro. Sitting across from him, she held out a hand. "May I see your identification, please?"

Rook handed over his badge case. A quick glance and it was handed back.

"Detective Rooker, how may I be of assistance?"

"I'd like to review your security footage of the incident here yesterday."

Gennaro nodded and handed over a CD in a paper envelope. The date was written in sharpie. She stood. "If there's anything else, reach back out."

"Were you here when it happened?"

Already walking away, Gennaro paused and turned. "I was not."

"Have you reviewed the footage?"

A hint of exasperation showed on her face. "Of course—but if there's nothing else, I'm quite busy."

"Did you see anything notable during your review? Beyond the shooting—"

Her eyes flashed at him. "Beyond the incident, no." She took a step away.

"Nothing?"

"Detective Rooker, I've answered your question. So, if..."

Having done the job long enough, Rook recognized when someone wanted him to go away. The reasons could be numerous, but it never ceased to irk him just the same. In moments like this, his desire to linger was in equal proportion to the person's desire to have him leave.

"Ms. Gennaro, in cases like this, I've found that reviewing the footage together helps us catch the little things—those blink-and-you-miss-it moments that separate good investigators from great ones. And with your background in corporate security, I'd bet you've already trained your eye to see what others don't." He leaned in slightly, voice dropping just enough to feel conspiratorial. "Look, you're clearly sharp, composed, and ambitious—I'd be shocked if your superiors haven't already pegged you for a fast-track." He smiled. "But this? This could be the moment they write about in your promotion announcement. The one that gets whispered about around the office like, 'Did you hear how she nailed that joint op with Five Below?'" He let the compliment linger, watching her reaction. "I say we make headlines."

Her expression was classic WTF.

"You're concerned about my career trajectory?"

Rook nodded. "As you should be. In the corporate world of the man, you're only as good as what you did today. This is a golden opportunity."

Gennaro checked her nails. "Last I checked my career was just fine. I'm 27, in charge of security for a major hotel in a major city. I'm single, own my own home, and have a diverse and comprehensive stock portfolio."

"You're single?"

There was that look again. "That's all you heard?"

"Well." He shrugged.

"I don't date cops." She started to turn away.

"You have this all wrong."

Gennaro hesitated.

"I wasn't asking because I wanted to date you. I was thinking of my brother. He's single too. But don't worry, he's not a cop."

Rook let a beat pass.

"He's in sanitation."

This time Gennaro didn't hesitate. She stormed off.

Rook noticed the front desk clerk Carli staring at him. She likely had heard the entire exchange. "Don't worry, we're old friends," he told her. "Ever since I broke up with her, she gets a little crabby when we run into each other."

Rook left the hotel smiling. He always enjoyed making friends.

11

Frank had called it a night. The storm was thick enough to hide a body but also thick enough to walk into traffic by mistake. Target lost, escape route erased. Time to regroup. There would be other opportunities. He had Fang's meeting schedule after all.

So far, the Minneapolis mission, codenamed Lakefront, had not been going spectacularly well. Frank wasn't surprised, and to be honest, neither should anyone else familiar with his work.

Mediocrity was sort of his brand.

His efforts were adequate but never exceptional. They were never terrible or incompetent either; however, he should never be anyone's first choice for an assassin. He'd started behind a desk, filing reports. One day someone handed him a gun, and he never managed to give it back. Right place, wrong time. Or maybe it was the other way around.

He would have liked to be better at his job, but it just wasn't in his DNA. He recognized this even if no one else did. But somehow, he'd stayed alive for twelve years, which was more than you could say for most of the A-listers.

His handler helped steer Frank away from his dumber instincts, but Tom could only do so much to mitigate the potential catastrophe that was Frank Perlmutter, professional assassin. Not every assassin could be elite.

Desiring nothing more from life than to get out of his job intact, Frank had no interest in martyrdom. He dreamed of heading to the Florida Keys with pension in hand. He'd like to live the rest of his days reeling in fish rather than killing people.

In the quiet lulls of a stakeout, Frank dreamed of a boat in the Keys, hauling in tarpon, snapper, bonefish—any fish that didn't shoot back. The sun on his face, a cold brew close at hand, maybe a cigar clenched in his teeth. So far in his forty years, he'd never had a cigar in his teeth.

When he dared to dream bigger, he thought the Keys would be a nice place to learn to paint. He imagined sitting on the edge of a dock with watercolors and a piña colada might be the perfect end to a perfect day.

Frank noticed that his dreams had never included female companionship. Other than having an awkward relationship with an awkward attorney—that ended because it was obvious there was no future there for either of them—he'd never made room for love in his life. Given the nature of his career, he'd stayed away from intimacy. He'd always been afraid to add love to his dreams, as it felt too far-fetched.

Fishing was enough for now.

Glancing at Rose asleep in the bed, Frank felt the spark of something dangerous: hope.

What if, when this was over, Rose found she'd developed feelings for him? By all accounts, that happened to people who endured harrowing events together. At least in the movies Frank had watched. Suppose they survived—big if—and she decided she'd had enough of Korea and wanted to stick around. Stranger things had happened. Maybe she'd embrace his dream of retiring to Florida to fish.

She was from a fishing village, after all.

Rose was a quiet sleeper, her steady breathing the only sound she'd made for the last hour as Frank watched her.

That was good—he was a light sleeper himself, and the last thing he needed was someone snoring or thrashing beside him. He could pick up the shift of a shadow across the room; a restless partner would be like sleeping next to a wind chime. But Rose was still. Peaceful. Like she belonged here.

If he was being honest with himself, what he liked most wasn't just the silence. It was the going to bed part. The waking up together part. That quiet stretch in between. It had been way too damn long.

Realizing that the woman of his dreams was right here in his bed ignited something in him. A plan of sorts. If he could help her by stopping Fang's plans while completing the Lakefront assignment, they could be together. The problem was that her situation violated his mantra of not getting involved in other people's problems.

But it didn't just violate it—it punched, kicked, shot, and backed over it with a 70-ton Abrams tank. Twice.

However.

His plan might be the only shot he had at getting the girl. It was reckless, sure—but what wasn't these days? Besides, it wasn't like a peaceful retirement in the Keys was panning out. If this was his last ride, it might as well be for something—or someone—worthwhile. Of course, that was assuming she felt the same way. And if not? Well, one impossible fantasy at a time.

Cade picked up a call from Rook, who got right to the point. "Hey, boss. You hungry?"

"Starving. I've been running on nothing but caffeine and hope. Please tell me you've got something better than vending machine peanuts."

"I've got meatballs and murder footage."

"Perfect."

They met at a neighborhood joint that Rook knew well. Marino's was an Italian deli tucked into the area north of downtown. His first visit, Cade stared at the menu. Rook told him to stop overthinking and just order the special. Cade did.

There were a handful of tables jammed in the small space, and they grabbed the last one.

Cade opened the to-go container. The smell hit him first—garlicky, cheesy heaven. He stared down at a mountain of pasta, two meatballs the size of baseballs drowning in sauce, and a golden slab of garlic bread. "I think I'm in love."

Rook nodded. He knew.

When Cade slowed down enough to speak, he looked up at Rook. "So, fill me in on the video footage from the hotel. Did you see anything?"

"Nah, man. It's not like watching a movie where the camera follows the action. It was just one wide-angle shot of the room." He took a bite and held up a finger. "I watched it through a dozen or so times. Saw the shooter, the dead bodyguards, Fang, and the executive assistant. Looked at who they interacted with. Like that."

"And?"

"One oddity. The shooter collided with a businesswoman. Dumped her purse. He was on his hands and knees picking up her belongings."

"Was it intentional? A diversion?" Cade asked. "Maybe something was passed between them."

"You never can tell, but it didn't seem like it. She was pissed and he became the center of attention. If you're planning to kill someone, it wasn't a great choice on his part."

"*Hmmm.* I'll file that away," Cade said. "It means something, but I don't know what. What else did you see with the shooter?"

"He was checking out the woman at the bar, Fang's executive assistant. She was a looker," Rook said. "His game wasn't strong though, if you know what I mean."

Cade laughed. "I have a pretty good idea what you mean."

"He was for sure checking her out. Started toward her, then did this awkward pivot like his swagger gave out mid-stride. Zero confidence with the ladies."

"Like me in high school," Cade said with a grin.

"Yeah, and then you went on to date Reynolds freakin' DeVries, the hottest television personality in the state." He shook his head. "I'll never figure out how that happened. Looks-wise, you're in completely different leagues. And being in law enforcement, it isn't that you're rich."

Cade leaned back with a grin on his face. "Do the math, you'll figure it out."

Rook waved a finger at him. "No. No. No. I'm not going there."

Cade was laughing now. "So, did our shooter finally overcome his fear of flying?"

A nod. "He did. Joined the Park woman at the bar. They got into a conversation pretty quickly. She was even touching his arm."

"That usually works on me."

"It did on him. He was looking at her like she was a lost puppy, all goo-goo eyes, right up until he clocked the two security guys headed his way. Then the mood changed. Real fast. Those guys weren't coming over to offer breath mints. As soon as they reached for their weapons, our shooter went for his, but it snagged on his belt. For a second, it looked like he was going to shoot himself in the balls."

"*Hmmm.*"

"Here's the other interesting part. When he got his weapon up, it looked like he was aiming at the man meeting with Fang." Rook paused as he replayed the events in his mind. "It was the woman. She had her hand on his shooting arm."

"Like she tried to stop him?"

Rook thought about it. "Like maybe she redirected his aim. I can't be sure, obviously, but that's what I think happened."

"And then she left with him. The man she just met. After he killed two of her coworkers. And she's abandoned her hotel room ever since." Cade shrugged. "I don't get it."

"It doesn't add up."

Cade stroked his chin. "The other thing I don't get is our shooter brought a silenced weapon, meaning he was no amateur. Yet, he acted like one, fumbling the draw. I'm not sure if this says more about him or more about the woman."

"Clearly, we need to find her," Rook said, swirling the last of his garlic bread in the red sauce.

Fidgeting, Frank checked the magazine again. He always got twitchy before a hit. The magazine was already loaded—he knew that—but his anxiety didn't care about facts. There was too much that could go wrong in something as complicated as assassinating someone, and he was unusually adept at finding all of them. Lose the target? Yep. Tail the wrong guy? Done that. Show up without a gun? Once. Only once—but still.

If it weren't for his handler, he'd have crashed and burned out of the agency long ago. Tom's main job was to save Frank from himself. It was necessary, Frank admitted in those dark moments of self-reflection we all have. Successful people often find that special person who balances them. Great duos elevated each other—think Hall & Oates, Simon & Garfunkel, Briggs & Stratton.

Each had strengths, each had weaknesses, and each brought out the best of the other.

Without Tom, Frank was more like Solo & Screwed.

Tom was his co-pilot. His tether. The guy who kept him from veering off the map. Without him, Frank knew his mistakes would mount until something went horribly wrong.

With Fang having a meeting in an hour, Frank knew he should call Tom. But going off-mission would piss him off—and this wasn't exactly mission-sanctioned. More like... mission adjacent.

Maybe he could thread the needle: take out Dazhao, stop Fang, and keep Rose safe. And maybe cocker spaniels could fly too. Worth a shot.

12

Frank stepped into the elevator with Rose, and just like that, the world narrowed to her silhouette in the stainless steel doors.

She was dressed to kill. Maybe not literally, but with Rose, you could never be sure. She wore danger like perfume—expensive, heady, impossible to ignore. Elegance clung to her like a second skin, each curve and contour framed by a black dress that whispered money and menace. Every detail, from the sweep of her hair to the red-soled heels, was calculated. Effortless.

She didn't smile, didn't speak. Just stared straight ahead like the floor below owed her something. Maybe it did.

He knew he looked like hell. His shirt clung to his back, collar limp, tie crooked like a noose that hadn't done its job. He couldn't stop looking at her. And that was a problem.

Because if she turned, if she saw the way he watched her—like a man glimpsing the last cigarette he'd ever smoke—she'd know. Know he was hooked. Know he was soft.

And in his world, soft got you dead. Frank knew he needed to regain focus.

When the world spun too fast, tai chi pulled him back. Frank practiced tai chi the way other men nursed addictions—quietly, religiously, and without apology. It quieted the noise, gave his mind something to grip when adrenaline threatened to hijack reason. In a job where panic got you killed and emotion got you used, staying centered wasn't optional—it was survival. Frank didn't believe in inner peace, but he believed in staying sharp.

Losing focus on a mission was a good way to get your face on a wall somewhere—maybe a nice plaque if HR was feeling generous. Frank had spent the last decade making damn sure that wouldn't be his exit strategy.

Ideals? Please. Those got stripped off him years ago. He didn't care who lived or died. That was above his clearance level.

Sometimes the target was a terrorist. Sometimes a politician who suddenly found his conscience—and a publisher. Frank didn't ask questions. Not because he lacked curiosity, but because questions tended to shorten life expectancy.

There were always more bad guys. The supply chain was solid.

But he did wonder, now and then, why this guy? Why now?

But he'd also remember the golden rule: don't look for logic in this business. You'll sleep better.

If the dictionary had pictures, Frank's face would be next to jaded, wearing a nametag that read "Yep. Still here."

Jad·ed:

tired, bored, or lacking enthusiasm, typically after having had too much of something. See also Frank Perlmutter.

The elevator opened to a softly lit lounge, where a smooth jazz pianist crooned "Autumn Leaves" while accompany himself on a baby grand piano. No one seemed to take notice. The room was three-quarters full, filled with the murmur of half-hearted networking at the tables. A couple of strays sat at the bar, nursing cocktails. Half a dozen servers attended to the room as Frank led Rose to a table near the bar.

"I don't see your boss, do you?"

Rose picked up a menu and shielded her face while she scanned the room. "No, he has not yet arrived." She checked her rose gold Bvlgari Serpenti watch, which looked like it outpriced Frank's annual salary. "His meeting is in 30 minutes, so he'll arrive momentarily. Mr. Fang prefers to arrive first."

And on cue, Fang swept into the room. He was accompanied by several men who didn't look as comfortable in dress clothing as they would in gym clothes. Their eyes scanned the room as they followed Fang to a table near the windows. One peeled off and went to the bar, where he chose a stool with a view of both the elevator and Fang. He waved the bartender away. The other two sat with Fang.

"Looks like your boss found a new security detail."

"I do not know these men," Rose said. "But Mr. Fang has considerable re-sources to hire whom he wants."

While they waited for Fang's guest, Frank's mind wandered to the woman sitting beside him. She was clearly out of his league, but yet she stayed with him. She was charming and unlike anyone he'd met. Although she was guarded about discussing her background, he chalked that up to different cultures. She had shared a little about the simple life she'd led before Fang's employment. Somehow, she'd gone from modest fishing village girl to fashion goddess, like it was a natural progression.

Frank was still struggling to upgrade from boxed wine.

Even her vocabulary was more sophisticated than he would have expected. When asked about it, Rose had shrugged and explained she'd always been a voracious reader. Frank wasn't sure he'd ever used *voracious* in a sentence before.

The memories of last night in his hotel room flooded back. Rose had tired of his questions and observed that he looked tense, especially before such an important undertaking as breaking up Fang's meeting. She had stood and came around behind his chair, her delicate fingers dancing along his shoulders. "Let me help you," she'd whispered. Her nails, tracing a path down his neck, brought shivers—and he was hers.

When she leaned in, her perfume was intoxicating. He'd caught notes of vanilla and cherry. If a perfume could be naked and sensual, this was it. He moaned and leaned into her as her lips brushed his neck. When he'd started to turn towards her, she'd told him to relax and let her take care of him. Her hand found his chest and slid underneath his shirt. If she was turned off by his dad bod, she didn't let on. Her hands continued their exploration, and soon, she'd unbuttoned and slipped off his shirt. Frank's body tingled at her soft touch, his every nerve on fire. It was nearly impossible to string together a coherent thought as her assault on his bare skin intensified.

Her fingernails wandered south. At that point, Frank wasn't just forgetting protocol—he was forgetting his own name.

"He's here."

It took a moment for Frank—and his body—to return to the present. It was a struggle. The memory felt so real he was sweating. Realizing Rose had said something, he looked into her dark eyes. "*Hmmm?*"

"Mr. Fang's meeting. His guest has arrived."

A tall man with spiky hair shook hands with Fang. He wore a dark blue suit that looked well-tailored. In other words, much better than the off-the-rack one Frank sported. But it was also unlikely he'd be able to hide a pistol under the tailored jacket. That meant the real threat was from the three-man security detail.

Frank stepped away from Rose, activating the comm link to bring in Tom. "We're going live," he said quietly.

The click in his ear told Frank his handler had come online. That and his profanity-laced greeting. "And you're just bringing me in now? That's not protocol. Frank, you can't go rogue on me here. There's too much riding on what we do in Minneapolis."

"I know, I know."

"Well, then, bring me up to speed. Where is Chen Dazhao? I don't see him."

Frank's lapel pin was a technological masterpiece—wide-angle enough for Tom to see the entire scene and sharp enough to zoom without losing resolution. His handler worked the controls with such speed and dexterity that he rarely missed anything.

"Dazhao isn't here. But the man he met with at the Hotel Theodore is."

"You mean at *the* shitshow."

It had been a shitshow, but he wasn't about to own up to it now. "Let's not play the blame game," Frank said, in the tone of someone very much at fault. "Mistakes happen, and I'm not pointing fingers."

"You'd be pointing at yourself, buddy boy."

"Maybe."

Tom snorted loudly, but Frank ignored him. Better that way.

"Dazhao met with Fang at the shitshow. I have intel that indicates Fang is planning a series of infrastructure attacks designed to manipulate the markets. That's why he met with Dazhao. My source tells me that Fang has set up meetings with other players to further this end. And that's why I'm here."

"Who's your source?"

"Rose Park. Chou Fang's executive assistant."

"The woman from the bar?"

Frank hesitated before answering. "Yes. She's cooperating and offering details of Fang's meeting schedule."

Tom's sigh rasped through the mic. "Frank, is this woman even vetted? Can her story hold up? Letting someone from outside the agency pick the targets is so far out of line that I can't see it anymore. Our protocols are in place to ensure the integrity of our information and prevent us from crossing the line."

"Being in the field means reacting to what's given you. There are things we can't plan for." Even as he said it, Frank wasn't sure how it would go over. Tom was a cover-your-ass kind of handler. Risk-averse, in other words.

"I don't take my position lightly. Before you step into the field, I plan, and plan again, with multiple contingencies accounted for." Tom was getting heated.

"But that's all academic at the moment. I'm here, with a target comparable to Dazhao. Who, you'll remember, was made our Alpha due to his Georgia cyberattack on our power grid."

"Not a grid. Dazhao went after a nuclear reactor."

"Same difference. This man is planning a similar attack. He's sitting across Fang right now, and according to my source, they are planning more attacks."

Tom sighed again. "I hate that we have zero corroboration on this. It's just her word. Do you have a name for this man? Has she even told you?"

"Xiang Li."

"What about specifics? Who has he worked with? What attacks are on his resume? Like that."

"Well…" The piano man finished his set and headed for the bar. The room got quieter, until a DJ started with "Brown Eyed Girl."

"Holy hell, Frank. This is not how we do things. We know everything possible before putting someone in your crosshairs."

There was movement at Fang's table. The men stood, shaking hands.

"I'll run facial recognition, but it's not always fast like the movies." Frank knew this, but Tom liked to over-explain things.

"Li's going to get away. I need to stop him."

"Frank, no. You can't."

"I have operational control," Frank started.

"No, I have OPCON, not you." Tom sounded angry.

With the security officers trailing, Fang and Li headed in Frank's direction. Fang's eyes brushed over him, but there was no flicker of recognition—no reason there would be. That was Frank's specialty. He had one of those faces familiar enough to be forgettable. The kind of man you'd sit next to on a train, then fail to pick out of a lineup ten minutes later. But Fang stopped in his tracks. He'd spotted Rose. He turned to his security detail and pointed her out. They beelined for her, hands on the weapons under their jackets.

Frank's gut tightened. "We need to slow them down," he murmured.

"You are not going to yell fire," Tom growled in his ear.

The DJ had switched to an up-tempo song, Kool & The Gang's "Celebration." Several couples got up to dance.

"I wasn't planning on it," Frank muttered, scanning the room. His gaze landed on a waiter threading through the crowd, tray stacked high with martinis and champagne. Perfect. He rose like he was going to dance and stepped deliberately into the server's path. Glass and liquor crashed to the floor in a glittering, boozy explosion. Gasps rippled. A woman shrieked as champagne foamed across the tiles.

"Watch the glass!" Frank barked, voice pitched with authority. Chairs scraped as guests scrambled.

Rose was already moving. She seized a linen tablecloth from a table and, instead of blotting, flung it wide across the spill, spreading the slick hazard into a treacherous path. The first guard lunged forward, hit the patch, and skidded. The second plowed into him, swearing as they both flailed for balance.

The third froze, sizing her up. Rose met his stare, calm and unblinking, as if daring him to cross. The pause bought her the second she needed.

"Come on," Frank hissed, reaching for her wrist.

But she didn't just follow. With a dancer's pivot, Rose steered them through the knot of startled businessmen, her grip guiding Frank like he was the liability to manage. To onlookers, she looked like a sharp woman hustling a clumsy date out of trouble—not a trained operative threading an escape route.

Behind them, guests surged toward the exits. Guards shouted, bottlenecked by toppled chairs and the spreading slick. When someone screamed "Gun!" panic detonated. The lounge became a stampede.

Rose glanced back once, her expression clinical, calculating. Predator, not prey. Then she slipped her hand into Frank's, a flicker of a smile ghosting her lips: *You may have started it, but I finished it.*

13

The Marshall Hotel was trying hard to impress. Cade stepped through its glowing, marble-wrapped entrance and took it in. Crystal chandeliers glowed above soaring ceilings, casting warm light over velvet sofas and armchairs strategically arranged for impromptu meetups. A valet marched purposefully across the lobby in a tailored uniform, footsteps echoing softly on polished stone. The air was laced with the faint scent of exotic blooms, and soft classical music floated through the lobby, doing its best to pretend nothing bad had happened.

Taking the elevator to the seventh floor, the doors opened onto a lavish lounge. A few hotel security officers in maroon blazers and double that in police officers stood around. Self-consciously doing nothing. A typical crime scene, in other words.

"Yo," Rook said when he saw Cade. "I just got here too. Something happened, but there's no dead bodies this time around."

"So, what did happen?"

Rook shrugged.

"Let's go watch some video, then. It might be more reliable than a witness."

"True that."

Shortly after, they found themselves in the hotel's security office. It smelled stale, like someone had been in there too long without opening a window. Possibly eating a baloney sandwich heavy on the mustard along the way. An older security staffer named Lorensen sat at the desk operating the surveillance video system. He had a half-empty 64-ounce bottle of diet soda sitting at his side. No cup, though. Cade and Rook stood on either side, watching over his shoulders.

"This here is the Praetorian Omni Security System. Its state-of-the-art lenses capture everything in exquisite detail. I can view each and every moment in 8K, which is 7680 x 4320 pixels. I once was able to zoom in a woman's notepad and—"

"We don't care," Rook said, shaking his head.

Cade looked at him in surprise.

"What? We don't care. All we want is to watch the video of the incident in the lounge."

Lorensen turned to Cade.

He held up his hands in a *what-can-I-do* gesture. "We're in a hurry, sorry."

"Fine," the security officer said with the petulance of a snubbed teenage drama queen. "Pulling up the lounge incident now."

The resolution was indeed quite good. As Lorensen zoomed in on the men holding pistols, he paused and then went in tight on a pistol. Cade didn't recognize the manufacturer. Lorensen snapped a picture with his phone, circled the weapon on his screen, and a search window popped up. "Rock Island Armory TAC Ultra CS 1911," Lorensen read. "It's a company out of the Philippines."

"Color me impressed," Rook said. "I take back everything I was thinking."

"No worries, kid," Lorensen said, picking up the diet soda and taking a surprisingly large swig.

"You know that stuff can rot out your insides?" Rook warned.

"We're not friends," Lorensen muttered, taking another defiant swig of chemical cola like it was holy water.

Rook glanced at Cade, a puzzled expression on his face.

"I don't need a stranger giving me lifestyle advice. Save it."

"We'll never be friends at this rate," Rook said sulkily.

"Can we get back to the men?" Cade asked. "Why did they pull their weapons in a crowded venue? What did they see? Who were they after? Can you see if there's anything?"

"On it," Lorensen said, deftly maneuvering through the time and space of the lounge footage.

"There," Cade said, pointing to the image of Fang. "He's talking to his security people. Watch him point. But at who?"

Lorensen panned as he pulled back from his zoom. Rook saw it first.

"There, it's Fang's wayward assistant. Rose Park. I thought she'd disappeared."

"She did disappear."

"Looks like you found her," Lorensen pointed out as he zoomed in on Rose. "But honestly, she looks difficult to lose." He let out a slow whistle.

"Dude, just stop." Rook shook his head.

"She was last seen leaving with the shooter at the Theodore," Cade pointed out. "Odds are then, he's here too."

"What does he look like?" Lorensen said. "I'll scan the place for him."

Cade and Rook shared a glance. "He's like everyone," Rook said after a moment's hesitation. "Nothing remarkable."

"Like everyone's dad."

"You're not being helpful."

"It is what it is," Cade said. "Let's keep looking."

They watched the footage several times, not seeing anything. "If they spotted him, there's no sign of it. They're focused on the Park woman."

"Notice that just as the men are pointed in her direction, the place gets clogged up as people get up to dance." Cade gestured to the screen. "They weren't dancing before. I wish there was sound so we could hear what was happening."

"Sorry," Lorensen said. "It's not normally needed."

They watched the collision and chaotic aftermath. "Did you see that? The guy gets up to dance but collides with the server. Was it on purpose?"

Lorensen brought the footage back.

"See how he turns and hip checks the guy with the server? But what is she doing with the tablecloth?"

"Maybe covering the spill," the security officer explained. "She didn't want anyone to get hurt."

"Can you show us her face?" Cade requested. "I have a feeling I know who she is."

After a brief wait, the video froze on a well-dressed Asian woman.

"That has to be her," Rook said. "Rose Park. That means the man she's with is our shooter."

"Interesting," Cade said. "So now he's around another of Fang's meetings, and just as the security team is sent after Rose Park, he creates a diversion."

"They're holding hands," Lorensen pointed out as the crowd filled the room.

"And now he's slipping out with the Park woman." Hand in hand, they disappeared out of view. Cade watched them vanish. Again. Like ghosts, who only showed up to make his job harder.

"Looks like his diversion worked," Rook said. "They slipped out while the crowd blocked the way."

"Let's talk about what we have." Cade gestured for Rook to go first.

"We have our Theodore shooter with Fang's executive assistant at a location where Fang just happens to be." He paused. "Not coincidentally."

"Agreed," Cade said. "She must have access to his schedule. Or, as his executive assistant, she set up the meetings in the first place."

"She must have it out for her boss. Except he's alive while his original security team are chilling in a morgue someplace."

"About that," Cade started. "There's something happening here we're not seeing. Our man appears to be a professional, as we talked about. But, man, if he has an objective, I don't see it. He shoots the security staff, but no one of any real importance. He shows up at a business meeting, and guns are drawn, but it's not him this time. They're after the woman he's with. And he creates a diversion—by colliding with a server—allowing them to slip away."

"He's either a genius or shockingly inept. It could go either way at this point."

Cade stared at his associate. "You might be onto something. I'm starting to believe he's not a genius, as much as he's flying by the seat of his pants."

Rook shook his head and sighed. "Never a good thing when you're a professional killer."

Chou Fang's expression didn't hide much. He wasn't happy having two law enforcement officers interrogating him. Again. He folded his arms and glared at Rook and Cade sitting across from him. "I am a busy man, here for a brief business trip. The sooner you ask your questions, the sooner I can get back to that business."

"Which is what?" Cade asked.

"The usual one finds at these mayoral conferences," Fang said, studying his nails. "Import, export. Each of us has our contacts, our resources, and we make connections to put together deals. All of us working together to make money."

"You make it sound like a beautiful thing," Cade said. "But yet you have armed bodyguards."

"Just the way the world is, as you gentlemen see every day. The world can be a violent place."

"You've managed to pop up at the heart of two separate incidents. In our experience, that's not luck or bad timing." Cade's eyes hardened. "When that happens, they are often the problem."

Rook jabbed a finger at Fang. "We know you're up to some crooked shit. Come clean."

Fang's eyes burned a hole into Rook's. "In my country, prominent business-men are shown respect. And those who don't... disappear. Law enforcement officials know their place. Perhaps you could take a page from their book."

Rook did not look happy. "You sound like a mob boss."

Wiping an imaginary speck of lint off his sleeve, Fang chuckled. "I am no mobster, and I can assure you that you're looking in the wrong direction. Perhaps your time may be better spent searching for my assistant, Ms. Park. And that man she left with. He killed my employees in cold blood. Bring them both to justice, and when you have completed your assignment, perhaps we can speak again."

He stood, buttoning his suit jacket, clearly dismissing the pair.

"Sit back down," Cade barked. "We are not done."

"But."

"Down." Cade gestured emphatically. When Fang reluctantly returned his butt to the chair, Cade continued. "Who did you meet with here?"

"It was nothing more than a casual meeting with a potential trade partner. He wasn't important."

Rook took a step forward. "Just answer the question. We need a name."

"Xiang Li."

"Spell it." Rook jotted down the name as Fang spelled it. "And where is Li from?"

"Xiang Li works the Asian markets. He's one of the largest importers of sugar."

"So, he's your sugar daddy?"

Fang looked confused and Cade nudged Rook. "Filter," he warned.

They asked Fang a few more questions about the meeting but got nothing of value. Cade wasn't convinced he was getting the entire truth from the man. After a few frustrating minutes, they cut him loose.

"That was painful," Cade said. "Didn't want us in his business—even though we're the ones trying to keep him breathing."

"He's dirty," Rook said. "Up to some shady shit."

"Yeah, more than likely. But it might be out of our scope to do something about it."

A woman approached. Cade had noticed her peripherally hanging out watching the controlled chaos of the crime scene. She looked to be in her mid-thirties and was dressed professionally in a navy pantsuit and heels. She had an olive complexion and dark, wavy hair. There was a hint of a smile as she held up her FBI credentials.

"You're with the Five Below Major Crimes task force?" she asked.

Cade nodded.

"I'm here to take over your case," she said, tucking away her ID. "It's the natural order of things, so you mustn't fret over it."

Cade studied her for a moment, wanting to get a read on her. "I didn't catch your name. My attention was grabbed by the large letters shouting FBI."

Her smile grew. "It happens." She held out a manicured hand. "I'm Kaz Hankee."

"No, you're not," Rook said. "No one with the name Hankee names their kid Kaz."

"Mine did." She gestured to the chair Fang had occupied. "May I?"

"I'm surprised you're asking." Rook shook his head. "You seem the taking type."

Hankee sat across from Cade and Rook and faced Rook, the hint of a smile back. "*Awww*, I hurt your feelings. How adorable."

Rook folded his arms, staying silent.

"So," Cade started, wanting to diffuse the tension. "You're not really here to take over the case, are you?" Between the coy look and the twinkle in her eye, he already had his answer. "I didn't think so."

Rook glanced at his partner, mouth open. "How did you know?"

Cade shrugged. "It seemed unlikely, that's all." He turned to face the FBI agent. "Why are you here? Just to bust our balls?"

Hankee straightened. "I came to offer my assistance. With the International Mayors Conference happening, there are a lot of global players here. We have a database that's considerably more extensive than any you're likely to have. I can offer context and perspective regarding people and scenarios—without strings attached."

Rook started to object, but Cade held up a hand. "I see some value in that," he conceded. "Let's begin with a name. Xiang Li."

"Xiang Li. North Korean by birth, but works sides of the Korean Demilitarized Zone, seemingly with tacit approval by both regimes. Li is a hacker suspected to be involved with infrastructure attacks in Paris and Tel Aviv."

"Why?" Cade asked. "Were the attacks ideological? Terrorism against Israel and the West?"

"Nothing more than a money grab. The attack manipulates the markets and, based on the positions held, betting against utilities and energy companies can produce windfalls."

"So, these are assholes then? Not giving a shit about anyone, just bottom lines?"

Hankee nodded. "Exactly that. Nothing more, nothing less. Ideology often is trumped by greed these days." She brushed her hair back. "Why did you ask about Li?"

Cade held her gaze. "Even though he wasn't directly involved, Li was in this room when the incident happened."

"Interesting. We'd be interested in chatting with Mr. Li if presented with the opportunity. He's rumored to have made advances in creating backdoors where there weren't any." She pushed a pair of business cards across the table. "If you run into him, don't hesitate to reach out. And maybe wear Kevlar."

"Just leave us the case," Rook said.

"You know I never was going to do that. Contrary to the movies, we don't go snatching cases. We prefer to work alongside locals to solve cases."

"I'd imagine Die Hard was a public relations nightmare for the agency then?" Cade asked.

"You might say that," Hankee acknowledged. "But it's Hollywood. Fact is far from their fiction. We are not cowboys swooping in with RVs and gunships."

She glanced around before pushing her phone across. "While I have you here." There was an Asian man in a candid photo, clearly taken without his knowledge, on her phone screen. "We're also looking for this man, Chen Dazhao, a Chinese national. He's a contemporary of Li's. Same sort of cyber-terrorism on infrastructure targets, but with a much more prolific history. Word is, he's also in town."

Of course he is.

"Given his history, should you encounter him, Dazhao should not be allowed to leave. Detain him, arrest him, shoot him. Any of these options would be considered acceptable."

"Damn, that's cold." Rook shook his head. "He must have some history. I take it he's not on your Christmas card list."

"He is not," Hankee said, eyes twinkling as she looked at Rook a beat too long, "but I'm Jewish. He did, however, make the Most Wanted list, if that helps."

Rook nodded, catching the look and matching her smile. "It does. And I forgive you for yanking our chains earlier."

"And I forgive you," she added, her tone teasing, "for assuming I play by anyone's rules but my own."

Rook arched a brow.

Cade glanced between them. Some sort of vibe was happening right in front of him. Whatever was happening, he was in third-wheel territory.

"If I had to guess, Dazhao is the reason you're here, not the shooting of two bodyguards." Cade studied her. "Am I correct?"

She nodded. "An astute observation, Detective Dawkins. The death of bodyguards is always going to be incidental. They were never the target. Ask yourself who was, and you'll be on your way to finding the shooter." She paused. "This is where our worlds intersect."

"Let's stay in touch, then. Maybe we can help each other," Cade said, standing. "Interesting meeting you."

"Likewise." Her expression became serious. "The conference offers us a small window with these players. At the end, they will scatter like rats. If we're going to apprehend these people, it needs to happen soon."

"Doing our best."

Cade looked to his partner, but Rook hadn't made an effort to move.

"I think I'm going to stay and talk to the agent a little longer."

Cade glanced at both, and that third-wheel feeling returned. He was more than happy to step away. Riding down the elevator, he enjoyed the silence and let his mind wander. A mystery shooter was still at large, and the governor's thin patience was wearing thinner by the minute. Cade could practically feel Ritter breathing down his neck, waiting for a win—or someone to blame. His father would've said that pressure builds character. His father would also say it's better than being bored. Like a lack of excitement was the worst thing in the world. Cade shook his head as the doors slid open. He could think of several things that were far worse. Like—

Barry Weiss.

Wearing his trademark vest with the *Barry Weiss Report* monogram on his chest, Cade's least favorite human stood in front of him.

Weiss was a local Fox affiliate news anchor with a flair for drama and a talent for getting under Cade's skin. During the hunt for the dark web's serial killers, Weiss had gone from being a nuisance to being a thorn in his side—giving thorns everywhere a bad name. His relentless on-air takedowns of Cade and the Five Below task force were bad enough, but things came to a head when Weiss tried to interfere with Cade's rescue of Rook. To temporarily placate him, Cade had promised Weiss an exclusive interview. Instead, he sent a ringer: a smooth-talking stand-in introduced as Five Below's new communications director. Gordy Stensrude, Cade's chosen stand-in, had all the polish of a conspiracy theorist on a Red Bull bender. He'd torpedoed Weiss' credibility—and humiliated Weiss—in a single, glorious broadcast on live television. The prank was a hit to Weiss' credibility that he was still trying to recover from.

It only sounds mean if you don't laugh. Weiss had deserved it.

"Dawkins."

"Weiss."

From the reporter's expression, none of his animosity from the prank had dissipated.

"Nice vest."

"Nice face."

"You sound angry."

"You set me up."

"You were a shithead and roasted me every day in the news."

Weiss shook his head, although none of his hair moved. "That's the business. I'm not out to make friends. If someone's not doing their job or verging on the incompetent, I say it out loud. I'm the advocate for the people."

Cade looked at him, cocking his head. "You don't believe the shit coming out of your mouth, do you? Three killers came to town. My task force stopped them. Remember? One of them in your coworker's living room."

Weiss looked like a child who'd just been told coloring on the living room wall was a bad idea. And interrupted in the midst of a promising masterpiece at that.

"About that. I'm guessing the killers were here because of you. Don't try to come off as all high and mighty when you're the reason people died." Weiss' pompous face stared back at him.

Cade stepped into Weiss' space and jabbed a finger into his monogrammed vest. "Stop." His voice was low but lost none of its menace. "You can't put the motivations of psychotic killers on me. That's not how life works. You have a grudge against me, fine. But let's deal with it like adults. When you go on your little radio show—"

"It's broadcast television."

Cade ignored the interruption. "And talking smack about me without facts is childish." His fingers balled into fists.

A small crowd had gathered to see if a fight would break out. It felt so very high school.

Cade took a step back and inhaled slowly, willing his hands to relax and unclench. It was only then that he noticed the photojournalist pointing a video camera in his direction.

"Perhaps if you articulated a question, I could answer it," Cade said evenly.

The look of triumph on Weiss' face triggered Cade's fingers once again. He took another deep breath.

Weiss nodded to the television audience. "It's been several days since two foreign nationals were gunned down at the Hotel Theodore. As a journalist with extensive experience, I know this to be unusual. How close are you to catching the perpetrator?"

"As you should well know, having extensive experience and all, I'm limited to what I can tell you about an active investigation. We are following up on every possible lead. It would appear the shooter made another appearance here at the Marshall earlier. There wasn't any violence, even though several other men had brandished pistols in his direction in the lounge."

"You're saying the killer didn't hurt anyone or threaten violence, even though he was being threatened?"

"He did play dump a tray of drinks, but that's as far as it went."

The camera pointed in Weiss' direction catching his reaction. Confusion colored his face.

"Unless you have any requests, I need to get moving." Cade grabbed the reporter's hand. "Always a pleasure, Barry. Stay golden, ponyboy."

Several snickers came from the onlookers as Cade held up a hand and walked out into the night smiling.

14

Frank expected the rebuke before she spoke it. Rose didn't need to raise her voice—the disappointment in her eyes carried more weight than a scream.

"You let Li walk away," she said evenly, her fingers brushing his hand. Not affection—contact. A test. "Do you understand what that means?"

Frank stiffened. He knew what she wanted: Li in the ground. He also knew what it sounded like—a deviation from his orders. "Rose," he began, but the word felt clumsy, inadequate. She always made him feel off-balance, like he was missing the real game beneath her words.

She didn't blink. "Li funds attacks. Fang wasn't just entertaining him. He was enabling him. You know what my grandfather taught me—that to ignore evil is to stand with it. Are you standing with it?"

Frank hated the heat rising in his neck. "I created the diversion back there to protect you. I wasn't about to let Fang's men tear into you."

Her expression softened, but not much. "And I thank you for that. But I don't need protecting, Frank—I need a partner who understands the stakes. Li is not some bystander. Every day he breathes, innocents pay the price. That blood doesn't wash off. Not mine. Not yours."

She turned slightly, her profile sharp as cut glass. "I arranged the meeting. If Li lives, it's on me. On us. I won't face my ancestors having stood idle." She looked back, eyes narrowing, testing him. "But maybe you can."

Frank exhaled. Damn, she was good—twisting guilt, duty, and heritage into a blade sharp enough to cut his excuses. And underneath it all, she was right: Li wasn't clean. Taking him out wasn't against the mission—it was just... adjacent.

Her gaze flicked over him like an appraisal. "I know where he is. The Barney Hotel, room 1248. Tonight, he's vulnerable. That's when you strike. Surprise Li with a nightcap."

"I don't think that's what that means."

Her eyes hardened. "It means you stick a gun in his face and he dies."

"That I understand."

She reached for his arm. "And when you end him, you don't just eliminate a threat. You protect the future. You honor the past. You prove you're the man who doesn't flinch from doing what's necessary."

Her hand lingered on his arm—calculated, not careless. "And you'll have my gratitude."

The way she said it left the meaning open but weighted. Not a promise, not nothing. A lure. Frank knew it. Knew he was being maneuvered. But the thing about being played was sometimes you still liked the odds.

He gave her a thin smile. "I'm in. Li's as good as dead."

Kristen Bednarek picked up Cade's call right away. Even though it was late, the detective sounded as chipper as always, which Cade appreciated. He started the FJ Cruiser but left it in park.

"Kristen, hey. Sorry for the late call. Figured if I'm not sleeping, I might as well ruin your night too."

She laughed. "It goes with the territory. I'm already used to it." Kristen had been a detective with St. Paul for several months now. After helping Five Below, she'd been working with the Family and Sexual Violence Division.

Cade walked her through the events of the hotel lounge.

Kristen whistled softly. "So, the shooter walks into a meeting he wasn't invited to with a silenced pistol and ends up dumping glassware everywhere? Either he's improvising or we're missing the whole damn point. But what's his game? Why was he there?" Kristen was good with asking the right questions.

"Seeing he was with Fang's former assistant, it wasn't coincidence they showed up at her boss's meeting. She brings the shooter, but rather than shooting anyone, he creates a diversion. It's weird."

"It is," Kristen agreed. "He sounds like a professional, yet he does some unprofessional things. There's likely a master plan we're not seeing. We're playing checkers while he's playing chess."

Cade wasn't so sure. "It feels more like he's playing tic-tac-toe. He's completely winging things, and his choices are not well thought out."

"Naw..."

"Could be." People were out walking in the cold, huddled under their parkas.

"You don't get to be a professional without training and at least some idea of what you're doing. The margin of error would bite his ass. He'd be dead, killed on his first job."

"Maybe this is his first job." The seat warmer kicked in, and Cade leaned back enjoying the feeling.

"I hadn't thought of that. But he isn't a young guy based on what I heard."

"Could be a midlife career change."

"Middle manager to assassin?" Kristen snorted. "Maybe his quarterly reviews pushed him over the edge."

"Maybe it was attorney to assassin. That career path makes more sense—moral ambiguity, long hours, lots of people wanting to kill you."

Kristen laughed—not the sort of laugh that was shy and reserved. It was spontaneous and loud, one of the things he liked best about her. When she settled, she asked, "Can you get a description together? Clearly, he's based in downtown Minneapolis, and if we get it out to the locals, maybe the hotels too, someone will bird-dog him for us."

Cade paused. "I could give a description, but it's not going to narrow things down much. He looks like a white suburban dad. Like everyone I've ever seen. There's nothing that stands out. He looks like everyone and no one at the same time."

"You sound frustrated."

"You think? Damn right I am. I was hoping he left town after the first incident, but he's still here getting into trouble. Which means it's likely he's not done with whatever brought him here in the first place."

"Wonderful."

"By the way, I met a woman from the FBI at the hotel. Special agent Hankee mentioned an interest in talking to Xiang Li, the man Fang met with. But she was especially interested in another man who's also in town, Chen Dazhao, a Chinese national. Both have resumes in cyber-terrorism, but Dazhao's is considerably more extensive. She basically said killing him would be an acceptable outcome."

A pause. "Really."

"Really."

She paused again. "I didn't think the feds were so pragmatic. But I'll add his info to the update. But back to the shooter—is he here to kill Fang's associates? Are more people going to die?"

Cade buckled his seat belt. "You bring a silenced weapon for one reason—to kill someone quietly. And if he brought it to the Theodore, he was planning on using it to kill someone. But not on a trio of bodyguards. That was reactionary."

"Feels that way. And with the Mayor's Conference underway, there could be a lot more collateral damage," Kristen said.

"Could be," Cade agreed. "Fang must be thinking the same thing. That's why he replaced his bodyguards so quickly. And if Fang's scared, that tells you something. Guys like him don't scare easily."

"You know what you've got to do next, right?"

Cade glanced over his shoulder and pulled out. "I need to talk to Fang. Before someone else gets hurt."

He gunned the truck, the snow swirling in front of his headlights.

15

Frank watched.

The Barney, the latest of Minneapolis's many hotels, stood gleaming under the neon glow and streetlights of Hennepin Avenue. Promising luxury and modern elegance, the hotel beckoned the rich and famous. Or at least those with an above-average expense account.

Frank was across the street, trying to be inconspicuous. The idea was to look for anything out of the ordinary. It could be as overt as a police presence, or it could be as subtle as someone watching the passersby. He'd already scoped out where he'd position himself if he were monitoring people approaching the hotel. There was no one there.

Satisfied, he moved to the skyway, entering a different hotel on Sixth. Dropping his parka on a lobby chair, he continued toward the Barney, smoothing his hair. Dressed in a conservative navy suit and carrying a briefcase, Frank blended in with the other businesspeople traversing the skyway. He added a pair of black glasses with clear lenses. It wasn't much, but the glasses added just enough misdirection. If it worked for Superman, Frank figured he'd get a pass.

He pulled out his phone and scrolled aimlessly—just another overworked business drone in a skyway full of them. Though his head was down, his eyes were everywhere as he strolled toward the Barney's skyway entrance. Men and women—mostly professionals, with the occasional bar-goer—and a busker played "Yesterday" in front of an open guitar case. But no red flags.

He entered the hotel, where lavish furnishings and Art Deco accents defined the Barney's aesthetic. It seemed to work—every detail a nod to old-world glamour, seamlessly blended with modern sophistication. The marble floors gleamed under soft, golden lighting, and plush velvet sofas invited the well-dressed guests to sink in and stay awhile.

Frank headed for the elevators, trying not to overthink things. He wasn't here for the decor.

When the doors opened, he blinked.

The mustached man from the other night—Roger Featherstone—stepped out. He didn't give Frank a second glance and strolled past like a man with nothing to hide.

Frank's pulse ticked up.

For days, he'd second-guessed everything about Rose—her motives, her story, her feelings for him. But seeing Featherstone confirmed it: Xiang Li had to be here. Rose had been telling the truth.

And if she was right about that, maybe she was right about everything else.

Maybe.

An older couple got into the elevator and Frank hurried in after them. When they used their keycard to activate the elevator's system, he added the twelfth floor after they'd pushed the button for 14. "Enjoy your evening," Frank said as he stepped off onto the twelfth floor. Following the signs, he rounded the corner, spotting a man in a security uniform reading a paperback on a folding chair. He was directly across from room 1248. The man's eyes tracked Frank as he moved down the hall.

Frank nodded absently as he pulled out his wallet and removed a plastic card. He gestured down the hall as he passed the guard. Just as the man returned to his paperback, Frank stuck the barrel of his gun against the man's cheek.

"What's your name?"

Voice quavering, he answered after a moment's hesitation. "Sam."

"Okay, Sam. Is he in there? Xiang Li."

Sam nodded.

"Stand up. I need your help," Frank whispered. Still clutching his book, Sam stood. One look at the guy's paperback and slouched posture told Frank everything. The rent-a-cop was more of an *I'm-not-paid-enough-for-this-shit* rather than an *I'm-going-to-try-to-stop-you* type. There'd be no heroics.

"Knock on the door and tell Li you need to use his bathroom. Sell it," Frank prompted, using the gun for emphasis.

Without hesitation, the guard rapped firmly on the door. Frank stepped out of view but kept his pistol trained on him.

"What is it?" The voice came from behind the door.

"Sorry, but it's an emergency. I have to pee, and I don't want to leave you alone while I run down to the lobby bathroom."

There was silence from the man inside 1248. Frank waved his pistol at the guard.

"I wouldn't ask if I could hold it."

Deadbolt. Chain. Click. The door cracked open. "This isn't very professional," Li said.

Frank stepped around the guard. One shot—clean, close, and practiced. Right in the eye. Li dropped like a puppet whose strings had been cut. The silk pajamas made a swishing sound as Li crumpled in the doorway.

"Give me your phone."

The guard fished it from his pants pocket and held it out, his hand shaking. Plucking it from him, Frank pocketed it and directed the guard to drag Li's body into the room.

He followed them in.

"Don't move."

As the guard stood over the body, Frank's eyes swept the room—clean, minimalist, expensive. He crouched beside Li, patting down the silk pockets, moving quickly and efficiently. A keycard. A money clip. And then, tucked inside the waistband of the pants, something hard and narrow.

A flash drive.

Frank palmed it without hesitation, slipping it into his coat pocket. It might be nothing. But if it was something—something connected to Li's backdoor access—it could be exactly what he needed.

He stood and pointed at the bathroom. "Sam, go wash your hands and sit down."

Frank slipped out, and as soon as the door latched behind him, he hurried down the hall. As he suspected, the elevator didn't require an access card to return to the lobby. He left the guard's phone in the elevator because he didn't want it—he just hadn't wanted the guard to have it.

Frank stepped off onto the skyway level. The guitar player was singing, "Let It Be," as he went past. After retrieving his parka, he rode the escalator to street level. With a last glance around, he pulled up his hood and stepped out into the night.

Frank didn't feel relief. Not yet. He never did until hours later—if at all. But the job was done. Quick. Clean. Mostly.

Cade picked up a call from the 911 dispatch center.

"It's Russ. We just received a call that there's been another shooting at a downtown Minneapolis hotel."

"Oh, shit. Which one?"

"The Barney on Hennepin. Room 1248. Minneapolis is on the way."

"I know the place. I'm close. Appreciate the heads up."

Cade did a U-turn, cutting off a taxi, and called Rook, filling him in. "You go up to the room. I'm going to cruise the area, looking for anyone in a hurry. Our guy's a pro, so he's not hanging out, he'll be getting out of Dodge."

He hung up and decided he'd get a better look at everyone if he were on foot. He pulled over and ran up Marquette. Sixth Street was just ahead, and that would take him to Hennepin, where the Barney Hotel was located.

Sirens echoed.

He briefly wondered if he should be up in the skyway but decided the shooter would prefer a more direct path. In its aim to be accessible, the skyway meandered through a lot of buildings. And there were cameras. No, the street was his best option.

At Sixth, Cade slowed to a walk, scanning every face, every stride, every flicker of movement. Winter in Minnesota made it tough—jackets, scarves, and knit caps turned people into walking bundles of wool and down. Features vanished. Gait and posture became the giveaways. He wasn't just hunting the shooter anymore—Fang's assistant might be in play too.

The shooter was a white male, which helped him rule people out fast, but Cade was looking for more than a match. He was looking for nerves. The stiff shoulders of someone expecting pursuit. A glance held too long. A stride that wanted to be faster but didn't dare.

Even bundled up, guilt showed in body language.

And Cade had gotten good at reading it.

The sound of running had Cade looking around, but it was Rook racing by. He never noticed Cade, so intent was he on getting to the scene. *Attaboy.*

The first siren started up almost as soon as Frank stepped onto the Hennepin Avenue sidewalk. The guard must have used the room phone, but it didn't matter. Taking his phone was always going to be a delaying tactic, nothing more. Frank kept moving, wanting distance between him and the scene.

The sirens grew louder as they raced to the Barney. Only when they realized he was no longer at the scene would they expand their search. But by then, he'd be back in his room with an appreciative Rose.

The moment he saw the guy sprinting toward the Barney, Frank knew he was a cop. Not because of a badge—he wasn't in uniform, and he sure as hell wasn't dressed for the weather. But the sprint gave it away. That, and the vibe. Cops had a certain energy, a posture, a purpose to their movement. Frank could spot it a block away. It was a talent that had kept him alive this long—and one he trusted more than most intel.

This cop ran right by without a glance in his direction. They'd been so close, Frank could have reached out and clotheslined him. But the cop had no idea. That was Frank's gift—he was a walking blind spot. People's eyes slid right over him and he never raised anyone's hackles or red flags.

He allowed himself a brief smile as he continued to distance himself from the scene of Xiang Li's execution.

Cade continued assessing everyone he encountered, but no one raised his cop's flag.

Until.

The businessman coming toward him wore a gray Canada Goose parka over a navy suit and carried a black leather attaché. He wore a pair of black-framed glasses. When Cade worked at the BCA, they had a staff lawyer, Calvin. An eccentric guy, he had many layers. Tough and unyielding when dispensing legal advice, but he was as soft as a marshmallow when you got to know him. Calvin wore the same frames.

Other than the glasses, this man was as bland as a beige house in a sea of taupe suburban homes.

But then the man smiled.

It was like a submarine in stealth mode, gliding through the North Atlantic beneath enemy ships. Even with powerful sonar, everyone above completely unaware. That was, until a sailor dropped a wrench. And then everyone above knew.

When his smug smile danced across his lips, it spoke without using a single word. Underneath the façade of blandness, a shark churned just below the still waters.

Frank barely registered the man approaching. "Excuse me," the man said. He looked like a barista who'd just worked a double. "Can you tell me where the Barney is?"

Before he could think about it, Frank found himself pointing. "Go down this street and turn left on Hennepin. Can't miss it."

The man smiled. "Thanks. I'm so turned around down here."

"I get that," Frank said, turning to continue his escape.

"Are you here for the mayor's conference?" the man asked, stopping Frank.

To be rude was to be noticed. He turned back. "I am. My firm provides accounting services for local-level governments. Here for the networking and free drinks."

Frank glanced over at Cade as the sirens grew. "Well, I should let you get back to whatever it was you were doing." Making coffee drinks most likely.

He turned away again.

"Where'd you learn to dance like that?"

Frank froze mid-step.

Damn it.

16

The question got him.

Maybe not a barista.

Something about the guy gnawed at him. His mind jumped back to the lounge at the Marshall. Had this guy been there? But he didn't look like the hotel's clientele—maybe behind the bar? A server?

He couldn't place the face—and Frank always remembered faces. That was part of what had kept him alive.

Which meant one thing: this was bad.

The man wasn't just some lost tourist or latte-slinger. He was here for Frank.

Frank's gun was zipped under his parka—useless right now. No easy play. No time.

His window was shrinking. Sirens would be here any second. The trap was springing shut.

He exhaled.

He hated this part—the shift from invisible man to target. But if there was one thing Frank Perlmutter could do it was survive.

Deal with it, he told himself.

He turned around.

Cade's desperate question stopped the businessman. He paused, not long, but long enough.

"Pardon me?" The man turned. "Dance?"

Cade nodded, needing this to continue. "You danced last night. At the Marshall. Before the unfortunate collision with the server."

The man smiled politely. Too politely. "I've never been much of a dancer, I'm afraid. In this life, you either have a head for numbers or you're creative. Not both. And I'm a numbers guy. You've mistaken me for someone else."

Cade studied him, still unsure. There was no way he could be absolutely sure he was the shooter, but man that smile. It was burned in his brain like a cattle brand. He needed a little more interaction to move the needle. "But isn't music and math deeply related? Maybe that's why I heard Paul Simon was originally an accountant. One would think that a high degree of aptitude in math would help in understanding and dancing to music."

The man smiled a very different smile from the one that stopped Cade cold. Softer. Less shark, more sheep. "One would think. But no, I never took the time. Or the lessons." He made a show of checking his watch. "If you'll excuse me, I promised the missus I'd call before she went to bed."

Dammit. Cade couldn't push harder without something concrete. His mind raced, but he couldn't come up with a reason to frisk him for a weapon. Even asking for ID felt pointless as it would likely be fake if he was truly a professional.

"Can't have you missing that. Where did you say you were from?" Cade asked, with one last desperate attempt.

"I don't think I ever said." His suspect opened the rear door of a waiting blue-and-white taxi, slipped inside, and was gone before Cade could even catch the license plate.

He stood for a moment longer, watching the car disappear. Then he sighed and went to find Rook.

"What do we have?" he asked Rook when he found his partner on the 12th floor of the Barney. There were a dozen uniformed cops around the elevator bank, milling and murmuring. Nobody was actually doing anything. Typical crime scene, in other words.

Rook nodded down the hall as he spoke. "Shooter forced a rent-a-cop to ask to use Li's bathroom. When Li opened it, bang. Shot to the eye. When the guard dragged the body into the room, the shooter left."

Cade nodded. "At least he left the witness breathing. Most don't. I want to talk to him."

"He's in the room across the hall. We have a uniformed officer sitting on him until we cut him loose." Rook led Cade down the hall. "A word of warning: he's not exactly loving life at the moment."

"I get that."

A tall, thin uniformed officer opened the door. Pittiglio, his nameplate read, looked like he hadn't seen a carb in a decade. He nodded and let them inside. The guard sat hunched on the edge of the bed, staring at his hands.

"This is Samuel Fischer," Rook said.

Cade sat across from Fischer on the other queen bed. "Sounds like you're having a day."

Fischer muttered, "I had one job—and now there's a body across the hall. Wait till Marty hears. Marty's the boss," he added.

"You did what you had to." Cade leaned forward. "The guy had a gun. Likely a professional hitter. If you'd gotten in the way, we'd be zipping up two body bags. You played it right."

Fischer looked up. "You really think so?"

"I do. You're still alive, aren't you?"

A faint smile. "Thanks."

"Sam, can you walk me through it? From the top. Don't skip the boring parts."

Sucking in air through clenched teeth, Fischer nodded.

"I was on post outside Xiang Li's room. I occupied a chair strategically stationed across from his door. To pass the time, I was reading *Rules of Prey* by John Sandford."

"Great book, go on," Cade said, wanting Fischer to get to the important part.

"Well, I saw a man coming down the hall. He looked pretty much the same as every suit walking through. Business type, you know, suit, tie, briefcase, sensible shoes. He nodded as he went past, but then he shoved a gun against my cheek." He paused. "It had a silencer. Like in the movies."

Cade didn't blink. "Then what?"

"He told me to knock and say I needed to use the bathroom. I wasn't thrilled about it, but honestly? I kinda did."

Cade cracked a faint smile.

"So, I knock. Say it's an emergency. Li opens the door—and the guy shoots him. One shot. Clean. Li drops right there. Silk pajamas and all. Not even three feet away from me." Fischer had the haunted look of a soldier who'd experienced combat for the first time.

"Then?"

"I guess that's when he took my phone. Told me to drag the body inside. I did. He told me to go wash my hands. When the door closed, I called 911 from the room phone." He looked between the three officers. "That was it. Never saw him again, but the asshole has my phone. Probably calling Guam and running up charges."

"Nah," Pittiglio said. "We got it. He dropped it in the elevator."

"He didn't want it as much as he didn't want you having it," Cade said.

"But I used the room phone. Not much of a plan, was it?" Fischer asked. "Guess I outsmarted him."

"Starting to think that's easier than we thought," Cade said to Rook.

"Sounds that way. Wouldn't have guessed it, but here we are."

"What did he look like?" Cade asked Fischer. "Describe him beyond what he wore."

"Well," the guard started, removing his tie.

"Nice clip-on," Rook said.

"It's a breakaway tie." Sam folded it carefully. "Designed to limit damage in hand-to-hand combat."

Rook scoffed. "Whatever, man. They gave them out because 99.9 percent of rent-a-cops couldn't tie a tie if their lives depended on it."

"And you know how to tie a tie?" Fischer threw it back.

"The description, please," Cade prompted to get things back on track.

"White guy, forties, medium brown hair—medium length. Wore glasses. Medium height. Medium weight. Looked like a dad."

"So, a medium dude?" Rook asked. "Very helpful."

Fischer shrugged. "Blame him, not me."

"Describe his glasses."

Fischer absently stroked his chin. "Thick black frames. Like, kind of hipster but also not."

"That narrows it down." Rook stopped typing his notes and put away his phone. "Can't thank you enough for all the time," he said to the guard. And then to the officer, "Make sure we have his contact info, and you can cut him loose."

"Hold on," Cade said. "Give me your boss's number." He handed his phone to Fischer, who typed in the digits and handed it back.

"What's his name?"

"Olivera, Marty Olivera."

Cade connected the call. "Mr. Olivera, this is Detective Cade Dawkins with the Five Below Major Crimes Task Force. There's been an incident involving your employee, Samuel Fischer. No, Mr. Fischer is fine, but the news is both good and bad. The good news is your employee prevented a double homicide. Not easy when you're dealing with a professional killer, but your guard handled himself well."

A pause while Cade listened.

"Yes, Mr. Fischer did very well. If he worked for me, I'd put him up for a commendation or raise. Or both, really."

Another pause.

"Well, I appreciate that. Oh, and the bad news. You can cancel sending any more guards for Xiang Li's protection." He ended the call.

"Hope that helped," he said to the guard.

Fischer blinked. "You didn't have to do that."

Cade stood. "No worries. You earned it."

Out in the hallway, Rook gave him a sidelong glance. "That's more than I would have done for the security guard."

"My mother always told me it doesn't hurt to be kind," Cade said.

As they stepped into the elevator, Rook shook his head. "But even though you did the rent-a-cop a solid, we got nothing of value."

"Oh, I got something," Cade said, hitting the lobby button. "Sam connected the dots for me."

"Yeah?"

"Yeah. I think I met the shooter tonight."

17

"Wait, you met the shooter?" Rook looked intrigued. "Do tell."

Cade ran a hand through his hair, not that it made any difference. Still messy. "When I arrived, I walked the area, thinking I might get lucky. After you sprinted by like a track star, I bumped into this guy on the street. He looked... average. Like aggressively average. Like if you graphed all the average men, he'd be right in the middle." Cade paused dramatically. "And he was wearing glasses."

"That's it? Feels kinda weak."

"But when I first saw him—right as you ran past—he smiled to himself."

"Okay, now I'm convinced." Rook's tone suggested otherwise.

Stepping out of the elevator, Cade shot Rook a look. "Let me finish, wiseass. It was one of those smug, self-satisfied smiles, like he'd accomplished something, something no one else knew about."

Rook narrowed his eyes. "You got all that from a smile? Maybe you should try tarot cards."

"Maybe I should. I'm telling you something was there."

"Did you talk to him?"

"Yeah, I asked if he knew the way to the Barney and he did. Didn't really want to talk though. But get this. He was walking away when I asked where he learned to dance."

Rook looked interested now.

"He paused mid-step, like he was running his options. I watched his hands, and his right moved reflexively to his waist, but it stopped. And then he turned around and said I must have him mixed up with someone else. His body language told a different story."

"Still." Rook shrugged. "Maybe not weak, but not strong either."

"Yeah, I had nothing to hold him, ID him, or check for weapons. I had to let him go."

Rook rubbed a spot on his white athletic shoes. "So. Where did he go?"

"He jumped into a taxi mid-block—like he couldn't get away from me fast enough."

"That can't be that unusual for you."

"True, but it was a guy this time."

"Don't give me that humble bull. Your last two girlfriends have been off-the-charts hot. Way out of your league, if I'm being honest."

"I should be offended, but strangely, I'm not."

Rook leaned against the elevator wall. "Would you recognize him again?"

Cade hesitated. Tired and not especially sharp, he struggled to picture the man clearly. "Man, I don't know. If he wore those glasses, maybe. With a silenced pistol in his hand, definitely. But beyond that? He's the embodiment of forgettable. It's probably his greatest asset."

"So how are we gonna catch him?"

"That is the question." Cade felt his frustration grow. "Of course, that's the problem with a professional. They don't have history here, no motive that intrinsically ties them to the victim. They come in, do their job, and then slip away."

"But, not our guy. He's still here. This was his third appearance that we know of."

"Maybe Xiang Li was his target, and now that he's taken care of, our shooter's in the wind." Cade paused by the lobby desk. "But it doesn't feel like it, does it?"

"No, it doesn't. If he wanted Li dead, then it's likely he wants Dazhao in a body bag, as well. They're both cyberterrorists cut from the same cloth. Taking out one and leaving the other doesn't make sense."

Cade gave a tight nod. "Agreed."

Rook looked up at the front desk clerk. "We're here to review security footage." He held up his badge.

The clerk waved a man in a gray blazer over. "Charles, these law enforcement officers have requested to view our security video. Can you help them?"

Charles gestured politely. "Certainly. Come this way." The security office was like every other one they'd seen: dim, windowless, stale. Rook explained what they needed and soon the video footage was up on the monitor.

"Here's the lift on 12," Charles said in a smooth baritone. He fast-forwarded until they saw a man exit the elevator. "Based on the time, that's your man. But he's not cooperating especially well." He spoke with a slight British accent that Cade hadn't noticed before.

"Yeah, notice how his eyes are down, and his face is never visible to the camera." Rook gestured to the screen. "What about the other cameras further down the hall?"

Charles shook his head. "Just lift cams and public lobby angles. Let me switch to those."

They watched as the shooter reappeared one minute later. Calm. Collected. No hint he'd just shot someone in the head. If there was anxiety, urgency, panic or paranoia, Cade didn't see it. After pushing the call button, the man stood with his hands in front of him, holding his briefcase.

"See how he only presses the button once?" Charles asked. "Usually, when someone's in a hurry, they jab the button multiple times like it'll make the lift arrive faster."

"You study elevator habits?" Rook asked.

"I have a lot of time," Charles deadpanned. "It comes with the job."

Charles pulled up the interior elevator feed. They watched the shooter step inside and press a floor button. A moment later, he bent down and placed a phone on the floor.

"That's the guard's phone," Cade pointed out. "Wait, which button did he push?"

"That's the skyway level."

"Not the ground level?"

"No, the button to the right is for street level. It has a star icon beside it." Charles spoke like a teacher explaining basic math to second graders. "Ground levels are the most requested destinations in elevators and therefore typically are installed with the star."

"Thanks, Holmes," Rook said.

"It's Charles," the older man reminded.

"So maybe it wasn't him on the street. Not if he exited on the skyway level." Cade shook his head. "I could have sworn..."

"Where did you encounter the gentleman you believed to be the shooter?" Charles asked. "He could have used the skyway system to remove himself from the scene before returning to street level."

"It was on Sixth near Marquette Avenue."

On the monitor, the elevator opened, and the man exited.

"If he got into the skyway and you saw him on Sixth, he likely exited from the Hotel Lily. That's the closest hotel to ours, and they have exits onto Sixth."

"Bring up the footage of his arrival at the hotel," Rook said.

The monitor showed the same man waiting at the elevator. Inside, he hit 12, took the pistol from his briefcase, disabled the safety, and hid the weapon under his arm. When the doors opened, he glanced both ways. Stepped out.

"That's our confirmation." Cade pointed out. "Let's see the skyway footage."

"Can do."

A moment later, the man strolled through the second-floor lobby, checking his watch. Once again, his head was down as he headed down a hallway.

"That leads to the Lily," Charles pointed out.

"Then that's our next stop," Cade said, rubbing his chin. "Also? He wasn't wearing a parka in this footage. But he had one on when I saw him. He must've stashed it somewhere along the way. We'll check the Lily."

He shook Charles' hand. "Thanks for the assist."

"Godspeed, gentlemen," Charles said. "Godspeed."

They took the skyway, that glass artery threading through downtown Minneapolis, and followed it to the Hotel Lily. The place screamed high-end—sleek facade, valet out front, the kind of lobby where everything looked expensive and no one made eye contact.

Inside, it was all marble floors that whispered with the footsteps of guests, chandeliers that dripped with crystal, and the faint hum of soft jazz filtering through the lobby.

Honestly, the place smelled like money.

The front desk clerk, crisp and professional, called for the hotel's head of security. Within moments, a woman appeared—tall, composed, and all business.

"I'm Amelia," she said, her tone efficient as she led them down a quiet hallway. "Follow me."

The monitoring room was dim and sterile, the air cool and humming with electricity. Rows of glowing screens bathed the space in blue light.

She gestured to a pair of chairs without breaking stride. "Let's pull the lobby feed."

No small talk. Cade liked that.

The footage played at double speed until Rook's voice cut through the quiet tension. "There," he said, jabbing a finger at the frozen image on the screen.

"Don't touch my screen," Amelia said. "You'll get your fingerprints all over it."

"Sorry," Rook said with all the petulance of a third grader chastised for grabbing an extra Snickers at Halloween.

Carrying a briefcase, the man came into view and strode purposefully to a cluster of chairs. He picked up a jacket and rode the down escalator out of view.

"I'll pick up his movement on the ground floor camera." She turned to Rook. "Don't get too excited when you see him. We don't want a repeat of your screen touching episode."

Cade's expression silenced whatever retort Rook was going to make.

Putting on his parka while he rode down, he stooped to retrieve his briefcase before stepping off. From there, he went to the revolving doors and stepped out into the night. At no point did he lift his face toward a camera.

"Is that Sixth?"

"It is," Amelia confirmed.

"Well, that closes the loop." Cade thanked the security officer.

"Try not to touch anything on the way out," Amelia added, eyes still on the screen.

"Next steps?" Rook nodded to the front desk clerk as they passed.

"I'll have Kristen check the cab companies and see if we can find the one he took and where he was dropped. I doubt we'll get a name or credit card, though."

"Highly unlikely," Rook agreed.

"Then, I think we go back to Fang. He's involved in all this. The shooter has turned up twice where he's been—and then killed the man Fang met with. Who's to say he won't show up a third time?"

"I'm betting it'll involve Dazhao and, of course, Fang," Rook said.

"I think you're right. Maybe we should reach out to the FBI agent, Hankee, see what she's got on Fang."

"I don't know." Rook shook his head. "Seems like we're playing with fire by bringing the FBI into this."

"Maybe, but we need all the resources we can get. I mean, if you can't trust the FBI, who can you trust?"

Rook zipped his coat and turned up the collar. "My point exactly. Who can you trust?"

"Mind if I ask you something?"

Rook gave a sideways glance to his partner. "Of course, but usually, when someone starts a conversation this way, we're headed for awkward moments. But yeah, knock yourself out."

"The FBI woman. Were you making a play earlier?"

"And there it is," Rook said evenly, not confirming, not denying.

"You were, weren't you?"

"I'm not saying I was." Rook pulled at his sleeve. "But I'm not saying I wasn't."

"You're not saying much, which is saying a lot." There may have been the slightest smirk playing on Cade's face.

Cade's phone buzzed. It was the governor's office. He showed the display to Rook, who shook his head. Cade put the call on speaker.

"Hold for Governor Winston Ritter."

Several moments of silence were followed by a click. Then, "Dawkins, I hear there's been an escalation in your case. Now we have another dead foreign national?"

"We do. Xiang Li was shot in the eye in his room at the Barney Hotel earlier tonight."

"That's effin' grand. What do we know about the victim?"

"Li was Korean—North Korean by birth—but he was also a suspect in several infrastructure attacks in Paris and Israel."

"I don't care if he clubbed baby seals." Ritter's anger was palpable. "You let a guy get executed in my city during an international conference. That's not exactly a Chamber of Commerce moment."

"It's not very Minnesota nice," Cade conceded.

Silence. Rook wagged a finger at him. *Naughty, naughty.*

"I hope you're not making light of the situation," Ritter growled.

"Not at all. I was agreeing with you."

"I put you on this case to contain things, so there wouldn't be any further killings. And yet, we have a dead Korean at the Barney. I had my campaign celebration soiree there."

"Wow. My first soiree snub." It came out before Cade thought about it. Rook covered his mouth.

"And at this rate, you'll never get an invitation." Ritter was seething. "Catch this killer before anything else happens. And I need you to hold a press conference to get out in front of the media."

Cade heard someone in the background.

"And don't use that guy you said was the task force communications director. He absolutely embarrassed Barry Weiss."

Cade's grin was immediate. "That may have been the idea. Weiss is an asshat." Rook did a double take.

"That asshat has a lot of power in this town." Ritter paused. "You'd be wise to remember that the media can make or destroy you. Your reputation is all you have. Lose that and no one will give a rat's ass about you."

"I appreciate the career advice," Cade said, not really caring if he was pushing his luck or not. "It means a lot."

"I don't know if you're being sincere or not. I really don't get sarcasm. But you should watch your step." Ritter's tone suggested he was both angry and annoyed. "One word from me and the Public Safety Commissioner will chop you off at the knees. I've already wasted too much time talking to you. Go catch the bastard." With that, the line went dead.

"That is not a nice human." Rook shook his head. "I'm not sure he likes you very much." Rook paused. "Say, whatever happened to our spokesman, anyway?"

Cade grinned at the memory. It had been epic. "I've lost touch with Gordy. I gave him several hundred for the prank and he was delighted. Said something about discovering hidden treasures and laughed giddily. Haven't crossed paths since."

"Did he say what kind of treasures?"

Cade shrugged. "Knowing Gordy, he could've been referring to almost anything from lost cities in Peru to prizes at the bottom of a cereal box."

Rook snorted. "True that. He's one of a kind."

"Probably safer that way. Can you imagine multiples of Gordy?"

"I just had a dark thought. What if Gordy's the next step in human evolution?"

"Good lord, that's dark. Apocalyptic even."

Rook cracked up.

"Well, that's an evil laugh."

The rebuke only spurred on Rook's laughter further.

18

As it so often happens, the case took a turn with a phone call.

Cade groaned as his phone buzzed on the nightstand, the sound slicing through the haze of sleep. He cracked one eye and winced at the daylight spilling through the blinds. It felt like he'd only just closed his eyes—twenty minutes, tops—but the sun said otherwise. Technically, he'd slept—but not the kind of sleep that did any good. His body had shut down, sure. His mind hadn't gotten the memo.

He stretched for the phone, not wanting to wake fully. Another hour of sleep might do the trick. The fantasy of going back to sleep was a strong pull. He answered with a noncommittal grunt.

"Mr. Dawkins, good morning. You don't know me." The man was a loud talker with too much energy for a morning.

"Should I?"

"No, not really. I'm more of a behind-the-scenes kind of guy." His voice projected, like he could have gotten a job in radio if he really wanted. There was a slight accent, Tennessee, Texas, like that.

"What's this regarding? If this is about my car's extended warranty, I'm covered." Cade had no idea or cared if it was or wasn't up to date.

"This regards the Korean national killed at the Barney."

Oh.

"Can I ask how you got my number?"

There was a dry chuckle. "Please."

Cade was annoyed. "It's a simple question. One I'd prefer you answered before we continue our conversation."

The caller inhaled loudly. "Alrighty, then. I'm an intelligence professional. Things like coming up with some rando's phone number—let alone their IP address, home address, work address, and internet history—is no big deal."

"Some rando?"

"That's what you took from that?"

"You were unusually dismissive, that's all. Harsh for a Tuesday morning." Cade slid out of bed, his knees cracking. "So, you have me. Talk."

"The killing yesterday at the hotel in Minneapolis. A foreign national by the name of Xiang Li. I'm concerned it was one of ours."

"The victim was an asset of yours?"

The caller paused.

Cade padded to the bathroom, remembering at the last second to mute the call.

"Unfortunately, no. You have it reversed. The person *behind* the gun was likely one of ours."

Cade unmuted the call. "How likely?"

"Pretty damn sure. He's in Minneapolis on assignment with a specific target."

Cade walked over to the window overlooking the backyard of his Stillwater home. It was mostly cloudy, but a few streams of sunlight broke through. The birdfeeder needed refilling.

"You're saying this man came to Minneapolis to kill someone? For the government?"

Another pause. Longer this time.

"That's what I'm trying *not* to say. Our government is big on diplomacy. There's an art to handling all sorts of people in a sensitive yet effective way. We reason, negotiate where we can, and coerce where we have to. As you may imagine, not everyone wants to be handled. However, when the situation can't be resolved by diplomatic means, we employ more of a blunt instrument. Don't get me wrong, even a blunt instrument can work with surgical precision. But the result's the same: someone who is an active threat to our country gets removed from the board."

"Removed?"

"Sorry, I'm a chess player. Meaning, we take their knight or bishop, thereby neutralizing future threats."

"Neutralizing is a safe word choice."

The caller cleared his throat. "Let me be clear here. Some people need killing. There's nothing redeemable about them and their continued presence will likely mean the death of innocents. It's a greater good thing."

"Sounds like a rationalization so you can sleep at night."

The caller laughed. "No, that's what the booze and hookers are for."

This wasn't a rabbit hole he wanted to go down, so he tried a different tactic. "So, let's summarize," Cade said, watching the White-throated Sparrow land at the empty feeder, glance up accusingly, and fly off. "You sent someone to our state to kill someone, and he's the one who murdered Xiang Li at the Barney."

Another pause.

"Yes, and no. Xiang Li was never the target. Our man has gone off-mission."

Cade moved into the kitchen and fired up the Keurig. He needed caffeine—badly. If the assassin didn't kill him, the caffeine withdrawal might. "That doesn't sound good. How dangerous is he?"

"To be honest with you, not all assassins are elite. It's not like the movies where every assassin dispatches evildoers with ruthless efficiency. Maybe some assassins are just average at their jobs, maybe even worried about their next performance review. But a good handler can make up for poor decision-making and a certain level of ineptness. I keep him on the straight and narrow, getting the most out of him. Except he turned me off when he went rogue. That goes against every protocol we have. Untethered, he's unpredictable. But if he's under foreign influence, it could be disastrous."

"Forgive me, but all I know about assassins is what I learned reading Mitch Rapp novels. Can't you just send another assassin to *"neutralize"* your rogue one?"

"We don't have another one." There was an exasperated-sounding sigh. "It's not like we kill that many people. One assassin was plenty."

"Maybe you should sharpen your blunt instrument. Just sayin'."

A note of anger crept into the caller's voice. "He's been doing this for easily a dozen years. And I've been his handler the entire time. Never an issue until now. He'd never go rogue unless he'd been compromised somehow."

Something in his voice made Cade wonder if he was getting the truth, the whole truth, and nothing but the truth here.

"What about the double killing at the Theodore? What happened there?"

"I'm not at liberty to discuss matters of national intelligence."

"Bullshit," Cade spat. "You called me specifically to discuss matters of national intelligence. Tell me what happened."

Another pause.

"This is not for public consumption."

"If you want my help, talk." Cade placed the cup on the coffee maker and pushed the button. The machine sputtered to life.

"Okay, but if you share our conversation, your browser history gets leaked to the media." The caller sighed loudly. "The target was responsible for numerous deaths amid infrastructure attacks. Our asset followed him to the hotel lounge, where he met with a man."

"Fang."

"Yes, Chou Fang. While Fang met with the target, our asset gathered intelligence about Fang from a woman in his party."

"Rose Park." He put the frother cup of milk in place and pushed the latte button. If nothing else, Cade was a fancy coffee drinker.

"Yes, Rose Park. When Fang's security detail went to intervene, they were killed."

"I studied the video, and it looked like there was more to it." Cade poured the now-frothed milk into the cup. "It appeared that your man aimed at another man, not Fang's security officers. But his arm was redirected by the Park woman, and he shot the first of the security detail. Then he killed the second on his own."

Another sigh. "That's essentially what happened."

"So, your target is still alive." Cade squirted in the chocolate syrup. "This woman influenced his choice of targets. And he left with her."

"Afraid so."

No one said anything for a long moment while Cade stirred his mocha. A quick dab of whipped cream and he took his first sip. *Okay, caffeine, do your magic.*

"Could Park be more than what she seems? Someone with an agenda?"

A pause. "That's my fear." To Cade, he sounded reluctant to make the admission.

"Where does this leave us?" Cade asked. "You must have had an outcome in mind when you decided to call me."

Tasting his mocha, the first sip was worthy of a love sonnet. The whole thing was insane—like casually chatting about Bigfoot while standing in line at a farmers market. How was he supposed to process an international assassin over chocolate syrup and latte foam?

A long silence stretched before the caller spoke. "This pains me, but I'm prepared to give you the alias and hotel information on our man. It's too dangerous to let him continue under possible foreign influence."

Cade set his cup down and ran for a pen.

Frank used the keycard and stepped inside. After killing Xiang Li, he'd holed up in an all-night diner, not willing to risk leading the authorities back to his hotel—or to Rose. Over blueberry waffles and too much coffee, he'd tried to make sense of what came next.

Frank's life had always been a series of cold, calculated choices. Emotions were liabilities, distractions that dulled his edge. But with Rose, it was different. It was raw, unsettling, and undeniable.

The moment their paths had crossed, Rose had become more than a loose end or a mere accomplice. She was a spark of heat against the ice that encased him, and that terrified him. The part of him that thrived in the shadows rebelled against this vulnerability, but the man who sat alone in an all-night diner, turning over every possible outcome, realized the truth he didn't want to say aloud.

He was already too far gone.

He returned to the room, unsure what he'd find—only hoping she was still there.

The only light came from the hallway behind him. If the room was dark, that meant she was likely gone. And he knew it. She wouldn't have gone to sleep knowing he was out killing someone—for her.

The door clicked shut behind him, sealing off the light, and leaving him in darkness.

He stood still for a beat, listening. Nothing.

His fingers, hesitant, found the switch.

Would she be there—or had she vanished, taking whatever connection they'd shared with her? Had he been used? Played?

Maybe the room would be stripped clean. Maybe she was already halfway to a new alias and another poor bastard willing to bleed for her.

The light clicked on—and whatever he'd expected, it sure as hell wasn't this.

19

The sky was still the color of steel wool when Cade stepped outside and made the call. Stillwater was just starting to stir, headlights cutting through the mist, a horn honk in the distance.

He pressed the phone to his ear. "Kristen, you're not going to believe this. We caught a break."

Her voice came through, thick with sleep. "I was wondering why you called at the ass crack of dawn. Tell me what you got."

He filled her in on the call. "We need to get our peeps to the Hallmark Hotel. It's on 12th in downtown Minneapolis." He checked his watch. It really was the ass crack of dawn. "Let's stage in the lobby at 0715."

"What about Minneapolis? And SWAT?"

"It's one guy. Bringing in SWAT might escalate things, and we lose control. More room for collateral casualties. I don't want that on my badge."

"We can hold off. Always bring them in if we need them," she said. "They're just a phone call away. What about Minneapolis?"

"Again, I don't want to lose control of a fluid situation. Give them a courtesy heads up that we're looking into a tip that may be nothing. We're not excluding them, only saving them from what could be nothing."

"I can sell that. Shouldn't be an issue."

"Perfect. We go in low-profile and try not to spook the herd."

"Okay, I'll get people rolling. See you there."

First things first, go back in and find his coffee.

Frank was dumbfounded.

Rose lay on her back, surrounded by a bed of soft flower petals. She hadn't left him after all. She was here, wearing black stockings, red-soled heels, and nothing else. Frank's breath caught in his throat.

It took him a moment to process what he was seeing. This didn't feel like reality. It felt like one of those dreams you wake from too early and then regret for the rest of the day.

Rose's eyes locked with his. "I've been waiting for you."

Frank immediately regretted the time spent away sipping mediocre diner coffee. Nothing in his average life had prepared him for this moment. Or for this woman. His body froze as he tried to imprint this sight onto his brain. He wanted it there forever.

For her part, Rose looked back, drawing her feet up as she ran a finger along her taut thigh. "It'll be better if you come over here," she purred. "Much better."

Frank moved.

When Cade arrived at the Hallmark, Rook was already there. If he was nervous about confronting a professional assassin, he hid it well. Rook sat back, halfway through a chocolate-covered glazed raised donut. He handed Cade a small white bag that was synonymous with bakery goods. "Got you one with sprinkles."

"Sprinkles?"

"Yeah, you're fancier than me."

"Dude, I'm a walking thrift store." He pulled out the donut. It did look good. "I'm a little surprised you have the stomach for a donut before we confront a stone-cold killer."

"I don't know about him being stone cold. He does dance poorly. But, being in violent crimes, I've done a lot of raids. You know why I eat before raids? It's more about psychology than hunger. Sharing a donut together establishes team cohesion. The act of eating signals to your brain that it's okay to reduce anxiety while it offers a sense of control as you work through the pastry. And, as you finish, it helps to mentally transition you into operational mode. Also, it gives your hands something to do besides shake."

"That's a lot of rationalization for a donut, but I'm fine with it." He took a bite. "I usually just go with blind optimism and caffeine."

Lorie and Kristen came in together, engaged in conversation. They stopped when they reached Cade and Rook. Lorie looked at the two with their donuts and shook her head. "I see how it is. You two men get pre-raid donuts and us women get left out. So disrespectful."

"So disrespectful," Kristen echoed.

"As difficult as women's journeys for equality have been, it's these little snubs that cut the deepest. When I think about how Ruth Bader Ginsburg fiercely advocated for gender equality and women's rights—"

Rook tossed her a white bakery bag. "Shut up and eat your damn donut." He handed another to Kristen. "Got you a bear claw."

Cade shook his head, but his team was all smiles.

While they ate, Cade watched the flow of the lobby as receptionists, bellhops, and guests started their day. If word got out about why they were here—and who they were after—this morning would dissolve into chaos. But for now, everything felt normal.

When the donuts were gone, he put his palms on his knees and announced, "Let's go get this guy. Our informant said the shooter is using the alias, Michael Weston. We'll find him in room 1609."

The elevator ride was tight with unspoken tension. Cade glanced at the mirrored walls, catching the team's determined gaze. They were ready. A hotel security officer rode up with them, unaware of the government assassin waiting on the 16th floor. He was to provide the keycard to access the room. The chime for their floor pulled him into focus, and he led the way into the hallway.

All four task force members pulled their weapons.

"Room 1609 is down the hall on the left," the officer said, pointing.

Cade nodded to the tea, and they went around the corner.

Unexpectedly, a pair of businessmen stood halfway down the hall. Cade lowered his weapon, but inexplicably, they raised theirs.

"Police. You're all under arrest," he announced with authority.

With no respect for his authority, they fired. Rook grabbed Cade's collar and pulled him out of the way. The wall behind him spat drywall, where a bullet struck inches from his ear.

"You do that again, I'm going to shoot you myself." Rook shook his head.

Cade turned to his partner. "I appreciate the help."

He turned to the security officer, who looked more than a little spooked. "Maybe you should sit this one out." His eyes wide, he nodded and handed over the access keycard. He hustled to the elevator and hammered the call button like it owed him money.

"Poor guy is rethinking his career choice," Cade said. "Five bucks says he punches out for the day the minute he gets out of the elevator."

Rook crept to the edge and glanced around the corner. Another shot rang out, surprisingly loud in the narrow hallway, and he ducked back. "They're in the recess near 1609—it looks like they're trying to get in."

"Who are they?" Lorie asked. "Is it our shooter?"

"I didn't get a good look, but I don't think so."

"That complicates things." Lorie shook her head. "If they aren't with our shooter, they're likely against him, meaning we're likely going to take fire from two different parties."

"Should I call in Minneapolis?" Kristen asked. "And SWAT?"

"Let me try a more direct route first," Cade said. He checked his Glock and knelt at the corner. He ventured a quick glance around the corner and, shaking his head, stood and lowered his weapon. "Both men are down."

"Could it be a trap?"

"Doesn't look like it. Let's see what we got." He followed Rook, Kristen, and Lorie as they led with their weapons.

Dressed in nearly identical navy suits, the two men were crumpled in the doorway of room 1609. One blocked the door from shutting while the other lay half under him in the area outside the door. With open eyes and bullet wounds to the head, they were not setting a trap.

Guns up, hearts thumping, they swept into the room, not expecting to find anyone, and they didn't. Cade turned to Lorie and Kristen. "Head downstairs.

The shooter's going to try to get out of the building. Call Minneapolis to blanket the area."

Cade knelt to check the men. He pulled their wallets and checked their IDs. No surprise, they had Korean passports. Which meant they were likely employed by their frequent troublemaker, Chou Fang. Had he sent his security team here?

"These have to be Fang's people," Rook said, echoing his thoughts. They stepped back into the room and Rook sniffed. "Smells like the honeymoon suite in here."

Cade cocked his head.

"C'mon, it can't have been that long. This place reeks of passion and overpriced perfume." Rook grinned. "I'm surprised, though. I thought you were punching over your weight, but Mr. Average has been commingling with Ms. World-class. Maybe not everything is average with him."

Cade laughed, shaking his head. "Nope, I'm not having this discussion. But I'd be willing to bet every last thing about him is average. Back to front." He paused. "It's way more likely it's an attraction to danger thing. Or she's using him."

"She could use me anytime."

Cade ignored him. "You know my tipster was worried about foreign influence being the reason for the shooter jumping over the guardrails. Maybe this confirms his fear."

"You may be right."

"One thing is for sure, we need to stop him. Bodies are piling up at an alarming rate."

They methodically worked through the room, finding little of value: a suitcase with generic clothes, toiletries in the bathroom, and a Stephen King paperback, *Billy Summers*, on the nightstand. They spent the next ten minutes checking the less obvious hiding places. They checked shoes, under the mattress, inside the toilet tank, even the curtain rods and minifridge. Nothing.

Rook ran a hand over his buzzed hair. "He had a go-bag. Everything of value, ready to go at a moment's notice."

"The guy's always two steps ahead. Let's head down. Maybe someone else caught the break we're still chasing."

But Cade had a feeling the only thing they were catching today was a higher body count, which seemed to be rising faster than the Mississippi in a spring thaw.

20

Trumpets blared, graphics sparkled, and there he was: Barry Weiss, the self-proclaimed rogue reporter. His smug face filled the screen, his hair coiffed, light makeup adding color to his cheeks. The signature beige vest was cinched over a pastel blue shirt like he'd wandered in from a Lands' End catalog shoot.

Cade groaned. "This guy again?" The shooting at the Hallmark had barely made it into evidence bags when Barry Weiss spun it into prime time.

The music reached a crescendo. On screen, the *Barry Weiss Report* graphic came up. Standing in front of the Hallmark Hotel, his hair was tousled to perfection yet didn't look likely to move in the breeze. Weiss turned to the camera, his expression serious.

"As a hard-charging journalist, I've built my reputation on telling the hard truths, championing the downtrodden and disadvantaged. In the metropolitan arena of corporate news, I'm the lone voice for the common person, unafraid of repercussions from the man. The rogue reporter, if you will."

"Someone thinks highly of himself," Cade spat.

"*Shhh*, listen," Rook said.

"In this swank downtown hotel," Weiss intoned, "two men were murdered. These men were in our beautiful city for the International Mayors Conference. Drawing dignitaries from around the globe, this conference serves as a platform for local government leaders to exchange knowledge and best practices. More private jets than a Super Bowl. That's how big this thing is. The International Mayors Conference has thrust Minnesota into the global spotlight."

He walked toward the hotel's entrance.

"At its best, the conference promotes collaboration, innovation, and networking opportunities. At its worst, we have imported sheep to the slaughter."

"That's not at all over the top."

"*Shhh*," Rook said.

"But these men weren't the only people murdered this week. There were three more killed recently at the Theodore. That makes five foreign businessmen here for the conference who were gunned down at luxury hotels. And what are we doing about it?"

Weiss looked into the camera, pausing for effect.

"Once again, Governor Ritter has unleashed his hand-picked disaster squad to stop these killings. Beyond the quite frankly juvenile name, the spectacularly inept major crimes task force, Five Below, is led by Cade Dawkins. Viewers will remember Dawkins as the Minnesota State Patrol investigator who killed Marlin Sweetwater—better known as the Blonde Killer. And then, he attracted three more of these deranged killers to our fair state to kill more of our innocent citizens. We know this man, Dawkins, is dangerous. But do we really want a glorified traffic cop to salvage our international reputation?"

Weiss' expression made his opinion obvious.

"One would think the FBI would be far better at handling this type of case," Weiss said as the screen showed a stock image of people wearing jackets with FBI emblazoned on the back. The screen transitioned to a zoomed-in shot showing Rook and Cade laughing. "It's an open secret that fellow law enforcement professionals don't take this task force seriously."

"What?" Cade fumed. "People love us."

"One has to wonder if the whole of the law enforcement community isn't right to worry about having this task force in charge of stopping the killers."

The image zoomed in on a tight shot of Cade, who clearly was having a bad hair day. "When the man leading the Five Below task force looks like a sleep-deprived barista who's had more than the legal limit of cough syrup, maybe the criminals feel a little too emboldened."

The image on the screen panned and then zoomed to show a tight, pixelated shot of Cade and Rook fist-bumping.

"I personally challenge Governor Ritter to do better. Perhaps assigning more serious investigators to work on this case will put a quicker end to these killings. We need to uphold our global reputation and keep all of its citizens safe from harm." Weiss was back on the screen. "This is Barry Weiss, watchdog for the world and our fair state."

Cade didn't care about Weiss' hair or voice or his ridiculous vest—but seeing his own tired face on screen, mid-laugh, made something twist behind his ribs. He was supposed to be stopping this. Not starring in the blooper reel. Worse, Ritter was probably watching with a smirk and a Scotch.

"I hate that guy." Cade stared at the screen as the weather segment began.

Rook patted his friend's shoulder. "I think the feeling is mutual."

"I suppose it didn't help that the shooter got away." Cade stared off into the distance.

"If those two goons hadn't shown up, the shooter and that woman would be in lockup. And calling them business leaders was more than a stretch. They were hired guns. Nothing more."

"They didn't deserve to die."

Rook narrowed his eyes. "They tried to kill you, remember?"

"Yeah, but if I wished death on all my enemies, suddenly I'm a B-movie villain. That's not my career path."

Rook cracked up. "Can't have that. We got no time for origin stories." They both laughed at this. "But what are you going to do about Weiss?"

Cade held up his hands. "Not much I can do. But I'm going to put a stop to these killings. We do that and everything's copacetic."

He paused, looking to Rook.

"Then I can cut back on my cough syrup consumption."

They both cracked up.

21

Cade frowned at the unknown number flashing on his screen. Nothing good ever came from mystery callers—unless you had a thing for telemarketers or subpoenas.

"The senator would like to meet with you."

"Which senator are we talking about?" he asked. He'd never dealt with either of Minnesota's senators but had heard good things about both.

The male voice was curt and professional. "Senator Fontaine. Please meet her at the Stone Arch Bridge this evening at 10:15 p.m." The call ended.

Cade shook his head. When a U.S. senator summoned you, you went—even if you didn't know why or what was on the agenda.

So, Cade went.

The icy November wind sliced through Cade's coat as he stepped onto the Stone Arch Bridge, the crunch of his boots on the frost-bitten path echoing into the night. Minneapolis glittered on either side, the river below cloaked in mist, like a scene from a noir film. Cade tightened his scarf, instinctively scanning the shadows as he moved forward.

The senator's choice of meeting spot told him she didn't want any record of their conversation. She had secrets to share.

Two figures emerged from the gloom ahead, their silhouettes imposing against the soft glow of the streetlights. Both wore dark suits beneath heavy wool over-coats, and the earpieces nestled in their ears were the giveaway. They were the senator's security.

"Detective Dawkins?" one of them asked, his voice curt and clipped as Cade approached.

"That's right," Cade replied, standing his ground.

"Follow me," the man said, his companion silently posting guard. Cade followed him as they moved deeper onto the bridge.

The wind seemed to grow colder as they walked, the only sound the rush of the river below. Other than the occasional passing car on the nearby freeway, no one was out. Ahead, a lone figure waited near the midpoint of the bridge, backlit by the faint glow of the city lights. Senator Evelyn Fontaine stood tall, her elegant silhouette betraying no sign of vulnerability despite the biting cold. Cade adjusted his pace, squaring his shoulders as the security officer peeled off, leaving him to approach her alone.

Senator Fontaine was a veteran senator in her fifties. The former Hennepin County prosecutor had a commanding presence on Capitol Hill and, by all accounts, was influential with peers on both sides of the aisle. She nodded as he approached.

"Detective."

"Senator."

Cade joined her at the railing, the Mississippi flowing loudly below.

Senator Fontaine didn't waste time. "I wanted to meet with you in my capacity as a member of the *United States Senate Select Committee on Intelligence*. We oversee the nation's intelligence activities—the CIA, FBI, NSA, and other agencies, seventeen in total. Our role is to provide oversight while protecting sensitive operations vital to national security." She paused, studying him. "I'm here unofficially to provide background and offer insight into an area that's often a high-stakes narrative involving espionage, geopolitics, and hidden truths within the corridors of power."

Cade nodded, suspecting where this might be headed.

"I'm going to take you at your word that our conversation will go no further. As a committee member, I've been privy to confidential intel as well as our community's intelligence strategy and tactics. I know where the bodies are buried and who put them there."

She held his gaze.

"Do I have your word?"

Cade nodded. "If this helps with my case, I'm in. You have my word."

"Okay, then I'll get started. My people have cordoned off both sides of the bridge, but we don't have all night. And it's colder than a witch's tit, as my eloquent father liked to say."

Cade was thankful he had added extra layers for the meeting.

"First, I want to give you a primer on spying. Our government is involved with intelligence gathering, espionage, and covert operations. We spy. They spy. Everyone spies. It's like the worst version of high school—but with guns and missiles. Spying is a low-cost, high-reward activity compared to overt military or political actions."

Cade nodded, resisting the urge to ask if this primer came with a study guide.

"But I want to focus on the counterintelligence that helps identify and neutralize foreign intelligence agents operating within our borders. It may sound like a game. We know they're here, and they know we know they're here. But it's no game. Billions of dollars are lost annually to intellectual property theft by foreign intelligence services. The FBI has around 2,000 active counterintelligence investigations related to China alone. But Russia, Iran, and North Korea are all active here too. Even allies such as Israel and Saudi Arabia are known to engage in intelligence-gathering activities on American soil."

Cade stared at the river while taking in the senator's words.

"The threats are mounting. It's not just stealing technology and secrets. Cyber-attacks aren't just common—they're crippling. Hit a bank or a grid the right way and suddenly you're living in the Dark Ages with an ATM card you can't use. We employ espionage to proactively engage adversaries by disrupting their operations in their own networks before they can launch attacks. In extreme cases, we've used targeted military strikes to achieve these ends, but in certain circumstances, a specialist is employed to neutralize threats." She paused. "A blunt instrument, if you follow me."

"I've read enough *Mitch Rapp* novels to understand the concept."

"I preferred his *Term Limits* novel. What a great concept." Cade raised an eyebrow. "But I digress. Our country is under unprecedented attack by cyber terrorists. When other methods to deter these attacks haven't achieved the desired result, our hand is forced. We kill the perpetrators." Senator Fontaine sighed. "We don't especially like this aspect of geopolitical relations, but it's cost-effective."

"I'm here today because our blunt instrument has gone rogue. His assignment was to remove Chen Dazhao, a Chinese national responsible for the cyberattack on the Hatch nuclear power plant in Georgia last year. Intelligence says he has more attacks in late-stage planning. He's here to meet with those who fund such operations, along with possible co-conspirators. People will die if those plans come to fruition." She wiped her glasses on her scarf. "No one knows why our asset has gone rogue, but our best guess is, he's fallen under foreign influence. Most likely from a North Korean operative who entered the country under the name Rose Park."

"Wait a moment. You're telling me Chou Fang's executive assistant is a North Korean spy?"

Fontaine nodded.

"That explains a lot, actually. We found listening devices hidden in her suitcase. And the hotel security footage made it look like she diverted your asset's aim to kill the security officers at the Theodore. But why?"

Fontaine didn't say anything for a long moment, staring at the mighty river. Then, "My educated guess—and it's just that—is she needed to be free from Fang to direct our asset. And so we're both clear, it's not her plan she's got him carrying out. It's the plan of her government, the Democratic People's Republic of Korea."

She paused. "That's bad. Their interests and ours don't align. Ever."

The weight of her words brought heavy silence. Cade spoke up first. "I can't say I ever met a spy before."

Senator Fontaine gave a brief chuckle. "That's the point, isn't it? If they're halfway decent at their craft, you won't ever know."

"Maybe I should stick to serial killers. Less complicated."

Fontaine laughed again. "I don't know about that. A different kind of complicated perhaps."

"What about the man he killed at the Barney, Li? When I interviewed Fang, he described Xiang Li as the largest importer of sugar in the Asian markets."

The senator snorted.

"But I got a completely different story from the FBI agent, Hankee. She said Li was responsible for attacks in Paris and Tel Aviv."

"You should believe her, at least about Li. Intelligence says he created a back-door entry method that other hackers could only wish for. Perhaps kill for, if I'm realistic. He's been involved with financially motivated attacks on infrastructure. These are cynical, not passionate, people."

"Not anymore—at least, not Li."

"The world is better off." She said it calmly, like she was reciting a fact. "We hoped to find something in his room or on his person when he was killed, but there was nothing. He may have hidden his entry tool in the cloud rather than keep it with him." She saw Cade's expression. "A federal agency visited the crime scene," she explained.

He shrugged. It wasn't unexpected. "Okay, what about Dazhao?"

"Like I said, he was our target." Her breath fogged in the cold air. "The world will not mourn his passing."

"The FBI agent said as much. She said he should be stopped from leaving if we ran across him. Lethal force would be fine."

"Doesn't surprise me. His Jerusalem attack killed hundreds."

"Fang has met with another man, Roger Featherstone. His identification said he's a Canadian citizen, but we know he traveled here under false credentials. Know anything about him?"

Fontaine cocked her head before shaking it. "Not a name I'm familiar with. But if he's in with this circle, he bears watching. Li and Dazhao are the cyber specialists, so perhaps Featherstone is the boots on the ground part of the planned attacks. If you have his picture, maybe run it by your Hankee contact. Her resources are considerable."

Cade nodded. "Chou Fang seems to be at the hub of things. Is he really just a businessman, like he claims?"

Senator Fontaine's gaze drifted toward the river, the faint glow of the city casting her in sharp relief. "There's a Japanese proverb: *When the character of a man is not clear, look at his friends.*"

Cade snorted. "His friends are shit."

Fontaine turned back to him, a small, knowing smile on her lips. "That's one way to put it. Fang hasn't been on our radar—until now. But if his associations tell us anything, it's that maybe he should've been all along."

She straightened her shoulders, the shift in posture as decisive as her words. The meeting was over. "I trust this has been helpful?"

"Very," Cade replied. "It gives me a strategy to work with."

"Good. You'll need one. The stakes aren't just high—they're personal. And the people involved? They don't do warnings. Just consequences." She offered her hand, her grip firm and brief, then turned away, already pulling out her phone.

Before Cade could process her parting words, the security escort reappeared. No time for follow-ups, no time for clarification. He glanced back at the senator, who was walking away, her voice low and steady as she spoke into the phone. Her presence felt even more enigmatic as she disappeared into the night.

Cade followed the escort off the bridge, his mind racing. He had come for answers and got a few. But the questions? They were multiplying like suspects in a locked-room murder mystery.

22

The November air bit at Cade's face as he stepped from his FJ Cruiser into chaos. Cameras flashed like a July thunderstorm. Reporters jostled, shouting questions before he reached the podium.

"Detective Dawkins, any leads on the killer?"

"Are the killings connected to organized crime?"

"Do you believe the public is in immediate danger?"

Welcome to the governor's requested press conference.

Cade pushed through the barrage, jaw tight, brushing his hair from his eyes as he closed in on the hastily assembled podium, the department's crest gleaming beneath the brutal glare of the floodlights. The motto, "To protect with courage, to serve with compassion," was etched underneath. Rook, Grace, Kristen, and Lorie stood behind him while a line of uniformed officers flanked them, their presence meant to convey control. To Cade, it felt more like a silent reminder of the weight on his shoulders.

He scanned the crowd. The usual faces were there—local reporters, national correspondents, even a few true crime bloggers with press badges dangling from their necks. He recognized many, from the crime-beat reporters for the Star-Tribune and Pioneer Press newspapers to television personalities Ava Anderson from the Fox affiliate, Maddie Leach, Reynold's replacement at the Five, and of course, Barry Weiss, from the *Barry Weiss Report*. But it wasn't the media that set him on edge. Somewhere, beyond the sea of microphones and notepads, Cade knew there were eyes watching this broadcast for a different reason.

Normally, killers liked attention. But this one? Cade didn't think so but hoped he was watching.

Gripping the edge of the podium, the cold metal grounded him as he leaned toward the microphone. Cade's voice was steady and practiced, his words designed to draw the media in.

"Good evening. I'm Cade Dawkins from the Five Below Major Crimes Task Force. Governor Winston Ritter has assigned us to investigate a series of killings that have shaken this city to its core. I want to start by saying this: we will find who's responsible."

He paused, letting the words hang in the chilled air. Members of the media furiously jotted notes in notebooks and tablets. He had them.

"Right now," Cade continued, forcing his gaze back to the cameras, "we're working tirelessly to connect the dots. We're following every lead and analyzing every detail. But I need to emphasize that this investigation is ongoing. For the safety of the community, I urge everyone to remain vigilant."

His words were measured, but his pulse quickened.

"Here's what we know. The two victims at the Theodore were South Korean nationals killed by a lone gunman. We don't believe they were the intended targets but were threatening the shooter. The same lone gunman murdered a North Korean at the Barney. All three victims were in the U.S. for the International Mayors Conference." Cade's grip on the podium tightened. "Here's where things get interesting. Sources have led us to believe the lone gunman may no longer be working alone but instead is being directed by a representative from a hostile government."

This had the media buzzing.

"At this time, we don't know if the shooter realizes he's being manipulated. Let me make this clear." Cade paused. "To the shooter from the Theodore and the Barney: if you're watching—and I suspect you are—don't trust the woman at your side. She's not who you think she is. She's a North Korean spy, and she's using you."

He looked up. "Any questions?"

Pandemonium reigned.

The game was on, and Cade hoped the killer was watching. He stepped aside to let his team field the questions.

"What woman? Who are you talking about?" This was from the blonde news-caster, Ava Anderson.

Rook answered. "We can't really discuss her details as she's a person of interest. But she was last seen with the shooter."

Anderson couldn't help herself. "I've never met a spy before."

"That's the point, really. You won't know if they are a spy if they are doing their job." Cade covered his smile.

"Maggie Delaney, StarTribune. Are other conference attendees in danger?"

"We don't believe so. The people involved are from a tight-knit group with a history of infrastructure cyberattacks." Rook paused. "But, if you're thinking about becoming a cyber-terrorist, you might want to rethink your career path."

Maddie Leach raised a hand, a confident smile lighting her face. The newest addition to the Twin Cities media scene, she'd quickly made a name for her-self—sharp reporting, sharper questions. Her jewel-toned coat popped against the gray backdrop. So did her reputation for cutting to the bone. "Maddie Leach, from the Five. This question is for Detective Dawkins. Why are you the one to stop this gunman?"

"Fair question, Ms. Leach. I'm tempted to say because the governor said so, but that's the easy way out. Not my style." Cade shook his head. "In my law enforcement career, I've been able to stop some truly evil individuals who've terrorized our state. In the Five Below, I've assembled a team of brilliant minds who are damn good at what they do. Together, we're relentless in our pursuit and won't rest until we've caught the perpetrator."

Barry Weiss waved his hand and spoke. "Barry Weiss, from the award-winning *Barry Weiss Report*. The law enforcement community has lost complete faith in your task force. Given their insider knowledge, why should we trust you?"

Cade looked like he was going to say something, but Grace spoke first. "I'm Grace Fox, with the Bureau of Criminal Apprehension. I'm their lead analyst. I've worked more crime scenes than you have vests, Barry," she told Weiss, drawing laughter from the crowd. "Since I work closely with law enforcement around the state, I know you're posturing for ratings. Law enforcement respects what we do and our results."

She was getting worked up as she went. "And Barry, I don't think you even understand how we work. When the governor activates the task force for the really difficult cases, we then work alongside local law enforcement. It's not us against them. It's us working with them. Together, we get results." She paused, staring at Weiss. "Care to restate your question?"

Weiss appeared flustered before blurting, "Are you sleeping with Dawkins?"

Her eyes narrowed as she stared at Weiss.

Cade held his breath, wondering what would happen. You don't mess with Grace.

"Seriously, Barry? We're all professionals here." She turned and paused before rounding on Barry. "You sound like a middle school virgin. Grow the hell up."

That shut it down. The press conference attendees scattered like dry leaves in the wind—questions forgotten, eager to break the story.

But two stayed behind: A red-faced Weiss, and Cade, who, for once, was satisfied.

Frank thought he might be finally content.

The television was on purely for background noise. The morning network show was starting its second hour and promised Thanksgiving recipes that every relative would love, a report on the NFL lineman who rescued stray dogs, and office style tips that would land you the next promotion. *Fluff, fluff, fluff.* But Frank didn't care. He traced his fingers over Rose's taut stomach, amazed to be enjoying post-carnal bliss with such an exotic woman. Life was pretty damn good.

Never mind that his career was tanking faster than Truth Social stock.

Working with Tom as his handler had been a strong pairing. Their skill sets meshing into a single, effective weapon. Their love-hate relationship strained at times, but it had never broken. Until now, maybe.

He wondered if he'd finally pushed Tom too far, forcing him to do the unthinkable: report to Sheila Ann that his asset had gone rogue. Protocol said he should. But Tom was a survivor, and survival meant treating contact with the dragon lady as the nuclear option—something to be avoided at all costs.

Frank knew his moment of reckoning was fast approaching. He'd need to decide if he could yet salvage his mission and get back into Tom's good graces. Either that or go with Rose and be forever done with his government job. Would she go with him to the Florida Keys and be content to live by the ocean as he always dreamed? Maybe today was the day to bring it up.

Her hand covered his and Ouija-boarded it south. She moaned.

Frank paused when he heard the broadcaster mention Minneapolis.

On screen, the nearly identical blonde television anchors spoke with a background image of the city and the words, Minneapolis Mayhem, over them.

"With several people gunned down in the City of Lakes, the governor has activated the aptly named Five Below Major Crimes Task Force. After the most recent shooting at the ultra-swank Barney Hotel and the iconic Hallmark, task force leader Cade Dawkins held a press conference."

The screen switched to the scene outside Minneapolis Police headquarters. A man with unkempt blondish hair stood in front of a podium while serious looking individuals stood behind him. "Good evening. I'm Cade Dawkins from the Five Below Major Crimes Task Force. Governor Winston Ritter has assigned us to investigate a series of killings that have shaken the city to its core. I want to start by saying this: we will find who's responsible."

The blonde broadcaster on the right spoke. "Viewers may remember Cade Dawkins as the detective who has stopped not one, two, or three, but four serial killers in the Twin Cities."

Cade was back on screen. "Right now, we're working tirelessly to connect the dots. We're following every lead and analyzing every detail. But I need to emphasize that this investigation is ongoing. For the safety of the community, I urge everyone to remain vigilant."

The camera zoomed in on Cade's face and froze. The broadcaster spoke again. "No stranger to controversy, Dawkins dropped a bombshell when he spoke directly to the shooter."

Frank pulled his hand away and sat up. He recognized Dawkins. This was the man he'd encountered on the street after the Xiang Li hit.

On screen, Dawkins looked directly into the camera.

"To the shooter from the Theodore and the Barney: if you're watching—and I suspect you are—don't trust the woman at your side. She's not who you think she is."

Frank's heart slammed against his chest.

"She's a North Korean spy, and she's using you."

His breath caught.

No.

Not possible.

Slowly, he turned to look at Rose.

Frank's eyes widened as his heart rate spiked. A chill ran down his spine, and he scanned her profile for any sign of recognition or deception. He looked for any sign that this was all a misunderstanding. Thoughts raced through his mind as he struggled to process the information.

"This can't be true," he finally managed to whisper, his voice barely audible.

The announcer spoke again. "As bombastic as this statement was, Dawkins was upstaged by another member of the task force, Grace Fox. When a local reporter challenged the task force's effectiveness, Fox took over the spokesperson duties."

A woman with long, glossy dark hair was shown, her look combining elements of classic beauty with a modern, edgy flair. "I'm Grace Fox, with the BCA, the Bureau of Criminal Apprehension, basically Minnesota's version of CSI. I'm their lead analyst. I've worked more crime scenes than you have vests." Laughter could be heard as the vest-wearing reporter fidgeted.

Keeping his eyes on the hotel television screen, Frank slid toward the edge a centimeter at a time. He wasn't sure what this new version of Rose was capable of.

On screen, Fox continued. "Since I work closely with law enforcement around the state, I know you're posturing for ratings. Law enforcement respects what we do and our results. I'm not convinced you understand how we work. When the governor activates the task force for the really difficult cases, we then work alongside local law enforcement. It's not us against them. It's us working with them. Together, we get results." She paused, staring at Weiss. "Care to restate your question?"

Frank knew his weapon was at hand. Could he reach it before she moved?

At the press conference, Weiss looked flustered as he asked, "Are you sleeping with Dawkins?"

Her eyes narrowed. "Seriously, Barry? We're all professionals here. You sound like a middle school virgin. Grow the hell up."

Frank edged away a bit more. If Rose were North Korean-trained, she was capable of close combat. But not only capable, but also certainly deadly.

The blonde anchor was back. "Our very own Reynolds DeVries came to us from Minneapolis. Full disclosure, she was in a romantic relationship with Dawkins before relocating. Reynolds, your thoughts?"

Frank paused, distracted by the drama unfolding on the screen. Reynolds gave a momentary look of surprise, but she reined it in. "Well, well." She turned to the other blonde anchor. "I don't know if this is the hard-hitting news you're used to covering in Buffalo, Charlotte, but here at Good Morning America, news is top priority, so let's move onto a breaking story."

DeVries turned to the camera. "In actual news, the mayor..."

Frank was ready to make a grab for his pistol when the television went dark. The remote was in Rose's hand when he glanced over. "We should talk," she said softly, patting the spot beside her. Her expression was unreadable.

Frank had braced for fireworks. After Dawkins outed Rose on live television, he'd expected her to lash out, bolt, or cut him loose. Instead, she sat down across from him in the bed, cool as a glacier, and folded her hands like she was about to negotiate a ceasefire.

"You think I'm the enemy now," she said. No question in her voice—just fact.

Frank leaned back, arms crossed, hiding the unease twisting in his gut. "Am I wrong?"

Her eyes flickered, sharp but steady. "I was raised to serve the Democratic People's Republic. That part is true. They took a girl from a fishing village, scrubbed her clean, and rebuilt her into what they needed. They gave me purpose. A mission."

"Which was what? Infiltrate Fang's circle? Cozy up to me?" His tone was harder than he felt.

"To watch Fang," she corrected, her voice low. "They thought he was an ally. But I saw what he was—an animal feeding off misery. The regime didn't care as long as the money flowed back north. That's when I realized loyalty meant nothing to them. Not loyalty to me, not loyalty to our people. Only greed."

Frank studied her, searching for cracks. "And now you want me to believe you've grown a conscience?"

Her jaw tightened. "Believe what you want. But I couldn't keep serving men who sell out their country for cash. Every death Fang profits from would be on me, too. I refuse that." She paused, eyes softening just enough. "And don't pretend you don't know what that feels like. You've told me about the things you regret. About the choices you've had to live with."

He cursed himself for opening up to her earlier, for giving her ammunition.

"You think I'm playing you," Rose continued, reading him as easily as a headline. "Maybe I am. But does that make me wrong? Fang deserves to fall. Li deserves to fall. You and I both know it."

Silence stretched. The mini fridge hummed, traffic sounds filtered in, and Frank realized his fists were clenched.

Finally, she leaned forward, voice dropping to something almost tender. "When this is over, I want a life. A real one. Not in Pyongyang, not in Beijing. Somewhere I can breathe. You once told me about Key West—the turquoise water, the sunsets, the rum. Do you know what that sounded like to me? Freedom."

She gave a faint smile, the kind that was either truth or the best lie he'd ever heard. "I'd even trade my Louboutins for flip-flops."

Frank barked a laugh despite himself. He hated how much he wanted to believe her.

"There's no reason you can't have both."

Maybe it was love, maybe lunacy. But when she finally stood and touched his arm—light, deliberate—he didn't pull away.

And when she left later, saying she needed air, needed to clear her head, he let her go. He told himself it was trust. Deep down, he knew it was surrender.

Part Two

23

A week ago.

It started with a question: could it be done?

Abduction had its challenges. She could fight, scream, carry mace. Someone might intervene. One lucky strike, and *he'd* be the one incapacitated.

He called himself Shadow. A worrier by nature. A planner by necessity. In his mind, one begat the other. Worry demanded planning to compensate for every possible failure, and planning fed new worries, new contingencies to consider. And he planned more. It was a cycle he trusted—one that had kept him alive.

After all, kidnapping was serious business, and he was new to this.

His planning was broken down into manageable steps:

Step one: isolate her. Reduce the odds of bystander intervention. He didn't want a group of buzzed frat boys handing out frontier justice. Or worse, some gun nut itching to justify their concealed carry, overjoyed to finally draw their Glock in the name of street justice. Or even worse, an off-duty law enforcement officer, trained and not the least hesitant to put him down when he made his move.

Step two: incapacitate. Fast, brutal, animalistic. A sudden strike taking away her ability to fight back would ease many of his most persistent worries. There would be no screaming, no fighting, and no lucky shot.

The first two steps were much like murdering someone. That he'd done.

Get them away from the herd and then pounce. Quick and deadly. Shadow was nothing if not efficient. But moving someone, someone still alive, that was different. He needed to have his vehicle close by. It wasn't like he could throw her body over his shoulder and carry her for blocks. Anyone witnessing that will call 911 without a second thought. There's no explaining that away.

Once he had her in his car, all obstacles fell away. Then it would be a matter of simply bringing her to the site.

The site.

Shadow couldn't help but smile. His planning began and ended with the site he had prepared. Meticulously researched, thoroughly prepared, devastatingly simple. Once he had her there, no one could stop him.

Maybe even more crucial, there was nothing *he* could do to stop him.

His worries came from the initial encounter and her abduction. These were the moments where it could all go horribly wrong. Hence this dry run.

In software, a dry run—or practice run—tested the system before full deployment.

In terrorism, it rehearsed an act of violence—without triggering it. It was used to determine whether a technique they were planning to use would be successful. Considered to be the heart of the planning stages of the terrorist attack, strengths and weaknesses in the plot are exposed, unforeseen obstacles can be detected, and techniques refined.

Both worlds were ones Shadow was familiar with.

November in Minnesota meant changing seasons, brilliant fall colors, dropping temperatures, and the earlier arrival of darkness. At 7:00 p.m., the sun was down, the pink of the sunset retreating. Since it was now approaching 8:00, the last of the day's light was gone and the streetlights were on. Shadow watched her bound down the steps in front of her Grand Avenue brownstone. Dressed in an open black coat over an untucked white blouse, short skirt, and heels, she looked immune to the below average temperatures and blustery winds that characterized the last week of October.

Watching from his car, he sat parallel parked in front of the neighboring building. He made no move to duck down when she came out. He knew he was virtually invisible. In these times of DoorDash, Lyft, and Uber drivers, a lone male sitting in an idling vehicle was not worth a second glance.

Her scanning of the surroundings before unlocking her Toyota wasn't missed. Situational awareness made his goal tougher but not impossible.

Five cars back, he waited while she belted in and started her vehicle. Blinker on, she pulled into the traffic flow. Shadow signaled and followed. A half dozen vehicles separating them, but that didn't concern him. He knew where she was headed. Although she didn't know it, this was his third time following her. It was too important not to get everything absolutely perfect.

At Lexington, she turned north. He followed, three cars back. She hit the westbound ramp onto I-94. Just like before. Shadow hung back, waiting for her to exit at Hamline. No surprises. That's how he liked it.

He cruised by as she was parallel parking. Looking over her right shoulder, she didn't notice him. The next street north was a roundabout, and he took that all the way around and turned into the alley just 100 feet from where she'd parked. Pulling into the shadows by a garage, he bolted from the car and knelt by the front passenger side.

The click of her heels on the pavement told him she was near. His pulse raced as he had a dangerous thought. Why not take her now?

She was here. Alone.

He was here. Ready.

Her heels clicked beside his car. Now or never.

He tensed, breath caught. His fingers flexed. One move—and she was his.

In the distance, a siren rang out.

He let her pass.

She strode confidently by, and Shadow exhaled. The important thing was she hadn't seen him, and he knew this phase of the dry run was a success. He could have her. Next time.

He watched her vanish into the Black Heart of St. Paul. She'd be inside for hours. Typically, when she left, she'd be in discussion with the other gamers. No doubt rehashing the strategies and gameplay of the night. The opportunity to take her was when she arrived, not when she left.

Next week, he'd be here, ready.

He checked his watch. Time for the next part of the dry run: the taking.

Next week, she was his.

Evening found Cade and Grace together. They grabbed a spot at the end of the row, away from the few others there. "This place hasn't caught on yet," Cade said, glancing around. "I would have thought it'd be busier on a Friday night."

"Well, it is a gun range after all," Grace said. "Not the trendiest date night spot." Her Glock G44 and extra magazines lay on the shooting bench. Cade's service weapon, a Glock 22, sat near it.

The air inside the indoor gun range was thick with the acrid scent of gunpowder, a distinct blend of metallic tang and earthy warmth. Fluorescent lights overhead cast a clinical brightness, stark against the black rubberized walls that absorbed the sharp cracks of gunfire. The rhythmic pops echoed, creating a symphony of controlled chaos.

"It was the most romantic spot I could imagine," he said.

Grace raised an eyebrow.

"They don't call me Mr. Romance for nothing."

She made a show of looking around. "The ambience is delightful," she added as the guy three stalls down emptied his magazine in rapid bursts. "And there's nothing like the sweet smell of gunfire to make me melt."

"You know, there's a no swooning policy at this range?" Cade teased.

Grace shook her head as she hung the paper target and brought it out to seven yards distance. "Who goes first?" she asked, picking up her pistol.

"By all means," Cade gestured, "Ladies first." Putting on her ear protection, Grace stepped up to the firing line. She took a breath and held it, squeezing the trigger. She fired five rounds and lowered the Glock. Her smile betrayed her confidence, which was borne out when Cade brought back the target. There was a single ragged hole an inch in diameter where her rounds were clustered.

"Very nice," Cade said. "You've done this before."

"Well, obviously. The BCA requires we qualify annually with our service weapons. Lab or field agent, we all qualify." Grace put a new target on the holder and sent it out to the same seven-yard mark. "Go ahead," she gestured.

Cade put on his hearing protection, picked up the Glock, and got into his two handed firing stance. He squeezed off five rounds.

When Grace brought the target back, none of the five rounds touched another. They were spread randomly around the target.

"Clearly, I have room for improvement," he said.

"Maybe a little," Grace acknowledged. "You flinch."

"I am not a flincher," he said, sounding personally offended.

"Are too," Grace said. "I've seen leaves steadier in the wind. But, there's no shame in it. It's something we can fix. Ever hear of the one bullet drill?"

Cade shook his head.

"Load one bullet in your magazine." She sent the target out.

"Insert the magazine."

"Rock the slide."

"Take your proper stance."

"Aim at the center of the target." He held his breath.

"Fire." The shot hit near the center ring.

"Aim again. And squeeze the trigger until it clicks."

He did.

"Did you notice the flinch?" she asked.

He nodded.

"You're anticipating the next shot. One of the most common reasons for flinching is the anticipation of the firearm's recoil. This anticipation can cause the shooter to involuntarily tense up or move the gun just as it fires. The one bullet drill forces you to concentrate more on the process rather than the outcome."

Cade nodded, still annoyed but curious.

"With only one bullet available, you'll need to take your time to aim, control your breathing, and execute a smooth trigger pull without knowing exactly when the gun will fire. Now let's repeat this until the flinch is gone."

They did this for the next ten minutes or so. By the end, the flinch was gone.

"Now," she said, "Load a full magazine. Get out of your head and just let the shots fly. Each one independent of the next."

Cade went to the firing line and squeezed off his five rounds. When Grace brought the target back, she smiled and handed him the paper. The circle was larger than hers, but there was just one opening.

"Well done."

They moved the targets out to 15 and 25 yards, each shooting several magazines. Cade's groupings had improved, but Grace's were consistently better than his. As they finished packing up, she bumped her shoulder lightly against his. "So, what's Detective Cade Dawkins doing this weekend that doesn't involve a crime scene?"

"I'm going to play some soccer. There's a Saturday morning pick-up game I'm going to join at the dome. It's been a while."

"You're gonna get your ass kicked, you know that, right?" She grinned, enjoying the teasing.

"I'm aware, believe me." He smiled, enjoying the tease.

"So, why then?"

"For the love of the game." He received an eye roll from Grace. "Okay, that and it keeps me in shape. If I don't play this week, then it'll be that much tougher if I wait until next week, next month, or next year."

"Makes sense."

"Then on Sunday, I'll probably do a little digging—go back over the Minneapolis shooter case. Unless something new pops, there's not much to do right now. You've got your nerd thing Sunday night, don't you?"

Grace folded her arms. "It's only nerdy if you've never played. And it's so much fun."

"Dungeons and Dragons, huh? I'll take your word for it. Sounds a little too Fifty Shades-like for my taste."

She punched him in the arm. "You don't have any idea what you're talking about. No one gets tied up. It's actually the safest night of my week."

Cade kept quiet and stowed his gear. Sometimes it was safer not to ask. Especially with Grace.

Shadow moved through the tunnel, his flashlight slicing a narrow path through the dark. Damp cinder block walls closed in around him, and each footfall echoed like a whisper. He paused occasionally to study the carvings in the walls—some were names, some unintelligible scratches; others, raw pleas etched by shaking hands.

HELP.

SOS.

Abandon all hope.

All is lost.

Lord have mercy.

Desperate words from desperate people. Shadow almost admired the honesty.

He reached the junction marked *"8"* by a rusted iron number bolted to the brick above a thick steel door. Shadow pushed the heavy door with his shoulder, eliciting a creak worthy of a horror movie sound effect. Inside, the air hit him like a wall: cold, wet, and rank with rot. He stepped into the basement.

Though he'd cleared the cobwebs at the door during an earlier visit, everything else had stayed the same. Filthy puddles seeped in from the brick walls. Dust coated the floor like fine ash. Animal bones littered the corners. But worst of all was the smell—a sour cocktail of mildew, old death, and something feral, something that didn't want to be found.

Shadow climbed the groaning staircase, the wood protesting at his weight. The first floor offered a trace of light through boarded-up windows. It filtered across decaying woodwork, peeling wallpaper, and water-stained ceilings. The stench was weaker here. But the silence? Still absolute.

He ascended to the second floor, where his real work had taken place.

For weeks, he'd come here night after night, hauling supplies, tools, insulation, wiring. He'd stripped one room down to the studs, then rebuilt it—better. Tighter. Every seam sealed. Every crack filled. No light would get in. No sound would get out.

He installed acoustic panels, thick fiberglass insulation, a steel-reinforced door with triple locks. The walls, the floor, the ceiling—he'd lined them all with his custom blend of quiet. The air in the room was still. Dead. Untouched by the outside world. A void. A cell.

No one would hear her scream in here.

He paused at the doorway, hand resting on the cold metal frame, eyes scanning the work. Every inch of it was perfect.

The space was complete. Sealed. Silent. Waiting.

All he needed now was her.

24

Shadow felt like someone had been sticking him with pins all day. He tried to shake it off. Nerves, sure—but not doubt. Never doubt. He had prepared for every contingency. No, he had this. It was more like the gravity of what he was undertaking. This was going to be a big deal. Yet it needed to be.

A BFD, as his dad would refer to any major event that he was personally involved in. A big fucking deal. But the man was textbook narcissistic and so everything and anything he was involved with was a big effing deal. To a narcissist, you're always the main character—no matter whose story you're in.

Maybe therapy would have been a good idea after all.

Knowing you see the world differently than everyone else doesn't make you normal—it just makes you aware of your abnormality. You can hide or pretend, but your abnormality will always be lurking under the surface veneer you show the world. Festering, growing, until the day arrives.

A day like today.

The fact that Shadow had hidden it, and yet thrived, felt miraculous. He'd risen to prominence in his organization and was well-respected. Or at least feared, if he was being honest with himself. Either was fine.

From his position on the ground, he watched a gray mouse moving along the edge of the alley. It would disappear from sight as it fell into shadow, then reappear a little closer when it moved into the light again. The mouse scurried in erratic zigzags, its whiskers twitching as it searched for scraps. At the rate it was meandering, it would be upon him in moments. Shadow checked the time—the girl should be arriving within minutes. His weeks of stalking revealed a roughly ten-minute arrival window. That window was upon him.

The mouse, tiny and earnest, was a half foot away from his boot. Setting down the syringe, he slid out his hunting knife. Cute or not, it was still vermin.

The mouse never saw it coming. With speed from extensive practice, he jabbed the knife and skewered it with the tip. It squeaked and squealed as Shadow watched it struggle and die, impaled on the knife. He flung the rodent into the bushes behind him as he heard the familiar heels on the alley's pavement.

Trading knife for a syringe, he got into a squat position. Ready to pounce.

As Grace Fox turned onto Lexington, she picked up a call.

"Go for Grace," she said, even though she saw Cade's name on caller ID.

"That sounds like an advertising slogan for the Catholic Church," Cade said laughing. "But you know me, I'm always going to go for Grace."

"You say that now," she said downshifting and going around a slower-moving BMW. "How's the investigation going today?"

"We haven't found a thing," Cade answered. "It's like they're trying to keep their whereabouts a secret."

"Well, as a law enforcement professional, I can confirm—criminals prefer the shadows."

"You know you sound like a textbook from the first day of the criminal justice program? But I guess if they didn't hide, I wouldn't have much of a career," he acknowledged. "But today is feeling mighty frustrating. I was hoping to have a little more tangible progress."

"Your day isn't over yet. You could still uncover something." She turned onto the interstate. "If you want, I'd be happy to take a look at what you've got after D&D. Maybe a second set of eyes will help."

"Couldn't hurt. What time are you done with your nerd fest?"

"I'll be home by 11:15 or so, if you want to stop by."

"I thought you'd never ask," he said huskily.

"Easy, big boy. Work first," she said with a giggle. "And then you'll get your punishment for calling me a nerd."

She took the exit and hit the corner hard turning onto Hamline. A St. Paul patrol officer was waiting at the light and waved as she cruised past. Having been the lead crime scene technician for the state's largest crime lab, she knew a lot of officers.

They talked for another minute while she was on University Avenue. After making the left onto Albert, she said, "Well, I'm here. I'm going to go nerd out."

"Have fun in that dungeon. I'll see you in a few."

Grace laughed and pocketed her phone. Keys in her fist, she headed down the alley.

Shadow willed his racing heart to slow as the woman walked alongside his vehicle.

Time slowed as her shadow splayed on the pavement at the Park Avenue's front corner.

He inhaled. And pounced.

Launching himself from the Buick's shadow, he slammed into her with bone-rattling force. The hit drove the air from Grace's lungs, her gasp breaking against the pavement as they crashed down together. Gravel tore at her palms. Shadow's weight pinned her before she could twist away, his breath a cold whisper above her ear as he landed on top of her.

The syringe aiming for her neck.

Grace's arm shot up, a key clenched between her fingers. She drove it toward his eye—but the needle was faster. He jabbed it into her neck, plunging the syringe, injecting the tranquilizer.

"You prick," she said, venom in her voice.

"Just relax and let it happen," he said. "It won't be long."

"It never is with you assholes," she hissed.

But her limbs were already slack. Her eyes rolled back. The fight drained from her as the drug took hold.

He rose in one fluid motion, scooped her into his arms, and carried her to the Buick's rear. With a practiced shove of his foot, the trunk swung open, and he set her inside the yawning compartment. He eased the lid down until it latched, the act efficient, noiseless, and devoid of hesitation.

A glance around told Shadow that no one was there. No one had seen a thing. The woman's keys were on the ground, where they had slipped from her hand. Picking them up, he went to toss them into the bushes with the mouse but then thought better of it. He tossed them instead by the driver's side door of her car—an invitation for joyriders. If someone stole the car, the cops would waste hours chasing a dead lead.

Shadow hurried to his vehicle, double-checked the trunk was latched, and climbed into the driver's seat. He drove down the alley for a few blocks, moving slowly, before turning onto Ashbury. Two minutes later, he was on Snelling Avenue. Traffic was light, and in a moment, he was accelerating onto 94.

In thirty minutes, Grace Fox would disappear—like she'd never existed. Shadow set the cruise control one mile over the limit, his smile faint but satisfied. Nothing felt better than a plan executed to perfection.

25

Grace woke in darkness. For a long moment, she didn't know if her eyes were open or closed—there was no difference. It was the confusion as much as anything, waking up groggy and not knowing where she was. Wherever she was, it was completely devoid of light.

What had happened?

Panic fluttered in her chest. Where was she?

Then, it hit her.

Oh God—she'd been on her way to D&D. She'd been talking to Cade when... No, they hadn't finished the conversation. They were going to meet afterward at her place. He'd know something was wrong when she didn't show.

But how could he find her, when she didn't even know where she was?

Fragments of memory returned, jagged and sudden. She'd gotten out of her car, taken the alley toward the bar, when—someone jumped her. She remembered slamming into the pavement. Her hand lashing out with the key between her fingers—because you never knew.

Didn't matter. He'd swatted her arm away like it was nothing.

And then... the sting. Her fingers went to her neck.

Injected.

She shuddered.

She remembered calling him a prick just before everything went blurry, his cold eyes boring into hers. He wore one of those generic medical masks and a knit cap, which meant she'd seen nothing but a pair of eyes.

No real description. Not much to go on. No way out.

Feeling overwhelmed, Grace fought the urge to cry. *Breathe, just breathe.* She did that, and only that, for what felt like 10 minutes. She wasn't going to cry.

But what was next? That's when her training kicked in. Grace was a crime scene technician—arguably one of the best in Minnesota—and this was a crime scene. She knew the order of operations mattered; following the steps kept chaos from swallowing you whole. The familiar structure steadied her breath, and she clung to that discipline like a lifeline. First, assess the scene.

She didn't appear to be in immediate danger. It felt like she was alone in the space where she was. She was lying on a rubbery surface, flooring of some kind. Reaching out, she waved her hand slowly, searching for an object, maybe furniture. On her hands and knees, she slowly turned around, grasping for something, anything.

But there was nothing.

She decided she needed to cast a wider net, so with one arm outstretched, she crawled until she made contact. She ran her hand along the surface. A wall, she decided. Crawling on, she encountered another one. She was in a corner.

Grace stood—and only then realized her shoes were missing. They were her high heel strap-ons, so they wouldn't have fallen off. Her abductor must have removed them, so they couldn't be used as a weapon.

She pondered that for a moment. That meant he planned on getting close. Close enough that she could hit him. Why get close? Another injection? Something worse? She'd damn well be ready to fight if he came close again.

Standing now, she walked heel-to-toe, counting steps. Twelve.

A square?

She turned the corner and did the same. Twelve steps. Another wall.

Her fingers found a vertical seam. A door. She ran her hand along it. No handle. No hinge.

She kept walking. Twelve steps again, then back to where she started. A 12x12 room. No bed. No windows. No light.

And no toilet.

Which, of course, made her need to pee. Grace swore under her breath.

It wasn't just the lack of light or space. It was the nothingness. A prison designed to strip her senses. The silence was thick, suffocating. She needed to break it.

She learned what little she could about her surroundings, now she needed to communicate with her captor.

She faced the door and knocked. No sound.

She kicked it. Same result. Solid and unyielding.

She cupped her hands and shouted. "Hey! You forgot a bathroom, genius. What kind of prison is this?"

The response was instant. Overhead spotlights flared on, blinding white. At the same time, screaming death metal exploded from hidden speakers.

She gasped, staggered back, hands flying to her eyes, then her ears. The noise was unbearable. The lights, somehow, were worse. But she stood her ground. Focusing on her breathing, she was determined to wait it out.

The music cut off.

The lights dimmed—except for a single beam, directly overhead.

Then the voice came. Amplified, modulated, and distorted.

"Grace Ann Fox. You are mine." The voice was deep and growly, like a low-budget movie's idea of what a demon sounded like.

"And you are?"

"Shadow," came the voice—distorted, smug, and utterly inhuman.

Of course. Every psycho had a name. This one picked something from a Marvel reject bin.

"Well, Mr. Shadow," Grace said, stepping into the spotlight. "I need a bath-room."

"Bathroom privileges must be earned."

"That's not going to happen. If you think I'm going to jump through hoops for you, you're delusional."

"Perhaps more death metal will soften you up."

"Bring it on. Morbid Angel is one of my favorite groups, so I don't mind. It'll help me relax."

There was a moment of silence before the spotlight clicked off, plunging Grace into darkness.

She peed in the corner. A small rebellion, but hers.

When she finished, she sat cross-legged on the floor and pressed her palms together in her lap.

It wasn't over.

This was her scene now.

She'd catalog everything she saw, heard, smelled, and felt. She'd map the room a hundred times in her head. She'd find a weakness.

There always was one.

She wasn't going to cry.

She was going to survive.

And when she got out—and she would—she'd be the last thing Shadow ever saw.

26

Something wasn't right.

Cade knew it the way a musician knows something was out of tune. Or a pilot knows when to abort a landing. The same way a person gets that tingly feeling when someone's watching from the dark. Grace was over 30 minutes later than she expected, but things happened. People lingered to talk, maybe traffic issues, things like that. But she hadn't called. And that wasn't like her at all.

The feeling had him edgy.

He called her, knowing she wouldn't answer. She didn't.

He couldn't stand it and got out of the truck. He paced, walking around the back of her building and then paced some more. At the one hour mark, he got back into the truck, tried calling her again, and then decided to head to the last place he knew she was going. The Black Heart of St. Paul.

He found Grace's car, parallel parked on the first side street over from the bar. Maybe she was still inside. He didn't think so, but he had to check. So, he parked in the alley—dark, narrow, and immediately suspicious—and went inside.

He'd never been to the Black Heart before and thought it had an interesting vibe. There was clearly a group of soccer fans who were cheering on an MLS match on the large screen. But on the mainstage, a drag show was going on. Both groups coexisting without a care.

The bearded guy behind the bar nodded when Cade approached. His name tag said he was Wes.

"I'm looking for the D&D group," Cade said.

"You missed them. They left about an hour ago."

"Maybe you can help. Looking for a woman."

Wes grinned. "Grace, right? Only one woman in that crew. She didn't show tonight, which is weird." The man shrugged.

"Yeah, but her car is parked outside," Cade said, feeling worse as he mentioned it.

"No shit?"

Cade nodded.

"I don't like the sound of that," Wes said. "Do you think I should call the cops?"

"I am the cops," Cade said, but he didn't feel inclined to pull out his ID. He headed out the rear exit and walked along the alley. Staying out of dark alleys felt like sound life advice, yet here he was. He flicked on his flashlight, scanning the alley and checking recessed areas. When he got to the end of it, he hadn't found anything.

Across the street, her car sat where she'd left it—silent, intact, and wrong without her.

He paused by the side of her car, noticing a glint of metal on the pavement. It was a set of keys. Pushing the fob unlocked the door and confirmed his fears.

Grace was gone.

"You know it's a school night, don't you?" Rob asked when he picked up, sounding sleepy. "I'm guessing something must have come up."

Cade swallowed hard. "It's Grace. She didn't show up to her weekly D&D session. Yet her car is parked the next block over. And I found her keys on the ground outside her locked car."

"Oh crap," Rob said, now sounding very much awake. "Where are you?"

"I'll send you a pin, but I'm by the furniture store across from the Black Heart of St. Paul."

"I know the place well." There was a rustling of fabric as Rob was on the move. "I'll be there inside of 10. I'm calling St. Paul to have squads meet you there."

"I'll be here."

Cade looked at his phone. There had to be more he could do. The thing about police work was that the pain was always someone else's. You helped where you could, but at the end of the day, you got to go home—and they didn't. And now he was the one worried, scared even. The world could be a tough place to live in.

While he waited, he walked around her car, looking underneath, shining the light inside. He didn't want to disturb the interior in case that was part of the crime scene. Grace was not the neatest of individuals, the debris of her life scattered inside. Fast food receipts, clothing, shoes, magazines, stuff like that. Everything looked amiss, but likely nothing was. The first time he'd walked into Grace's apartment, he'd whistled, saying it looked like her place had been searched and they hadn't found what they were looking for. He got an arm punch for that one.

I'm not a slob, just organizationally challenged, she'd said.

Yet, her lab was as pristine. Organized like someone with industrial-strength OCD on a three-day cleaning bender, it was polished beyond food service standards. You could eat from any surface, and it shone like the queen's own silver. Total opposite of her car.

Yep, Grace was an enigma at times, but she was also the most amazing person he'd ever met.

Cade took a deep breath. He knew he had to hold it together if he was going to do what needed doing.

A St. Paul black and white rolled up, emergency lights flashing. Rolling down the window, the officer asked, "You him, Dawkins?"

"Yeah, Cade Dawkins, State Patrol."

"Nick Rodriguez. Let me get out."

Officer Rodriguez exited the squad and came over. He wore the professional concerned look of law enforcement officers everywhere. "What do we have?"

Cade walked him through the situation as he knew it, Rodriguez nodding along. As he finished, Rob pulled up and another squad fell in behind him. Cade walked them through what he knew.

Rob rubbed the back of his neck, eyes scanning the street. "There's a chance this is something else," he said. "But it sure doesn't feel like it."

"Agreed," the second officer, Hamdan said. "Not with her keys lying here."

"Next steps?" Rob asked.

"We need detectives and crime scene here," Cade said. "Knock on doors, look for cameras. If we can find a vehicle, then we have a start. Otherwise..." His voice broke.

"Otherwise," Rob continued for him. "We don't have any idea where to look. Unless we hear from the kidnapper."

"If it's a kidnapping," Hamdan said, "There's a number of motivations why someone gets abducted. Especially a woman," she added wryly.

"I'll get things rolling with the department," Rob said. "Call in to the duty officer and get a watch commander out here." He looked at Cade. "Hang on buddy, help is coming." He got on his phone and was immediately talking with someone.

"I'm going to walk the neighborhood," Hamdan said, "see who's out." She paused. "I know who you are and respect what you've done. We'll get her back." Without waiting for a response, she turned and headed up the block.

Rob cleared his throat. "Detective Thao is on her way. She recommended using the BCA's crime scene people. Given the circumstances."

Cade nodded.

"So, that's happening," Rob said, restless, needing to do something. "Was she here by her vehicle when she was grabbed? Is this the crime scene? It seems likely if her keys were dropped here."

Cade nodded, thinking. "She'd always carry her keys in her fist like they were some sort of personal protection device. She wouldn't have accidentally dropped them, especially if she was walking alone." He knelt down. "There would have been a struggle. See any signs of that?"

Kneeling down himself, Rob ran a light over Grace's car. "See how dusty it is? No sign her car was touched. If it happened here, they didn't touch the vehicle during the course of the struggle."

Both investigators shone their lights on the road surface next to the door.

"Not seeing anything," Cade said. "But crime scene will find things we can't. That's their superpower."

Standing, Cade stared toward the Black Heart. "Would she have walked the long way around to the front door? Unlikely. She's going to be wary of taking a dark alley, but would that stop her?"

"Doubtful. She's a cop."

"Right. She'd take the most efficient path—even if it was dark."

An unmarked car pulled in behind the squads. "That's the detective," Rodriguez said.

"I've worked with her," Cade said. He met the Asian detective. "Hey, Lorie."

"Awww, Cade." She wrapped him up in a big hug.

Fresh from taking the detective exam, Lorie Thao had joined the Five Below Major Crimes task force with fellow St. Paul detective, Kristen Bednarek. Both had contributed greatly in finding the killers terrorizing the Twin Cities.

"We'll find her. Since she's one of theirs, I thought best to bring in the BCA's crime scene crew. We'll have a half a dozen officers here on scene within the next half hour. You know what they say: get boots on the ground, knocking on doors. I'll coordinate things with the watch commander who's en route."

She took a deep breath. "Walk me through what you know so far. I'd also like to get a sense for Grace's habits and tendencies. We've obviously met and worked together, even drank together once, but you know her far better. Help me get into her head."

"I can do that." Cade glanced to Rob. "Can you guys do a thorough sweep along the alley, see if you see anything? I walked it, but I was looking for … something larger," he said after a moment's hesitation.

Rob understood. "We'll look for anything. Take your time. Give her all the info you can."

For the next ten minutes, Cade leaned against a squad and went through the situation, what the bartender had said and finding the keys by Grace's car. Lorie took notes, stopping him occasionally for clarification. He talked about Grace for a while as Lorie nodded along. She stopped taking notes while he talked. Her eyes were watery when she glanced at him.

"You've got it bad, don't you?" she asked.

Cade stared down the alley. "I just want her back." Rob's return saved him from further self-examination.

"Hey, found something. It may be nothing, but it might be something too."

"Show me."

Detective Thao followed as they went into the alley and past Cade's truck, where they met up with Rodriguez.

"There are tire marks, like a vehicle was parked here. By the garage," Rob said, pointing with the flashlight beam.

"I see that," Cade said, crouching down and using his own flashlight to look around the markings. "This area is disturbed too. Assuming the vehicle was parked in the right direction, this is the front of the vehicle here."

"Maybe somebody was working on their car. Had the hood up, standing here. There are shoe prints here and here," Rob pointed. "But look at the orientation—they're perpendicular to the vehicle. Why stand in front of your car without facing it? Unless you weren't looking at the car...you were looking down the alley. Waiting."

"Okay, I'm calling this a secondary scene," Lorie said. "We need to let crime scene do their thing. If we keep trampling the scene, we'll be shooting ourselves in the foot and will lose valuable evidence."

Everyone nodded in agreement.

"Nick, stay here," she said to the officer. "Preserve the scene until the BCA gets here. I'm going to meet the watch commander and get our people canvassing." She checked her watch. "Let's wake up some neighbors."

Cade stayed behind for a beat, resting a hand on the scuffed gravel, grounding himself. "Hold on, Grace," he whispered. "I'm coming."

27

Frank couldn't shake the feeling he was being played.

Rose had gone out on another of her shopping trips. She claimed shopping helped her decompress—but she never looked stressed. She had the unnerving calm of a predator who knew the prey would walk into the kill zone.

He stood by the window, one hand gripping the edge of the curtain as he peeked out at the street below. The city hummed with the usual chaos—car horns blaring, pedestrians weaving through traffic, and buses spewing exhaust. Somewhere in that commotion, Rose was out there, shopping as if the weight of two predators—Fang and the police—weren't closing in.

He let the curtain drop and rubbed a hand across his jaw, his stubble scratching against his palm. It wasn't like Rose to leave a trail, but her brazenness unnerved him. She didn't flinch at cop cars, didn't glance over her shoulder in boutiques, didn't seem to worry at all. If anything, she moved through the city like she owned it, as if this cat-and-mouse game was one she'd already won. She carried herself like a hunter in the tall grass, her steps deliberate, her every movement purposeful. The aura of invincibility clung to her now, a woman untouchable, unflinching, unafraid.

After Dawkins outed her as a North Korean operative, Frank had expected chaos—panic, denial, even violence. Instead, Rose had wanted to talk.

She'd told him she was from a fishing village on North Korea's eastern coast. That the RGB found her, trained her, and placed her with Chou Fang to monitor his network. But what they didn't count on, she said, was how disgusted she had become with Fang's greed. If ideology drove them, it may have been different. But lives meant nothing to them in their pursuit of financial gain.

Her voice had cracked, and for the first time, Frank saw her falter. She said doing nothing would make her complicit. She had to act—even if it meant betraying the country that made her.

Rose told him that she was breaking from the RGB and was willing to start a new life in the U.S. when the threats were neutralized. She'd been captivated by his stories of life in the Florida Keys and thought Key West sounded delightful. She could embrace the salt-life mindset—one that valued relaxation, adventure, and the beauty of the ocean. She even joked she'd trade K-pop for Jimmy Buffett. And trade her Louboutins for flip-flops.

It may have been a masterclass of manipulation, but it worked.

He didn't know if it was love or lunacy—but whatever it was, it owned him now.

28

Grace groaned.

She wasn't sure when she'd drifted off—maybe minutes, maybe hours. Time was a lie here. The absence of sound, light, sensation—it stripped her awareness down to a raw nerve. She had curled on her side, her arm folded beneath her head like a makeshift pillow, and at some point, exhaustion had won. Her dreams were dark and chaotic, leaving her more restless than rested.

Reflexively, she lifted her wrist. No Apple Watch. Of course. He'd taken that too.

The room remained a tomb. No light. No sound. No time.

She recognized the playbook her captor was using. People's imagination was often worse than reality. She'd think she'd been in the room for days or weeks when it was more likely hours or days. And then, the next time the stimuli hit, it would be music so loud she couldn't think, light so bright she couldn't see. The harsh white light would pierce her closed eyelids, stealing the only respite they could offer.

Because she was familiar with the music, she was able to catch him off guard when she mentioned the band. Like most people, she'd had various phases in her musical journey of discovery. Death metal, jazz, old-school soul, she'd listened and loved it all. For some reason, she'd studied best with loud metal playing in the background. Stephen King wrote with loud rock music playing. She totally got that.

If the music was meant to unsettle her, he'd underestimated her.

When her captor mentioned that bathroom privileges must be earned, she let him know that she wouldn't roll over for him. That was important. And it gave her back some power and possibly the ability to negotiate. His statement also told her that he wanted something from her. He wasn't going to simply use her.

But what did he want? Was there something larger going on here than psycho kidnaps woman? She sincerely hoped so.

When the light came, it stabbed. A solitary spotlight flared to life, blinding white. She covered her eyes and blinked against it. The room—cell, really—was the same. But new additions stood in the corner.

A bucket.

Two bottles of water.

Two peanut butter Clif bars.

Cracking the seal, Grace drank like she hadn't had a drop in years. She didn't even stop to inspect the bottle. If he wanted to drug her, he'd had his chance.

She poked her finger inside the bucket. Of course. No toilet paper.

"Classy," she muttered.

She took a moment to examine the protein bar before tearing into it and taking a bite. She forced herself to slow down and take her time chewing. This may have been the best protein bar she'd ever enjoyed. When she finished the first bar, she slid down the wall and pondered while she drank the rest of the water.

Should she conserve the second bar? She didn't know when there might be more food brought in. It seemed likely that it might happen at night when she slept. But night was meaningless here. Only her captor would know when that was. But for sure, there'd be more food. He wanted her life for something.

A small orange dot lit up on the ceiling. That hadn't been there before.

"Hello, Grace," the distorted voice said.

She didn't acknowledge him.

He laughed, but it didn't come out as joyful. "Not talkative, are you?"

Again, she didn't reply.

"Unfortunately, I need you to talk to me. I'm testing a new communication system."

Grace shook her head.

"I see you've discovered I brought you food and drink. Even a place for you to use the bathroom."

"But no toilet paper," she blurted.

More distorted laughter. "Thank you. That helped. I'll bring you a roll if you tell me something."

Grace looked up but refused to take the bait.

"Give me your login for the BCA system, and you'll have your precious toilet paper. Hold out, and you'll be using your fingers instead."

There was a smirk in his tone she didn't like. She couldn't resist pushing back. "Sure. I'll give you the login." She took a breath. "Right after you crawl out of your hidey-hole and kiss my ass."

Grace mulled things over. He'd likely get bounced pretty quick by the system, but still. It went against everything to give aid to the enemy. "Let me think about it."

"Fine. But no toilet paper until you comply."

Grace got to her feet, feeling her muscles fighting her. She was going to need exercise if she was going to be able to function at a higher capacity at some point.

"Is that the reason I'm here? Because you want to break into the BCA's computer system? Kind of a lazy way to be a hacker, don't you think?"

No reply from above, but Grace wasn't going to let it go.

"Our IT people will see your intrusion. Not only will they kick your lazy ass out, but they'll track you back here to this shithole."

She paused, wondering if she'd pushed too far. Part of her considered giving him the login and letting the tech team trace the intrusion back to him—but she wasn't entirely sure the system could do that. She used computers, sure, but she wasn't a back-end guru. She needed to think carefully before giving him anything.

"For the time being, this shithole is your home," the voice said. "Get used to it."

The light snapped off. Darkness swallowed her again.

29

"I'm so sorry," Rejene said as Cade entered her office. Despite having had a week off, she didn't look particularly rested. "Any news?"

Captain Leah Rejene oversaw the East Metro State Patrol division. Her brown eyes hinted at the intelligence behind them. She was a quick study and was adept at navigating the political side of law enforcement. When he wasn't running the task force, Cade worked under Rejene.

"Nothing that points us in a direction." Cade ran a hand through his hair. "Crime Scene said a vehicle had definitely been parked adjacent to the area, where they believe she was abducted. Nothing had disturbed the tire tracks. They're working up a profile on the tires to identify them. The homeowner there said she hadn't parked in the alley. No one on the block had a camera pointed to the alley."

"Maybe they need to widen the search. The vehicle had to drive in and out of there," Rejene pointed out. "Traffic cams, business surveillance—anything that picks up movement in or out. Casting a wider net will get vehicles that went through the area. At least it's a database of possibilities."

Cade nodded, already thinking ahead.

"There was one odd detail," he added. "In a hedge near the vehicle, they found a mouse that had recently been skewered. Fresh blood, but no trail. It had been stabbed and tossed."

Rejene frowned.

"Yeah, I don't know what it means either." Cade plopped down in one of the chairs across from her desk. "But it doesn't feel random."

Rejene sat, not saying anything for a long moment.

"Yeah." Cade sighed. "It's looking like I'm not going to be back to help Rob anytime soon. The Minneapolis shooter case is still ongoing, but now with Grace..."

Rejene nodded, studying him. "Take the time you need. We all know the first 48 hours are the most important." She hesitated. "Have you considered activating the task force to help find her?"

Cade exhaled. "It's a Governor Ritter decision. And we both know how he feels about me."

Rejene nodded grimly. "Still, it may be worth the call. Pitch him on the idea."

"For now, St. Paul and the BCA have it. They have plenty of resources. The longer I avoid Ritter, the better."

The spotlight came on—then two more. Grace blinked against the glare. This time, the music was different. Neil Diamond's "Holly Holy" trickled in—not ear-shattering but unsettling in its normalcy. It floated across the stale air like some twisted lullaby.

The small orange dot lit up again. The new communication system had been activated. Grace wanted to see if he would communicate with her—maybe push her for the login—but her abductor remained silent.

Shadow was being shy.

She stood slowly, stretched out the tightness in her legs, and twisted open her second bottle of Fiji Water. She drank deliberately, then broke off a piece of the protein bar and chewed it slowly, savoring every bite like a quiet act of defiance.

But Grace could be stubborn. It was her superpower.

Let him wait.

Cade's phone vibrated with a text message. He glanced at the screen—it was from an unknown number—and tucked the phone back into his coat. Sitting back in his office chair, he rubbed his eyes. Running on zero sleep, he was struggling, and fought a losing battle with a yawn.

"I know how you feel," Rob said as he came in. The investigators shared opposite sides of the same desk. Though often working different shifts, they overlapped several times a week to promote continuity. Today was one of those overlap days. "Have you considered getting a dedicated task force office? Not that I mind seeing your smiling face around here."

"I have. But, so far, we don't have any full-time staff to justify an office. Ritter's not going to spend money he doesn't need to."

"He is a cheap bastard."

"Got that right. Ritter is a frugal sort of guy," Cade said. "I'm willing to bet he still has—and wears—all of the Sam's Club six-pack of underwear he bought back in the 90s."

"Thanks for that visual," Rob muttered. "Maybe you should have kept Gordy on as communications director."

Cade snorted. "Life would never be boring."

Rob tossed over the kind of white paper bag that cops the world over would be familiar with. "Brought you a donut. Gonna check in with Rejene. Bring me up to speed about Grace when I get back."

Cade looked into the bag. A chocolate iced glazed donut with sprinkles looked back at him.

Enjoying the first bite, his phone buzzed again. When he pulled out his phone, it was another text—same as before. No message. Just a link.

He froze mid-bite, staring at the link. Clicking could expose him to malware. It could be a trap, but it could also be everything—Grace's life. He tapped it.

He swallowed as his browser launched. The page started to load but was redirected. On the new page, a list of soccer game feeds was displayed. All were from Europe and Asia. He scrolled, then stopped cold.

Shadow v. Fox.

Swallowing hard, he clicked the live feed link. The page was slow to display, with the shell of a viewer appearing first. He clicked the play triangle. At first, it was difficult to discern what he was seeing. The overhead view showed someone sitting motionless, legs splayed, their face obscured. Frozen. Unmoving.

Even from above, even through the grainy stream—he knew that shape.

It was Grace.

Everything else vanished—his exhaustion, the donut, the office—and he sprinted for Captain Rejene's office.

30

"You need to see this." Rob and Captain Rejene glanced up when Cade burst in, holding up the phone. They crowded around and watched as the small figure sat unmoving.

"This feed came as a link from an unknown texter," he explained.

"Do you think it's her?" Rob asked, leaning in to get a better look. "It's so small I can't tell."

"The link was labeled 'Shadow v. Fox,'" Cade said, then explained how it had been hidden in a list of soccer matches.

"Can you zoom in?" Rejene asked.

Cade rotated the screen, going full frame. The video was from above—a small figure sat still in a bare square room. Larger now, the unmoving figure was still a mystery.

"I can't tell if this is a still or a live feed," Rob said. "If the person would move even a little."

As if on cue, the figure moved—lifting a bottle, taking a drink. Frustrated, Cade tried to use his fingers to zoom, but nothing happened. However, a small orange box that hadn't been there before appeared. The box was labeled "COMM."

Cade touched the button, and it went green.

Grace thought Shadow must be otherwise occupied if he wasn't talking to her. Both times the light came on previously, he had spoken. But not today. And the music was different. Neil Diamond was vastly different from Morbid Angel. Maybe he thought if she liked death metal, she'd hate Neil Diamond. She didn't. He had some decent songs.

She took a sip, then heard a soft click above her. The orange light was now green. As the song's chorus came on, she found herself singing along. But then, a loud voice boomed from above. A very familiar voice.

"Grace?"

Music played from the phone's speaker. Cade quickly turned up the volume. Even though he didn't know the name, he recognized the Neil Diamond song playing. Then, a softer, feminine voice began singing along with Neil's rich baritone.

"Grace?" Cade glanced at his partner and then his boss. Both wore the same astonished look.

"Cade?" her voice came through the speaker. The figure, now certainly Grace, was up and waving at the camera. "Is that really you?"

"Yes, it's me," he said, his voice cracking with emotion. "Are you okay? Have you been hurt?"

"I was drugged, but otherwise I'm fine. But I don't know where I am. All I know is this room I woke up in." Grace gestured around her.

All they could see was a bare, featureless square of a room. Something round—maybe a bucket—sat in one corner. It looked like a holding cell.

"We're trying to figure out where you are," Cade said. "When I found your car, I called in both the BCA and St. Paul. And we're not going to stop looking. Grace, can you tell me what happened?"

"I knew you'd figure out I was missing," she said. She ran a hand through her hair and continued. "After I parked, I was tackled in the alley. I fought and tried to use my keys to hurt him, but he managed to stick me with a needle. After that, I was out and woke up here. Wherever this is."

"I found your keys on the ground next to your car," Cade said. "He must have moved them, hoping someone would take your car. It's a good thing no one did."

"You're saying there's hope for humanity after all?"

"Perhaps, but then we still have creeps like the guy who took you." He leaned forward. "Did you see him? What can you tell us about him?"

"Sadly, not much at all. He wore a surgical mask and a stocking cap. Couldn't see much other than his eyes." She paused, remembering. "He referred to himself as Shadow. Whenever he talks, his voice is distorted, like in the movies. I can't tell you if he's young or old, has an accent or not. Nothing."

"It's all right. Has he said why he took you? What he wants?"

Grace shook her head. "No, but he asked for my—"

The video froze.

Damnit.

Words appeared: "Event ended."

Cade stared at the screen.

"He cut the feed," Rob said. "Right before she could finish."

"Yeah." Cade's voice was low. "He didn't want us to hear the rest."

He let out a sigh. What a day. He felt relieved, angry, frustrated, and horribly exhausted. And it was only Monday.

"I think you no longer have a choice. You need to have that conversation with Ritter," Captain Rejene said. "Get him to activate the task force. Use their resources for locating Grace."

"She's right," Rob said. "We can help."

"Okay, I'll talk to the prick," Cade said, already heading out the door.

"He asked for my work login," she whispered, staring at the orange light as it blinked out.

"No," she growled, throwing the empty water bottle across the room. It clattered and rolled before silence swallowed the room again.

Grace curled into herself, the tears coming hard now—hot, angry, helpless.

The lights shut off. And the dark was absolute.

The Governor's residence looked to be hosting an event, as the lot and on-street parking along Summit Avenue were full. Blocking in a blue Audi, Cade headed inside. As usual, he was met by Sarah. But unusually, she was dressed formally in a ruby cocktail dress.

"Feels a little early in the day for a fancy cocktail party," Cade said. There were a number of people, all dressed to impress, wandering around. A string quartet played in the corner.

"This is our kickoff celebration for the Governor's re-election campaign. Some of the largest donors in the state are here. Because they are primarily an older demographic, the Governor thought it best to make it a brunch event. And really, who doesn't love a brunch?"

Cade shrugged. "Makes sense." He lowered his voice. "I need a minute of the Governor's time. Something important came up."

Frowning, Sarah shook her head. "Winston hates to be interrupted when he's with his people."

"His people?"

"The donors."

Cade folded his arms. "This is a matter of life and death."

"So is his re-election." She held his gaze. "And if he isn't re-elected, it may be more than just me that's out of a job."

"It's not like he ever wanted me in this position. I was appointed by the Commissioner for the Department of Public Safety, meaning only he can remove me. Not everything is political, you know."

Sarah laughed. "You're so naïve. Everything is political."

The Governor stepped around a pair of women in their eighties, glanced at Sarah, noticed Cade, rolled his eyes, but came over.

"Dawkins," he said with a nod. "Here to say you caught the shooter?"

Feeling his leverage slipping away, Cade shook his head. "Another urgent matter has come up."

Ritter stepped closer. "More urgent than stopping a killer before he ruins the state's largest event on the global stage? This I have to hear."

"You don't need to worry. I have the best and brightest on the case. We'll have him in custody soon. But this urgent matter—"

Ritter shared a glance with his assistant. "Dawkins believes everything is urgent. He doesn't have any idea the urgent business I have to run this state." He lifted his glass to a judge and held up a finger.

"Maybe a kidnapped law enforcement officer is more urgent than scheduling your next photo op," Cade said.

"You have no idea what it takes to be elected, so I'd hold your tongue if I were you." Ritter's voice dripped with contempt as he studied Cade. "You look like shit. Bags under your eyes, hair like a first shift barista, and clothes that look slept in. Take care of yourself, and people will give you more respect."

"I haven't slept in the last 24 hours. Not since Grace was abducted." He wanted to say more but thought the words that would escape wouldn't be good for anyone.

Ritter's gaze softened. "I'm sorry to hear what happened. But bad things happen to people all the time. It's why you have a job." He studied Cade for a moment. "Wait, you're here to get the major crimes task force activated for her case, too."

Cade nodded. He didn't trust himself to say more.

"I'm not convinced it's warranted."

"Really."

"Really. First, it's for major crimes and this is one crime. One victim." Ritter acted like he was lecturing a high schooler. "It would set an unmatchable precedent if we were to activate the Five Below—love the name, by the way—major crimes task force for a one-off."

"One-off?"

"A one-off, Dawkins. One crime. One victim. Not a statewide crisis."

Cade took a breath. "There are things you don't know. The abductor sent me a link to a live feed of Grace's holding cell. I could see her and talk to her. She could talk to me."

Ritter leaned closer. "Show me."

Cade pulled up the text and handed over his phone. Ritter touched the link and brought up the page of world soccer feeds. The earlier link of Shadow v. Fox wasn't there.

"I'm sure it was there," Ritter said, handing the phone back. "But it's gone now."

Cade frowned. He knew what he saw. Cade explained what he'd seen earlier.

"Still, not worthy of a task force," Ritter said when Cade finished. "It's just one person."

"You're missing the point. This Shadow person has gone to a lot of trouble to abduct one of the state's premier crime scene investigators. Someone who's a valuable member of our task force. Who's to say he won't take more or there's not a larger agenda behind it?"

Ritter shrugged and checked his watch. "Who's to say there is? And it's concerning that this criminal reached out to you. Maybe you're part of the problem."

Cade's eyes flashed at Ritter. "Not fair. I had nothing to do with this. But an undertaking of this magnitude is what the task force was designed for. Our resources can work this better and faster than the locals."

Ritter shrugged. "I'm not convinced. And it's my understanding Ms. Fox was abducted on her own time. She wasn't on duty."

Cade's jaw muscles tensed. He squeezed his hands into fists. "Why would that possibly matter?"

"C'mon, Dawkins. Even you can't be this clueless. It's the optics. We can't be showing favoritism to law enforcement. People notice these things. *Voters* notice these things." Ritter checked his watch again. "If there's nothing else, I promised one of my largest donors I'd take a look at his development proposal. It's the least I can do."

Clearly dismissed, Cade headed for the exit.

"I'm not heartless," Ritter called out. "If anything changes, I'll reconsider activating the task force for this case. But until then, stand down and do the job I gave you. St. Paul can handle the Fox thing."

The Fox thing.

Fists clenched, Cade pushed the door open and stormed past an open-mouthed Sarah. She looked as if she was going to say something, but he didn't wait to hear it.

31

Cade pushed out of the governor's residence, rage thrumming in his veins, and dialed Rook before the door even shut behind him.

Rook answered with his usual greeting: "How ya doin', boss?"

"I've been better. You heard about Grace?"

"Heard what?" His tone was wary.

When Cade hesitated, Rook blew out a breath. "Don't be giving me any bad news. And on a Monday, too?"

"Grace was taken last night. She was grabbed in an alley in St. Paul."

"Wait, what? Tell me what happened."

Cade briefed him on what he knew and what he didn't. Unfortunately, there were more questions than answers.

"We'll get Five Below on it right away," Rook said.

"Can't. I met with Ritter, and he shot down the idea of using the task force to help find her. Said it set a dangerous precedent to use Five Below to locate one law enforcement officer who was abducted while off duty."

Rook scoffed. "Off duty? That sanctimonious prick. He really said that?"

"He did. Said to stand down on 'the Fox thing,' as he put it." Cade turned onto Lexington, headed toward the interstate.

"Eff him," Rook spat. "We'll run our own op. Off the books. We work parallel with St. Paul. Feed them anything we find."

"I'm in. It's better than standing around while everyone else is doing something." Cade accelerated down the ramp onto 94. "Let's meet and figure out what we can do."

"We can talk about the Theodore security footage as well." Rook paused. "Where are you now?"

"Just going to cross the river into Minneapolis."

"Let's meet at Graze. It's a food hall in my neighborhood."

"So, lots of hipsters, you're telling me?"

Rook laughed. "I'm not saying there won't be. They're everywhere." Rook lived in the North Loop area near Target Field, home of the Minnesota Twins. It was considered the up-and-coming area of Minneapolis. Hence the hipster invasion.

There was a surprisingly small amount of plaid as it turned out. Cade briefly pondered the possibility that it was no longer hip to wear plaid, and, as a herd, the hipsters had now moved on to newer, hipper styles. But that opened a larger can of worms—what if he'd accidentally become hip himself? He shut that thought down immediately. One crisis at a time.

Rook came through the front doors, and Cade waved him over. They awkwardly hugged. Rook's face made his concern evident.

"Tell me." He gestured them to a nearby sitting area.

Cade filled him in, talking through the abduction and the subsequent video feed, Rook nodding grimly. Bad things happening to good people was part and parcel of a cop's life, but it didn't always hit this close to home.

"So, our esteemed governor didn't think this met the threshold of a major crime?" Rook shook his head. "What a dick."

"Can't argue with that. In a perfect world your boss isn't the largest asshole in the state."

Rook stood. "C'mon. Let me buy you lunch, and we'll figure out how to get Grace back."

Ten minutes later, they continued the conversation over Korean braised beef tips and a carnitas bowl. "How can I help?" Rook asked. "Task force or not, we're working this."

"I appreciate that more than you'll ever know." Cade took a bite of the beef tips and after a moment said, "Grace's attacker used a syringe to inject her with a tranquilizer."

"Oh, shit," Rook said. "That happened here last week. A woman leaving work was attacked with a syringe. Someone jumped her, tranqed her, and then left. But no effin' way that was a coincidence."

"I think it was a practice run," Cade said. "Why else would the attacker leave her behind?"

Rook nodded, looking at his friend. "Hurry up and eat. Let's go talk to the victim."

"I was hoping you could take this one. I want to meet with Crocker over at the U. If anyone can trace the feed, it's him."

"That makes perfect sense," Rook agreed. "I'll meet with the victim and catch up with you afterwards."

Cade nodded.

"I'm surprised Grace's abduction hasn't hit the media yet. This would be a big story." Rook pushed his bowl away and leaned back.

"I'm not sure that wouldn't be a bad idea." Cade stroked his chin. "Shining a light on it might bring in tips. Maybe someone saw something."

"And it might put pressure on Ritter to authorize using Five Below to find her," Rook pointed out.

"Gotta be careful with that. Ritter's a snake. If he feels we're manipulating him, he's going to go berserk. Bite us in the ass."

"Bite you, you mean," Rook said. "He doesn't give a lick about me."

"True statement."

Rook stroked his chin. "Maybe you use your ex-girlfriend's media leverage. Have her help you out and, who knows, maybe rekindle things." Rook wriggled his eyebrows.

"Nah, that ship is long gone. And besides, I'm dating someone."

Rook studied his face for a moment before his expression lit up. "You're dating Grace."

"Guilty."

Rook made a show of shaking his head. "Man, I don't get it," he said with a grin. "Maybe they think you're funny. Women like a man with a sense of humor."

"I'm sure that's it," Cade said. "So, we have to bring her home safely. I'm not letting anything happen to Grace." He paused. "Not again."

Rook stood. "Alright, I'll check in when I know more. Keep me up to speed. Five Below is on it," he added, bumping fists.

Cade held a finger to his lips.

On his way to the U, Cade's phone rang.

"Cade, this is Kristen Bednarek. Lorie filled me in on what's going on. Just... shit on a stick. Grace?"

Along with Lorie Thao, Kristen had joined the team during Five Below's first case. Both had been brand new St. Paul detectives and had made an immense impact. Kristen's unflagging positivity had helped the team during some of the toughest times hunting the killers.

"I appreciate the call, Kristen." His voice cracked, but he was trying to hold it together. But failing miserably. He took a shaky breath. "It means a lot."

"I'm in," she said. "For whatever you need."

"The governor declined to activate the task force for this case," Cade said, still bitter.

"Well, screw him. Pardon my French. We can still help each other. That's what cops—and friends—do for each other. So, how can I help?"

He thought about it a moment. "We're stretched thin. Honestly, we need someone to keep track of leads, coordinate updates, and share intel across the board. Like a project manager." Cade drove through the University of Minnesota campus, weaving past clusters of backpack-wearing students.

"I can do that," she said enthusiastically. "That's totally in my wheelhouse. I'll build a shared case file, keep everyone looped in. *Ooo*, I'm so pumped."

Cade pulled the truck into a spot by the loading dock near the library. He tossed a State Patrol card on his dash. "Kristen," he said with a smile, "You have no idea how much I appreciate you."

"Let's bring her home." Her voice cracked with emotion.

Cade headed for the library to meet Crocker. He needed a miracle—and fast.

32

Professor Darius Crocker met Cade at the library's entrance. Walter Library—one of the University of Minnesota's oldest buildings—housed Crocker's state-of-the-art computer lab, tucked deep in the sub-basement past all the dusty relics no one thought to throw away. Being chair of the computer science department had its privileges, and he used them. Racks of computers and networking equipment filled this space.

The man himself looked to be a former football player based on his build. However, his sedentary occupation had contributed to his midsection since his playing days. He had the beginnings of a salt and pepper goatee and kind eyes that didn't miss much. They were joined by Crocker's friend, Clement Tubbs, chair of the U's Psychology Department. Like his colleague, Tubbs was a Black man approaching fifty, with a thoughtful demeanor and the calm precision of someone used to reading people for a living.

Cade had history with both men. Crocker's computer expertise and Tubbs's psychological insight had been instrumental in his last case, when they'd helped him track the killers behind the Orbiting Cortex site. The professors had first uncovered the site, then reached out to Cade because of his recent takedown of the serial predator targeting blonde women. That victory put Cade in the crosshairs—the site's killers marked him as their next target. It hadn't ended the way they'd planned.

"Thanks for meeting," Cade said. "Something's come up that you might be able to help with."

"Good lord, not another serial killer, I hope," Tubbs said.

"No, thankfully. But I'd rather have this discussion in the lab. More privacy."

They rode the elevator down in silence, listening to the piped-in music. When the doors opened, Cade exclaimed, "It should be illegal to turn "American Idiot" into elevator music."

"Still feeling strongly about your music, I see," Crocker said with a laugh.

Inside the lab, the three men sat around a conference table, each of them taking the same chairs as in previous meetings there.

"Grace Fox from the BCA has been abducted," Cade said. He filled them in with what he knew. "But there's been a development that could be in your wheelhouse. Earlier today, I received a text message with a link from an unknown number."

"It was a number you didn't recognize?" Crocker asked. "Trying to clarify the circumstances."

"There wasn't a number to see. It said unknown caller."

"That means whoever they were, they blocked their caller ID." Crocker shook his head. "Clicking a link from a blocked number is a recipe for disaster. But you know that."

"Yeah, normally I wouldn't ever click one, but with a possible ransom request coming, I felt I had to."

Both professors nodded in understanding.

"The link took me to a site with multiple soccer feeds. It listed matches from England, Spain, and Asia. One of the games was listed as Shadow v Fox. When I clicked it, I got a live feed of the room where Grace is held."

"Interesting."

"It gets more interesting. When I tried to pinch and zoom the screen to see if it was her, a box appeared that said COMM." He spelled it out: C-O-M-M. "When I touched it, Grace and I could talk to each other."

"So, she's okay?"

Cade nodded, his breath catching as he relived the moment. "Yeah. She's okay. For now."

"Fascinating. Did she give a clue to her whereabouts?"

"She had no idea where she was. And when she tried to say what this Shadow—that's how he referred to himself with Grace—wanted from her, the feed was cut mid-sentence."

"Let me take a look," Crocker said. Cade passed him the phone with the messaging app pulled up. When Crocker clicked the link, it brought up the page with the game feeds. The Shadow v Fox feed wasn't on the list.

"It was there earlier," Cade said.

"You were redirected a few times, right?"

Cade nodded.

"Then I'd bet he hacked the site and inserted his feed. A real-time plant. Disguised within normal-looking traffic."

"But," Tubbs said, leaning in, "wouldn't others be able to access Grace's feed?"

"Only if they happened upon the page at the right time. I'm guessing most people go there to watch a certain game. It's like if you wanted to catch the Arsenal game, for instance. You wouldn't click any of the other links. You're looking for Arsenal."

"Makes sense."

"People are going to ignore the ones that don't interest them. There might be a stray person around the world who has clicked on it, but what are they gonna do? Nothing."

"I'd imagine it's the same with the COMM button. It's not there unless you interact with the screen. The odds of someone finding it have to be infinitesimal," Tubbs said.

"I found it," Cade pointed out. "I was frustrated I couldn't see her face, so I tried to zoom."

"Clearly, he wanted you to find it," Tubbs said. "He wouldn't have incorporated it otherwise. I'm guessing you would have been prompted if you hadn't found it on your own."

Crocker leaned back, stroking his chin. "I see why you reached out—this is my area of expertise."

"And I can help with the abductor's mindset," Tubbs said. "Try to figure out what he's about."

"So, send me the link," Crocker said, "and I will research the smack out of this site. And then, if and when you receive a new link, forward it to me. No guarantees, but I just might be able to trace him."

"Crocker and Tubbs to the rescue." Cade smiled.

"You had to go there, didn't you?" Crocker said, but he was laughing.

"A note of caution here," Tubbs said. "This shadow person abducted Grace and then built a way for you to communicate with her. He did it for a reason, and it's not to benefit you. He wants you involved for some reason. He could have simply hidden her away and froze you out. Yet, he's drawing you in instead. You have to ask yourself why. What's in play here, and what's Shadow's endgame? Tubbs tapped the table. "Because right now, you're not just looking for Grace. You're playing *his* game."

The three men glanced at each other, the implications weighing heavily on them. It was the unknowns that could kill you.

Rook lifted the phone and punched in the code for apartment 211. He stood in the entryway to one of the hundreds of new apartment complexes in Minneapolis. They were springing up like ... well ... cheap commercial real estate projects.

"I don't want any," the woman's voice said over the phone's tiny speaker. "Go bother someone else."

"I don't have any," Rook replied. Reluctant witnesses were nothing new. "Ma'am, I'm the law, let me in."

The woman laughed. "You're the law? You've watched too many Westerns."

"It's a forgotten art form. Westerns, that is. Yellowstone is hitting some good notes."

She laughed. "It's a soap opera on horses. Tombstone was a classic, but beyond that, I don't know." A pause, then, "Why are you here specifically?"

"I'm following up on your attack last week. There's been another," Rook added.

Silence.

Then, *buzz.*

Rook took the stairs. When he knocked on her door, she made him wait. He covered the peephole when he noticed she was looking at him.

"You're a pain in my ass," she said but opened the door. "It's my day off and I'm trying to sleep in."

"It's 3 p.m.," Rook pointed out.

"Your point?"

"Just let me in." Rook held up his ID. "I'm Terrance Rooker."

"Fine." She opened the door. Asia Winters looked to be in her late twenties. She was dressed in a sweatshirt and shorts, which did nothing to hide her curves. She looked half asleep despite the hour.

"I wanted to talk to you about what happened last week. Yeah, I know you told this to other cops," he said, seeing her reaction. "But the same thing happened again yesterday, but this time the woman was abducted."

"Oh shit. She's missing?"

"She is. So, walk me through your evening up to the moment you were attacked. Maybe your attacker was around before he made his move, and you saw something." Rook had his phone out to take notes and jotted down her name.

"Why don't you record this instead? That way you'll get all my nuances. There's an app on your phone if you didn't know."

"Witness claims to have nuances," Rook said aloud, tapping a note into his phone. "Attending officer remains skeptical."

Asia gave him a look. "You don't play well with others, do you?"

Rook ignored her question. "Go ahead."

Asia sighed, leaning forward, chin on her hand. "I was working my usual Sunday night shift at Sisyphus Brewing across from the sculpture garden. Nothing out of the ordinary. Sundays are mostly regulars dropping in. Playing games, watching football, and decompressing before the work week. I don't remember anyone being there that I didn't know. Not recently, anyway. I was back at work again last night, and it was the same crowd. Same as the week before."

Rook typed into his phone and looked up. "Okay, tell me about when you left."

"I'm cleaning during my shift, and so around 10 p.m., I'm pretty much done with my closing chores. The regulars know the routine, and they were all gone by then. Sam and I locked up. He parked on the street, and I was around the corner in the lot."

"He didn't walk you to your car?"

"No, I parked in the corner spot near the side entrance. Sam was on the street—maybe 50 yards away. We could both see our cars. We do this every damn week. He said see ya, and I got to the lot and…"

Asia's face clouded, and she wrapped herself up in a hug. Rook stayed silent, wanting to give her space.

After a brief pause, she continued. "He hit me. Knocked me down."

"Hit you?"

"Tackled me. Like when I played football with my brother and his friends. We landed hard, and he was on me." Her voice faltered. She hugged herself tighter. "I tried to fight, but he had me pinned."

"Pinned how?"

"Like the school bully has you on your back, sitting on you. He had one hand pressing me down, and the other was reaching behind his back—like fumbling for something. Then I saw the syringe."

"What did he look like?"

"His face was covered with a COVID mask."

"Hair color?"

"Knit cap."

"Eye color?"

Asia hesitated, shaking her head. "I remember looking into his eyes when I asked him why. I thought they were blue, but then I remembered green too. So, I guess I'm not much help there either."

"Did he answer you?"

She nodded, her eyes darting. Rook had seen this before when a witness shared a traumatic account. Their bodies rebelled as they relived the moment. "That's when I saw the syringe. Things never go well for people in movies when that happens."

"What did he say?" Rook prompted.

"It's not personal." Tears ran down her cheeks, and she shook as sobs wracked her. Her hands twisted in her lap, knuckles white, as if she were holding on to keep from shattering apart. "How could it not be personal? He attacked me." A tremor rippled through her voice, her eyes darting to the door as though she half-expected him to walk in.

Rook put a hand on hers. "I mentioned earlier that another woman was abducted. It happened last night. Her attacker injected her with something. A syringe to the neck."

Asia involuntarily put a hand on her neck.

"But rather than being left behind, she was taken." Rook held her gaze. "I hope there's something in your account we can use to find her."

"You think I was practice? Like he used me to perfect his technique?"

He nodded.

Asia studied him for a long moment. "But how did you know she was injected? Did he leave the syringe behind?"

Rook shook his head.

"Was there a witness or a camera?"

Again, he shook his head.

"You'd suck as a poker player," she said, taking a step toward him. "What aren't you telling me?"

"It's what I can't tell you."

Her eyes burned into his as tears rolled down her flushed cheeks. "Has anyone ever told you you're an asshole?"

"You're the first this week, but it's Monday."

"Leave."

Rook left, muttering under his breath that Mondays really needed to go extinct.

33

Shadow sat in the dark of the control room. The lights were on in the woman's cell, casting long, stark shadows across her bare walls. She was moving again—more squats. He noted the depth of her bend, the precision of her form. She'd already cycled through lunges, burpees, and pushups with military discipline.

He couldn't fault her. In her place, he'd do the same—stay strong, stay alert, stay alive. She was adapting. Trying to stay sharp. Preparing to fight.

He liked that.

"You're not a prisoner," he murmured, eyes fixed on the screen. "You're a participant."

And that, he couldn't wait for.

Grace dropped to the cold concrete floor of the holding cell, her palms braced against the rough surface as she began a set of push-ups. Her movements were steady, controlled—each rise and fall marked by a sharp inhale and exhale. Sweat beaded on her brow, but her expression was stoic, her jaw tight with focus. The dim light overhead cast shadows along her toned arms, highlighting the strength she refused to let falter.

She shifted into a plank position, her core trembling slightly but holding firm. This wasn't just about physical fitness; it was about control, about pushing back against the helplessness that threatened to creep in. She refused to let the four suffocating walls of the cell strip her of her resolve.

Switching to a set of squats, she moved with deliberate precision, her eyes fixed on an unseen horizon. Determination radiated off her in waves. Her breaths came faster now, but the faint smirk tugging at the corner of her lips betrayed the satisfaction she felt in reclaiming even this small semblance of power.

Grace's resilience wasn't just in her muscles—it was in the fire that burned in her eyes, in the refusal to let her circumstances define her. Each repetition was a statement, a silent vow: she wasn't done fighting. Not even close.

When the lights came on, she paused her exercise routine and squinted. Shadow had used these brighter lights previously when she spoke with Cade, so she thought of them as stage lights for a show. Unfortunately, she was the show.

And, same as before, an orange light popped on. She'd be talking to Cade soon.

Grace had been working out in her mind what she could say to Cade that could help locate her. But the trouble was she didn't know anything. She'd been unconscious during transport. The room felt like new construction, but she couldn't tell if it was above ground, below, or in another damn country. And maybe worse, she couldn't pick out her abductor from a lineup if her life depended on it.

She took a deep breath, telling her body that now wasn't the time for her anxiety to take over.

Okay, if she was working the case from outside, she'd look for someone who had recently purchased the materials to build her holding cell, especially the lighting and soundproofing components. Had he done it himself or hired it out? A survey of construction firms and remodelers might prove fruitful. Also, it would take someone with specialized skills to create a communication system like the one used here. She guessed it had to be encrypted otherwise she'd already be back sleeping in her own bed. That wasn't something your average DIY-er could accomplish. So, who had the capability?

The light went from orange to green.

"Grace?"

She'd never been so glad to hear a voice. Relief washed over her.

"Cade, I'm here." Grace waved to the ceiling, unsure exactly of the camera's location. In the upper corner of the room, a tiny red light blinked—one she hadn't noticed before. Probably part of the camera system, she guessed, but it gave her the creeping sense that something was watching... and counting.

"Grace!" The excitement and relief were evident in his tone.

"Tell me you're outside with the entire Minnesota National Guard ready to storm the castle."

"I wish." Cade sounded like a teenage boy wishing the Homecoming Queen had picked him instead of the douchebag they typically picked.

"How about the State Patrol Special Response Team rolling up with their urban assault vehicles?"

"Not today."

"What about a troop of Boy Scouts and their den mother in a tricked-out minivan?"

"As soon as you tell me where you are, I'll make it happen."

"The trouble is, I have zero idea where I'm being imprisoned. Why don't you ask Shadow?" Grace said, a flicker of sarcasm in her voice.

There was a brief silence before Cade spoke. "Mr. Shadow. I'm sure you can hear me. Would you please tell me where Grace is being held?"

He waited and hoped, but there was only silence.

"Looks like you're going to have to figure it out on your own then," Grace said.

"And with my best researcher unavailable. I'm talking about you," he added unnecessarily.

"You say the kindest things. But you need to think like me." Grace paced. "Ask yourself what I'd be researching if I wasn't stuck having a spa day here. I'd want to know how this room came together. Not everyone could pull it off. Specialized materials, knowledge, and capabilities were needed to put this place together. Look into that."

"Already started."

"Started but not finished. Shadow didn't Home Depot this place together in an afternoon. Someone either helped him or sold him the pieces. My bathroom is a Home Depot bucket. Maybe the materials came from there. Look for recent specialized lighting and sound-dampening purchases."

"Will do."

Grace paused. "Tell me about how you were able to talk to me. How did you know what to do?"

Cade walked her through receiving the text message with the link and the page it brought him to. He explained discovering the COMM button and realizing what it meant.

"Okay, let's assume it's encrypted," Grace said, cutting him off before he could respond. "Start with the number that sent the text. Then find out who has access to that webpage of feeds. Can you trace the IP address?"

"Good questions."

Grace wasn't finished. "My abductor's vehicle had to be close to the spot I was grabbed. No way he threw me over a shoulder and walked to his car a block away. Ring cameras and the like must be prevalent in the neighborhood. One of them had to catch something."

"Done."

"Lastly, let's examine the why. I have to ask the question: why me? It's not like I'm the kind of woman you kidnap just to stare at. No, he wants something. It could have been something random, but I doubt it. It's unlikely he just happened to see me and decided, why not grab this woman to hold in my state-of-the-art detention facility?"

"Grace, he had what we believe was a practice run with a Minneapolis woman before you. But after injecting her, he left her behind."

She paused. "That's interesting. But it also tells me several things. He's a planner. He wanted things to go smoothly. It also tells me he hasn't done this before."

"First time abductor. And he wanted you specifically."

Grace pondered for a moment. "Okay, then. He wanted me, but why? If he's not using me for anything, then he wanted me away from something."

"From the task force's shooter case? Or is there something you're working for the BCA?" Cade asked.

"Nothing unusual. Certainly nothing warranting this extreme," she said, gesturing around the small space. "No, it has to be the task force's case because you've been invited into this situation too. Think about it. Your focus is divided, and you're not chasing down the shooter fulltime."

"So, you think it's the Hotel Theodore shooter doing this?"

Grace shrugged. "I mean, it makes a certain amount of sense. He stands to gain from this situation."

Cade sighed. "I don't know. This feels too organized and too planned for the shooter. He—"

Cade's voice was gone as the green light switched to orange. The spotlights turned off with a click, plunging Grace back into darkness.

She wanted to scream, but after a few deep breaths, she dropped silently back into her routine. The dark didn't care, and neither would she.

"Did you get that?" Cade asked when Crocker picked up.

The university professor sounded out of breath when he answered. "Yes, we listened in. Clement was here too. You're on speaker, by the way."

"Hello," Cade said. "What did you think?"

It was Clement Tubbs who spoke. "I was impressed with Ms. Fox's resiliency. She's held prisoner, yet she remains sharp enough to process the ramifications of her situation. The questions she raised are astute. And she's pointing you in the directions she would take to solve her abduction. A remarkable young woman."

"That she is," Cade agreed. "What about the backend of this communication link? Can you track where it's coming from?"

Crocker spoke. "It looks like the feed itself was encrypted. But I'm looking at the code used to insert the feed link on the webpage. I'll let you know if I uncover anything. There are a lot of steps involved to make this happen, and the odds of the abductor slipping up at some point are good."

"Okay." Cade paused, thinking things through. "How likely is it that the shooter took Grace? That he planned and built the room and the communication system?"

There was momentary silence on the line before Crocker spoke. "That's a lot of things for one person to be good at. Even James Bond had help from Q on the technology side. One person can't do it all. At least not well."

"That's my thought, too. Does the shooter have help? An accomplice perhaps? Or is someone involved with the International Mayors Conference doing this? I get the feeling this Fang businessman, whose security detail was killed, might be up to something. Maybe he has something to hide." Cade ran a hand through his hair. "Either way, Grace has given us several paths to go down."

"Let us work on our part," Crocker said. "You do yours and we'll reconnect."

There was something in his pause that bothered Cade. "What is it?"

"I saw something. Wondering if you saw it? I didn't at first, as I was so focused on Ms. Fox."

Unsure what the professor was referring to, Cade ran through Grace's video in his head. There was nothing but Grace in a small room. "I don't know. I don't think so."

Crocker sighed loudly. "There was a countdown timer in the upper left of the screen. It was at 71:28 when I noticed it."

Cade swallowed hard.

"It could be nothing."

"It could be everything."

Both men were silent as they processed the implications of the timer. Crocker broke the silence. "I hope it's nothing more than battery life, but I fear it may mean something far worse. You may have just a three-day window to rescue her. To be cautious, let's set timers for 71:28," he said after a pause.

As Cade set a timer on his watch, he got another call. It was Rook.

"Hey, let's meet. Where ya at?"

"In the parking lot outside Crocker and Tubbs's lab."

"Less than ten minutes away. See you there."

Cade leaned against his truck. Thinking.

The timer meant something—it had to. Seventy-one hours sounded generous until you realized how fast time moved when someone's life was ticking down. But if Shadow thought he was the only one playing against the clock, he was about to learn what a desperate man could do with every second.

34

Cade leaned against his truck, parked near Walter Library on the University of Minnesota campus. The sun had set over an hour ago, and the breeze off the Mississippi had teeth. He zipped up his coat, but the chill he felt ran deeper. His mind was somewhere else—where it always seemed to be these days.

"You're thinking about Grace, aren't you?" Rook adjusted his cap, his voice low. "I get it. If it were me, I'd be consumed too."

Cade nodded, staring at nothing. "I keep spinning my wheels. Nothing I've learned has made a lick of difference. Every clue I've chased, every angle I've played—it's like trying to solve a puzzle with half the pieces missing. My mind hasn't stopped running through possibilities, but I don't know enough. The bastard took her, but why? He hasn't hurt her but hasn't released her either."

Rook nodded but kept quiet.

"But you had a reason for asking to meet." He looked at Rook. "So, what's on your mind?"

Rook put a foot on his bumper, meeting Cade's stare head-on. "I'm going to be straight with you. It's too much. Shadow took Grace for a reason. We can't underestimate her value in any of our cases. And then he involved you with the comm link. Now, two of the arguably highest-profile law enforcement agents in the state are effectively off the grid or seriously derailed. Like it or not, you're hopelessly wrapped up with Grace's abduction."

"How could I not be?"

Rook held up his hands in a surrender gesture. "I'm not saying you shouldn't be. But you need to hand off the shooter case to the rest of the team. You're not doing anyone any good. We don't need a headline about a grieving cop pulling the trigger too fast."

Cade was going to object, but Rook wagged a finger at him. "You need your head in the game. It's for your own good."

Before he could reply, Rook continued. "We can handle things. I can lead the task force while you focus on Grace."

"I'm fine with that, but I'm supposed to lead the task force. I can't just walk away."

"No one said you're walking away. You're still the leader, but now you lead from the top. Leave the day-to-day stuff to me. Don't worry, when we need you, we'll call."

"I don't know."

"I'm throwing you a lifeline here. You keep pushing like this, you'll crash and burn." He looked to Cade and shook his head. "Get Kristen and Lorie on the phone."

Cade didn't move.

"Do it," Rook barked, slipping into full coach mode.

Cade shot him a look but pulled out his phone. He brought in Lorie and Kristen, putting them on speaker. "Hey, boss. What's happening?"

Cade ran a hand over his stubble. "Hey, Kristen, Lorie. I have Rook here. He wants a word."

"Hey, Rook."

"Hey, we were talking, and it would be better for Cade if he stepped back to a more strategic role with Five Below. Have you two handle the day-to-day until Grace is found."

"Not a problem. We can handle it."

"He's a little fragile," Rook said. "I mean, understandably."

Cade cocked his head, listening to Rook, not liking the direction the conversation was headed.

"Of course," Lorie said. "We've got this until he's ready to come back."

Cade leaned in. "I'm right here."

"That would be best. His head hasn't been fully in the game."

"You know I'm on this call, right?" Cade looked at Rook. "And my head has been fully in the game."

"That's the problem. You can't have your head fully in more than one case. It's impossible to maintain. No matter who you are." Rook put a hand on his friend's shoulder. "You trust me, right? Then trust me now. Let us carry this for a while. You focus on bringing Grace home."

Kristen spoke up. "Cade, don't worry. We'll run down the shooter. And we'll keep you looped in."

"And we'll call the moment something breaks." Rook paused. "Are we good?"

Cade met his eyes and gave a weary shrug. "We'll have to be."

Detectives Kristen Bednarek and Lorie Thao sat outside the City Center shopping mall sipping identical lattes, their eyes scanning the ebb and flow of shoppers: a young woman in a flowing floral dress juggling a cluster of glossy shopping bags; a group of teenagers strolling by, their laughter echoing as they shared bites of giant pretzels, their outfits a chaotic blend of oversized hoodies and brightly colored sneakers. Kristen's gaze lingered on a woman in a long trench coat and sunglasses, her movements deliberate as she slipped into a clothing store. Lorie raised an eyebrow, silently questioning whether this casual observation would soon turn into something more.

"This feels like we're waiting around for bad shit to happen." Kristen leaned closer to Lorie. "Like a damned death watch."

Lorie nodded. "That's because it is. I don't know how you get ahead of a killer like this. We follow up best we can, but unless we know who the targets are, what can we do?"

"At least Rook is keeping an eye on Fang. Bad things seem to happen around him."

"That's because he's bad. We can't prove it, but we both know it."

Kristen bumped coffee cups with Lorie. "The thing I don't like about police work is the fundamental lack of proactivity. We always come in after the fact."

"But I'd argue that the patrol officers are the proactive part of the force. With highly visible uniforms and marked vehicles, they are meant to deter criminals proactively."

Kristen scoffed. "Yeah, and how's that working?"

"There's no way to quantify that. Take away the visible part of the force for a period, and see how many more crimes happen compared to the previous period? That's never going to happen." Lorie leaned back, clearly enjoying the theoretical part of her job. "And I'd postulate that, at first, crime would go down as the criminal element would be wary, believing a cop was hiding behind every corner. However, it wouldn't be long before they were emboldened by the lack of consequences and returned to their ways, bringing along the ones who previously weighed the risk/reward and found it unsatisfactory."

"You've given this a lot of thought."

Lorie looked proud—until Kristen continued. "You need to get laid more often."

"There is that. Wait a minute." She turned to Kristen. "So you're saying you don't need it more often?"

Kristen let loose with a loud, unfiltered laugh. "No, I am most definitely not saying that. I'm an every day and twice on Tuesday kinda gal. Brandon hasn't realized it. But he will."

They bumped cups again.

They were silent for a few minutes until Kristen said, "You know what proactive policing really looks like? Robocop busting down doors announcing arrests for future criminal activity."

She stood and gave her best cyborg impression: "You're guilty and sentenced to *immediate* termination, punk." She held out an imaginary Auto-9 pistol and took aim at several imaginary targets. "*Boom. Boom. Boom.*"

On the last *boom*, the woman coming out of the clothing store gasped, flinched backward, and ran off in the opposite direction. The click of her high heels lingered as she lost herself in the crowd.

Kristen's eyes widened. She lowered her imaginary pistol and turned to Lorie. "You don't suppose..."

Lorie was already nodding. They bolted after her.

35

A grinding, mechanical whine jolted Grace upright in the dark. It came from the wall beside her—loud, close, unfamiliar. Heart pounding, she pressed her ear to the surface and ran her hand along the seam of the door. The sound grew louder, more urgent, but offered no answers.

And then the unimaginable happened. The door swung open, and a man stepped inside.

Grace backpedaled, instinct screaming for distance. If he was here—inside with her—bad things were going to happen.

It was a matter of whether the bad things were going to happen to her or to him.

Her captor loomed over her, a towering figure wrapped in menace. His broad shoulders filled the doorway, and the dim light cast jagged shadows across his frame. Every inch of him was concealed in dark, heavy fabric, from the thick gloves on his hands to the combat boots that scraped against the floor. A hood hung low over his face, the smooth, featureless mask beneath it erasing every trace of humanity. His breathing, slow and measured, was the only sound in the room, amplified by the suffocating silence.

Her skin crawled. Something about his stillness, his size, the inhuman smoothness of his mask—it wasn't just that he looked dangerous. He felt... wrong. Predatory in a way her body recognized before her brain did.

Grace stood. Facing her captor, she sized him up. If his face was covered, maybe it meant he wasn't planning to kill her. Or maybe the mask was just there to terrify her. Either way, not enough information.

"You're coming with me." His voice was gravel, low, and guttural.

Grace wanted to mouth off, but curiosity overrode sarcasm. If she could see beyond her cell, she might find something useful—an exit, a clue, a weakness. "Fine, lead the way."

But he wasn't taking any chances. "I insist." He gestured for her to go.

"But do me a favor, I want to hear you say, 'I'm Batman.'"

Getting no reaction, Grace stepped out of the cell for the first time. Outside her prison, the place was rundown to the point of being decrepit. Crumbling walls, cracked cement floors, and cobwebs thick enough to catch a bear brought home the fact this was way off the beaten path. She was unlikely to be discovered here. It was going to be up to her.

"Love what you've done with the place. Just needs a fresh coat of paint, some furniture, and an exorcist."

Evidently not amused, her captor nudged her forward.

"Hey Mr. Shadow, you don't have to push. Use your big boy words."

They came to a dimly lit stairwell. "Down."

She didn't bother pointing out the lack of an "up." Grace bit down on the snark rising in her throat. God, she wanted to say something, anything—but snark wouldn't get her out of here. Intel might. If she stayed smart, if she listened, if she kept him talking... she might learn something useful. "I'd imagine the rental cost here wouldn't break your bank. Or did you buy the place as an investment?"

They descended until a room opened up—dark, low-ceilinged, and rank with rot. The air was damp and musty, thick enough to taste, and the floor was strewn with debris. The place reeked of decay and death. "Your landlord isn't keeping up his end of the deal."

"I know what you're trying to do. But there's no landlord, this place has been abandoned. No one will find you here." He nudged her again.

She edged past an animal carcass and saw something larger slumped in the shadows. Grace covered her mouth to stop herself from calling out. A body lay among the debris. Wearing the dusty green overalls of maintenance men everywhere, the face and head were shrouded in shadow. Drag marks on the floor indicated the man had died elsewhere. If Shadow had noticed her discovery, he kept silent.

They came to a door. It was the kind of door that wasn't made any-more—thick, solid oak reinforced with iron bands, its surface scarred with deep grooves that told of years of use or abuse. The heavy, rusted handle was worn smooth, polished by countless hands over decades. Faint scratch marks clawed at the wood near the base, as if something—or someone—had once tried to escape. The air around it was colder, heavier, as if whatever lay beyond was leeching the warmth from the room.

Shadow pushed past her and pulled the door open. Based on the sound, the door didn't want to be opened. A wall of rot and shadow waited beyond.

"Go."

But Grace's body locked up. Her prison cell was bad. The basement, worse. But this—this was something else entirely. "I'm not going in there." Hearing the shake in her voice, she didn't care. "Kill me, but I'm not going in that room."

Shadow loomed over her, staring.

Grace held herself together through sheer force of will. After several seconds of hellish imaginings, he spoke.

"This isn't a room. It's a tunnel between buildings." His voice sounded painful; it was so gravelly. "I'm not locking you up here. We're practicing the route in case I have to move you. If that happens, we'll need speed—this walkthrough ensures you won't slow me down."

He stepped through the door and hooked a finger for her to follow.

Cinder block walls stretched out in both directions, disappearing into the oppressive darkness. The faint, rhythmic drip of water echoed through the cavernous space, each drop amplifying the suffocating silence. A dank, musty odor clung to the air, thick and relentless, clawing at her senses. She squinted at the gray wall. Scratched into the surface, just outside the doorway, were three words:

They never left.

The letters, uneven and etched with desperate force, seemed to pulse in the dim light. A chill prickled her skin, and she stepped back instinctively, her breath hitching in her throat.

"It's supposed to be haunted here," Shadow whispered, as the air seemed to grow colder, heavier with every passing second. "But the dead never scare me."

Grace shivered.

"Time for you to go back. If the need arises, I know you'll move fast. It's either that or be left in these tunnels with those who remain."

Grace followed, the stench of the tunnels clinging to her skin. Relief didn't come until the door shut, sealing the tunnels behind her again.

36

Rook had barely gotten through a page of his Carl Hiaasen paperback when his cell buzzed. With a glance toward Fang and his entourage in the hotel's restaurant, he set down the novel. The book was more cover than actual entertainment. He answered the call.

Kristen's voice sparked with energy, breathless and electric: "We got her."

Rook sat up.

"She didn't have any ID on her, just a credit card. But in those So Kates, it's definitely her."

"I'm not following. Who is Kate?"

"Uncultured heathen. They're the pinnacle of Christian Louboutin's designs."

Rook slouched, feeling like he'd stepped into a country where they spoke a language that resembled English, but none of it made sense. He decided if it came up again, he'd ask someone less judgmental later. Better to move on for now.

"I see."

He did not.

"Could you humor me and start from the beginning? Who did you arrest?"

"Seriously, Rook. You got to start getting more sleep." She made an exasperated sigh. "The executive assistant to Fang. Rose Park."

Rook straightened in his seat.

"What should we do with her? Book her at the nearest Minneapolis precinct?"

Rook was on his feet and headed for the exit. "No, hold on. Word will spread too fast. Half the jailers are paid stringers for the media. Not judging. It helps beef up the retirement portfolio. Bring her to St. Paul, where it's quieter. Let's sit her down and talk sense with her. Maybe she'll give up her boy toy."

With a last glance toward Fang, Rook ran for his car. He'd catch up with him later.

On the road, Rook called Special Agent Hankee.

"Detective." The background was loud, like she was near a crowd.

"We've detained the Park woman, and I was wondering if you wanted to sit in when we talk to her. Thought you could offer some international context."

The background grew considerably quieter as Rook accelerated up the ramp to merge onto 94.

"And you're not concerned the Bureau will take over your case?" There was a lilt of humor in her tone. "I could scoop it right out of your hand."

Rook wasn't in the mood. "Do you want in on the interrogation or not?"

"Someone needs to get more sleep."

"I'm going to hang up and call the CIA."

"Alright, alright. Text me the address, and I'll be there." She paused. "Life is too short to be so grumpy."

Rook hung up on her and accelerated around a Tesla.

About fifteen minutes later, he pulled into the Law Enforcement Center's parking lot, grateful for one of its few perks: plenty of space. That wasn't always the case in downtown St. Paul—but it was still a dream compared to the City of Lakes. If he weren't a cop with the freedom to park just about anywhere, it would be a nightmare.

Lorie's car came in right after him. He walked over and gave her and Kristen a fist bump, saying, "Nice work."

"Luck. Sheer luck," Kristen said. "But I'll take it."

Rook grinned. "Don't underestimate it. Lots of police work is luck. It's being prepped, ready, and knowing enough to put yourself in the right spot for the luck to find you. You're doing the right things."

Lorie opened the rear door and helped Rose Park slide out. She was elegant, more polished than any detainee who'd ever been in Rook's squad. She gave him a slow once-over, her gaze so sharp and lingering that Rook was sure he'd never been assessed so thoroughly in his life. Maybe it was a spy thing. Always looking for weaknesses to exploit, strengths to co-opt, or advantages to gain. What did she find in him?

"Welcome to St. Paul, Ms. Park. Let's go have a chat and see what you've been up to." Rook gestured and then followed the three women.

A lieutenant handed them a conference room. Rook had Park sit across from him and Lorie while Kristen took her usual spot between the suspect and the door—silent, steady, and just close enough to make Park think twice.

They'd barely handed Park a glass of water when there was a light knock and the door eased open. Special Agent Hankee stepped in, moving like someone who didn't need to announce herself to take control. Navy suit, neat ponytail, and that cold, unreadable look she wore like armor. The silver flash of her watch caught the light as she sized up the room. She carried a worn leather folder under one arm—the kind that had seen years of classified conversations. No pleasantries, no small talk.

Hankee gave them a nod. "Let's get to it."

Lorie cleared her throat. "Ms. Park. We're with the state's Five Below Major Crimes Task Force. You're being detained due to your involvement with the perpetrator of several murders of foreign nationals in Minneapolis."

She paused to see if the woman had something to say. She didn't.

"Who is the man you were with?"

Park's expression softened, looking more like she was answering a pageant softball question rather than an interrogator's demand. "I am here at the behest of my employer, Chou Fang. I am his executive assistant. As such, I travel with him." She smiled.

Lorie shook her head. "You're misunderstanding my question. We want to know about the man you left with following the shooting of Mr. Fang's security detail."

"I did not leave with him. He was armed and coerced me to leave with him to provide cover in case there were other shooters. I did nothing wrong." She didn't smile, but it was close.

"I am sorry for your bad experience in our country," Lorie said. "But can you tell us about the man who abducted you?"

"I can." Park not-quite-smiled again.

There were several beats as the officers in the room waited for her to elaborate. Glances were exchanged when she didn't. Rook felt his irritation grow.

Lorie cleared her throat. "Please tell us about the man."

"There's much to share and also little to tell. He was a private man."

"Tell us something." Lorie sounded exasperated. "Anything."

"What would you like to know?" Park's expression edged closer to a smile.

Rook had enough. "Tell us anything. His name. Where he's from. Who he works for. The reason he's killing people here. Where he's staying. Who his next target is."

Rook shook his head when Rose hesitated. "*Anything*. Does he have any scars or tattoos? Does he prefer Coke or Pepsi? Wine, beer, or prison hooch? Does he pray to Jesus, Buddha, or his mother? Does he prefer metaphysics to theology? What are his hopes and dreams? Is he more likely to read Hemingway or People? Is he more interested in soft porn or commercial real estate? Does he snore?" He leaned forward. "Do you find him easy to manipulate?"

Rose's expression moved into Mona Lisa territory. "He said his name was Frank. A security guard by trade."

Rook scoffed. "Do you know many mall cops who carry silenced weapons?"

Her gaze shifted toward Rook. "Not in my country, but this isn't my country. There are different rules and customs here."

"Since you brought it up, let's talk about your country. Where are you from, exactly?"

"I grew up near Orang in North Hamgyong Province."

"That's in North Korea?"

Rose nodded. "It's a remote village on the eastern coastline of North Korea."

"Your English is quite good." This observation came from Hankee.

"Thank you."

"It was not meant as a compliment," Hankee said with a sharp tone.

The room seemed to shrink around the two women, the air thick with unspoken tension. Hankee leaned back from the table, her arms loosely crossed, her posture deceptively casual, while Rose leaned forward. Their eyes locked, and for a moment, neither moved, their silence louder than words.

Rook was riveted.

They were two lionesses in the savanna, circling, each assessing the other's strength. Hankee's gaze was steady, unblinking, her lips curved in a faint, knowing smile—a predator unafraid to show her teeth. Rose, clad in sharp, immaculate lines of designer authority, mirrored the pose with her chin raised slightly higher, her own smile sharp and cold, as if to say, *Are you sure you want to do this?*

The hum of the air conditioner was the only sound between them, like the restless rustle of leaves in a windless jungle. Their eyes locked. Neither flinched.

It was a duel of instincts and dominance, fought with stillness and glances.

Hankee narrowed her eyes, seemingly everyone else forgotten. "The Reconnaissance General Bureau taught you well. But that's what the RGB is known for. Taking raw recruits and transforming them into deadly Disney princesses."

"I might say the same about the Mossad."

Rook glanced between the two women, wondering what the hell was going on. It was like he'd shown up uninvited to a chess match—and he'd brought checkers.

Frustrated, he wanted to get back to the shooter, not listen to these two posturing. He turned to Rose. "Just so we understand each other, Ms. Park, we both know the man isn't a security guard. He works for the U.S. government, killing people. You hijacked his mission to accomplish your own. And now, he's been—perhaps unwittingly—working for the North Korean government. You are in a heap of trouble."

Rose smiled. "Please name any U.S. law I've broken."

Kristen shyly held up her hand. "Conspiracy to commit murder. It's a crime when people agree to intentionally and unlawfully kill someone. Conspiracy focuses on the planning and intention behind the act, even if the murder itself does not occur. The key elements include an agreement between two or more individuals to commit murder. This agreement doesn't need to be explicitly stated and can be inferred from actions, but the participants must have the specific intent to cause someone's death. With your partner carrying out the killings, the agreement has been realized."

Rook gave her a thumbs up.

All eyes turned to Park, who offered a shrug. "This sounds like a substantial amount of guesswork. To say I had planned a U.S. government assassin's target is to say the unprovable. We both know he'll never see the interior of a courtroom." She folded her arms. "And you are mistaken. I am nothing more than a business-man's executive assistant. I handle travel arrangements, make appointments, and keep the business operating."

"And what is his business, exactly?"

"Mr. Fang is an international trade consultant. He provides expert advice and services to companies looking to enter foreign markets."

Hankee cleared her throat. "Could you explain why he met with Xiang Li and Chen Dazhao? Both men are infamous cyber-terrorists."

Park blinked, her mouth falling open. "That's news to me if it's true."

"It's true."

"I will have to take you at your word. This world of espionage and terrorism is unfamiliar to me."

Rook thought Park was a pretty good actor. She played the part well, though every now and then a hint of cynicism showed. "Can you tell us where this man is now? He was at the Hallmark but slipped away in the commotion."

"That's where he held me. But when those men tried to break into the room, he shot them. In the chaos, I slipped out. I found a maid's cart and hid in a room with the housekeeper until it felt safe to leave. She understood what was happening and gave me a uniform to help me get out without drawing attention."

"Very well done," Lorie said. "But why were you shopping instead of going to the police?"

"I needed a change of clothes before I went to the authorities. I wanted to be comfortable." She smiled again.

"Excuse us," Rook said. "Kristen, will you stay with Ms. Park while we confer outside?"

She nodded and the others stepped out. Rook studied the faces of his colleagues. "I'm not convinced she is who she says she is, but lacking proof, what can we do?"

Hankee spoke first. "She's 100 percent RGB. But I don't see that she's broken any immigration laws or harmed the interests of the U.S. She's good at what she does."

Lorie nodded. "I have to agree. The question then is what do we do with her?"

Rook stroked his chin, which needed a trim. He'd been running hard, with no time for even basic self-maintenance. "Kick her loose and see if she reunites with our assassin? She could lead us to him." He looked around for responses.

Lorie shook her head. "I don't have any other bright ideas. We could hold her for a day, but the district attorney won't press charges. Not in an election year." She paused. "Should we call in Cade? See if he has any ideas?"

"Nope. He's tied up," Rook said. "Let's cut her loose and only bring Cade in if something develops. Everyone agree?"

No one looked especially happy, but no one had any other solutions. Holding her might feel like a win, but without leverage, it'd only tip their hand. Better to let her think she was in the clear—and follow her. An hour later, Rose Park was released.

Hankee pulled Rook aside as everyone was getting ready to depart. Her hand lingered on his arm as she spoke. "Chou Fang is the key. He has been the common thread here. He's got something brewing."

"Agreed."

"Keep him under surveillance, and I'm willing to bet if Dazhao shows up, so will the shooter. I'd like to know about it when it happens." She squeezed his arm. "Keep in touch."

Rook walked out to his car, shaking his head. It was hard to know who to trust when everyone carried their own agendas.

37

November weather in Minnesota was like a grizzly bear—docile one moment, vicious the next. On calm days, it lumbered along peacefully but stir its mood with a cold front or biting wind, and it lashed out, all claws and fury. With Minnesota weather—like grizzlies—there's no mercy when it strikes.

Cade glanced up at the gray skies swirling overhead and zipped up. The breeze had become a strong wind, and Cade was starting to know what ice in the veins might feel like.

He'd returned to the St. Paul neighborhood where Grace had been taken. It was beyond frustrating that so little had surfaced. Lorie and Kristen had uncovered no large purchases of sound-dampening materials from any Home Depot in the metro area. The search for Ring camera footage had yielded nothing. The problem? These days, most people either didn't answer the door—or flat-out refused to share their footage. Hence, Cade's return to the neighborhood.

Kristen had given him a grid of the neighborhood and a list of homeowners they'd made contact with. Studying the map, Cade considered the possibilities. Shadow could've taken any number of routes to get out—but if he were trying to vanish fast, he'd want to hit the interstate as quickly as possible. That meant heading west.

Still, a smart move would've been staying in the alley as long as possible to avoid cameras and curious neighbors. Which brought Cade to Ashbury—the last chance to turn left before hitting Snelling Avenue, a busy thoroughfare that would force a right turn away from the freeway.

No, this was the street. This was where Shadow would've gone.

The neighborhood was quiet, save for the traffic noise coming from the nearby Snelling and University Avenues. To the right of the alley, away from the interstate, was a duplex. On the left, a brick two-story with retail, a bar, and likely second story apartments. Cade headed that way.

He almost missed it. A camera mounted high on the wall. Cade went inside the retail store. A bored clerk looked up and then back down to the graphic novel he was holding.

"Hey," Cade said, as he felt his phone vibrate in his pocket. "Can I get a look at your surveillance footage?" He showed his badge.

"Our owner is a fussy little prick. He won't cooperate without a warrant. Says showing our video opens us to litigation. Come back with a warrant and then he'll show you himself."

Cade's shoulders sagged, but he wasn't going to give up that easy. He looked around the sales floor, noting all the drastic inventory reduction signs. "Is your owner here? Maybe I could convince him."

"Nah, he's on a cruise. Bahamas I think." *Of course he is.*

Nodding, Cade saw an opening. "So, he wouldn't know if you gave me a peek over your shoulder."

The clerk shook his head. "He'll know. He claims he's hidden cameras all over the store. I don't want to lose my job."

Cade leaned on the counter. "When I see a store plastered with drastic inventory-reduction signs, I wonder how long the business will continue."

"That's fair. It's not public knowledge, but we are going out of business. Selling to a developer."

"What I hear is that you're already losing your job. Helping me might be the only useful thing you do this week. So, showing me your video to help get my kidnapped girlfriend back shouldn't be a problem."

Cade held his gaze.

"Should it?"

The man shrugged. "I'll grab the store laptop."

Cade's pocket buzzed again. He ignored it for the moment as the clerk returned with a heavy-looking laptop. "I can pull things up by date and time. Give me an idea when to search."

With Cade's instruction, the clerk pulled up Sunday evening and ran through the hour window of Grace's abduction. Sunday evening was a quiet time on a quiet street, and just two vehicles were caught on video. He had the clerk slow and then stop the video for each, but the quality was less than ideal. One was a light-colored conversion van, the other a larger sedan, likely decades old. Maybe an Olds Aurora or a Buick like the LeSabre or Park Avenue. Hard to tell based on the grainy footage.

He'd send the vehicle information to Kristen. Maybe it would be helpful.

Pocket buzzing again, Cade pulled out his cell and saw a new message had arrived. It was from an unknown number. He opened it and saw it was a link. Grace.

First thing he did was forward the link to Crocker.

"Sorry, but I need to take this," Cade said and stepped out. He clicked the link and was redirected to a list of soccer matches, although it was on a different site than before. Halfway down, he spotted the familiar Shadow v Fox link. He clicked the link while heading for the quiet of his truck.

As before, the video showed a small space with someone on the floor. She wasn't moving. Not even a twitch. His heart raced as he found the comm link and activated it.

"Grace? Grace, are you there?"

The figure moved. *Relief, sweet relief.*

"Cade, I'm here." Her voice sounded surprisingly calm. "Tell me you're here, too."

"I wish, but traffic is bad, so I'm running late." He noted the countdown timer was down to 27:42:00. Just over a day.

"Typical."

"But I grabbed a tea for you." Inside the truck, Cade thought he should be headed somewhere, but he didn't know where.

"So, it's not so much the traffic as your coffee stop."

"I grabbed a tea for you too, remember?"

"Always appreciated." Grace paused. "Do you remember how to get here?"

"I'm a little fuzzy on the details to be honest."

"You don't remember? It's a charming little place." Knowing her captor was listening and likely had his finger poised over the disconnect switch, Cade was sure Grace would be careful. "I haven't had much of a chance to look around.

With my room's luxurious amenities, I haven't wanted to leave. Though I was taken on a brief tour of the basement, but that wasn't anything to write home about."

Cade perked up. This was something new.

Grace continued. "My tour guide mentioned a tunnel to another building and warned me the place could be haunted." She touched her chest. "With the dead."

"Sounds spooky."

"More gross than spooky. You won't find this place on Yelp, at least recently." She patted her chest again and held it for a beat—longer than natural. Something in that gesture meant something. "You know I'm looking forward to seeing you again. It's been too long. How soon before you're here?"

Cade looked out the window and wished he had a better answer. "Hopefully soon. Rook is leading the charge in Minneapolis so that I can focus on you. You're my only priority."

"As I should be." The video froze, and words appeared on the screen.

Event ended.

He stared at the screen. The timer read twenty-seven hours and change. But it didn't feel like a deadline—it felt like a countdown. A fuse already lit. And when it hit zero, something terrible was going to happen.

Crocker called. "What do you think?"

Cade ran a hand through his hair. "We're down to just over a day, without getting any closer. It was interesting when she mentioned getting out of her cell for a tour. That was new."

"I recorded the stream and watched it back through twice. She never mentions why he brought her to the basement, but I noticed something else."

"What's that?"

"She touches her chest—over her heart—while she spoke. She did it twice. Once when she said the place was haunted with the dead. And the other when she talked about no recent Yelp reviews." He paused. "What do you make of it?"

"I saw that too." Cade started his truck to get the heater running. "No recent reviews could mean the place she's being held isn't in use anymore. I read recently that Minneapolis alone has over 300 abandoned buildings, and the number could swell to nearly a thousand if you go statewide. But we don't know if the building is even abandoned. It could be owned by Shadow or someone else and it hasn't been kept up."

"Agreed. She mentions a tunnel, though."

"I'll look into that. Tunnels could be something."

"I've heard stories of urban explorers navigating forgotten tunnels under the city." Crocker exhaled. "Maybe it's something. Thoughts on the haunted part?"

"She said haunted with the dead."

"That's when she touched her chest again, saying the word dead."

Cade drummed his fingers on the steering wheel. "I'm not sure what she's getting at. Places aren't haunted by the living, are they?"

"I've been known to haunt a few taverns in my time, but that's a story for another day. Could she mean a cemetery? Are there abandoned cemeteries?"

Cade nodded to Crocker's words. "That's worth checking into. But would they have basements or tunnels?"

"Maybe her captor made his own tunnel, which wouldn't be in the public record."

"I'll have the team look into cemeteries." He paused, considering her meaning. "Maybe when Grace emphasized the word dead, she was telling us about a threat. Either to herself or someone else."

"So many unknowns," Crocker said.

"Well, one thing's for sure. We won't know for certain until we rescue Grace." Cade sighed and opened up a pad, jotting down some notes. Then, "What about the technology aspect of this? Anything yet?"

It was Crocker's turn to sigh. "As I mentioned earlier, Grace's captor is using encryption reminiscent of code we've encountered on the dark web."

"Like the Orbiting Cortex site?" A chill ran through Cade. Orbiting Cortex was a site comprised of serial killers that Crocker had discovered. But now, there were three fewer killers on the site due to Cade's last case involving the dark website.

"Exactly." Crocker paused. "I may have to revisit the site. See if there's a connection. In the meantime, I'll get Clement down here to watch Miss Fox. See if he picks up anything from her mannerisms."

"Let's keep in touch."

Rose leaned back against the velvet headboard of her suite at the Saint Paul Hotel, the weight of the silver tray still on the table beside her. Room service had delivered again—another club sandwich, another bottle of wine she didn't intend to finish.

It wasn't indulgence. It was theater.

The Saint Paul Hotel was a magnet for scrutiny—business leaders, politicians, journalists all moving through the lobby, staff trained to notice and remember faces. If the police were watching, she wanted them watching her here. Let them trace her credit card, let them note the endless deliveries. Let the spotlight follow Rose so it didn't fall on Frank.

She flipped the room service menu absently, as if debating her next order, while her mind raced. Every plate she ordered bought Frank a little more distance, another layer of insulation from the manhunt swirling outside.

She knew what he would think: that she'd abandoned him, or worse, been taken by Fang. Good. Better he believe that than try to play the hero and stumble into a dragnet.

Still, isolation gnawed at her. Each knock on the door set her pulse jumping, each tray wheeled in felt like a countdown. For now, she had the advantage of choosing where the eyes would fall. But she also knew attention was a fire—once lit, it could burn out of control.

38

The rhythmic thrum of tires on the I-94 bridge over the Mississippi was a steady counterpoint to Rook's thoughts as Minneapolis loomed ahead, its skyline silhouetted against the fading light of dusk. His grip on the steering wheel tightened as his mind churned over the surveillance setup they'd arranged for Fang. The man was as slippery as he was dangerous, and tonight, Rook was determined to catch him in a misstep—anything to put him away.

His phone on the passenger seat vibrated, the screen flashing Lorie Thao's name. Rook glanced at it, hesitating for a moment before answering with a clipped, "Talk to me."

"Rose Park," Lorie began without preamble, her voice steady but tinged with curiosity. "Just checked into the St. Paul Hotel. Corner suite on the sixth floor."

Rook frowned, his eyes darting to his rearview mirror as if Fang might materialize there. "The St. Paul Hotel? That's interesting. I would have expected her to return to Minneapolis."

"Me too. Did she meet anyone before heading there?"

"No. Just a quick stop at a boutique. She left with a few bags—clothes, I think—and went straight to the hotel." She paused, the faint hum of traffic audible on her end. "And then she called room service," Lorie added, a hint of amusement creeping into her tone. "She ordered enough food for three people. A half-dozen appetizers, two filet mignons, a bottle of wine, and three cheesecakes. Either she's stress-eating or someone's joining her."

Rook chuckled dryly, the tension in his chest easing, if only slightly.

"You think she's baiting us?"

"Could be," Rook said, his mind already spinning possibilities. "She's bold enough to make a move like that. But she's also clever enough to make it look like she's baiting us when it's really something else. Stay on her. If she's meeting someone, I want to know who."

"Got it," Lorie replied. "What about you? Any progress on Fang?"

"Not yet," Rook admitted, irritation seeping into his voice. "Heading to his supposed meeting spot now. If he shows, I'll be ready."

Lorie's laugh was soft but knowing. "Careful, Rook. You're starting to sound as confident as Rose."

"Luck's not usually my plus-one, but here's hoping," he shot back.

The call ended, and Rook set the phone back on the seat, his focus sharpening as he merged onto a crowded Minneapolis street. The city lights were flickering to life, casting a harsh glow on the alleys and storefronts. Tonight, he needed more than luck—he needed Fang to make a mistake, and if Rose was playing her own game, it was one more reason to stay sharp.

The diner hummed with the late-morning lull—coffee cups clinking, silverware scraping plates, a faint oldies tune wheezing out of the jukebox like it had emphysema. Grease and bacon hung in the air, mixing with the sharp scent of coffee that smelled better than it tasted. Cade had slid into his booth expecting nothing more than a forgettable breakfast, but the high-back vinyl seats turned the place into a row of padded confessionals—perfect for overhearing sins, secrets, and the occasional gem of outdated slang.

"Listen. You ain't getting diddlysquat."

Cade perked up. Diddlysquat? Nobody under seventy said that anymore—unless they were trying to make a point, and Cade had a sneaking suspicion he knew exactly who was. But the diner had high-back booths, and he hadn't seen who was in the adjoining booth when he sat down. While he normally wasn't one to eavesdrop, diddlysquat wasn't a word you heard often.

Clearly, he wasn't the only one, as whoever was on the other end of the call must have expressed their confusion. "Diddlysquat. What do you mean, you don't know the word? How can you call yourself a chief executive officer with such a limited vocabulary? Diddlysquat means nothing."

The server arrived, but Cade didn't want to miss anything and politely waved her away.

"All words mean something," the voice said, clearly repeating what he'd heard. "But diddlysquat quite literally means nothing. Zero, zip, zilch. Let me use it in a sentence for you. If you're looking for a refund for my executive coaching services, you are getting diddlysquat. That idea should be removed from your head and escorted from the building by security."

The voice was so familiar that Cade wanted to peek over the partition.

"Sorry, you're not happy, but my waffles have arrived. Gotta go, buffalo."

He knew that voice. It could only be one person.

He slid out of the booth and looked.

The spiky, bleached blond-haired Gordy Stensrude, a forkful of waffle on its way into his mouth, stared back at him with wide eyes. He broke out into a massive grin and gestured for Cade to join him.

Cade slid across from Gordy.

He first met Gordy Stensrude when he'd been a witness in the Blonde Killer case. Unusually colorful, Cade had liked him right away, but to call him colorful was a massive understatement along the scale of calling the Grand Canyon a rather large ditch. It went beyond his bright fashion choices; it was more his unique take on life and his willingness to speak whatever was on his mind. And his mind was the Willy Wonka's chocolate factory of minds.

Gordy had served briefly as the task force's communications director. The job lasted twenty minutes and one live TV ambush, but it had put Barry Weiss in his place, and for that, Cade would be eternally thankful.

Gesturing to his plate, Gordy said, "Those Belgians were way ahead of their time. Syrup reservoirs, what brilliance. So, what's up, lawman?"

Before he could reply, Sabine, the server, had returned. "Would you like to order? I can get your menu."

"Dude, just get the Belgians."

"Waffles it is, thank you." He paused. "And coffee, please."

Gordy held up a finger. "My friend doesn't want a coffee. He wants a peppermint mocha but is too embarrassed to ask for it. He drinks them all year long."

"I'm not one to judge," Sabine said and headed off.

Cade fist bumped with Gordy. "I caught the end of your call. Executive coaching now? Last I remember, you were a Microsoft call center person."

He shrugged. "It got old. Same shit each day. I just needed to find a new way to tell them to reboot. After that, I volunteered at the paranoid helpline, but I got fired for answering every call demanding to know how they got the number."

Cade shook his head but grinned.

"It was hysterical. But after my gig as your communications director, I parlayed that experience into an executive coaching business."

"What experience? You did it for a whopping twenty minutes."

He grinned. "What can I say? It looked good on paper."

Cade could only shake his head as Sabine delivered his mocha. "And you get paid for this?"

"Quite well, in fact. I charge between $600 and $800 an hour."

Almost spitting out his coffee, Cade looked up sharply. "No way."

"Way."

"And people pay it?"

"They do. I have a half dozen clients. Well, five now." He shrugged but didn't look particularly upset about losing a client.

Cade looked him over. "Well, it's nice to see that money hasn't messed up your fashion sense." Gordy's stocky build was covered in a Hawaiian shirt that Jackson Pollack would have certainly appreciated, over red cargo shorts and yellow rubber rain boots.

"A man has to be true to his self." His hands made the namaste gesture.

"Yeah, can't have you looking like The Man just because you're coaching The Man."

Gordy cocked his head, likely wondering if Cade was messing with him. He was.

"I'm curious how you help these C-level types," Cade asked after taking a drink and enjoying that first sip feeling. "You'd think that by the time they reached the pinnacle of the corporate world, they'd have life figured out."

Gordy took another bite of waffle and talked with his mouth full. "You'd think that, but you'd be wrong. Outside of high school freshman, these are some of the most insecure people on the planet. Most don't know if they have all the information they need to make decisions—or if they have the correct information. Can they trust the people around them? What if they're only being told what people think they want to hear?" Gordy gestured with his fork, syrup oozing its way down it. "Imposter syndrome is alive and well. They wake up each day wondering if today is the day their empire is going to finally come crashing down."

"Not how I like to start my day," Sabine remarked, dropping off Cade's breakfast. The waffles, with sliced banana and strawberries, looked to be a good choice.

"But the other executives?" Gordy swirled his fork loaded with waffle in the lake of syrup that was his plate. It looked like he'd used the entire bottle. "The other half suffer from the god complex. These prima donnas won't listen to anyone underneath them, utterly convinced they are gifted leaders who can do no wrong."

"I'm surprised they would listen or, for that matter, hire an outside consultant."

"They do, though, because I tell them things they don't get from anyone else. I abuse them. It helps ground them."

Cade shrugged, not getting it, but considering it was Gordy, it wasn't a total stretch either.

Gordy accurately read his expression. "Let me demonstrate. I'm due for a client check-in with Charles Hopper, CEO of VentureStock. He's firmly in the second camp." He poked at his phone after sticking an AirPod in one ear. After a moment, he spoke. "Hopper, you are a piece of shit. I wouldn't listen to you if you told me my hair was on fire and I smelled smoke. Have a nice day."

Gordy ended the call and looked up at Cade.

Cade had to know. "What did he say? What was his reaction?"

Gordy took a large swig of his orange juice. "That was his voicemail. Now he's got it recorded and can listen to it as often as he wants."

"And he wants to?"

Gordy nodded confidently. "Yes, sir."

"Let me guess—he pays you for that?"

"Not just pays—he pays *more*. I charge $800 to insult the rich."

Sabine had stopped by the table and heard both Gordy's call and his hourly fee. Cade looked up at her. "I am in the wrong business."

She touched his shoulder. "I say the same thing at least twice a shift. People forget what they ordered and then blame me."

"Part of the job, I imagine," Cade said.

"It doesn't have to be." Gordy leaned forward. "People don't know what they want. Not usually. You're doing them a service if you tell them. Next time someone complains about receiving the wrong meal, simply smile and say, 'This is what's best for you.' 99 percent of the time, they'll thank you."

Sabine didn't look so convinced, but said she'd try it.

Gordy put his fingers together, studying Cade. "So, lawman, what are you working on? Something's draining your energy. You look wrung out."

He nodded. "It's Grace. Someone's abducted her, but I can't figure out where she's being held. It's all I can think about. I can't even deal with my other case." Cade sighed as he ran a hand through his hair. "I have a few clues, but they haven't helped."

Eyes sparkling, Gordy leaned forward. "My brain is attuned to psychic vibrations. Maybe I can help. Tell me about it." He gestured for Cade to continue.

Cade shrugged. Nothing else was working, so why not? He told Gordy what he knew about the abduction, the tunnels, and the talk of the place being haunted. Listening with fingertips pressed to his temples, eyes closed, Gordy didn't move when Cade stopped talking. He wondered if Gordy had drifted off.

Cade cleared his throat.

Gordy's eyes fluttered open. "Sorry, dude. I couldn't pick up anything. There must be something wrong with the perp's brain."

Cade was trying not to let his frustration show. "Yeah, that's it. His brain is not wired correctly."

"Sorry."

"Not your fault. But I had better get moving." He slid out of the booth and grabbed both checks. "I got your breakfast."

Gordy caught up to him right after he'd settled the bills. "I had an idea. Someone who can help you. Here's her number." Gordy handed over a piece of paper. The name Abbey Hill was written above a local number. "She's a ghost hunter. If the place is haunted, she'll know it."

"Ghost hunter," Cade repeated, like the words had lost meaning halfway through. This was it. He was officially out of ideas.

"Yes, she's a real ghost hunter."

Cade wasn't sure he wanted to know, but he couldn't help himself. "How is it you have her number?"

"She's on Twin Cities Live, and I'm commingling with a producer," Gordy said with a hint of a smile. "She had it on speed dial."

"I don't know, it sounds kinda out there. A ghost hunter." He shrugged, suddenly weary. "Aren't all of them frauds?"

"Maybe not all of them. It can't hurt to call."

Cade shrugged. "Can't hurt," he repeated and tucked the paper in his wallet along with his credit card.

They bumped fists, Gordy adding an explosion sound. "See ya, lawman."

With a flash of color worthy of a Jackson Pollack, Gordy left.

39

The call came early.

As much as Cade wanted to ignore it, he knew he couldn't. It came with the job. Matters of life and death didn't keep office hours, which meant that neither did he.

"Dawkins." A glance at the screen told him it was a few minutes after seven and it was the governor's office. Sarah's voice confirmed this.

"Governor Winston Ritter has requested you be present for a 9 a.m. meeting at his residence."

Cade had that wary feeling he often had when he was around the governor. "Really. This meeting, do you have any idea what it's regarding?"

Sarah's hesitation came through loudly.

"How about his mood this morning?" More hesitation. "Would you say it's sunny or cloudy in the governor's world? I just want to get a sense of what I'm headed into."

"Well," Sarah began. "Put it this way. It's not only cloudy, but the wind has picked up and fat drops of rain are pelting anyone crazy enough to be out."

Not good.

"Also, the sky has turned green and there's a funnel cloud waiting to drop."

Not good at all.

"And you live in a mobile home. See you at nine."

The call lasted approximately 35 seconds, but it was long enough to get the picture of where his day was headed. Cade got up. If it was going to be that kind of day, he was going to go for a run. He needed a clear head for what was coming.

He'd spent a frustrating day yesterday going to every hardware, lumberyard, and home improvement store in the metro area. Whoever had built Grace's cell had to get the material somewhere. Kristen had provided a list of nearly a hundred stores in the Twin Cities metro area that sold these types of materials. Lorie had taken the Minneapolis side of the list while he took the St. Paul side. When they'd shared notes last night, they weren't any closer.

But between them, they'd impulse-purchased scented candles, string lights, Gorilla Glue, and Monkey Hooks. Oddly, they each bought a compact LED flashlight.

That was how investigations went. Lots of miles, lots of talking. Lots of crossing things off the list. Tedious, but necessary. But it would all be worth it when the break came.

He put on his running shoes and headed out into the cold morning air.

At 9:00 a.m. sharp, he walked into the governor's reception area. Sarah was there, as she always was, and gestured for him to go on in. Cade wore a black wool shirt over a heather-gray Henley, jeans, and black boots. Ritter wore a navy suit, as did his guest.

"Hello, Andrew. I wasn't expecting to see you."

Though he should have. It was Andrew Tyroler who had appointed him to head the task force, and he was the only one who could unappoint him. If Ritter was looking to dump him from the task force, he was going to need the commissioner of the Department of Public Safety.

Commissioner Tyroler reached out a hand. "I wish it were under better circumstances."

Ritter gestured for Cade to sit. He did.

The men exchanged glances and Tyroler nodded. Ritter cleared his throat, locking eyes with Cade. "Everyone knows I'm not usually swayed by the media."

Cade bit his lip.

"But, as governor, I need to be aware of the mood of our state's voters. And frankly, they're in a bad mood."

He pointed a remote at the large screen that dominated his bookshelves.

Barry Weiss came on screen.

This wasn't going to be fair or unbiased.

The familiar jingle and graphics for *The Barry Weiss Report* rolled across the screen. Weiss appeared in studio, wearing his trademark vest, his expression grave.

"Good evening. I'm Barry Weiss. Tonight, we take a closer look at the Five Below Task Force—a unit that, in my view, has failed the people of Minnesota. I'm calling for its immediate review, if not outright termination."

On the split screen, crime scene tape fluttered in front of a Minneapolis hotel. Weiss's voice continued over the footage:

"Since the task force was activated, Minneapolis has endured six high-profile killings—murders that have cast a shadow over the International Mayors Conference. With the eyes of the world on our city, business leaders and civic advocates have been targeted and killed. Yet arrests have been few and answers even fewer."

Back in studio, Weiss lifted a stack of papers. "This is the task force's record to date. Pages of press releases and promises—but little else." He set the papers aside with a pointed glance. "By any measure, that's not good enough."

The program cut to man-on-the-street interviews. In a downtown skyway, Weiss asked a passerby in his fifties: "How would you rate the task force's response to these murders?"

The man shook his head. "It doesn't seem like anything's happening. Somebody should be held accountable."

The segment shifted to two older women leaving a grocery store. Weiss prompted: "Critics say the task force has been ineffective. Do you agree?"

One adjusted her scarf. "It feels like nothing's being done. They need to fix it—or shut it down."

The second woman pointed at the camera. "If our leaders can't keep people safe, why should we trust them with anything else?"

The broadcast returned to Weiss, his tone final. "The people are speaking. And they deserve better."

Ritter paused the video on the woman's sneering face and turned to Cade. "This isn't just public opinion. The media narrative has turned. You're not the hero anymore—they think you're the problem." He glanced to the commissioner. "Andrew, your thoughts?"

"It's concerning that you don't have any results to show. Six murders."

"Technically three. We were activated after the first three." The disconnect between his mouth and brain didn't help his cause.

"Fine. Three murders after you were put on the case doesn't exactly inspire confidence."

"I'm not inspired," Ritter added.

Cade ignored him.

Tyroler stroked his chin. "I know Winston would like to act right now. Make a clean break. But..."

Ritter glanced over sharply, not looking pleased.

"I'm giving you 24 hours. Deliver tangible results or you're done."

He held Cade's eyes.

"And I'll likely shutter the task force at that time. Are we clear?"

"Crystal."

"Is there anything you'd like to say? Now's your opportunity."

There was a moment where Cade was going to say something. He was going to do it. Tell Ritter what he thought of him. Use words and phrases like shit-for-brains, political weasel, dick-slap, and one he'd been wanting to try out for a while now: douche-canoe.

He was ready, the phrases locked and loaded.

But.

There were others to think about, not the least of them being Grace, and he was relying on task force resources in the search. Also, he didn't want to undercut Rook, Kristen, Lorie, and the Crocker and Tubbs team. Everyone was working their asses off to find the shooter. He couldn't do it.

"Nah, I'm good."

But it would have been glorious.

Palms on his thighs, Cade said, "If there's nothing else..." as he stood.

"Wait a damn minute," Ritter growled. "Are you taking this seriously?"

"I'm taking this situation very seriously," Cade replied evenly. *I'm just not taking you seriously.*

Ritter waved dismissively. "Then off you go."

Cade didn't wait.

He left.

40

Frank was unraveling, one restless lap of the hotel room at a time.

She'd said she was going shopping. That was hours ago. And she hadn't come back. Rose wouldn't have vanished without reason—not when she had made such a show of pulling him into her bed last night. If her plan had been to ditch him, she'd have done it cleanly, not after peeling away every layer of his defenses.

Which meant something had gone wrong.

He stopped mid-stride. The only name that fit the equation dropped into his mind with the weight of lead.

Fang.

Rose had enemies everywhere, but Fang had motive and reach. If she wasn't back, Fang had her. Frank's gut told him as much, and that instinct—paranoid or not—was what had kept him alive in cities darker than this one.

Would Fang harm her? Trade her? Hand her over to the authorities to curry favor? None of the answers ended with Frank seeing her again. And against all reason, he wanted to. Needed to. He told himself it was professional—she had intel, leverage, value—but that was a lie he couldn't keep straight. The truth was simpler. He'd fallen, fast and stupid.

But he wasn't ready to accept that she was gone.

He went to the window, staring at the gray skyline pressing in like prison bars. Every option circled back to Fang. Going in guns blazing was suicide; Fang's men would cut them both down before Frank crossed the lobby.

No, the only card left was the reckless one. Negotiation.

Frank, who usually solved problems with a steady aim and a steady trigger finger, would try diplomacy. He'd bluff leverage he didn't have, sell Fang a deal he couldn't refuse, and pray Rose stayed alive long enough to cash it in.

He picked up the phone.

Fang answered on the second ring. "Chou Fang." His voice was smooth, clipped, assured.

Frank forced calm into his voice. "This is Rose's friend. We haven't met, but I've had dealings with your bodyguards."

"Dealings is a generous way to say it," Fang replied dryly.

"They threatened, I shot. Call it even."

Fang let the silence stretch before asking, "Why are you calling?"

"You have something of mine."

"I have many things."

"Rose."

A pause. Long enough for Frank to hear the pounding of his own pulse.

"This surprises me," Fang said finally. "I wouldn't have pegged you as senti-mental."

"I'm pragmatic," Frank countered. "Rose is useful. I want her back."

"In life, we can't all have what we desire."

Frank's jaw tightened. He couldn't afford to blink. "This isn't a request, Fang."

"Nor is it a confession. Hypothetically—if I did have her, what's in it for me?"

Frank took a steadying breath. Time to bait the hook. "I have a flash drive I pulled off Li's body."

The line went quiet. Then, "You have my attention."

"It contains Li's backdoor protocols. With it, you own access to systems no-body else can touch."

"And you're offering this... for a woman?" Fang spat the last word like an insult.

"You mistake leverage for romance. Rose has intelligence that matters more to me than code. Trade her for the drive, or I gift-wrap it for the NSA."

A soft exhale, almost a growl. "Fine. She's alive. Bring the drive, and we'll trade."

"Not so fast. If she's harmed, I walk."

"And if you don't show, she floats in the Mississippi."

Frank pressed. "It'll be neutral ground, my choice. You'll have your details by tomorrow."

Another pause, laced with Fang's suspicion. "How do I know this isn't a bluff?"

"You don't. But if I'm bluffing, you won't know until it's too late."

"And you?" Fang asked.

Frank swallowed hard. "Same answer."

They both knew it was theater. Frank didn't have the drive, but he had the guts to make Fang believe he did.

"One warning, Fang," Frank said, letting steel edge his words. "Play me, and all you get is a bullet."

"Likewise."

The smile in Fang's voice chilled him more than the threat itself.

41

The clock was ticking.

Cade sat in his truck outside the Governor's residence, not ready to deal with other drivers quite yet. He'd tried to keep his cool in there with Ritter, but man. That guy was programmed to push every damn button Cade had.

Push might be too mild. Ritter poked, kicked, and stomped every one of them.

But Cade wasn't just angry. He was exhausted. Burnt to the damn wick. Ritter had that effect on people—a man so smug he could weaponize his smile. Meanwhile, Ritter had given him a 24-hour clock on the Minneapolis shooter, let alone Shadow's apparent countdown on Grace's existence.

When it rains, it pours, as his grandma used to say when things went south. Bless her heart, she was right.

He dialed Rook. Time to share the good news.

"Yo, boss. How are you doing this morning?"

"Not especially great. You? What are you up to?"

"Just having a large bowl of Cap'n Crunch and watching the Saturday morning cartoons."

"Really."

"No, not really. I'm on Fang. Something seems to be happening. He's added three new men, and based on their size and bearing, they're not business consultants. These guys look like they eat drywall for breakfast."

Cade watched Andrew Tyroler, the commissioner, leave. He would be headed to his office at the state capitol, as would Ritter soon enough.

"This might be good news, actually. We need something to happen. Desperately. Having no developments in this case is killing us." He paused. "Or it will."

"Interesting." Rook was no slouch. "Talk. What's happening?"

"I just got out of a meeting with Ritter. And the commissioner of the Department of Public Safety."

"He's your boss."

"Yep. Ritter's been drinking the Barry Weiss Kool-Aid. Says I'm dead weight. Thinks the task force is a waste."

"Weiss makes up shit for ratings."

"Exactly. But the governor is listening to him."

"Why was Tyroler at the meeting?"

"I think he was there to temper Ritter's aggressive instincts. Ritter made it clear he wanted to fire me and shut down the task force completely."

"But it's not up to him." Rook sounded angry.

"No, but he has influence. And by God, he was using it."

"What's the upshot?"

"We've been given 24 hours to produce tangible results, whatever that means."

"Damn."

"And then Ritter said this could end my career if I'm not careful."

"Double damn."

"So, that's why it's a good thing something's happening. Call me when you know something. And then bring in the entire team. Whatever is happening, we need to be all over it."

"Done." Rook paused. "Where are you with Grace?"

Cade stared out the windshield. "Frustrated beyond belief. Lorie and I are hitting every hardware and home improvement store in the area looking for purchases of likely materials used to build Grace's cell."

"And?"

"We got diddlysquat."

"Diddlysquat?"

"Sorry, we've got nothing. I ran into our old friend, Gordy Stensrude, and he used the word to great effect."

"Gordy? That guy's a walking acid trip."

"Get this. He is an executive coach now. Charges $600 to $800 an hour."

"We're in the wrong business."

"Some days—take today, for instance—I wonder."

"Hang in there. Your ancestors had to survive before you could be here now. In this body. In this lifetime. Call it fate, divine timing, logic, magic—whatever you believe. But what's for sure is that you're here, right now, on earth, for a reason. You're here to make the world a better place."

Cade smiled despite himself. He could always count on Rook to mix tough love with TED Talk energy. "I appreciate the pep talk."

"Not a problem." Rook switched gears. "I'm assuming Gordy was his usual colorful self, spouting lunacy and conspiracies."

Cade smiled at the memory. "Ohh, yeah. Gordy never disappoints. But get this, he gave me the number for a ghost hunter."

"What?" Rook laughed. "Why?"

"Remember, Grace said the place was supposed to be haunted? Well, Gordy said his ghost hunter would know the place then."

"Ridiculous."

"I know."

"Are you going to call this ghost hunter?"

Cade stayed silent. He'd never considered actually calling the ghost hunter because it reeked of craziness and desperation.

Rook didn't let it go. "Let me ask you: what do you have to lose?"

Cade stared at the card in his hand, Gordy's cursive letters spelling out the name of a woman, who made her living as a ghost hunter for a local news and feature television program.

Abbey Hill.

This felt crazy, but the idea of heading back into yet another Home Depot felt crazier. And in investigations, you did your due diligence. You checked every possibility and crossed each off the list.

He ran a thumb across her name. Abbey Hill.

This was a possibility.

Sigh.

Sometimes desperation makes room for possibility.

He dialed her number.

Abbey sounded skeptical, but there was a spark of intrigue when Cade mentioned she could help with an active investigation. He asked to meet in person—no details over the phone. What if she showed up in a tinfoil hat, muttering about government mind control? He needed to rule out crazy first. After all, she had been recommended by Gordy. Eventually, she agreed and named a local coffee shop.

Parking across the street, Cade shook his head at the absurdity of it, but here he was. Meeting with a ghost hunter.

The Wild Bean was a cute little coffee shop in a row of cute little shops on the main drag in suburban Mahtomedi. He excused himself to slide past a man and his teenage daughter who were standing in front of the entrance. Inside, he saw a woman in her early forties wearing a colorful sweater seated by herself in the back of the shop. He headed her way.

She looked up from her novel when he approached.

"Are you Abbey Hill?"

"I'm Abbey." A voice behind him answered, and when he turned, he found the teenager he'd passed at the entrance.

"You're a policeman?" she asked with no small amount of incredulity in her tone.

"I am. And you're a ghost hunter?"

She nodded, and Cade introduced himself.

The man, clearly her father, stepped up. "Can I see your identification?"

Cade handed over his badge case. His Minnesota State Patrol badge and Five Below major crimes task force ID. The man studied both briefly and handed it back.

"Thank you. I'm Abbey's father, Constantine Hill. You can't be too careful."

"I got it from here, Dad." Abbey had the tone teenagers worldwide use like a weapon with their parents. "He's legit."

"Okay." He shook hands with Cade. "I'll leave you to it. See you at home."

After they had their drinks, they grabbed a table by the window. Cade looked across the floral tablecloth and studied the teenage ghost hunter. Abbey looked young but carried herself like someone older. Her wavy auburn hair flowed past her shoulders, and she had a pleasant, curious face. She studied him right back.

Cade broke the ice.

"I was expecting someone much older."

"I saw that," she said with a giggle. "Didn't they teach you about assumptions in detective school?"

Cade had to laugh. "You know, there's not really a detective school?"

"Well, clearly there should be." She took a sip of her way-too-pink drink. "You said you needed help with a missing person case. I'm here, so let's hear about it."

He appreciated her straightforwardness, but he had questions. "Can we back up? I'm curious about you. How old are you, and how did you fall into the ghost hunting gig? Feels like an unusual career path for a high schooler."

Abbey studied him for a moment. Looking like she had come to a decision, she nodded. "Don't let my age fool you. I know what I'm doing."

Cade held up his hands in what he hoped was a calming gesture. "I never said you didn't. I'm simply curious. You don't meet a teenage ghost hunter every day. Especially such a badass one."

Eyes narrowing, Abbey fixed him with a look. "Flattery will get you bonus points. Good move, Detective."

Cade grinned.

"I'm 15, a freshman at Pine Ridge High School. The show? My friends Lexi and Kelly talked me into entering the contest to replace Twin Cities Live's retiring ghost hunter. We ended up winning, and now the Spook Squad is a regular feature. We visit haunted locales around the area."

Cade nodded through a sip of his mocha. "So, you walk around looking for ghosts while waving those paranormal detection gadgets and pronounce the place haunted? Nice gig."

Cocking her head, Abbey fixed him with a look considerably north of annoyed.

"Please. I don't need those stupid toys."

Intrigued, he leaned closer. "Really. Do tell."

She paused before speaking. "I have... instincts. That's enough to do the job." She took a large pull on her drink before continuing. "Why don't you tell me what you're looking for?"

Cade leaned back with a sigh. "Not long ago, a coworker of mine, Grace, was abducted. Snatched from an alley in St. Paul, injected with something. When she came to, she was in a windowless room, no idea where she was or why she was taken."

Abbey nodded, processing.

"There's a reason people tell you to stay out of dark alleys." She ran a finger along the cup's condensation. "The fact that you know she was sedated and ended up in a windowless cell means you've had contact with either her or her captor. Tell me about that."

Cade described what he saw after receiving the link.

"Why do you suppose this Shadow gave you access? Seems like he has an ulterior motive."

Cade held onto his cup with both hands. "If so, he hasn't made it especially clear. If I had to guess, it's tied to our current task force case, maybe to divert my attention from the shooter. There have been some shootings in Minneapolis involving attendees for the International Mayors Conference."

"I've heard about that. You're working on that?"

"I was, but with Grace..." He stared at his hands. "It was just too much to do both. For the moment, my only focus is bringing Grace home."

Abbey hesitated.

"I can see that you're hurting."

Cade didn't trust himself to answer.

"This might be a good time to share what Grace said that made you reach out to me."

"She mentioned taking a brief tour of the basement. She said there was a tunnel to another building. Apparently, her guide warned her the place was haunted, but she said it was more gross than spooky. She emphasized that we wouldn't find any recent Yelp reviews about the place."

He glanced at the teenager. "And that's it."

"Okay, not on Yelp. At least recently." She leaned back processing. "Logic says it's not a residence, and it's abandoned. There's more than one building that's connected by a tunnel. That rules out many of the places I've been to. My first thought was it could be the Nopeng Sanatorium near Duluth. It's creepy and gross. Abandoned. But there's one main building, large and in charge. So, no reason for a tunnel."

She ran a hand through her hair. As she paused, her expression transformed from frustration to joy.

"Hold on. You know where she is?"

Abbey nodded, her grin widening as she leaned forward, like she couldn't get the words out fast enough.

"Tell me," he said, bracing himself.

She dropped her voice, eyes gleaming with something between awe and dread. "The Anoka Asylum."

Cade cocked his head, goosebumps doing their thing. "I don't know it."

"There's no reason you should. It's creepy AF."

She leaned forward. "For nearly a hundred years, they treated mentally ill patients considered incurably insane. We're talking leather restraints and straitjackets, lobotomies, and electroshock. The place was overcrowded and underfunded. It was brutal."

"And you think this is the place where Grace is being held?"

"I know it is. It's old. It's abandoned. It's haunted. And get this, there's a series of tunnels connecting the buildings."

"You've been there?"

"I have. We filmed a Halloween feature there. Anoka is the Halloween capital. The asylum campus has like a dozen buildings. Some are being used, but the majority are boarded up. Ideal if you wanted a private place to hold someone."

"Okay, I'm sold." He slammed the rest of his coffee and stood. "Thanks for your help. I need to go check it out. Right now."

Her reply stopped him. "Not without me."

When Cade turned, she continued. "I've been there. Hell, I've been *in* there. I can show you what you need to know. Which buildings are most likely, which are not. I can guide you, save you precious time. Let me be your Tenzing Norgay."

Cade's expression made her laugh.

"Tenzing Norgay. He was Sir Edmund Hillary's guide. Mount Everest? Maybe you need more than detective school."

He briefly considered rejecting her offer. Bringing a teenager into a possible hostage situation wasn't a good look, but her comment about precious time made him think of the countdown clock. And his mind was made up.

"You can tell me about it on the way. Let's go."

42

When they were in Cade's truck and the Anoka Asylum was entered in the GPS, Cade smiled. "Oh. That Tenzing Norgay. I was thinking of the other one."

Abbey's expression suggested she didn't believe him either.

The drive to Anoka had taken nearly an hour, and after she relaxed a bit, Abbey bombarded him with questions about his law enforcement career. She was particularly curious about his involvement with serial killers.

She dodged questions about ghost hunting, claiming some secrets were proprietary, but they found common ground talking about soccer. It turned out that she'd played at her high school.

They'd been driving through the usual suburban sprawl—gas stations, dental offices, a liquor store with faded signage—when the road narrowed, twisted, and disappeared into a canopy of large trees. Set back from the winding roads and thick groves of oak and maple, the cottages of the Anoka Asylum formed a quiet, unsettling village. It felt like entering another world.

After parking, they followed the cracked sidewalk to the first building, aptly named Cottage No. 1. Each step toward the cottage deepened the silence, and Cade couldn't help but shiver.

From a distance, the cottages looked oddly quaint—like colonial relics nestled among the trees. But up close, the charm faded. The brick facades, streaked with age and shadow, felt watchful. Windows sat like dead eyes, dark and impenetrable. The air thickened with something old and unfinished.

"Can you feel that?" Abbey murmured. "There's a weight here."

Cade nodded. He felt it, though he'd never have been able to put words to it. Weight fit, but so did importance, darkness, and desperation. The complete absence of hope.

Abbey stared at the imposing structure. "People suffered here. They were scared and tormented."

He didn't know how she knew, but he accepted it. Because he felt something.

"Rather than have one large industrial institution, they broke up the living quarters into cottages that housed up to 50 patients."

The cottage they faced was an imposing brick building with nearly a dozen steps that brought visitors up to the first floor entrance. There was another story above that with dormers perched on top.

There were identical cottages spread around the large grassy park at its hub. Thick vines crept up the walls, and the pathways between buildings were cracked and overgrown, nature slowly reclaiming what the state had left behind.

"Those over there are occupied. Haven For Heroes houses veterans, and the county workhouse has a minimum-security facility down at that end." Abbey gestured and then pivoted. "That's an auditorium, and just past that are several boarded up cottages. The entrances are blocked with fences. They're just about ideal to hide someone. There are other options here, but ..."

She pointed like a prosecutor revealing the guilty party to the jury. "That's where I think she is."

"Then, let's go." Without waiting, Cade started across the park. Abbey didn't move.

Pausing, he gestured for her to follow.

She didn't. "Hold on. I watch Law & Order. Shouldn't you be calling for backup?"

Cade paused, amused. "No offense, but I've seen a shit-ton of Scooby-Doo episodes. You won't see me questioning how you do your job."

"I see how it is. But it was a fair question."

He gestured. "Let's walk and talk."

They walked, he talked. "I have every intention of calling when and *if* we discover something. A crime in progress, for instance. But, and this is a massively big but."

Abbey giggled.

"If I call the locals in and explain that my ghost hunter consultant said she has a feeling this was where an abductee was being held and they should help us break in, how do you see that going?"

"Wait, I'm a consultant?"

He cocked his head. "That's all you heard?"

Abbey shrugged. "I've never been a consultant."

"But yes, you are my consultant. But when I tell the local police, the conversation—and subsequent media circus—wouldn't go well."

"You have a warrant, though. Right?"

"Maybe you should watch less TV."

"Now you sound like my dad."

"Smart man. But, no. I don't have a warrant. You didn't notice when we stopped by the Washington County Courthouse to ask a judge for one, did you?"

Abbey folded her arms. "I know a rhetorical question when I hear one."

"This is a scouting mission. Nothing more. We're here to see if this is a likely possibility for Grace's location."

"It is." Her eyes held his, conviction written all over her expression.

"Let's find something concrete then."

The path to Cottage No. 9 was broken and buckled by years of frost, choked with weeds and brittle twigs that snapped like bones underfoot. The cottage's lower windows were boarded-up with stained plywood. It was dead quiet.

They moved to number 8. It was the same, but worse. The cement steps had collapsed, making it impassable.

"How do we get in?"

"That's what the tunnels are for."

"Okay, how do we get into the tunnels?"

She pointed to a low brick structure the size of a bathtub. "Open that up and we're in the tunnels. They've sealed off the tunnels, but you're resourceful."

Cade rubbed his chin while walking around the structure. If he had to guess, it was designed for access and light into the tunnels, at least before it was bricked shut. One thing was for sure; he wasn't getting in with just his bare hands.

"C'mon. We're going back to my truck."

"It does seem like a job for tools."

They turned and headed back the way they'd come. "Which building did you visit when you were here for your television gig? How did you get into the tunnels?"

"There's an administrative building by the auditorium. Our crew was given permission to explore that one building and the grounds. We went to the basement, but the tunnel entrance had been sealed off."

"Did you find any ghosts?"

"Don't you watch the show? Not even as research when you knew we were meeting?"

Cade held up his palms. "I was busy. And I didn't want to taint my perception of you having watched your theatrics."

"*Taint? Theatrics?* That's cold."

"I'm skeptical but trying to keep an open mind."

"Uh-huh."

They walked in silence for a long moment.

Abbey spoke first. "Well, I research everything. My father's an investigative journalist, and I got it from him. As soon as I knew the show wanted to do a segment here, I was in research mode."

They got to the truck, and Cade gestured for her to get in. He started the truck and headed back to the brick structure. "What did you learn?"

"The history was unusual. At first, it seemed that the asylum was a great place for patients to heal from the traumas of the outside world. No treatment, no stress. The patients were well cared for and given time to recover. They had nearly 400 acres along the scenic Rum River to explore and be with nature." Abbey gestured toward where Cade assumed the river was.

He backed up the FJ Cruiser to the brick structure and hopped out.

"You said the place was great at first ..."

Abbey nodded.

"But then came the 1920s, the golden age of commitment. People could commit other family members for nearly any reason. And they came up with plenty of reasons. What made it so despicable was that the patient could only be released if a family member came to claim them. Imagine a husband wanting to get rid of his wife. If no one knew where she was, the asylum was her prison."

Cade opened the tailgate and slid on gloves, pulling out a heavy chain.

"Security was tightened, and the earlier freedoms were taken away."

He hesitated before looping the chain around the structure. This wasn't just another brick wall—it was the threshold to whatever horror had been keeping Grace hidden. He shoved the thought aside and went to work.

"As you might imagine, without constraints, the population swelled. Over 1,000 patients. The staff couldn't keep up with the overcrowding. Conditions were horrendous. Patients left in straitjackets for days, others strapped to beds without anyone changing soiled sheets."

"Sounds horrible." Cade grunted with the effort as he secured the chain to his trailer hitch.

Abbey nodded, her gaze distant. "Some patients tried to escape the conditions any way they could. A few made it across the grounds to the Rum River—only to drown in the current. Others disappeared into the tunnels beneath the asylum."

Cade gestured. "Get in. It's safer if something goes wrong."

He wiped the sweat from his brow with the back of his glove and started the engine.

Abbey continued. "The tunnels were dark, twisted, and daunting. Even those patients with unimpaired mental faculties couldn't find their way out. Many got lost in the never-ending maze and gave up. Disoriented and defeated, suicide was an option for many. Dozens were discovered hanging from the large pipes that ran through the tunnel's ceiling."

"Hold on," Cade said and started the truck. It rumbled to life, and he shifted into low gear. He eased forward, feeling the resistance immediately—until the chain was at full stretch. The truck groaned, tires spitting gravel as they fought for traction. For a moment, the structure held fast, unmoved. Cade gritted his teeth and gave it more gas.

There was a creak, then a loud crack.

The truck lurched forward as the tension released, and Cade hit the brakes, dust rising in clouds around him.

He climbed out, heart thudding, as the bricks lay strewn around what was left of the tunnel entrance. He glanced at Abbey.

"Are you sure you want to go into the tunnels? It sounds horrible." He studied her. "Now's the time to speak."

She wasn't having it. "No way. I didn't sign up to be the ghost hunter who waits in the car."

Cade held her gaze, wanting to be sure.

"Girls just want to have fun." She hooked a thumb toward the tunnel entrance. "C'mon, let's go. You can debate the merits of taking a 15-year-old into the lair of a known kidnapper later."

After stowing the chain, he handed her a flashlight.

"I'd rather have a gun."

He narrowed his eyes at her.

"But a flashlight is good, too."

Cade went down into the tunnel first. The moment his boots hit the concrete floor, the air changed—heavy, stale, weighty with memory. He turned, shining his flashlight down the stretch of gray cinder block walls, but the beam barely pierced the gloom. The light felt weak, like it was trying and failing to matter. The darkness didn't seem to reflect any of the light—it absorbed it instead.

He stood still, listening. Nothing but the low hum of silence and his own breath.

"Are you going to help me down or what?"

Her voice yanked him from the fever dream that had gripped him and got him moving. When she'd joined him, he glanced around, already unsure which way to go.

Accurately reading his indecision, Abbey pointed.

"You sure?"

"Quite sure."

The gravel underneath their feet was damp and uneven. The tunnel smelled of mold, mildew, and a faint odor of rust. The cinder blocks dripped water that ran down the uneven surface. As they moved into the tunnel, it was apparent that no thought or effort had been given to keep the path straight. In the first twenty feet, it veered right and hooked to the left. Twice.

"Stay close."

"Where do you think I'd go? Take a break in the solarium?"

Cade wasn't sure he even knew what a solarium was when he was 15. "Just keep up."

Other than the crunch of gravel, the silence was oppressively, aggressively loud. Cade heard nothing, yet he seemed to hear everything. He shook his head and kept moving.

They reached an intersection of sorts. He'd missed it, but Abbey tugged on his arm. A heavy-looking door marked with a faded 9 sat recessed into a dark space. Despite his attempts, the door wouldn't budge.

"Remember, tunnel access was sealed. But it doesn't matter, that's not our door."

He was going to ask but thought better of it, and they resumed moving.

When she grabbed his arm again, he stopped and looked at her. Abbey's eyes were wide.

"What is it?"

There wasn't an intersection, door, or anything else. She raised her light to the pipes running overhead. He didn't comprehend why he was seeing it, but he could swear he saw the thin shadow of a cord that descended from the pipes.

Shivering, he faced Abbey. "My mind is playing tricks again."

She nudged him forward.

After another hard left, and after a pair of dead rats, they saw a number. A rusted iron number 8 bolted to the brick above a thick steel door. He saw something that chilled him. Words were scratched into the damp brick like claw marks.

They never left.

Goosebumps rose, and he fought a shiver.

"This is our door."

"Hold on." Cade knelt and came back up, holding a purple hair tie. He held it out. "Yours?"

Abbey shook her head.

"Then I'd bet anything Grace dropped it out here to mark the door."

"That's what I'd do," Abbey said. She glanced up. "Time to call reinforcements?"

"Not yet. A found hair tie does not equal calling the cavalry. Let's keep going."

Cade placed his hand on the door. The metal was cold. Unforgiving. He turned to Abbey. "No turning back now."

She raised her light. "I was never turning back."

43

When he pushed it open, it creaked like the door to a vampire's lair—so loud and theatrical, it practically demanded a thunderclap.

"Just once, I'd like to enter a haunted place without the door auditioning for a horror soundtrack."

Inside, it was everything he expected from a hundred-year-old basement. Standing water, musty odors, debris, and cobwebs the size of Cleveland. The dead maintenance man was a surprise, though.

The man's throat had been sliced open. Kneeling to examine the body dressed in dusty green overalls, Cade couldn't help but think of Walt, the Méridien Chambers maintenance man who'd been so helpful. Walt or not, nobody deserved this fate.

Abbey cleared her throat. "About that cavalry."

Taking her offered hand, Cade stood. "I agree, it's time to get help rolling."

"Who are you calling? Your task force or the local police?"

Good question. The task force is at a critical point, but I'll update them. Calling the locals gets people here fast, locking down the perimeter so Shadow can't escape.

But when he pulled out his phone, he frowned.

"What?"

"No signal."

Abbey sighed loudly. "Of course. Nothing in my life goes that easy. If it did, I would definitely be someone else."

"It's not you. It's because we're in the basement of a brick building."

"Or it's because I'm jamming cell signals."

At the sound of the third voice, Cade whirled and Abbey gasped.

A towering silhouette stood at the base of the stairs. Filling the doorway like a Viking's defensive lineman, the man exuded menace. As Abbey lifted her flashlight, details emerged. Dressed in all black, he wore combat boots, tactical pants, and a hoodie pulled low. Even though he gripped an unusually large knife in his gloved hand, it was the pale, featureless mask hiding any sign of humanity that most chilled Cade to the bone.

So, this was Shadow.

Cade slid his hand toward his service pistol.

The voice was low, cold, and commanding. "Don't. I'll impale her before you can draw your weapon."

He was right. Abbey was closer to Shadow than he was. One wrong move would get her killed.

Cade moved his hand away.

"That's better, Detective Dawkins."

The use of his name landed like a slap, but Cade didn't flinch. He kept his eyes firmly locked on the man.

"We're here for Grace," he said, voice clear, every word weighted with intent. "We're taking her home."

Grace was on the floor, hair damp with sweat from calisthenics. Breathing calmly, eyes laser-focused, she listened. The audio feed had unexpectedly kicked in moments ago. It began with Shadow announcing that he was jamming cell signals. Familiar with the jamming tech, she knew it transmitted a noise signal on the cell phone frequencies. It had a limited range but was devastatingly effective. But why was he telling her this?

When he threatened to impale a woman, Grace knew Shadow wasn't alone. But who else was down here—and whose life was on the line?

Logic told her that if Shadow wanted Grace to hear the exchange, he had a reason. It would mean something to her.

Then, there it was. Shadow mentioned Detective Dawkins, then she heard his voice over the intercom, the familiar tension in Cade's tone. She closed her eyes in relief.

Of course he'd come.

Grace stood, needing to do something. Looking around her cell, there wasn't much she could do. The only thing in there was her Home Depot bathroom bucket.

So, she listened.

Shadow didn't seem particularly moved by Cade's announcement.

He stood as stoic as a palace guard for a moment before speaking. "Good luck with that. She belongs to me now."

With that, he stepped backward, and the metal door slammed into the doorframe, the deep *thrummp* of mechanical locks engaging. Cade ran to the door, pulling and pounding. The door wouldn't open. He kicked it in frustration.

His heart raced. So close, but now he was cut off. What would happen to Grace now that Shadow knew he was here?

Abbey joined him at the door. "How are we going to get in? That door looks pretty badass."

"We find another way." He shone his light along the wall. A century of damp conditions had taken its toll. He stopped at a section slick with black mildew, where the crumbling limestone blocks had eroded. The mortar had dissolved into gritty dust, leaving deep gaps between the blocks. Water trickled down in thin, steady rivulets.

"Sometimes the wall is less secure than the door."

He plucked a robust screwdriver from the slain maintenance man's tool belt. Cade jammed the tip into a gap between the limestone blocks and used his hip to knock out a chunk of mortar.

Abbey clapped her hands. "Yes, we can get in."

Cade stopped and turned to her. "Not *we*. I need you to do something more important. We've lost control of this, and we're going to need backup. Fast. Head back through the tunnels, far enough to get past his signal jammer. As soon as you've got a cell signal, call 911 and tell them to send everyone."

"I can do that." Her eyes shone in the light, steady and assured.

Glancing at his watch, his eyes caught the timer he'd set. He didn't know what zero would bring, but he suspected it wouldn't be good. It showed less than 30 minutes.

He handed her the truck keys. "When you get outside, get inside and lock the doors until help arrives. I need you to be safe."

"Are you sure you don't want to come with?"

With his decision already made, Cade was calm. "Grace is in here. I'm not leaving without her."

"Catch you outside then." Abbey hurried for the tunnel entrance.

Returning to the wall, Cade attacked it like a man clawing his way out of a coffin—desperate, determined, and not entirely sure what he'd find on the other side.

She knew he was coming.

Shadow's last words before he cut off the audio feed were ominous.

"She belongs to me now."

And then hearing the finality of the slamming door meant he was coming. For her.

Grace didn't have much to work with in her small cell, but she was ready when she heard the grinding mechanical whine of the door opening. She couldn't overpower him in a fight. But surprise was her weapon—and timing was everything.

She dumped the bucket.

Days of piss and shit.

Right in front of the door.

When Shadow stepped inside, he looked down.

He was standing in sewage.

Seizing the opportunity, she jumped on his back, the metal wire of the bucket handle going over his head. She yanked it hard, digging the wire into his throat.

"I am not yours," she grunted through gritted teeth.

He brought up his massive arms, trying to claw the wire from his throat. Grace was ready and drove her knee into his back.

Shadow twisted, frantic to dislodge her, but lost his footing. Going down hard, he went to his knees before face-planting into the bucket's disgusting contents.

"Eat shit," she spat as she hung onto his back, the wire wrapped around his throat. Then she was up, stomping on the back of his neck before racing out the open door.

Sweat ran into his eyes, his hands cramping as his muscles burned, but Cade was through the wall. From what he could see through the opening, Shadow wasn't waiting, just stairs rising into the dark. The jagged limestone scratching and tearing at him, he fought his way through the opening.

Abbey hurried back down the tunnel, feeling disoriented as she made her way. The light barely gave her a yard or two of illumination, but the stakes were too high to slow down. Passing Cottage No. 9, she slowed to see if she had cell service.

"Damn it."

She kept going.

Grace didn't wait to see if Shadow would get up.

Her pulse thundered as she bolted from the cell, the bucket handle still clenched in her hand, now streaked with blood. Her shoes skidded across the concrete floor as she flew down the corridor, back toward the decrepit stairwell. The dim light flickered overhead, casting jerky shadows that made everything feel alive and closing in.

Behind her, she heard the groan of movement.

He was getting up.

She ran harder.

The main floor was worse than she remembered. Darker. The cold bit deeper. The walls seemed to close in, the rot more aggressive. She ran down a narrow hallway, past the remains of a gutted kitchen, past a doorway where floorboards gaped like teeth.

A flash of light caught her eye. The front of the house.

She veered toward it, but a sound—low and wet—rose behind her. Not words. Just intent. Rage made into sound.

He was closer.

She flung herself into a side room and shoved the door shut behind her, heart in her throat. She fumbled for anything—anything—to wedge beneath the knob. Her hand landed on an old chair leg, and she jammed it into place. It held. For now.

Breathing hard, she looked around the room. Dust, plaster, broken glass. The walls were bare, and cables slithered along the floor like vines in an abandoned greenhouse.

But something else, too.

A glow.

Monitors. Dozens of them. Stacked like some kind of surveillance shrine.

A central desk dominated the space, cluttered with keyboards, hard drives, and scraps of paper filled with scribbled notations and times. The monitors displayed live feeds from various cameras—some from the tunnel, some from the cell, others showing exterior angles: the alley where she'd been abducted, the road leading to the building, and even what looked like an interior stairwell Grace hadn't yet seen.

One monitor looped old footage—clips of her pacing, sleeping, working out in the cell—an unsettling reminder that she'd been studied like a lab rat.

Her stomach turned. He had been watching everything.

Every detail screamed of his preparation, his surveillance. His obsession.

Another screen pulsed with a digital timer: 00:13:04 and counting down.

Just as she saw a figure emerge on the video feed of the stairwell, she heard Shadow coming. She needed to move.

Cade moved cautiously, every sense alert. Arms crossed at the wrist, he gripped his service pistol, barrel angled slightly upward. In his support hand, he carried a tactical flashlight, a method drilled into muscle memory from years of training. The beam of light tracked with the barrel, cutting through the dark in tight arcs as he swept corners, doorways, and every shadowed stretch ahead of him. Moving with deliberate steps, his footfalls soft, he scanned for movement. His breath slow, and controlled, he listened for the slightest noise.

He was at the stairs.

He took the first step as it creaked under his weight. Moving to the outside edge, he needed to be as silent as possible. Halfway up the stairs, he paused, feeling the step give. He leaned back to take his weight off it.

Something wasn't right.

Kneeling, he swept his flashlight over the structure of the stairs. Sawdust gathered on this step and the one above it. Glancing at the railing, it had also been nearly sawn through.

It was booby trapped.

Abbey reached the brick structure, where she and Cade had entered the tunnel. As she moved up the rusted metal steps, the change in weather slapped her in the face. As it often happened when fall headed into winter, sleet was the result of the near-freezing temperatures. She ran for the shelter of the truck, checking her phone.

She had service.

Punching in the three digits that would bring help, she waited for them to pick up.

"9-1-1. What's your emergency?"

Grace realized she should have questioned why there was a floor mat on an otherwise bare floor. Normally, she was methodical—trained to notice details, to analyze and anticipate. She noticed things like the out of place floor mat but priorities changed when you were running for your life.

Time slowed as Grace's weight triggered the pressure pad.

A sawhorse—one with protruding knife blades—flew at her.

Because she was running, the majority of the blades missed.

But not all. Two got her.

One sliced the triceps on her right arm, the other stabbed deep into her shoulder.

Grace called out in pain as she tried to free her shoulder from the blade.

There was no time to be gentle. Shadow was coming.

"I'm at the Anoka Asylum. At Cottage 8. A woman is prisoner here. She's the kidnapped police officer, Grace Fox." Abbey recognized the nerves in her voice, not liking the tremble.

"Are you safe?" the woman asked.

"I am, but Detective Cade Dawkins of the Five Below Task Force is inside. He's with the man who took Grace. And we found a body of someone he's killed."

"Where's the body located?"

"It's in the basement. He's wearing maintenance man overalls." She wiped the sleet from her face. "You need to send everyone you can. This man, he calls himself Shadow. He's massively huge, and he's got a Crocodile Dundee kind of knife. He threatened to impale me on it."

"Where are you?"

"Outside."

"Good. Stay where you are. Help is on the way."

"Send every damn squad."

Abbey took a deep breath. Help was coming, but how would they get past the fence and get inside?

She glanced around, a smile forming. Maybe there was something she could do.

There was only one way to get past Shadow's crude booby trap. He'd have to leap. It wasn't far, but there was no room for error either.

He took a deep breath.

One. Two. Three.

Go.

Wrenching herself free, Grace swore and ran further into the darkness.

Should I stay? Should I go? Hell no, I'm going. Abbey opened Cade's truck.

Cade's leap was enough, and he cleared the doctored steps. But his trailing foot brushed the step and, with a groan, it plummeted to the basement. Staring into the abyss, he shook his head. He'd been lucky to see the sawdust. No way he'd have discovered it if he'd been descending the stairs.

He continued cautiously. If this place had one booby trap, it probably had a dozen more. He'd seen *Home Alone* enough times to know that once the marbles start rolling, the paint cans weren't far behind.

Abbey slid into the driver's seat of Cade's truck and stared at the ignition like it was some ancient artifact. The keys jingled in her hand—Cade had given them to her earlier in case she needed to wait in the truck. Somehow, *"just in case"* had turned into *"ram the fence down like an action thriller."*

"Okay, Abbey," she muttered, fumbling the key in and turning it. "You've got this. You've seen *every* Fast and Furious movie and at least three Dukes of Hazzard reruns."

The engine sputtered, then died.

"Are you kidding me?" She cranked it again, this time giving it a little gas like she thought she remembered from a YouTube video on "Things Everyone Pretends They Know." The truck growled to life.

"Yes! Like a virgin, touched for the very first time." She gave the dashboard a pat. "Don't make it weird, Madonna."

Abbey yanked the gearshift—then immediately slammed the brakes when the truck lurched backward.

"No, no, no. Not reverse!"

She took a calming breath. "You are a professional. Maybe not getaway driver professional, but a professional ghost hunter, close enough." She bumped the lever into *D* and nodded. "Okay. Forward is our friend. Ghosts behind me, Cade in the basement of death in front of me."

Foot to the pedal, she gunned it.

The truck roared like an angry dragon as she bounced across the grass toward the fence, white-knuckled, hair in her face, heart somewhere in her throat.

Shadow's voice taunted from hidden speakers. "You're clever, but not clever enough." Both Cade and Grace had goosebumps hearing it.

On the main floor now, Cade advanced warily, his pistol sweeping in front of him. The flashlight cut a swath through the gloom, dust swirling in its beam like ash from a fire long since burned out. The floorboards creaked underfoot—soft in places, spongy in others. He didn't trust a single inch of it.

He pivoted past a collapsed coat rack, his light dancing over broken furniture, piles of rubble, and what looked like a stack of moldy newspapers from decades ago. The silence was heavy, the kind that muffled your own thoughts and made your heartbeat sound like a bass drum in your ears.

Every doorway was a potential ambush, every shadow a place for Shadow to hide.

A narrow hallway loomed ahead. The wallpaper was peeling in long strips like dead skin, revealing cracked plaster underneath. Cade's breath fogged in the cold air as he moved forward, clearing each doorway with a quick sweep of the muzzle.

Suddenly, something *thunked* to the floor behind him. He spun, gun up, light flaring—just a shattered light fixture dangling by a thread of wire.

"Home Alone, my ass," he muttered.

Pressing forward, his nerves hummed with anticipation. It was like going through the State Fair haunted house, knowing someone was waiting to jump out. Only this someone had an unusually large knife.

Then, he saw the open door.

The control room.

He crept closer, every muscle tight, pistol ready. He had no idea what waited inside. But, if Grace was still in this place, he was running out of time.

Abbey floored it.

The tires screeched in protest as Cade's truck lurched forward, rattling like an old cassette deck forced to play Bon Jovi on full blast. She gritted her teeth, eyes locked on the sagging chain-link fence that separated her from the asylum grounds. Her grip was tight—both hands clenched on the wheel like it might fly off and smack her if she let go.

"I cannot believe I'm doing this," she muttered. "I don't even have my learner's permit."

The truck bounced hard over the curb and fishtailed slightly on the loose gravel.

The fence loomed.

She braced, screamed, and slammed her foot down harder. "*Livin' on a Prayer,*" she wailed as the front bumper met metal with a horrific crunch.

The fence folded like bad origami. Posts groaned. One snapped. The truck didn't stop until it bulldozed halfway into the overgrown yard beyond, its bumper dragging a snarl of bent steel mesh.

Steam hissed from the hood.

"Nailed it," she yelled, breathless, heart pounding partly in disbelief that she was still alive. "Cade better buy me so many waffles."

She shoved open the door, boots hitting the ground, and ran full tilt toward the crumbling building.

"Hang on, Grace. We're coming."

Cade swept the beam of his flashlight down the crumbling corridor, pistol steady in his other hand. The creak of the warped floorboards under his boots echoed like a threat. Somewhere ahead—he knew it—Grace was close.

"Grace!" he called out, low but urgent.

A voice called back. "Cade?"

He turned, heart pounding.

She appeared at the top of a shadowed stairwell, dirt-smudged, eyes wide, a jagged cut above her brow. She was breathing hard, but thankfully, standing.

"I'm here," she said.

He ran to her, holstering the pistol just long enough to catch her in his arms.

"I knew you'd find me," she whispered into his shoulder.

"Of course I did," he said, his voice tight with emotion. "We're getting out of here. Now."

Then they heard it—a slow, deliberate clap from the hallway behind them.

Cade turned, flashlight sweeping to find Shadow standing at the far end of the corridor, framed by the decaying archway. His hood was down now, mask still in place, the light glinting off the expressionless plastic. He said nothing.

Cade pulled Grace behind him, leveling the pistol. "Don't."

Shadow tilted his head.

And then—

CRASH.

A massive metallic screech echoed through the building. It was unmistakable: someone had just driven a truck through a fence.

Cade's heart surged. "Abbey," he breathed.

A sharp *beep* pierced the silence, and Shadow's gaze flicked to his wrist. He looked at Cade. "You think this ends with me? Tick-tock, Detective."

Cade's stomach dropped.

The *beep* sounded again—more urgent now. A small red light blinked rapidly on the watch face.

"Sixty seconds," Shadow said, voice flat behind the mask. "You should run."

And then he was gone, vanishing into the dark like smoke.

"Go!" Cade shouted, grabbing Grace's hand. They bolted down the hallway, boots slamming against warped wood.

A faint ticking seemed to echo from the walls as they ran. They turned a corner, burst through a half-hinged door, and slammed through the exit.

Abbey stood wide-eyed by the truck, steam still hissing from its crumpled hood. "You found her!"

Cade didn't stop moving. "Get behind the truck!"

They dove, hitting the ground just as—

The night held its breath.

BOOM.

The asylum behind them exploded in a bloom of orange and black. The force rattled the truck and shattered the building's remaining windows. Fire belched from the basement windows as bricks pelted the truck and smoke filled the night air.

Abbey got to her feet, phone out to video the aftermath. "Holy crap."

Cade held Grace close as they stood, the heat of the blaze washing over them, but neither willing to let the other go. They said nothing, just staring into the inferno, the roar of the flames echoing the chaos they'd just survived.

Shadow was gone.

But they were alive.

44

The truck idled in a lot down the block from the blast crater. Smoke rose into the night like a fading scream. Sirens howled from every direction, growing louder by the second. Grace curled up in the back seat, wrapped in a blanket. Her face was pale, blank—but not broken. She stared out the window like her ordeal hadn't fully ended yet. Abbey glanced at her, looking unsure what to say. Cade was outside, phone pressed to his ear, adrenaline still spiking in his veins.

"Crocker?" he said, voice raw. "We got her. She's safe."

There was a long pause on the other end.

"That's good," Crocker said quietly. "But you're not going to like what I found."

Cade felt his stomach knot. "Go ahead."

"We traced the last video feed through the Tor relay it was bouncing across." Crocker let out a breath. "One of the exit nodes linked to a mirror of Orbiting Cortex."

Cade didn't speak. Couldn't.

"You remember that site better than anyone," Crocker continued. "Serial killers use it to share exploits, brag, and offer challenges to each other."

Cade closed his eyes, pulse thudding in his ears. The area swarmed with responders, their lights flashing red and blue through the smoke.

"Someone uploaded Grace's photo and bio six months ago. This contributor—ChokeHalo—has been prolific. Multiple posts. Personal commentary. Trophy photos. Timelines."

"Recent posts suggested something bad was coming. He had a plan that was close to fruition," Crocker said. "The timer in the corner of the feed? That wasn't a countdown to an escape or a deadline for you. That was a kill timer."

A beat of silence.

"He's not a distraction from your case, Cade," Crocker added. "He *is* the case. Shadow is a full-blown serial killer. And he's been on Orbiting Cortex the whole time."

Cade stared out across the dark lot as the sleet returned, the aftermath of the explosion still fresh in his mind.

"So, Grace wasn't leverage," he said quietly.

"No. She was the target. He didn't stumble onto Grace—he selected her. The comm link, the feeds, the tunnels—it was all part of the performance. And you were his audience."

Cade's hand clenched the phone tighter.

"I'm sending everything we've found to your inbox," Crocker said, breaking the connection.

Cade lowered the phone slowly, his reflection dim and hollow in the truck window. Inside, Grace looked up, her expression shifting—she could feel it too. Something had changed.

He didn't speak. Didn't have to. The past week had wrung him out—sleepless nights, nonstop pressure, and now this.

The truth of Crocker's discovery hit hard.

This wasn't over. With Shadow, it might only be the beginning.

45

Rook swung across the street for a greasy sandwich and bad coffee. He flipped to public radio, letting the drone of fiscal policy debates be background as he watched Fang's SUV.

Feeling his breakfast sandwich expanding uncomfortably in his stomach and fighting some serious fatigue, Rook needed to do something and got out of his car. Maybe Fang had the right idea. He bought a newspaper from the pay box as well. Tossing it onto the passenger seat, he leaned against the vehicle's frame and stretched his legs. Sitting in the car for such extended periods took its toll.

Another half hour passed uneventfully. Rook kept one eye on the Pioneer Press newspaper and the other on the restaurant's front door. With Fang's men being so large, one eye should be enough.

The lull broke. Fang's men emerged, scanning the lot with precision. Rook sat up straighter. Show time.

After a moment, Fang followed, the newspaper folded under his arm. Rook continued reading his newspaper, not wanting to draw attention to himself. He watched Fang's slow journey to his SUV.

Rook followed them out of the lot as they made their way to 94 and headed east. In a routine surveillance operation, a team of vehicles rotated so the suspect did not have the opportunity to identify a specific vehicle. Being alone, Rook stayed a quarter-mile distance behind. He thought about calling in the team but decided to wait for something more concrete.

Fang made his way along 94, crossing into St. Paul. Before they reached the downtown of St. Paul, Fang took the Marion Street ramp. Rook followed as they headed downtown, the Xcel Energy Center directly down the hill. At John Ireland Boulevard, Fang signaled right and turned, the Cathedral of St. Paul looming majestically on the hill. As they drew alongside the Cathedral, Fang took another right onto Selby Avenue.

Sunday morning, directly in front of the city's largest Catholic church, as one might have guessed, was a busy location. It looked to Rook like a service had just finished, with a second service following shortly. Cars were pulling onto the already busy avenue while others waited for their spots. Two blocks from the cathedral, Fang slid into a freshly vacated spot. Almost immediately, he exited the SUV as Rook cruised by. Using his rearview mirror, he saw Fang's men gathered by the Suburban's open hatch.

Finding an empty spot a block further down, Rook hustled back toward the cathedral at a light jog, making up the ground between them. The security men stood by the vehicle, but Fang was gone. After a nerve-wracking minute, he spotted him up ahead. Walking alone, hands in the pockets of his long wool coat, Fang was headed for church.

Maybe he was seeking absolution. Maybe not. Rook had tailed too many killers into too many sanctuaries to believe that stepping into a church washed the blood off your hands.

What was more likely was that this was where Fang chose to meet to finalize things. Picking a crowded public area for a sensitive meeting was sound strategy, and from the looks of things, this had to be the most crowded spot in the Twin Cities on a Sunday morning. At least until the Vikings game started at noon, anyway.

Knowing that Fang was meeting someone—likely Dazhao—energized Rook. He would be watching Fang like a hawk. If these players were here, odds were the shooter would be too.

He called Kristen and told her to get the team rolling. It looked like things were happening. She surprised him with the news of Grace's late-night rescue.

"Should I call him? He's probably still sound asleep."

Rook hesitated. "I was going to say let him sleep, but if it were me, I'd want the head's-up. He can choose if he wants to join the fun."

Kristen giggled. "I'll call him. See you soon."

People were streaming toward the entrance in droves. Rook checked his watch—10:30. The service was just beginning. He positioned himself about twenty feet off to the side and back from Fang's location. That angle gave him a clean sightline without putting him directly in the man's periphery—close enough to track, far enough to stay invisible.

When Rook entered the sanctuary, he scanned the crowded room, finding Fang right away. Leaning against the wall, arms folded and fidgeting, Fang didn't look exactly comfortable.

Rook checked his watch—nothing to do now but wait. One glance down confirmed what he already felt: a night spent in the car had left him rumpled, wrinkled, and in serious need of a shower. He didn't exactly blend in with the Sunday-best crowd filing into the church. They'd have to take him as they found him.

It had been a long twenty-four hours, and Rook was counting on it all coming to a head soon. Lately, it had felt like the tide was finally turning—breaks were coming, leads were clicking into place, and for once, luck seemed to be leaning his way.

But then came Ritter.

Cade's recounting of his threats still gnawed at him. It was a sharp reminder that politics could unravel everything they'd built. Shut down the task force? Strip Rook of his authority? It wasn't just pressure—it was a loaded gun aimed squarely at his future. And now, that hopeful shift he'd been feeling? It might've just reversed course.

His career was hanging by a thread, and he knew it. When the dust settled, he wasn't sure if he'd still have a badge.

He didn't want to, but he knew he had to.

Frank put on the conference pin, slipped in his earpiece, and activated the system. The slight crackle confirmed the commlink was live—not that he needed confirmation with Tom's profanity-laced tirade blaring in his ear like something out of a longshoremen's union meeting.

When Tom finally paused to take a breath, which took surprisingly long—think Navy SEAL on testing day—Frank interrupted. "Good to hear your voice, Tom."

"Holy hell, Frank. I thought you were dead or ran off with that saucy North Korean spy."

"You heard?"

"Trust me, everyone heard. That press conference was ratings gold and everyone carried the story." Tom hesitated. "I'm surprised. I never expected you to resume the Lakefront mission."

There was a wary pause, where no one spoke. "You are resuming the mission?"

Frank stared at the cathedral, glowing pale in the morning light. The sort of place meant for confessions. Regrets. Maybe redemption, if you still believed in that sort of thing. "Yes, sir."

"Alright, we're back in the saddle. Sit rep?"

Frank adjusted the cuff of his jacket, eyes scanning the plaza outside the Cathedral of St. Paul. "I have an 11:30 meeting with Chou Fang to trade him the flash drive I took off Xiang Li."

He heard Tom's hesitation in his earpiece. "Wait, you destroyed it. I watched you."

"Fang doesn't know that."

A city bus rumbled by, and Frank watched it head up the hill.

"Okay, a dangerous game, but it is what it is."

"He's going to need someone to authenticate the drive."

"There's so little trust these days."

"That someone would be familiar with hacker backdoor protocols."

Tom exhaled through his teeth. "Chen Dazhao."

"Exactly."

"Frank, that's brilliant. Risky as hell, but still brilliant."

Another wary pause. Tom specialized in those. "Wait, what's Fang trading with you?"

"Not what, who. The saucy North Korean spy."

It sounded like the longshoremen's union meeting had started up again.

Frank let him get it out of his system. Once Tom wound down, he asked, "Aren't you the same Frank Perlmutter who always said keep your head down? Don't get involved in other people's problems. That's you, right?"

"It's a fluid situation."

Tom burst out laughing. "Fluid? How so?"

Frank paused, not quite willing to admit what drove him to this place. "Maybe I never wanted to get involved with someone else's problems because I never found someone I cared about."

"And now you have."

"And now I have."

Tom sighed wearily. Frank knew him long enough to picture him shaking his head. "Understood. People don't risk their lives for nothing."

"I'm sorry, Tom."

"Don't apologize for what love does. We'll roll with what we got."

Frank didn't trust himself to say anything.

"I'm assuming you're going to dispatch Alpha and leave with the girl. Exit strategy?"

"You know me. I like to blend in."

"That is your superpower."

"But I told Fang that I'd be wearing the same blue shirt and orange vest that the cathedral traffic control staff wears. I want him to focus on that. Someone following me around the corner, looking for an orange vest, will be in for a surprise."

"How is that?"

"I placed an ad on Craigslist, offering $38 an hour for a half-day road construction project. I arranged for them to arrive around 11:15 and requested that they wear a blue shirt and an orange vest. They're meeting around the corner from the cathedral."

Frank was glad he could still make Tom laugh. "You're pulling an Istanbul? Love it. That should ensure plenty of suspects.

"What's your next step?"

"I'm going to put my exfil vehicle in place and then head inside. See who's shown up."

"Love it. I'll get into the church's surveillance system."

"The Cathedral of St. Paul has a surveillance system?"

"Everyone has a surveillance system these days. Especially the Catholic Church."

Frank wasn't going to ask. He started the rental and headed up the hill.

It was supposed to go down like this:

Frank would meet Rose's boss, Chou Fang, just before noon outside of the Cathedral of St. Paul. The handoff would take place in front of the city's largest church. Services would be just letting out, so there would be plenty of activity to blend in with.

Having never met each other, Frank would be wearing a blue work shirt and an orange vest, the uniform of the church's traffic control volunteers. He would be waiting at the bottom of the front steps. They would meet long enough to hand off the drive when he saw Rose, and then they would go their separate ways. Just two friends passing on the steps. Nothing to raise an eyebrow.

It actually went down like this:

Frank arrived just after the 10:30 a.m. service had started. Even though the street was lined with parked cars as far as he could see, he was able to park just around the corner from the Cathedral. Frank moved the orange traffic cones and the road construction sign that held his preferred spot and placed them in the roadway just behind his parked car. This would block the lane and effectively bring traffic to a standstill after the service let out, sending a thousand people out onto the local roads.

He locked his newly rented Ford, thinking about the future. Could he and Rose survive this and start a new chapter in the Florida Keys? Leave their dangerous lives behind and settle into a quiet one that would make Jimmy Buffett proud?

He made his way down to the corner of John Ireland Boulevard. The Cathedral loomed, stone and shadow spread across the highest point in St. Paul. Built over a century ago, it felt carved into the sky. In his youth, Frank had been brought up in the Catholic Church. Though it had been years since he'd been inside a church, it was not difficult to get caught up in the memories of his youth. His family had been a fixture at their local church. Each Sunday he would climb the front steps of their small church holding his father's hand. Simpler times.

Frank slipped off his vest, folded it with care, and tucked it under his arm. A quick glance at his watch—10:45 a.m. He stepped through the doors into the sanctuary.

The sheer scale of it hit him first.

Vaulted ceilings stretched above like a stone sky, and the pews were packed. Even the back wall was lined with people—standing room only. Church was big business here in St. Paul.

Frank joined the others at the back, listening to the congregation sing. He scanned the crowd that stood at the back of the sanctuary. As in much of his life, he was an observer, not a participant, but it was a role he was comfortable with. His keen observation skills had served him well over the years. He could study a scene and get a feel for what fit as well as what didn't. It allowed him to blend in and anticipate movements and reactions.

For the most part, the people in the back were alone, and the majority were male. They seemed to be of varying social and economic statuses. Some even appeared to be homeless, drawn here for both the comfort of the religion and the warmth the large church offered. As he studied the crowd, Frank found Fang near the opposite entrance. Arms folded, still wearing his overcoat, he didn't look comfortable at all. He fidgeted, checking his watch every few minutes and kept glancing around. Though Fang had never seen him before, nerves made men unpredictable. A hard stare might spook him—or worse, blow the meet. Frank moved closer to the slightly rumpled man next to him.

He forced himself to keep facing the priest delivering the message. Some might find it odd that Frank wouldn't remember a single word, but his mind was elsewhere, locked on the plan that was about to unfold.

What Frank did find odd was the man next to him. Black, late thirties, with sharp eyes and rumpled clothes that didn't match the Sunday-best crowd. He wasn't listening to the sermon. He wasn't looking at the altar. He was watching Fang.

Was he one of Fang's men? A cop?

Either way, he wasn't part of Frank's plan. And complications, in Frank's world, rarely ended well.

46

The man beside him smelled ripe—unshaven, rumpled, and twitchy—but his clothes and shoes told a different story. Not homeless. More like someone who'd spent the night in his car. Which, come to think of it, was exactly what Frank looked like after a surveillance op.

The priest offered his blessing as the service drew to a close. Several people, who'd been standing at the back, pushed through the doors, leaving early to beat the rush. Frank walked with a small group of twenty-somethings, who were laughing and talking about getting some coffee. He stayed close, blending in as if he were part of their group.

As the group made their way out the front doors, Frank separated and moved to the side. He slipped into his orange vest, moving down the steps. The crowd flooded out the front doors, a sea of people moving in a single direction.

Cade and Grace walked together, bumping shoulders, hands finding each other's as they headed towards the cathedral. The closer they got, the more imposing the structure became. Cade supposed that was the idea. If you wanted to get the idea of God being large and in charge, you built the biggest building you could. It worked.

"I've never been to the cathedral before, have you?" he asked.

"Oh yeah. I'm here every week for Friday bingo night."

"Wait, what?"

"Yeah, me and the blue haired ladies." But her expression gave her away. "I've been here but not for bingo." She left it at that.

The service was still in session, but there were still quite a few people congregating around the entrance and the steps.

"Rook's inside. Let's grab a bench and see who arrives."

The transition from fall into winter in Minnesota was anything but linear. They'd already had snow, but it had melted and now it was roughly 50°. A day designed for bench sitting and people watching.

He studied her as they chatted. She'd lost weight, her face looking particularly gaunt. Dark circles were under her eyes, where only laugh lines had been. But she was here, alive and physically unharmed. He hadn't broached the subject of talking to a professional yet. He wasn't ready for that discussion.

"Are you even listening?"

Never the words anyone wanted to hear, Cade snapped to attention. "I'm sorry, it's just so damn good to have you back. It was incredibly difficult." He paused, unable to continue.

Grace patted his hand, content to let the comfortable silence stretch between them.

After a minute, she spoke. "I knew you'd come."

"I had to. It took longer than I hoped, but I'm glad you held on to your hope."

Grace shook her head. "People speak of hope as if it's this delicate, ethereal thing made of whispers and spider webs. It's not. Hope has dirt on her face, blood on her knuckles, the grit of cobblestone in her hair, and just spit out a tooth as she rises for another go."

"Sounds more like you, if I'm being honest."

Cade recognized Grace's smile for what it was: not joy exactly, but something steadier. A thank you without words.

After a moment, Cade nodded toward a pair of women taking a selfie. Kristen and Lorie took a few more and giggled as they looked at the shots.

"Good," Cade said. "We're going to need them."

"Because of those guys?" She nodded subtly. Fang's bodyguards were not designed to blend in. Too many muscles. Too small suits. Decidedly unfriendly demeanors.

"Yep, those guys."

"What about the shooter? You've encountered him. Anyone here resemble him?"

Cade leaned back and ran his fingers through his already messy hair. "Man. Doubt it, but I don't know. The problem is, the church going crowd is so homogeneous. Makes an average human nearly invisible. Like picking out a cow from the herd. Impossible. I'll likely only pick him out by his actions."

"Which would be too late."

"Yep. Hole in the head, brains on the sidewalk kind of late."

Grace leaned closer. "I don't think so. The shooter's used a silenced 9mm so far. It's unlikely to blow out the back of anyone's skull and send brains to the sidewalk. Now, if he used a .44..."

She paused, seeing his expression. "What?"

"Grace. No offense, but you need a hobby. Have you thought about taking up watercolors? Pole dancing? Learning to play the harp?"

This had her giggling. Probably his favorite sound.

A half-dozen men wearing orange vests came out, propped open the doors, and positioned themselves along the sidewalk.

"Service is ending."

People, thousands, all leaving at the same time. Young, old, singles, couples, families. Fashion choices ranged from decked out, to casual, to dumpster diving fashion.

A second glance. Wait, that was Rook. Overnight stakeout problems.

"There's Fang. Rook's behind him."

They tracked the pair as they left the building.

"Fang's scanning the crowd. Looking for someone." Grace talked low, like a golf announcer. "Looking left. Looking right. Looking high, looking low. Wait. He's locked in and moving. Headed for the guy in the vest."

The pair faced each other for a moment, whatever words exchanged unheard. Fang glanced over his shoulder, vest guy following his gaze. A dark-haired woman in a silk head scarf stood by one of Fang's boy toys.

"Is that...?" Grace asked.

"Could be."

"Think vest guy is the shooter?"

"Could be. But he could be the Pope or Ronald McDonald."

"They're greeting each other like old friends."

"The two-handed handshake. Recommended the world over for passing hidden intel."

One of the bodyguards appeared at his boss's side. Took something small. Handed it off to another, albeit smaller, Asian man.

Behind them, Cade spotted the FBI woman, Kaz Hankee. Her eyes were laser-focused on the man plugging a flash drive into a handheld device. It felt like everyone took a collective breath as he navigated a screen.

Time slowed.

"That's Chen Dazhao," Cade said. "The one Hankee said to detain, arrest, or shoot. Let's go talk to him."

They stood.

"Hold on, he's checking the flash drive. Typically, it's a pass or fail kind of thing."

Dazhao lifted his gaze. Gave a subtle shake.

Fail.

Time sped.

Cade froze. Guns were out—everywhere. Fang. His men. Dazhao. Hankee. Kristen. Rook. Grace. Even the damn vest guy. It felt like someone had shouted "draw" in an old western. Giving in to peer pressure, Cade drew his.

Rook yelled for everyone to get down. His voice carried the authority of a pissed-off high school gym teacher.

Chaos. Many obeyed. Some ran instead. Others screamed.

Shots fired. Like this. Pop. Pop, pop, pop. Pop.

Many more screams.

Cade and Grace tackled the closest bodyguard.

Rook slapped Fang's gun away. Pushed his gun into Fang's neck.

Kristen and Lorie wrestled another bodyguard to the pavement.

The third bodyguard on his knees. No fight in him.

Hankee stood over Dazhao, who lay dead. No sidewalk brains, but he had a new hole in his forehead. Blood spread from around his torso.

"The shooter." Grace pointed. A blue-shirted, vest-wearing figure darted through the throng. Disappearing around the corner.

"I'm on it." Cade ran.

"Not without me." Grace sprinted after him.

Neck and neck when they reached the corner. Some twenty seconds behind fleeing vest guy. They had him. The vest made their job easy.

That was. Until.

Cade stopped dead, Grace took a few more steps before she froze.

Cade blinked, chest heaving. "What the hell…"

The street was flooded with orange vests.

Dozens of men—forty, maybe more—milled around the blocked-off intersection. Some leaned on traffic barricades. Others checked their phones. Most looked bored. All wore blue work shirts and identical high-vis orange vests.

Contractors?

Crowd control?

Something else?

Grace stepped forward, scanning faces. "He's not here."

Cade's eyes swept the scene like a radar dish, searching for that one twitchy move, that flick of panic that would give someone away. But everyone looked perfectly, irritatingly normal.

And then Grace saw it.

There, abandoned in the gutter, lay an orange vest—crumpled and empty.

She pointed. "There. He ditched it."

Realization dawned, sick and electric.

"Oh no," Cade whispered. "We didn't lose him. We never had him."

He turned in a slow circle, taking in the dozen exits, the hundreds of people now spilling from the church, moving in all directions. Families, couples, kids in dress shoes, and old men in hats. Any one of them could be him. Or none of them.

The shooter hadn't escaped.

He'd vanished.

The vest had done its job.

Grace stepped beside Cade, breathless. "He ghosted us."

"No," Cade said, jaw tightening. "He outplayed us."

47

A week later, with most of the dust settled and the media circus having moved on, Cade lifted his mug. His friends and fellow Five Below colleagues lifted theirs. Rook, Grace, Kristen, and Lorie sat around the table at the Woodbury Hope Breakfast Bar. At the far end, Crocker and Tubbs—the resident profs of data and psych—nodded along, content to listen and sip their black coffee.

Kristen peered over her coffee at the passing server's tray. "Did you see the French toast? It looks so good I'd swipe right on it—and I don't even date carbs." She leaned back, content. "We should do all our case postmortems here."

"I'm good with that," Cade said, taking a sip of his peanut butter cup latte. "This is amazing."

After everyone ordered, Cade kicked off the discussion. "Let's take stock of the case and the Cathedral's aftermath. Be honest, good or bad, it's the only way to improve." He nodded to Rook.

"Okay then, boss. Let's start with bad: The shooter got away. Really thought we were going to catch that guy. How did he slip away?"

"I followed up on that," Kristen said. "All those people wearing orange safety vests in the construction zone by the cathedral answered an ad. $38 an hour cash for a half-day road construction project. No experience needed. They showed up en masse." Pushing up her glasses, she paused. "Think about it. What the shooter did was brilliant. Made us focus on his vest and then ditched it around the corner. From there, he did what he does best: blended in with the church crowds. When you blitzed around the corner, you were looking for that vest. And he gave you plenty to look at."

Rook sighed. "Bloomington PD found his rental at the MOA ramp. Of course, before he vanished on us, he put a bullet into Dazhao's brain. If that bullet didn't do the job, the other four did."

Lorie spoke up. "The ME said of the four bullets in his torso, one came from Kristen's service weapon."

"He shot first." Kristen shrugged.

Lorie rolled her eyes, but she was smiling.

"The other three were from the FBI special agent's gun."

Cade shook his head. "She's not actually FBI." Everyone gaped at him.

Rook leaned forward. "But she gave us the files on Fang and Dazhao. They'd planned to attack infrastructure with Xiang Li. Targets were major financial centers. New York, London, Paris, and Tel Aviv."

"Not many cases with global implications fall into local law enforcement's lap," Grace said. "But explain. If she wasn't FBI…"

Cade paused as breakfast was delivered. Everyone dug in, but Rook gestured with his fork. "Keep talking."

"You're curious about your girlfriend, are you?"

Rook sputtered but wisely didn't say anything.

"Remember I got a call from the shooter's handler when he was worried about his asset going rogue?" Cade snuck a quick bite of his banana churro waffles. "Well, he called back today. Said not to worry, his asset had left the state. There wouldn't be further shootings. Said he expected his asset was quitting the business entirely. I got the sense this was a relief. He apologized for the cluster, but before he hung up, he dropped the Kaz Hankee bombshell. She wasn't FBI, but Mossad. Here for retribution for Dazhao and Li's previous attack on her country, but she got wind of Fang's plan."

"You slept with the Mossad?" Grace asked Rook.

He didn't look like he wanted to answer, but he didn't look unimpressed either.

Cade continued. "The plan may not have come together with Li getting executed. The shooter recovered a drive with Li's backdoor protocols, and at the handler's insistence, he destroyed it. Too dangerous in the wrong hands. But the shooter used the promise of trading the drive to lure Fang and Dazhao to the Cathedral."

"Trade for what?"

"Rose Park."

"I thought I saw her in the cathedral crowd."

"No," Lorie said. "She was at the St. Paul Grand Hotel."

"She was Fang's bluff. An escort hired to fool the shooter."

"But the shooter was bluffing too. The drive he handed over was blank."

"He's got some balls."

Grace held up a hand. "I think the shooter fell for the Park woman. Whatever happened that brought them together, stuck."

Tubbs laughed. "Professor of psychology here. It's science. Bonding over shared trauma makes powerful connections. The complex interplay of emotional connection and survival mechanisms can create intense feelings of intimacy."

"See? They're in love. Where is she now?"

Lorie spoke. "Park fled the hotel while we were at the cathedral. Where? Anyone's guess." She turned to Grace. "How are you doing after your horrible ordeal?"

Grace looked off into the distance. "That was an experience all right. Turns out you can lose weight living off protein bars and bottled water. But I don't recommend it."

Kristen reached out a hand, placing it over Grace's. "You don't have to joke. Not here."

Grace gave a tired smile. "I'm just glad to be sitting at this table."

Rook spoke. "Understandable. Knee deep in the shooter case and then you get taken. Cade was beside himself."

"Why did that Shadow person grab you to begin with?" Kristen asked.

Grace reflexively put a hand to her neck. "He never said."

Cade reached out a hand and took hers. "At first, I thought your abduction was tied to the shooter case. It made sense because it took us both off the game board. Crippling the task force. But Crocker here," he gestured to the large man sitting at the end of the table, "Found something that pointed in a different direction."

Crocker glanced at the waiting faces. "Yeah. Grace's personal info was on the Orbiting Cortex site. Videos of her in captivity."

"That means..."

"Yes. Shadow is one of them."

No one spoke.

"A serial killer."

"One who, unfortunately, escaped the explosion at the Anoka Asylum."

They all looked back at Cade. Shocked.

"Oh shit. What does that mean?" Everyone at the table knew how dangerous and unpredictable these killers could be. What pain they could cause. What cost the victims endured.

"The fact we haven't heard anything, no contact or threats, hopefully means he's gone. Slunk back into the hole he crawled from."

Tubbs spoke. "There's a dominance theory based on lobster behavior—believe me, I know—that says defeated lobsters, like humans, experience reduced serotonin, adopt submissive postures, and are considerably more likely to lose subsequent encounters. There's a good chance Shadow has gone back to where he feels more at home. Seeking comfort."

"Lobsters, huh?" Cade shrugged. "We combed the asylum grounds. The buildings, tunnels, even the river. Diddlysquat."

Grace mouthed the word.

"Shadow is football lineman large, but because he always wore a mask, we don't have a lot to go on. Maybe he'll turn up, but it's not looking likely."

"There's something I wondered about," Crocker said. "We couldn't trace the feed, yet you found this young lady. How?"

Grace covered her smile, gesturing to Cade. "Well, don't keep him waiting."

Cade had the look of someone forced to admit their dissertation paper was solely sourced by Wikipedia.

"*Umm*, I had the help of a ghost hunter."

"And how old was this ghost hunter?" Grace prompted with no small amount of delight.

"If you can believe it, Abbey is 15 years old. A freshman at Pine Ridge High School. I'd run into our old friend Gordy and told him about my frustrating hunt for Grace. But when I mentioned the place was supposed to be haunted, he suggested a ghost hunter might be the right call."

"Looks like he was right." Crocker laughed. "It doesn't matter how you got there, it's that you got there."

Grace smiled. "I hope Abbey's charging consulting rates."

"That kid's going places. And not just haunted ones." Rook leaned back, clasping his hands. "So, where are you with the Governor?"

Cade paused, thinking it over. "Good question," he said, taking another sip of coffee. "Although we didn't stop or technically solve the shooter case, it's over. No more killings. And that's what Ritter wanted."

"Stopping a major terror attack has to be worth something," Grace pointed out.

"It was redemption. Our little task force suddenly ended up on the international media landscape. Ritter couldn't have been happier. He's been interviewed by the BBC, the New York Times, CNN, Al Jazeera, and People. Suddenly, he's everywhere taking the credit."

"That's a nice change from calling us a failed experiment." Rook shook his head. "Threatening to shut us down."

"He was going to do that?" Lorie looked pissed. "The bastard."

"That's behind us now. Ritter got his precious media attention, and maybe unfortunately, his reelection looks promising. We're going to be stuck with each other."

Rook made a face worthy of someone tasting gas station sushi for the first time.

Cade paused. "Ritter did insist on one change to the Five Below Task Force."

Everyone looked back warily.

"We need to hire a media consultant. To control "the narrative," as he put it." Cade made air quotes. He let that sink in.

"Gordy?" Rook asked after a moment.

Laughing, Cade shook his head. "That was the very next thing Ritter said. 'Don't bring back that weirdo communications guy.'"

"Awww. Gordy's not... well, maybe a bit," Rook said. "But he's entertaining."

"He's better than Ritter's suggestion for the job."

"Naw..." Rook had the gas station sushi expression again.

Cade glanced around the table, seeing dawning looks of horror.

"Barry Weiss."

It wasn't a name he could say easily. The guy was nails to Cade's personal chalkboard.

Everyone laughed hearing Weiss's name, but it was Kristen who spoke up.

"It's not such a bad idea. Think about it. Now he works for you, he has to do what you say. He's finally off the air. No more *Barry Weiss Report* smear campaigns." She was on a roll, her eyes twinkling with her unique energy. "We can take him under our wings, nurture him. Help him find his inner peace and donate those awful vests to the Goodwill."

They all stared at her.

"Kristen, you're far too nice for your own good."

She looked like she was going to say something, but it was Grace who spoke first. "One thing you need to understand about nice people like Kristen. Yes, she's extremely kind and loving, but her other side is just as extreme. It's the hell they've survived that made them so gentle. Don't mistake her self-control for weakness. The beast in her is sleeping, not dead."

Kristen smiled sweetly. "So, if Barry gets out of line, I'm going to punch him in the dick."

"That a girl," Cade said as everyone cracked up. He reached for Grace's hand and squeezed it gently. Thankful for her return. Thankful for her.

He looked at the smiling faces around the table. The people most important to him.

He was happy. Grace squeezed his hand.

So thankful.

The evening brought a sunset for the ages. Salty ocean air blew in with the breeze, warm and thick. Sitting at the edge of the dock, Frank cast his line into the bay with a gentle *plop*. He didn't care if the fish were biting. Catching anything was beside the point.

What mattered was this: he was here. He was alive. And he was out.

He rolled his bare shoulders, loosening muscles that had been wound tight for most of his life. No more listening for footsteps behind him. No more contingency protocols, kills, or voice in his ear. Just the whisper of waves slapping wood, the creak of the dock under his weight, and the occasional gull overhead. For a man who had lived in shadows, the light took some getting used to.

From the nearby speaker, Jimmy Buffett sang semi-wistfully about a pirate looking at forty. Frank's retired toes skimmed the water, moving to the rhythm.

Life was better here.

Sunshine. Water. Survival.

His former life was over. Years of successful kills. But he wasn't anyone's legend. Just a man who walked away and kept walking. Hopefully far enough that no one would come looking. In his profession, retirement usually meant a shallow grave. No one wanted a tell-all book making waves.

The only waves Frank wanted were the ones tickling his toes.

The slight tug on his line brought him back to the present, but he was content to let the fish have their nibble.

Soft footfalls. A creaking board. The presence of someone behind him.

Frank turned, accepting the offered piña colada.

Rose, sun kissed and radiant, sat beside him. Comfortable in just a bikini top, shorts, and flip-flops, she lifted her glass.

"Cheers."

Frank clinked glasses, thinking about the twisty road that had brought them here.

He watched her, trying to read the smile behind her sunglasses. She looked content, maybe even happy, to be far from the shadows of their old lives. Frank liked to think it was because she trusted him, because he offered her something simpler, something safe. Maybe she wanted a life where secrets were just stories, not survival.

But, as the sun slipped below the horizon and laughter drifted up from the boardwalk, a sliver of doubt settled in. There was an intelligence axiom: Once a spy, always a spy. Rose played the long game better than anyone he knew. If she ever needed a loyal, lovestruck pawn, he fit the bill. Frank wasn't sure what worried him more: that she might be playing him or that a part of him wouldn't mind. But for now, with Rose beside him and the world finally quiet, he decided not to ask. Not yet.

They sat in comfortable silence, sipping matching piña coladas, their toes in the water, faces toward the horizon.

Dusk. Wind swirled dry leaves. The mournful cry of Canadian geese echoed across the deserted grounds.

Inside Cottage No. 9, a light turned on. A screen flickered to life.

The Orbiting Cortex site beckoned.

Shadow smiled.

Game on.

Acknowledgements

Every so often, a character insists on writing themselves—which, frankly, is a gift to any author. In keeping with my usual tradition, I'm handing the mic to one of them. This time, Rook has graciously volunteered to deliver the acknowledgments.

Yo, Rook here. Let's be real: Allan probably just wanted someone likable to kick off this section, but whatever—here we are.

First, congrats on finishing the book—seriously, well done. Now hit pause on your life and go leave a review. Allan claims it's not for his ego (sure, buddy), but it really does help this book find more readers. I'll hang out here till you return.

See? Not so difficult, was it? As long as you spelled my name right, we're good. A side note to movie producers: Michael B. Jordan would make an excellent Rook in the movie version. Let's make that happen.

Allan would like to thank Jen, his family, and friends. Your support and tolerance of his borderline-obsessive writing habits are deeply appreciated.

And a huge thank-you to the wonderfully talented Stephen Black, editor extraordinaire, for pushing Allan to make this story sharper, smarter, and better on every page. Your insights were pure gold.

Huge thanks to Stillwater Story House for choosing Killer Instinct as your very first book. I'm not saying you launched your press with peak excellence... but you launched your press with peak excellence. Trust me, your instincts are clearly killer.

A shoutout to the people who work in the Starbucks he frequents. Without you and the caffeine you so wondrously deliver, Allan would still be staring at a blank page. There's magic in those peppermint mochas.

He also asked me to thank a bunch of people—because apparently, he thinks acknowledgments should read like an Oscar speech. Here we go: the coaching family and players of the St. Croix Soccer Club; the local bookstores he basically lives in—Inkwell Booksellers, Valley Booksellers, the Woodbury Barnes & Noble, and Magers & Quinn; John Sandford and the Prey books for jump-starting his writing career; his neighbors Jim, Nancy, and Theresa for their unwavering support; his dog Tucker for sharing his chair at his writing desk; Mike Flanagan and Quentin Tarantino for the storytelling masterclass; Eric Ramsay for (mostly) fixing Minnesota United's vibes; Jeff Probst; the entire Stranger Things cast; and whoever invented Nutella. (Okay, I added a few.)

And the friends who inspired many of this book's characters. To paraphrase a common legal disclaimer: any resemblance to actual persons, living or dead, is meant to be a compliment. Love to you all.

Okay, he's done. Finally.

Thanks for sticking with us. You're greatly appreciated.

Rook (on behalf of Allan)

About the author

Allan Evans writes the twisty thrillers your friends warn you not to start before bed. He's the author of two other Cade Dawkins thrillers, Killer Blonde and Killer Smile, along with several young adult and middle-grade novels—including Abnormally Abbey, Class Clown, and Spook Squad, which have earned him a wonderfully surprising number of young readers who think he's cooler than he probably is.

Allan's diverse professional background—encompassing undercover investigator, bodyguard, advertising creative, and more—provides the raw material behind the realism and edge of his crime fiction. When he isn't writing, he's coaching middle-school soccer or diving into research that inevitably finds its way into his books.

He lives in Minnesota, where winter is cold, crime is complicated, and stories are never in short supply.

Follow Allan on socials (Facebook, X/Twitter, Instagram, Threads, TikTok) using evanswriter.

Also by Allan Evans

The Cade Dawkins Thrillers
Killer Blonde
Killer Smile
Killer Instinct

The Abbey Series (Young Adult)
Abnormally Abbey
Class Clown
Spook Squad